For
Barbara
and
Fernando

Harriet (HA-ree-eht)
Keeper of the hearth, ruler of the home

~

Felix Mendelssohn in a letter to his mother describes a meeting with Queen Victoria and Prince Albert at Buckingham Palace on the 9th of July, 1842 (Fanny is his sister).

"The Duchess of Kent came in, and while they were all talking I rummaged about among the music on the piano and soon discovered my first set of songs; so of course I asked the Queen to sing one of these instead of the Gluck, and she agreed. [...]

And which of my songs did she choose? 'Schöner und schöner schmückt sich' – and sang it quite charmingly, strictly in time and in tune, and very nicely enunciated. [...]

Then I had to confess – I found it very hard, but pride goeth before a fall – that Fanny had written that song, and would she now sing one of mine? She said she would gladly try, so long as I gave her plenty of help, and then she sang 'Lass dich nur nichts dauern' really quite faultlessly and with much feeling and expression."

~

"From my knowledge of Fanny I should say that she has neither inclination nor vocation for authorship. She is too much all that a woman ought to be for this. She regulates her house, and neither thinks of the public nor of the musical world, nor even of music at all, until her first duties are fulfilled. Publishing would only disturb her in these, and I cannot say that I approve of it." – **Felix Mendelssohn**.

~

"Music chooses her musicians." - ***Patricia Barber***

~

www.redwayacres.com

Author's Note

The Redway Acres series of books is designed to be read in order.
It is my hope that any book within the series
can be picked up and read without prior knowledge
of the previous books.
However, plot details in previous books
will be mentioned in subsequent books, and therefore
the suspense or enjoyment of those books may be reduced
if read out of sequence.

Thank you.
Trish Butler

Table of Contents

Map

Wyndham Estate, near Bath, Somerset

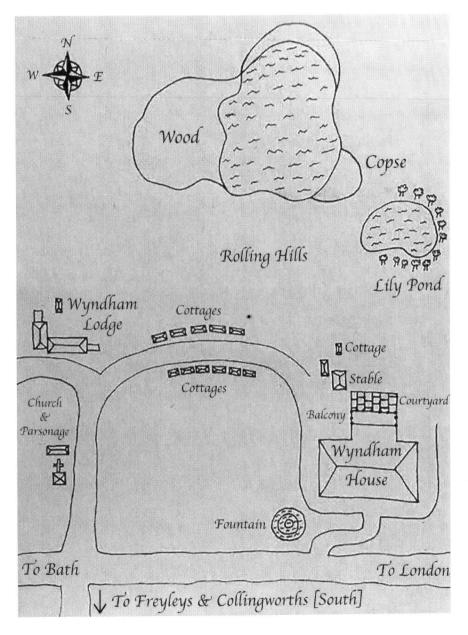

Prologue

On a warm but cloudy, early summer day in 1817, Harriet Wyndham stood at the graveside of her identical twin, Maria. While Helena Ackley, sang a stirring hymn, Harriet's lips twitched into a brief smile as red tendrils of hair escaped Helena's bonnet, wafting gently around her face in the slight breeze. Her friend never could keep a tidy appearance. Their group of mourners, shrouded in black, watched as the stone masons set the headstone in place, only two months after Maria's death. On the Wyndham side of the family Harriet alone remained.

Her mother's family, the Marshams, disowned Eliza and consequently Harriet and Maria, when she rushed into marriage with Ernest Eldridge. The sickly man died on the day of the twins' birth. For years Harriet thought him her father, until her cousin, Nathaniel Ackley, revealed that he believed his friend, Lieutenant Mark Wyndham, could be her true father. With Mark at sea when Eliza Marsham discovered she would bear his child, Nathaniel, knowing his cousin Ernest loved her desperately, encouraged him to step up and spare her the ignominy of bearing a child out of wedlock. On the day Eliza's year of mourning for

3

Ernest came to an end, Mark proposed marriage and became the twins' stepfather.

Harriet stood tall and straight-backed, her pale, blonde hair neat beneath her bonnet, blue eyes glistening with the ever-present tears for her beloved sister. Harriet's colouring, inherited from her mother, and slender physique and tall stature, inherited from the lieutenant, lent her a noble outer appearance that she did not feel within. She remembered Mark's long, brown hair tied back at the nape of his neck, and his bright, green eyes. He accepted, even encouraged, her exuberant and tenacious behaviour as a child. She had missed him when he went to sea, and even more so after he died.

The people Harriet currently considered family, gathered in the tidy graveyard surrounded by a stone wall. From the time of the twins' sixth birthday, after the death of their mother and her baby in childbirth, Mark entrusted Alexander Harker and Nathaniel Ackley, to be as fathers to her and Maria. The two tall men became their guardians and they moved from London to the large Harker estate of Eastease, in Lincolnshire. Their stepfather visited whenever he could, until the day he died at the battle of Trafalgar, three years later. As she looked at the pale headstone of her twin, Harriet felt old despite her few one-and-twenty years.

For fifteen of those years, she lived in the house of Alexander and the last five of those with his wife, Genevieve, too. Harriet turned her gaze to them. The tears welled in Alexander's dark eyes; his brown, curly hair left unruly after removing his hat. He towered over his wife, her figure rounded since bearing their two children. Ordered, light brown hair could barely be seen beneath her bonnet, and her pale blue eyes also swam with tears. Gennie's hands grasped those of her youngest sister and Harriet's dearest friend, Amelia.

Previously a colonel in the army, Nathaniel, her second cousin once removed and second son of the Earl of Aysthill, lost most of his right leg at Waterloo two years prior. Everyone still referred to him as 'the colonel'. He and Helena ran Redway Acres, the stable Helena inherited from her grandfather. Nathaniel stood half a head shorter than Harker, his sandy hair blowing in the breeze, his brilliant-blue eyes glistening. Harriet could not recall seeing him cry more than twice, each time when one of her parents died. If she closed her eyes, she could almost feel his arms holding her tightly to him as she and Maria cried on his strong shoulders.

Mr. Eliot Brooks, Maria's widower, and Harriet's family member through marriage, held the position of clergyman of the quaint, little church to which this graveyard belonged. As Helena's singing drew to a close, the tears poured down his cheeks. He seemed a shadow of the man that Maria filled up with her love.

Mr. Brooks fell in love with Maria the moment he laid eyes on her nearly two years ago, when she returned to Eastease unhappily married to another man whose child she carried. It made no difference to Mr. Brooks, who assisted in getting the marriage annulled. After the birth of her son, Mark, he proposed and accepted the baby as his own. Maria then bore him a daughter, Eliza, named after her grandmother.

Harriet thought it odd that she never appealed to him when she looked exactly as Maria, but he never afforded her a glance. Neither his seriousness, nor his softly waved, brown hair, nor his deep, brown eyes with gold flecks that so enamoured Maria, appealed to Harriet.

With the hymn at an end, Helena clasped Harriet's hands in her own, her green eyes fixing on her intently. "Mr. Brooks is coming to Redway for tea. You are welcome, too, of course, but you look contemplative. I wonder if you need a little more time with her?"

"You are right," Harriet replied, grateful for her friend's understanding. "Please tell Alexander not to wait for me, as I might be a while. I will walk back to Eastease across the fields." Harriet could not yet sever the bond she felt with her twin, despite death's most cruel attempt.

"I would suggest you should not do so alone, but I believe you might have some company." Helena turned towards the road, affording Harriet a clear view of Mr. Luke Parker sitting on the stone wall next to the gate. As Nathaniel spoke with him, he placed a friendly hand on the younger man's broad shoulder. The sun that finally managed to slant through the clouds, glinted on his mop of straw-coloured hair which fell forward when he nodded towards the colonel.

Helena, squeezing her hands again, gave Harriet some comfort. "I will let him know you may be some time. Come for a visit to Redway soon, my dear."

"I will."

Helena joined her husband as Harriet looked back at the headstone. *'Maria Wyndham Brooks'* read the name chiselled in the cold, marble. How odd to see her own name on a headstone. To be the one alive, standing above it and not the one buried beneath it. Although now known as Harriet, she laid claim to the name Maria from birth until four days after her sixteenth birthday...

Chapter One

Four days after her sixteenth birthday at the beginning of April 1812, Maria Wyndham rode over the fields of Eastease to the eastside shelter, the long grass, a lush green from recent spring rain. Her horse, Henry, ran easily over the gently undulating ground and she enjoyed the rush of the cool air upon her face, flushed with excitement as much as the exertion of the ride.

At Eastease the night before, she enjoyed the ball held to celebrate the birthday of herself and her twin sister Harriet. A longtime friend of Alexander and Nathaniel, Mr. Robert Davenport, arrived unexpectedly the previous week and stayed for the celebrations. Though twelve years their senior, Harriet and Maria enjoyed his charms and fun-loving antics. She and her twin both found him interesting and talked in their rooms at night of his gleaming, brown hair, and hazel eyes with glints of green and amber. Certainly a handsome man, Mr. Davenport dressed well and danced superbly. He called them beautiful ladies, not girls, the moniker most often on the lips of their guardians. He made them feel grown up.

Maria felt the flush of desirability as she descended the wide curved staircase with Mr. Davenport's eyes watching her intently. The halls and ballroom of Eastease shone with the light of hundreds of candles flickering over the shimmering fabrics of the ladies' gowns and the multitude of jewels that adorned their bodies and hair. Her own gown, a light shade of pink rose, barely graced her shoulders and scooped low across the small mounds of her breasts. The corsage of rosebuds affixed to the right shoulder of the gown tickled that delicate skin as it cascaded down the neckline. Harriet's gown mirrored hers, with the rosebuds on its left shoulder.

After completing her duty of dancing firstly with Nathaniel and then Alexander, Maria found Robert Davenport standing in front of her offering his arm.

"My dear, Miss Maria Wyndham, I believe you promised me the next pair." His wide smile reached sparkling eyes that roamed down the gown's neckline before looking back at her face. The feeling of warmth that spread across her body at the caress of his glance could not have been any greater if his fingertips followed the same course.

"You are quite right, sir! I did." Teasingly, she smiled widely and slid her hand through the crook of his elbow with a stroke of fingers around his bicep and over his forearm. The squeeze as he pulled her into his side pleased her, though she scowled as he placed them further down the line of dancers than she hoped. Maria wanted to pass some sly glances at her sister, knowing Harriet would be frustrated that she danced with Mr. Davenport first. With Mr. Woodhead and Amelia Hopwood between themselves and Harriet dancing with Luke Parker, that opportunity was not afforded her.

"Do not be angry with me, Miss Wyndham," Robert whispered as they passed each other for the first turn. "I must be forgiven for wishing to talk to you without your sister overhearing."

She gasped at his audacity, but nodded, eyes wide as he grasped a gloved hand firmly and turned fluidly. They returned to their original positions in the dancing line. The dancers next to them performed a complicated manoeuvre inserting themselves the other side of Maria and Mr. Davenport, thus moving further down the line of partners. At each turn they continued to talk in low voices, thankful that they knew the dance well enough to perform it without thinking.

"I am sure, Miss Maria, that you must laugh at such an old fool as I, looking at you with such desire."

"I could never consider you old, Mr. Davenport."

"I can hardly take my eyes off you for a moment. You must have noticed when you danced with Harker and Ackers."

Maria nodded quickly, but truthfully in her excitement for the evening, she did not look to him at all during those dances. She did feel that if she turned to him, she would have seen his gaze upon her and he now confirmed it to be true.

"Can I possibly hope? No, I am too foolish."

She shook her head and looked across at him unable to speak the words she wanted to in case someone heard. Instead at her next opportunity she encouraged him.

"You are right to hope, sir. Not foolish, not foolish at all. I assure you." Though whispered as they joined hands and turned, her words tumbled out earnestly. Once again the dance demanded he release her, though he took no pleasure in it, she could tell from his expression.

"You return my feelings then?"

"Yes!"

"Do I have your permission to speak to Alexander tomorrow?"

She could hardly hold her countenance, he just proposed! As her hand slid from his, though every fibre wished it could remain in his grasp forever, she nodded, the flush high on her cheeks now as a smile spread across her face.

"Ride out with your sister in the morning when I do so. Find some excuse to continue alone and meet me at the eastside shelter."

"Why?"

"I am so much older than you, Harker may object. If we meet there we can plan to elope. Assuming you wish it. You do wish it?"

"Yes! Yes of course, Mr. Davenport."

"Robert, please."

The dance came to an end and the second of the pair began. Talking became almost impossible. Robert only managed to request she speak to no one of it and that she not be upset with his lack of attention for the remainder of the evening. He did not wish to raise suspicions before talking to his friend. However, he would be thinking only of her. When she thought of it, her body heated and her skin tingled with anticipation.

Harriet rode with her a short way the following morning before claiming to be unwell, insisting Maria continue to ride without her. How fortuitous that she did not need to think up some excuse? The old, worn shelter came into view, but the passion and excitement in her eyes and heart, stopped Maria from seeing its dilapidated appearance.

She finished placing a colourful blanket on the bunk and candles on the little table when he arrived and tied up his horse. As exuberant as she, he gathered her into his arms when he entered the shelter and complimented the efforts she made to brighten it. Stepping back again, he proffered a bunch of wild, spring flowers that he picked on his way to her.

Touched, she set about placing them carefully in an empty tankard, as he slumped upon the bunk with a sigh. She looked over to him at the noise and anticipated his words.

"Alexander refused his permission, did he not?"

"He knows you have to grow up eventually. I cannot think for looking at you, how well you have grown." He smiled as she walked to him and cradled his head against her stomach. Easily, he wrapped his arms around her and she did feel grown up, providing him comfort in this way.

Then he drew her down to his level on the bunk and kissed her, all other concerns forgotten. His hands explored her curves causing sensations to soar through her. They would elope and marry, she saw no reason to wait, when her body felt so strong and powerful.

He laid her on the bunk on top of that pretty blanket, the air around them fragrant with the spring flowers, and the lit candles casting a pleasant glow across their faces. As their actions became more passionate, her body responded. Then he pushed their clothes aside and she knew this moment would connect them together forever. She wanted it, she wanted him, but he paused and looked at her.

"What is it, Robert?" though concerned, she thought to encourage him. "Please do not stop."

His face changed in front of her, he sneered and laughed. Suddenly alarmed, she tried to pull away from him.

"Tell Harker this is for him," he growled out the words as he thrust into her and she screamed. Scared now, she tried to get away, but he

10

pinned her arms down and used his weight to keep her body in place. As he moved within her, the pleasure melted away. She did not understand what happened. Why did he change?

"Please, stop," she said quietly.

He put his face close to hers, but she turned her head.

"What happened to *'Robert, please do not stop'*? You could not get enough of me a moment ago," he taunted her. She shook her head and silent tears slid out of the sides of her eyes, into her hair.

When he finished, he knelt and wiped himself on the blanket, standing to button up his breeches. Maria curled into a ball and stared at the tankard of wildflowers that, without water to sustain them, wilted in the same way her tender feelings wilted and died. She may as well die too if her life would be reduced to marrying this man.

"I will not marry you." *Surely Alexander should not force her to accept him?*

"Marry you? No, never my plan."

"Then why did you...?" Oddly the thought of him compromising her without marriage ever being his intention shocked her more than having to marry him.

"Always the one with the questions, Maria. No, I decided I should marry Harriet. I am meeting her on the north road and we will ride to Scotland. Did you not question the ease with which I separated the two of you today? Harriet will not ask as many questions as you. She is quiet and undemanding. She would never have given herself without a promise, as you have just done."

"You did promise, you said you would ask for Alexander's permission, that you loved me, that you wanted me." As Maria spoke the words, she knew they sounded childish. What possessed her to meet him here? Why did she not wait and talk to Alexander after he refused his permission? A hard stone formed in her stomach and she felt sick with the anxiety of what would happen next.

"I said none of that, you assumed it all. Ah, maybe that last part I am guilty of, what man would not want such a succulent rose as yourself presented to him so willingly? You behaved exactly as I predicted you should, as a silly, young girl who has been far too sheltered. You cannot blame me for that. You can only blame yourself and, of course, your guardians, though I do not see them doing much guarding of the two of you. I have taken you here, and tonight on the road at an inn, I will take Harriet. Then we will marry and her dowry will be mine."

"You only want money? I can give you money. Please, do not take Harriet." She hated to plead, but a panic overtook her at the thought that he would deceive her wonderful sister.

"You do not see. Although I do want money, I want the additional satisfaction of hurting Harker as he has done to me."

"How has Alexander hurt you? He has been nothing but pleasant and welcoming towards you." When he made no reply, she continued. "You are hurting Nathaniel, too. Have you not considered him?" She grasped at the small hope that this horrible man might be persuaded by the thought of his friendship being ruined, for surely Nathaniel would not react well to Mr. Davenport's actions.

Robert looked a little crestfallen but regained himself quickly. "It cannot be helped. He should have watched over you more carefully, instead of fawning over that Hopwood girl." Maria thought Nathaniel seemed to be taken with Martha Hopwood, too.

"I hate you." She sounded petulant, but it seemed her passion for this man now ran as cold as it had hot merely moments ago.

"Get in line, right behind my father." He moistened his thumb and finger and pinched each flame of the candles to snuff them out, turned and left. The removal of the soft, flickering flame lifted the final veil from her eyes to reveal the truly derelict and dirty room, as well as the depth of his deception. How could she have given her body to this repulsive man in such a location as this? Her disgust with herself could not be worse under any circumstances.

Maria lay on the bunk and gave in to her tears for a few moments, before realising she should ride back to Eastease and warn Harriet not to leave. She would have to tell her sister what happened on this bunk and Harriet would hate her forever, but better that than her twin leaving and marrying Mr. Davenport.

"Too late." Harriet stood looking at Maria's headstone, wiping at the tears that coursed down her cheeks as she relived those moments with Davenport. "I wasted precious moments wallowing in my misery before heading back to the house. Could I have stopped you? Would you have listened? When you came back to us I asked for your forgiveness, but you said, *No need, my dearest,* in that soft way of yours."

She thought back to that frantic search for her sister, in the stable, in their music room and some other rooms downstairs, while avoiding the Hopwood family who attended the ball and stayed overnight. Finally, she made it to the rooms they shared and found Harriet's letter on her table.

"I never told you, Sister, but I felt relief. If you did not leave with him, would he have revealed what happened between us? Would I be forced to marry him instead? I am so sorry, so disgusted with myself for even thinking such a thing, and that, more than anything else, led me to pretend to be you. I did not know if we would ever see the Hopwoods again. Would it not be better for them to leave thinking ill of me, rather than you? Did I not deserve their contempt?

Nathaniel knew of course, he always did when we played that joke on anyone. He did not say anything, until the Hopwoods left and Alexander followed you to Scotland. I confessed everything to him. He asked me to keep the pretence as he thought it might aid you if you needed to escape your marriage, and it worked! Now, you will be Maria forever more, it says so here."

Harriet waved her hand at the hard, unforgiving stone before starting at a movement near the road. Mr. Parker waited to walk her back to Eastease and she watched as he stood, stretched his legs, and rubbed at his behind where it rested on the stone wall. He gave a slight bow when he saw her attention upon him and she smiled a small smile in return, before sitting down on the grass, indicating that she did not yet feel an inclination to leave. Her long coat protected her gown, though the ground felt dry but cool.

"Poor Mr. Parker. He left to travel the world right after word reached our friends of your elopement and did not return for over a year. He always favoured you of course." Harriet followed his route as he picked up the reins of his horse and walked the mare around the outside of the graveyard wall, his course would take him behind the church.

Shaking her head, she turned her attention back to the grave. She thought back to the day after the elopement, when the colonel's anger became palpable and he took himself out for a ride.

"Did I ever tell you Nathaniel burned down the eastside shelter for me?" In her mind's eye, she could see her cousin, still with both of his legs and dressed in his red coat, riding his large, chestnut stallion over the same route she rode the day before...

Nathaniel squeezed Thor into a gallop across the east side of Eastease land. The powerful, beast ran happily for him and the colonel once again felt the mutual respect and affinity they shared of preferring the charge and fight, to work off their frustrations. His anger raged so hot within him that he considered murder. He knew himself capable of it but this would be different from killing on the battlefield. He directed his anger at Davenport for what he did to Maria, and then leaving with Harriet, but truthfully it should also be directed at himself. He felt Robert to be more his friend than Alexander's, he should have stopped him. The lack of any action he could take in that moment made him feel impotent.

The offending structure appeared in his eyeline as Thor cantered in that direction. The greyed wooden slats, shrunk away from the joints, making him certain the rain penetrated inside often, and one good windy day should see the whole structure come down. Dismounting, he entered the small room and surveyed the scene. How he hated the thought that Maria, Harriet as he must now think of her, lost her innocence in such a way and in such a sorry location. Some wildflowers, wilted almost to nothing in a dry tankard, and two candles stood on a small table. He recognised Maria's sweet blanket that still lay on the bunk with a dark, dried bloodstain smeared upon it.

The anger that dissipated somewhat in the exertion of the ride, swelled up in his chest once more and he turned to a wall to smash a gloved fist into the wooden slats. Surprisingly, only a slight splintering occurred, insufficient to dampen his anger. In fact, it acted as a flint's spark on tinder and as his rage flamed, he turned it onto the scant furniture. He overturned the bunk with a roar and then pounded his fist into the brittle wood of the little table, sending flowers and candles flying as its legs parted company with each other.

When no more remained within the room to destroy, he put his booted foot through a slatted section of the wooden wall. He gained more satisfaction from that and continued to kick and tear at the fabric of the structure, using the slats to lever the nails from their snug holes. Removing his coat when the exertion began to warm him; his hands ached and the sweat trickled down his back, by the time only the posts and the roof they held up remained.

His chest heaving, he spread his arms wide, grasped two of the posts and bowed his head, resting there for a moment and reviewing the level of his anger. The white-hot spears of it dimmed with the destruction of the shelter, but the impotence remained. Grunting, he pushed against the posts, the muscles in his strong arms and across his back strained against the restrictions of the fabric of his damp shirt, but the stubborn posts remained upright.

Straightening, he picked up his coat and walked over to Thor, who stood there disinterested in the proceedings. Draping the coat over the saddle, he removed the thick rope he procured from the stable before he headed out. He looped it around two posts, realising that, in bringing it with him, he knew his intention when he rode in this direction. Tying it to Thor's saddle securely, he took hold of his horse's reins and walked him forward. The strong stallion made quick work of it and the posts came up out of the ground, bringing the roof down.

Nathaniel continued to push and pull at the remaining posts, adding them to the pile and as the final licks of frustration escaped him, he tied the rope to those remaining. Eventually, with the whole structure down, he glanced over it wondering what his explanation to Harker should be.

As though taunting him, he spotted the blood-stained blanket poking through the pile of kindling he created. Pulling matches out of his coat pocket, he bent to light the corner of it. The fire caught quickly beneath the cover of the roof and soon the whole pile blazed. Nathaniel watched from a good distance away, feeling the heat of it on his face and holding Thor securely. He wished for Davenport to be trapped under it screaming for his help. *"I would let the bastard burn.*

He stood watching the consuming flames lick until satisfied there would be nothing left to salvage. A few drops of rain rapidly became a steady downpour plastering his shirt to his body and his hair into his eyes. Droplets fell from the end of his nose, but he stood there, immovable, until the fire subsided. Confident the rain, which finally dampened his anger, should finish the fire, he returned to Eastease.

The stable manager ran out to him as he approached. "We saw smoke over the east side, Colonel. Did ya see the fire? Do I send men out?"

"No. The eastside shelter is burned to the ground. It will have to be replaced, but the rain took care of the fire."

"Yes, sir. I will get men on it, soon as there be a good day for it."

It should cost Harker, but Nathaniel felt confident that if his friend knew why, he should consider it worth it.

Harriet sat on the grass at Maria's graveside, remembering how grateful she felt to Nathaniel for burning down that shelter. She still avoided entering the new structure, but his action freed her of all evidence of her indiscretion.

"Annie told me of the shelter being destroyed while she helped me dress for bed that night…"

The petite maid, Annie Brown, stood behind Harriet as she unpinned her hair. Harriet, used to the easy conversation with her own maid, sat in front of the mirror and sought her mind for a suitable subject matter.

"I suppose the discussion between all the servants is of Maria?"

"Mrs. Hopkins warned us not to speak of it. Today's news is that the eastside shelter burned down."

"Really?" Harriet could not hide her astonishment. "How did that happen?"

"No one knows. Colonel Ackley went out for a ride and said the rain took care of the fire, but it will have to be replaced."

Harriet considered as she stood and removed her chemise. On her tiptoes, Annie placed a nightgown over a distracted Harriet's head. Before feeding her arms through the sleeves, Harriet undid her drawers and allowed them to fall to the floor. *Nathaniel destroyed the shelter for me!*

Annie bent to pick up the discarded drawers, casting a frown up to Harriet's face as she straightened. Alarmed, Harriet wondered if it could be possible to tell from her drawers what happened the day before?

"I thought your menses started yesterday, Miss, but there is nothing here. Are you well?"

Of course! The blood from what happened the previous day dried in her drawers. What could be done except to tell Annie and impose on her trust again? Earlier that day the maid withstood the revelation of her being Maria. Harriet decided to tell her as she supposed, over time, the fair haired woman, with doll like features, would come to that realisation herself. Now at least Harriet could ask someone what to expect should she be with child.

"Annie..." she began hesitantly. Her shame must have broken through in her tone.

"Oh no, Miss. The colonel?"

"Certainly not!" Horrified at the suggestion, Harriet covered her mouth with her hands. Her reaction made her realise what a bad situation it would be to marry Nathaniel, as he offered, should there be consequences to her liaison. "I met Davenport at the eastside shelter when I thought he would marry me, not my sister. He deceived me, but before I realised my mistake he held me down. Annie, I could not stop him. I am so ashamed."

At this Harriet sat on the bed with her head in her hands, but she did not cry. Silently, the smaller woman moved to her side and placed her arm around her. "It is that man who should be ashamed, Miss, not you. He is no gentleman, that is sure. I am sorry to my core that your sister has to marry him."

Harriet nodded at that, then chanced her question. "Annie, if I am... if there are to be consequences, how will I know?"

"I do not know, Miss. I have no experience of that and both of my parents are gone now. I am youngest by far in my family. Whatever happens, I will be here to serve you. Surely, Mr. Harker and the colonel will take care of you. Do they know?"

"Only the colonel, you and I, and of course Davenport." She practically spat the name, she hated to have it grace her lips. "The colonel says he will marry me if there is a child, but I cannot see how we can make that work when he is as a father to me."

"Well, one thing at a time. Firstly, we should wait to see what happens."

"Annie, could you keep this to yourself, please?"

"Of course. Goodnight, Miss." Annie, left the room.

"Goodnight, Annie." Harriet spoke to a closed door, before the sobbing overtook her once again, though unsure why she cried, she could not seem to stop. Certainly her tears fell over what Davenport did, and of course her sister being lost to them, but also the uncertainty of what her future held. As Annie said, she would have to wait and see what happened, but waiting would be hard.

Harriet looked up from the headstone to check upon Mr. Parker's progress. As she watched, his tall figure appeared around the other side of the church. He tied his horse to the tree closest to the wall and sat facing away from her, looking out over the fields of Eastease. She recalled them both swinging from that tree as youngsters. Her sister never dared. Both she and the tree grew considerably in the intervening years, and she doubted she could reach the lowest branch to do so now. Mr. Parker, being taller even than Alexander, could probably grasp it.

"After you left, we did not see Luke Parker for quite some time. His father attended Alexander's wedding and informed us he left to travel the world. We held a Christmas ball after the birth of Jacob Harker well over a year later, Mr. Parker returned shortly before that and attended."

Harriet recalled her astonishment at the changes in him, from the pimply, skinny boy she danced with at her sixteenth birthday ball. He must have gained a foot in height, and nearly as much across his shoulders! No more pimples and his hair very stylish. *He does like to wear it long.* They danced the first pair and he surprised her with his improvement.

"You did not see Nathaniel dance with Helena for the first time at that ball. Who knew he could be so romantic? I love him so much for offering to marry me, if I carried Davenport's child, but thank goodness I did not. It is funny to think that I said to Nathaniel, back then, that I hoped for someone for him to love and for him to have children. I thought he should make a wonderful father for his own children, I always thought him a good father to us. Then only days later I met Helena..."

Two days after Nathaniel shocked Harriet with the realisation that she could be with child, she decided to take a ride out on her horse. Henry and Hudson, liver chestnuts with flaxen manes and tails, belonged to the twins. They wore four white socks each and white blazes on their faces. As with their owners, no one could tell them apart.

When her sister eloped, she took her horse, Hudson, with her. As Harriet would be pretending to be her sister, her horse, Henry, would have to become Hudson. She wondered if the animal would mind his change of name? While she rode, she would have to try it out.

The rain continued throughout the previous day made the morning fresh and the vegetation green. Despite the eastside shelter being a pile of ashes, according to the report from Annie, Harriet endeavoured to ride away from it and headed instead to the boundary between Eastease and Redway Acres. The north road ran down the west boundary of Eastease, and several cottages and the church bordered it.

Riding out behind those buildings, Harriet reached the Redway border and turned her horse to ride along it. The animal's comfort in the familiar territory evident in his easy canter, as Redway Acres raised 'Hudson' until Harriet's birthday just last week. The owner, George Stockton, visited Eastease often, and holed up with Alexander in his study talking business.

As Harriet turned and started along the boundary, she noticed a woman riding a large grey from the direction of Redway's outbuildings. She squinted as she watched, sure the woman did not ride sidesaddle. Indeed Harriet confirmed it when she drew up to her, not getting too close in case the animals did not wish to be friendly.

"My goodness, you are riding astride! As a man!" Harriet said it rather rudely due to her shock at seeing a woman ride this way.

"Am I?" The woman smiled, blowing tendrils of her red hair out of her eyes. "Thank you for pointing that out, I was unsure."

"I apologise. I am not normally quite so rude as that. I am Harriet Wyndham. It is nice to meet you. That is a handsome stallion."

"Thank you, yes he is beautiful." She rubbed at the neck of the stallion with a gloved hand. "You are Harriet you say? I thought I understood from my grandfather that Harriet rode Hudson, not Henry."

"This is Hudson!" Harriet felt a little panicked. How could this woman tell the horses apart? No one at Eastease could.

"I beg to differ, Miss Wyndham. I should know, I raised and trained both Henry and Hudson myself. This is Henry, which is the horse ridden by Miss Maria Wyndham, not Harriet."

Harriet thought quickly, sure by now the news of her sister's elopement reached many households in the neighbourhood.

"I apologise, again. Please do not breathe a word, but yes this is Henry. Of course, you are right. However, when my sister left Eastease the other day, she did so in a hurry and took Hudson with her by mistake. No one at Eastease could tell the difference and I prefer the name Hudson, so I hoped I could change his name. Do you think he minds? Will he respond to Hudson?" Suddenly realising the woman did not introduce herself she added. "What is your name? You did not say."

"No, I did not."

Harriet looked into the green eyes that seemed to be pondering a decision. Perhaps she did not wish to know her after her sister's elopement, but why then ride over to talk to her? Harriet felt tears prick her eyes and she turned her head while she tried to gain control of herself. She felt at such a loss without her twin whom she spent just about every waking moment with for the past sixteen years. It would be nice to make a friend.

"My name is Mrs. Helena Andrews." The woman's voice held some sympathy. "I am a widow and I have a young daughter, Isabella. We have lived here with my grandfather for almost four years. As to your other questions, no he will not mind, and yes, he will respond to Hudson. Try saying it in the same way that your sister used to say Henry."

"What is your stallion's name? They seem to be getting on well." Harriet indicated towards the two stallions and Mrs. Andrews agreed, walking her horse closer. The animals tolerated each other well.

"This is Perseus, he can be rather headstrong, but usually around men. Henry, sorry Hudson, he seems to like, but that is probably because he remembers him and there is no mare in the vicinity! Are you almost finished with your ride? Hudson still looks quite fresh. Maybe he would be happy to stretch his legs some more? I planned to ride to our stream further north, it is a pleasant spot at which Isabella likes to picnic. I need to see how firm the ground is to determine whether it is something we can do in another week or so. Would you join me?"

"Yes, that should be wonderful, thank you. Lead the way."

They rode north across the fields. As with Eastease, the mainly flat Redway land included the occasional rise that could barely be called a hill. The ground, soft enough to make it an easy ride for Hudson and Perseus as they raced in friendly competition, gave way to a muddier earth as they arrived at a copse of trees bordering a stream. It would seem that Miss Isabella Andrews would have a longer wait for her outing. Mrs. Andrews indicated the point at which the trees ended and the green fields took over and Harriet could see why it would be idyllic for a picnic. Dismounting to allow the horses some respite, the older woman suggested they walk them along the bank of the stream.

"You are an excellent rider, Miss Wyndham. If you do not mind me saying so, however, Hudson has a soft mouth and works better with light contact. Lighten your hands by relaxing your grip slightly. He is very responsive and only requires soft aids. As you get to know each other you will see how quickly he learns and is eager to please. It has only been a week after all."

"I will try. He is much bigger and more powerful than any horse I have ridden before. It is daunting." It comforted Harriet to talk to Mrs. Andrews of her riding ability and take advantage of her considerable knowledge.

"You are more than capable of handling him. I could tell straightaway. He likes you and will look after you, trust him a little more. I am sorry I will not be seeing his brother any time soon. I am glad to see him looking so well." She looked fondly back at the horse, before noticing tears in the younger girl's eyes. "I am so sorry. Of course, you will miss your sister far more."

"Yes, I keep thinking how our lives have been so similar up until this point, but now her life will be very different from mine. She will no longer live here, she will be married and have babies. I have no idea what that will feel like."

"Very painful!"

"It is?" Harriet looked horrified.

"Oh, again I am apologising. I must learn to think before I speak. It is a wonderful experience to have a baby, in the right circumstances. However, the birthing is painful, but worth it."

"How do you know when you are going to have a baby?" Harriet suddenly saw her opportunity to ask someone. A stranger, too, which seemed to make it easier to talk of.

"The pain of childbirth is unmistakable, I assure you."

"No, I mean, if you do not mind me asking, early on, how do you know?"

"I see, well let me think back. Ruth Robertson, our housekeeper here at Redway talked to me of it. She asked me several questions." Mrs. Andrews counted points on her fingers as she recalled them. "Have your menses stopped? Do you feel sick, especially in the mornings? Do you feel hungry in between the sickness? Are your breasts tender and do they feel larger? Then of course your waistline gets larger and you feel the baby move within you. That is when you know for certain, when the baby moves, around four months. It is a very odd sensation at first."

"Thank you." Harriet looked up at the sky to judge the time. "I should be going, I did not expect such a long ride as this. I do not want anyone to be concerned."

"Well, please come and visit Redway and bring Hudson with you. Isabella misses him terribly."

They rode back and parted when the roofs of Redway could be seen. Then Harriet rode to Eastease alone. She felt a little happier. Pleased she made a new acquaintance, although she thought the woman a little older than her, and found out how to change Henry's name to Hudson. In addition, she now knew what to look for if she might be with child.

She wondered whether to mention Mrs. Andrews to Nathaniel but decided against it. A cloud hung over Eastease until her sister could be found and married, and she should not be socialising. Not that she felt the daring Mrs. Andrews would give it a thought!

Harriet looked up, startled that Mr. Parker looked directly at her from his position on the wall where he turned to face the graveyard. She blushed as she smiled at him. What must he think of her sitting here talking to a grave?

"And what, dear sister, am I supposed to do with him? He thinks I am you, of course. He always favoured you. I know you said his grandmother desired the match between you, but she has passed now and he is free to choose as he pleases." Sighing, she wondered how much time she passed sitting there? Mr. Parker must surely be tiring of waiting.

At the beginning of the year, their uncle's solicitor informed the twins of his death and their inheritance of the Wyndham estate just outside of Bath, in Somerset. Phillip Wyndham, brother of Lieutenant Mark Wyndham, died six months ago and without any family of his own, left the Wyndham property to them. His only request that his friend, Bertram Horncastle, be allowed to live out his life there if he so chose.

"I should go to Wyndham House and see exactly what we have inherited. Nathaniel knows only that it is a large property, at least as large as Eastease. Anything other than that, he says he cannot recall. Can you forgive me for going whilst still in mourning for you? If I wait, it will be cold for travel and for assessing the extent of the property. Truthfully, I will feel like a piece of me is missing forever."

Harriet tried to push herself up from the ground before realising the discomfort in her legs and behind, sinking back down quickly.

"Miss Wyndham, please allow me to assist you," Mr. Parker called. He stood up, ambling over to do just that.

She loved to watch his easy gait, his long legs eating up the ground quickly to come to her assistance. Often in these intervening years she considered her pretence of being Harriet most unfair to the two of them.

She endured his attentions on his frequent visits after that Christmas ball when he returned from his travels. Bitter sweet it could be termed, because as much as she enjoyed his company, he thought her to be Harriet. She wasted four years of his life, allowing him to pursue a Harriet Wyndham that no longer existed.

Her carefree, exuberant and adventurous Maria died in the eastside shelter at the hands of Robert Davenport. He squeezed the life out of her on that bunk in the shelter in much the same way he did to the Maria her sister became. She could no longer pretend to be the Harriet of her sister's youth, she must become her own version of Harriet, born from the two deaths of Maria.

She could not do that here at Eastease, so close to Mr. Parker whose expectations would be of a different woman. Nor could she do that so close to Mr. Brooks, when she looked exactly as his wife.

She would forgive herself, finally, for what occurred with Robert Davenport, for who could be blamed for behaving as an innocent sixteen-year-old girl, when that was what you were?

"Miss Wyndham?"

She looked up at the large hand stretched out to help her stand. She grasped it, her pulse quickening at their connection, even though only through gloved hands.

"Thank you, Mr. Parker, and thank you for your patience, waiting such a long time." They walked towards his horse.

"I am happy to do so. The day is fine, so not an onerous task. Should we walk across the fields?"

She nodded and he hopped over the wall, then assisted her climb over the stile. She would enjoy his attentions, their easy conversation and the closeness of him, before she would tell him her plan to leave for Bath. It would be better for everyone if they could simply forget each other.

Chapter Two

At the end of July 1817, Harriet Wyndham began a six-day journey from her home of Eastease; her destination Wyndham House, five miles outside of Bath in Somerset. Mr. Brooks professed no interest in the property, except for the income it would provide his and Maria's two children. Therefore he left the running of it to Harriet, asking only that she keep him abreast of activities via regular correspondence.

The entourage that accompanied her consisted of two carriages with various passengers, and a cart full of Harriet's belongings including much horse paraphernalia. Her current companions, Helena and her eight year old daughter from her first marriage, Isabella, as well as their maid, Rebecca Robertson, rode in the first carriage. Isabella took after her mother in colouring with red curls and green eyes, Rebecca's thick chestnut hair pinned up tightly under her bonnet, her brown eyes sparkling as she played a game with the youngster. Jacky Robertson, Rebecca's husband and Redway Acres stableman, drove them.

"What do you plan to do with yourself in this big house once we are gone?" Helena enquired.

"I do not know yet, but I filled my time amply at Eastease, I cannot imagine doing less there." Harriet hoped she sounded confident, though wondered the same thing herself in the times when she doubted her decision to move to Wyndham House. She would have much to learn about the running of her new home, as well as new people to meet, but would she be lonely?

"You spend a considerable amount of time with the school and at Bernier. You will not have them or Redway to visit near Bath."

"But Bath itself is a very busy town, especially during the season and I hope I might find some scheme to occupy me. Not a school perhaps, but something else. I need to see the estate before I decide, but I will know what I want when it comes to me. It will feel right."

"I should imagine they will have a grand music room. You will enjoy that."

"Yes, I am hoping that there will be a master in Bath that can teach me further." She began improving her musical skills when she became Harriet, as her sister's skills surpassed her own. Soon she found comfort from the pastime and as she improved, she sought more instruction from teachers and musicians. Luckily Alexander's enjoyment of music found him happy to provide all the expertise he could for her.

"Your last two instructors said you outstripped even them and they learned more from you than they taught!"

Harriet blushed at Helena's compliment. She felt those men too kind in their praise, if they truly said those things.

"There might be more people to perform in front of, if I decide to hold dinner parties or even a ball. They must have a ballroom; do you not think?" Harriet's eyes gleamed at the prospect. Though she felt modesty over her own accomplishments, she did enjoy performing in the hope that she could instill in an audience a fraction of the emotion music provided her.

"Most certainly," Helena agreed.

"And you will stay for at least a month? You must."

"Nathaniel has agreed to stay that long. If you are not happy, you can simply return with us. I am sure he will not wish to make this return journey too soon. I thought he might suggest a ride this afternoon, given Davy's agitation."

As if on cue, a large, grey stallion passed the carriage on one side, with a red coated Nathaniel Ackley mounted upon it. Harriet could see the stump of his right amputated leg pushed firmly into the top of the wooden leg strapped to the saddle. Davy followed behind on his black mare, Coal.

Helena looked relieved to see the smile on the ten year old's face and admired his riding prowess. Davy arrived at Redway over three years prior, a mistreated chimney boy that Nathaniel rescued. Harriet suspected, because he looked so much like Nathaniel, her friend could not resist taking Davy in as her own son. Once she married the colonel, both children referred to Nathaniel only as their father, and he loved them as much as he did the son he and Helena produced together. Little Nate, only recently turned two years old, remained in the care of those at Redway and Mr. Brooks.

Harriet felt relieved that Nathaniel agreed to make this journey with her. As much as she loved Alexander, she felt he would be inclined to take charge, rather than allow her to learn at her own pace. He ran Eastease from when he turned eighteen, much younger than Harriet now, so he held considerable knowledge of running a large estate. They talked often before her leaving and she stored the knowledge away.

Helena pushed down the window on her side of the carriage and peered back at the other vehicles. "The others are not far behind. I can see Annie sitting next to Charlie Mickleson, he will be happy with that!"

"Really? Annie has said nothing of it to me." She smiled. With Annie so fair and small and Mickleson a dark, hulking muscular man, they would make an unusual sight. What if they did wish to marry? Harriet hoped Annie would stay with her at Wyndham House, but might she prefer to return to Redway with Mr. Mickleson? She knew Helena valued his services at Redway as much as she did Annie's services to her as her loyal maid. Perhaps she could find him employment on her estate?

"They are both rather reticent. I think they might be in their thirties before he makes his intentions known. She might have her hands full though, if still waters run as deep as they say."

"I take it James is riding on the cart with Peter?" It pleased Harriet that James Dawley asked to accompany them, it would be nice to have familiar servants in the house and the stable as she got used to her role in charge of a large estate. James served Nathaniel and Davy on this trip, and proved himself invaluable in organising all their belongings, as well as the requirements for them and their servants at each stop.

"I am looking forward to seeing Peter Robinson coming into his own on this trip, as he will be out from under the, let us call it 'firm', hand of his father," Helena mused, still looking back at those following. "We are considering him for Redway when we have the need. This will be a good opportunity for him to show us what he is made of."

"Mama, what kind of horse will we be getting for me?" Helena closed the window and looked at her daughter with a smile as the conversation turned to the favourite subject of the ladies, horses.

As each day rolled by, Harriet's anticipation, excitement and nerves raised their heads in turn and with equal intensity. On the final day of travel, her courage rose and she felt ready for the challenge of running Wyndham House and all it entailed.

The carriages pulled up to the front door in the late morning. When Harriet descended she stared open mouthed at her new home, at least double the size of Eastease. Nathaniel looked towards Harriet apologetically and she realised his memory of the large property failed him when he spoke of it.

She stood there awed by the house she owned. Three rows of windows looked down on her expectantly, with more attic room windows above those. It continued around the sides into two large wings towards the back of the property that she could not see. She wondered how many other houses and cottages stood on her land? How would she manage this by herself? How foolish to think that she could.

If she wanted to start her new life as a new Harriet, it would be best not to fall at the first step. Symbolically, she placed her foot on the first of the half dozen, wide steps that led to the large, front door. Before she reached it, the dark-wood door opened and a distinguished looking butler in his late twenties appeared. As tall as the colonel, though slimly built, he addressed them with the soft burr of a Scottish accent, his blonde hair touched with red, and his bright, blue eyes, friendly.

"Miss Harriet Wyndham, I assume? I am Mckinnon, the butler."

"Yes, I am she. Thank you, Mckinnon. This is my cousin, Colonel Nathaniel Ackley, his wife, Mrs. Helena Ackley, and their children Davy and Isabella." She stepped through the door and gestured behind her while making the introductions.

"Whatever happened to Lewis?" Nathaniel recalled an older butler at Wyndham House in his younger days.

"He left, sir. Did nae wish to serve Mr. Horncastle. Only tolerated him because of Mr. Wyndham. Stable manager left, too, sir. Though in my opinion nae much of a loss."

"Strictly speaking, Lewis would have been working for me. Why should he not serve Mr. Horncastle?" Harriet interjected into the proceedings. Though glad of Nathaniel's support, she owned this home. The servants should have to learn to answer to her, not Nathaniel or this Mr. Horncastle.

"He is an unusual man, Miss Wyndham. He is... let me take you to him. If you would follow me, please."

Harriet allowed a servant to assist with her outerwear, frowning slightly at what the butler said of Mr. Horncastle. The Scot did not seem disturbed by his revelations, in fact she felt him rather amused.

They followed Mckinnon to a parlour, its overall appearance rather manly due to the dark, bulky furniture within it. Detracting from the masculinity, golden-yellow, embossed wallpaper covered one wall from floor to ceiling. It held a decorative pattern, upon which the expansive windows cast enough light to brighten the room considerably.

Harriet found her attention caught immediately by the magnificent views of the back of the property, and away from Mckinnon's announcement of them. The gardens continued for some time before rolling hills dipped out of sight. The horizon beyond, a mass of trees, must have been miles away. A man cleared his throat behind her and she turned, but saw no one until she looked down.

A handsome man, with fair hair, of possibly thirty years old stood over a foot shorter than she and looked up at her, his face pleasant and his smile large. His body seemed of regular size, but his arms and legs much shorter than one might expect. Harriet looked down at him, noting his superior style of dress despite his odd size, and found his blue eyes and wide smile too much to resist.

She broke into a smile of her own. "I apologise, Mr. Horncastle. The view is captivating."

"I agree, Miss Wyndham. If I may be so bold as to say so." Nathaniel harrumphed at the obvious flattery, causing Harriet to scowl at him.

"I apologise again, Mr. Horncastle. We did not expect you to be…"

"Short?" he seemed amused at their astonishment.

Nathaniel made to open his mouth, but Harriet cut across him. "Of short stature, sir. If I may say so."

"You may. I like the sound of it! I have been called much worse."

Harriet liked Mr. Horncastle immediately. He told them amusing tales in a most entertaining fashion, seemingly enjoying the company. Isabella, of similar height as he, vowed to not grow an inch more in order to remain so.

However, Nathaniel did not hide his contempt for this little fellow. Harriet, quite astonished at his intolerance, suspected that he wondered why her Uncle Phillip left Mr. Horncastle in charge of Wyndham House. Prior to their journey, however, he and Alexander expressed their satisfaction with the shorter man's reports.

After refreshments, Mr. Horncastle showed them to their rooms to prepare for some luncheon. He spoke as they made their way to the wide stairs, "Miss Wyndham, Mckinnon suggested the green room for you and I concurred, the views are spectacular from its windows."

At the head of the stairs, Mr. Horncastle gestured to the doors in front of them that would be Miss Wyndham's rooms. Set back from the corridor that ran across the top of the stairs from one wing to the other, the upper windows of the front entryway provided plenty of light for the conversational seating that occupied the open hallway.

"However, you must peruse all the rooms and determine which you like the best," Mr. Horncastle insisted.

Turning left at the top of the stairs, he spoke again, "Colonel, Mrs. Ackley, you are down this corridor." He gestured to the two open doors, with a door presumably to a dressing or sitting room between them. Then he turned to the other side of the corridor, opening doors as he spoke. "We did not know if you wanted the nursery rooms opened up for the children or whether they should be on this floor with yourselves, so we have done both."

"I am not a baby and do not need nursery rooms!" Davy spoke out, apparently disgusted with such a suggestion. Harriet considered that anyone who did not know them might easily assume that Davy must be the colonel's son, not only his colouring, but several of his mannerisms reflected that of his father. It would seem, that his physique would match the colonel's, too, although he did not seem particularly tall yet. Since living at Redway and working with horses, his muscles gained much strength. Davy who, though over a full year older than Isabella was no taller than she, did not take well to Mr. Horncastle.

"Of course you are not!" agreed Nathaniel with unnecessary vigour.

"It is very good of you to give us all your consideration, Mr. Horncastle. I am sure we will be able to keep everyone happy. There are rooms enough in this house for an army!" Harriet interjected scowling at her cousin.

"It would seem we already have the colonel to command it for us, Miss Wyndham," to her relief Mr. Horncastle agreed with her amiably, before gesturing to the corridor the other side of the stairs and confirming his own rooms lay in that direction. After the women, at least, thanked him, everyone dispersed.

Harriet gasped when she entered the *'green room'* and took in the view. Half a dozen windows ranged across the back wall, giving her a panoramic view of that she admired from the parlour below. She felt her annoyance at Nathaniel's attitude toward Mr. Horncastle drain away as she looked at it. *"Home,"* she thought and did not think she could ever tire of seeing it. A set of French doors in the middle of the windows allowed access to the balcony, which covered the rooms that extended below. The enormous room contained a large bed that lined one wall covered with green wallpaper. She wandered to double doors that stood opposite it and found herself in a dressing room. Easily as big as her room at Eastease, it contained ample hanging space for more than the clothing she brought with her. Her maid already within it, emptied Harriet's many trunks and bags. Annie placed piles of things on an additional bed within this room, presumably for any maid to rest upon when not needed. Though she certainly must have her own room in the servants' quarters, Harriet suspected it would be quite a distance away.

"Have you seen my room, Annie? It is so big I might get lost in it."

"The whole house is enormous, Miss. I think I may get lost once or twice a day at least. To think you own all of this!"

"I know, it is daunting. I am glad that you are with me. Are you sure that you will be happy moving here?"

"You will manage it admirably, and I am happy wherever you are, Miss. I never thought I should be lady's maid to the mistress of such an estate as this. I hope that I am up to the task."

"Of course you are! I have never felt the need to complain of anything with you. We must endeavour to assure each other in this manner anytime either of us has doubts! Now I must go and take a look at some of the other rooms and please forewarn James and the others that Mr. Horncastle is of short stature and I will not stand for them disrespecting him, no matter the opinions of Colonel Ackley!"

"Miss, I must insist that we first refresh your appearance from the journey and change that gown, I can see the road dust on it from here."

"Well, I must start as I mean to go on I suppose," she grumbled at her explorations of the house being delayed as she submitted herself to Annie's talented ministrations.

James Dawley moved easily around the dressing room that stood between two large bedrooms intended for the use of Colonel and Mrs. Ackley. In all his twenty-five years he never encountered such a large property as Wyndham House. When they approached it, he sat upon the hard bench seat of the cart driven by Peter with his mouth agape. Quickly recovering his wits, he directed the young lad beside him to drive the cart to a side road that led to the back of the house. It would not do for the vehicle packed with furniture and other belongings, to be seen by any occupants of the house, although he understood they only expected a Mr. Horncastle to be present.

James did not wish to miss the opportunity to travel to Bath and it pleased him that Miss Wyndham agreed to his accompanying them. For seven years he performed footman duties at Eastease, or when the colonel or another gentleman stayed there, he acted as a valet. His mother, his only remaining family, moved to one of the cottages at Redway, four years prior. Back then, he aided the colonel in protecting Mrs. Ackley from Lord Aysthill and, as was her way, that lady helped his family in return. After that, his mother's health improved. She found a friend in Enid Smithson, and they worked together taking in mending and washing for Redway, and surrounding houses. With his mother settled, he gave more consideration to pursuing his own happiness. James realised that footman at Eastease, though a comfortable circumstance, did not fit his modest ambitions. When he left with the group travelling to Bath, he suspected he might never return. His mother cried when he told her, but he promised to write.

James moved easily around the dressing room unpacking the colonel's luggage. Though not especially tall, his strength belied his slim build and he handled the trunk easily. Lifting a large pile of shirts and breeches from it and placing them on the small bed, he began storing them in the wardrobe and chest of drawers. His dark hair flopped in his brown eyes, the latter showing thick dark lashes as he revealed them by running his hands through the unruly mop. Loyal to Colonel and Mrs. Ackley for the kindness they showed to people of all ilk, he hoped they would not be disappointed in his new life choices.

As he continued with his task setting aside those items that should need refreshing after the journey, James heard Colonel Ackley enter a bedroom. He could tell the man's moods easily and showed no surprise when the colonel walked into the dressing room shortly after with a frown on his handsome face.

"Do I look as if I need freshening up to you, James?" he barked.

"It is protocol in a house as grand as this I expect, sir. Your boot and leg are rather dusty." James did not mind the colonel's anger, he knew it not to be directed towards him. Suggesting simple options soothed the man when in a disagreeable mood, which happened more often since the loss of his leg. James, having seen the stump of that leg, suspected the colonel felt some degree of pain more often than not.

"I will probably go for a ride this afternoon, what is the point in changing them? It is as if I am living at Aysthill under my mother's thumb!"

"I could set out your riding clothes, sir and you could wear those to luncheon with your riding boot, if you let me quickly clean that leg." He pointed to the dirt on the jointed wooden leg and the colonel unbuckled its strap before sitting on a bench to allow James to pull it off him. Then he took the crutch James offered as he stood again. They heard Mrs. Ackley enter the adjoining room and he looked up at the colonel when he harrumphed.

"They have us in separate rooms, as though we never share a bed. Put out the change of clothes, James. I will change in a moment. I must speak to my wife about these arrangements." The colonel hopped into Mrs. Ackley's room with the aid of the crutch.

Helena inspected the children's rooms that faced the front of the house. She stood at the window of Isabella's room and considered the picturesque view of an ornamental, small pond in the well-tended garden beyond. At her first view of the house she stifled a laugh thinking how her estranged mother would not believe she, who so disgraced the family, might be welcome at such a prestigious location. Closing the curtains, leaving a small opening to see by, she turned to see her daughter's pouting face.

"Thank you, Rebecca." She dismissed the maid with a rueful smile indicating Isabella's countenance, before nodding at the younger woman's rounded stomach. "Be sure to ask James to help you with any heavy lifting and make sure you rest, too."

"Thank you, Mrs. Ackley." Rebecca bobbed and exited the room.

"I don't want to lie down. I want to explore with Davy." Despite her protests, the young girl climbed up on the bed tucking her legs under the blankets, Isabella knew her well enough to know she would not yield.

"You felt unwell last night and did not sleep much. I know, I tried to sleep next to you!" Isabella complained of stomach pains the night before and would not settle unless she laid in the bed between her parents. Nathaniel, more prone to indulging her, obligingly rubbed the little girl's tummy to help her sleep.

Isabella and Nathaniel fell in love the moment they met. From that day, she wished desperately for him to be her father and he in turn would, if he could, have given her the world, as any father should do for a beloved daughter.

"I will wake you before luncheon, sweet girl." Helena closed the door behind her, noting with satisfaction her daughter's eyes closing as she left. Davy exited the next room and grinned at her.

"Do not go far, you only have thirty minutes before luncheon." He scampered away and she called to his retreating back, "do not disturb any of the servants at their work."

Crossing the hall, Helena entered her own room. The rich colours on the walls suited her style, with the dark wood of a large four poster bed. Moving to the window, she looked down onto a courtyard. To the right she could see where Harriet's rooms must be, a beautiful balcony extended over the rooms below. She felt very proud of her friend being mistress of this enormous house.

Double doors, which presumably led to the dressing room, opened suddenly. Nathaniel stood within them leaning on his crutch and scowling, as petulant as their daughter a moment ago. "I do not want a room of my own. We share a room at Redway and when we stay at Eastease, why can we not do so here?"

"There is no reason we cannot do so here, Nathaniel. You can simply walk across the dressing room or I can. Think of it as having options of sleeping locations. You have been disagreeable since we met Mr. Horncastle, why is that?" She kept her tone even, there would be little point in matching his mood with one of her own.

"He is a freak. He belongs in a show, not Harriet's house. It is unreasonable that Phillip foisted his friend upon her."

"Nathaniel, he is a person. Any decent person is worthy of our respect, no matter their height. You felt him perfectly amiable in your correspondence with him, before you found out how tall he is."

"How tall he is not."

"Nathaniel." She sighed. Sometimes reasoning with him proved impossible.

"If Harriet is to stay here when we leave, he will be the only gentleman, if indeed he is a gentleman, here to protect her. How is he to accomplish that?"

"I am sure he is perfectly capable. I expect he has come up against plenty of people who think as you do and has proven them wrong. Harriet likes him and your cousin wanted him to stay here for as long as he wishes. There is certainly enough room here. Give it some time and remember, if you want him to keep you abreast of Harriet's activities after we leave, then you need to prove to him your amiability and capability as much as he needs to prove his. Now let us freshen up."

He looked to the bed and she shook her head. "There is not time, Nathaniel." Helena could tell by the way his eyes roamed down her body that his thoughts shifted from Mr. Horncastle to their entanglement in their carriage earlier in the day when they managed to be alone.

He turned to close the doors to the dressing room, and she realised that he recalled she still wore nothing beneath her skirts.

Chapter Three

Harriet roamed some of the ground floor of the house, after Annie deemed her suitably attired, but when she finally found the music room, she groaned. Happily she found the instruments sound, although dusty and out of tune. The walls, covered in dark panelling, made the room seem small in comparison with others in the house, leaving little doubt Mr. Phillip Wyndham did not place prodigious emphasis upon music.

She tried singing in the room and found the sound quality dulled by the wood panelling. So, she wandered from room to room, singing in each one, before settling upon the parlour where they enjoyed refreshments upon their arrival.

She discovered another room that, though similar to the parlour with similar views, did not have such a good sound resonance. The added benefit, if they made that room the parlour instead, would be the courtyard directly outside its French doors.

Luncheon passed pleasantly, with Harriet asking Mr. Horncastle many questions about the house. The man seemed happy to regale them all with what he knew of the house's history and tales of Phillip.

"I found the music room, sir." Harriet approached her true interest cautiously. This would be her first time at making changes and she hoped Mr. Horncastle would not object.

"Yes, Phillip attended recitals and operas mainly to be seen at the right places, not a true connoisseur, but I enjoyed them. I cannot, I regret to say, turn my hand to an instrument. You, on the other hand, have an excellent singing voice. I admit I did listen at a couple of rooms in which you tried your singing. I think I am right in saying you favour the parlour for your music room?"

"If changing it will not cause you too much discomfort? I thought the room along the corridor should do as a parlour. It does not seem to be used for any particular purpose, but does provide access to the courtyard. It might be pretty to sit out there in nicer weather."

"Harriet, this is your house, damn it all. Have your music room wherever you wish. Mr. Horncastle is lucky to be living here." Nathaniel seemed determined to undermine her gentler approach to achieving her goal of the best music room she ever hoped for, which she felt the 'gold room' as she thought of it would provide.

"Nathaniel, please allow me to approach these decisions in my own way. Mr. Horncastle is allowed an opinion as this has been his home for so long. How should I have felt if, after Genevieve married Alexander, she came to Eastease and wanted me to leave, or wanted to move my music room or my bedroom?"

"Genevieve never would have done that!" he exclaimed in easy defence of the sweet wife of his friend.

"Then why do you consider it acceptable that I do so to Mr. Horncastle?" He would not concede the point, but did not say anything further. "How do you feel about that change, Mr. Horncastle? Music is important to me and that room provides the best sound in my opinion."

"As I was saying," Horncastle cast a derisive glance at the colonel, but Harriet could not blame him for that. "I did enjoy the musical soirées I attended with Phillip. If it means hearing more of your singing, and if your playing is as good, I would be most happy to relinquish the room. Would you allow me the honour of hearing some of your playing, whenever possible?"

"When it is a piece I am confident with, yes. I do not appreciate an audience when I am learning a piece, however."

"Thank you, Miss Wyndham. What do you say to asking Mckinnon to make those changes as soon as possible?"

"And dusting the instruments, too?"

"Most certainly." He chortled at that.

"Once everything is moved, perhaps Mckinnon would see to finding a tuner in town to visit and take care of that?" Harriet could not have been more thrilled. She achieved her goal of using the best room for her favourite pastime and Mr. Horncastle seemed equally happy.

"Perfect, and as soon as possible, as I am looking forward to hearing you play and sing."

"I can play the pianoforte, too, Mr. Horncastle. And Mama can sing beautifully." Isabella, it would seem, wanted to have her say.

"Isabella! I may not wish to sing, you should not volunteer someone else's performance," her mother admonished her.

"Well I certainly will not be performing for everyone here." Nathaniel made his intentions clear, but Harriet felt some disappointment. She loved to sing while her cousin played. Though not as talented as her, he always managed to put such fun into their pieces and knew some rather risqué songs that she suspected Mr. Horncastle would enjoy.

Relief flooded Harriet when Helena, ignoring her husband's surliness, got to her real point of interest. "Mr. Horncastle, I understand from Mckinnon that your stable manager recently left your employ." Harriet glared at her, so she corrected herself quickly. "I apologise, Harriet. I mean *your* employ of course."

"He did indeed, although the few horses we have currently are rather old. Phillip rode somewhat, but not towards the end. Mostly we used the carriage if we went anywhere. I, of course, do not ride." He said it as a matter of fact, but Harriet felt she detected some disappointment. With a glance at Helena she noticed the quiver of a smile at the corners of her friend's mouth. If anyone could get this little man upon a horse, she would be the one to do it.

"Why not?" Helena asked gently.

"You have noticed my size I am sure. In particular, my arms and legs."

"At four years old Isabella rode independently, her legs then as short as yours are now."

"Mama, we should have brought my pony with us, Mr. Horncastle could have ridden her!" Isabella's intentions though good, raised a snorted laugh from Nathaniel, and Mr. Horncastle frowned.

Harriet wanted to kick her cousin, but as she sat to his right she should surely stub her toe on his wooden leg. "Isabella, Mr. Horncastle is a man and a pony is for a child to ride."

"I thank you, Miss Wyndham."

She noticed his back straighten and he sat taller. Nathaniel harrumphed, but she did not care. He would be leaving and she would be staying at Wyndham House with Mr. Horncastle. She knew which man she needed to keep on her good side.

"But Elpis is wonderful and if you are scared riding at first, she should soon put you at ease." Isabella defended her much loved pony.

"You are quite right, sweet girl." Her mother soothed her. "Elpis is a very docile pony, nethertheless, we could certainly find a suitable horse for Mr. Horncastle when we look for one for you, as promised on this trip. You are far too tall for Elpis now."

"Let us take a walk out to the stable." Harriet suggested and they all agreed to walk off their meal by doing so.

When the guests went down to their luncheon, James decided to hunt for Mr. Horncastle's valet to ask him for some help with a stubborn stain. He knew the supplies he needed, but not where to find them. He finally came across the butler, finished with overseeing the serving of the luncheon trays, and asked him of the identity of the other valet and where he might be found. Astonishingly, the valet left after the death of Phillip Wyndham, feeling his loyalty to the household, and in particular Mr. Horncastle, died, too.

"Who is acting as Mr. Horncastle's valet in the meantime, Mr. Mckinnon?"

"Mr. Horncastle insists on taking care of these things himself. Given his unusual physicality, he tends to be private about who sees him without clothes. He manages quite well, although I have to say, it is not entirely to the standard I should expect in a household such as this. Still, we have been in mourning for six months with no visitors. Your party is the first since Mr. Wyndham's passing."

James explained his situation at Eastease, and with his mother settled, his preference to become entirely a valet, not just one on an as needed basis. He wondered if he could be considered for the position when the colonel left? In the meantime, perhaps he could help Mr. Horncastle in a limited capacity? Mckinnon nodded and suggested he might try and ingratiate himself with Mr. Horncastle in a small way, to encourage the man to be less independent in these matters.

"I have not, as yet, mentioned it to the colonel, Mr. Mckinnon. If you would not mind keeping this conversation to yourself?"

"I should suggest you keep it that way for now. Your colonel does not seem to like Mr. Horncastle much as yet, though he may, in time, be swayed by his wife's opinion."

James scurried away to the kitchens in the hopes of finding what supplies he needed with the help of the housekeeper or the cook.

The Wyndham stable, over half the size of Redway, impressed Helena. She could see that with proper care, the high-quality wood, fittings and fixtures in the stable should gleam and shine, making it a very handsome building indeed. The recent stable manager obviously did not consider these matters warranted his attentions. She watched disheartened as Nathaniel ran his eyes over it and the horses contained therein and shrugged. In his current mood Harriet could not rely on his help, even though Helena disagreed with what caused his mood, there it was.

"I am taking Perseus for a ride," he announced and promptly went to the stallion's stall to tack him up himself.

"May I assist you, Colonel?" Mickleson appeared with his master's saddle slung across a thick forearm, reins grasped in his other fist.

"I can do it myself, man!" Nathaniel dismissed him curtly, taking the saddle, while Helena shrugged at the look Mickleson gave her. She would not get in Nathaniel's way with this black mood upon him and a ride would help him work it off.

"I want to ride with you, Papa." Davy requested.

"I want to ride, too!" Isabella of course did not want to be left out.

Nathaniel looked to Helena, she knew he hated to disappoint their children in anything, but she needed him to blow off this bad temper.

41

"Davy?" she offered and he nodded before curtly instructing Mickleson to tack up Coal. Davy moved to go to his mount's stall, but Helena hooked a finger around his coat collar, holding him back and speaking quietly in his ear. "Your father is in a mood. If he rides hell for leather, you do not try to match him. Follow at a distance and catch up, when he has run his course."

"What if I am in a mood?"

"You do not know the terrain here. Agree or stay here with me."

"Yes, Mama." She released him and he ran to his beloved mare.

"I want to ride!" Isabella pouted, but for once her father would not indulge her.

"We will ride tomorrow, sweet girl, I promise, but for now let us take a look at Harriet's new horses. You know how we love to meet new ones." Helena watched her husband mount his stallion and head off to the fields with barely a backward glance to Davy and certainly not a look to her. It would be a long month at this beautiful house if he did not work out his issues with Mr. Horncastle.

The horses, certainly past their prime, seemed healthy mainly due to the efforts of a young stableman called Benjamin Bramley. Helena thought him probably eighteen. His lean, long frame meant he had grown into his big hands and feet, but his face still showed some softness and his beard growth showed minimally. His light-brown eyes held an innocent yet mischievous look, and he smiled easily and widely. He flicked his brown hair out of his eyes as he talked knowledgeably about the animals for which he cared. Mickleson, who rejoined them after Davy followed his father, looked towards Helena and she raised her eyebrows. He nodded wryly as they both acknowledged the young man's enthusiasm for horses and dedication to their care.

The half doors to the stalls seemed overly high and Helena noticed Mr. Horncastle kick a wide stool towards each one, stepping upon it before peering over the door at the horse within.

"Harriet," she said to her friend, as Isabella stepped up on the stool with the small man to peer into the stall with him. "I think you could lower the height of all these doors, they do seem exceptionally tall."

"I agree."

This stall housed a gelding that Mr. Horncastle informed them Phillip Wyndham rode most often. The slim thoroughbred took to

Helena quickly, as most horses did, and enjoyed a treat from several she procured from the kitchens.

"What do you think of trying this gelding tomorrow, Mr. Horncastle? He is gentle and slim enough for your leg length. We can wrap the stirrup leathers around the stirrup to shorten them for you. How brave are you feeling?"

"I think you are having the same effect upon me as you are the horses, calming. I would be honoured to try riding Theo in memory of dear Phillip. Thank you."

"Thank you, sir, for your patience with my husband. It is not in his usual manner to be this way with someone, I do not know what has gotten into him. Perhaps the six days cooped up in a carriage or he might be in pain, which he is often with his leg."

"Do not concern yourself over the colonel and I. We will have a confrontation soon enough."

"That is what I am afraid of." She gave her own harrumph at that, knowing what a confrontation might mean for Nathaniel.

"He is a fighter?"

"Yes, he is. Near Redway we have a neighbour who opened her house to men who have lost a limb. Nathaniel helps them learn to ride and fight, so they can be men again, and find a purpose in life. He certainly leads by example."

"And how good a fighter is he?"

"Mostly unbeaten. When I first knew him, someone described him as formidable, since losing a leg that description has not lessened."

"Hmmm, well we will see about that." She looked at Mr. Horncastle in surprise, but felt the man did not seem worried. She planned to have a word with Mickleson to ensure that Nathaniel did not hurt this smaller man.

Nathaniel and Perseus rode hard across the fields, up and down the slopes. Used to the flatter fields and gentle slopes of Redway, they enjoyed the harder work going uphill and the speed down the other side. If he bothered to stop atop any hill, he should have seen picturesque views of fields and trees in all directions. When he approached an expansive wood at the bottom of the steepest hill, he slowed Perseus gradually, finally trotting to the tree line and turning right. Seeing a lake to that side, he headed towards it. After stopping close to its edge, he looked back to see Davy and Coal careening down the final hill. The boy learned well in the past three and a half years and handled the mare easily.

The run blew away the colonel's mood. Out of the sight of the little man who irked him, he smiled as his son brought Coal to them. He held pride for the achievements of the boy he thought of only as his son.

"You and Coal are looking good together, you did well with the different terrain. How did it feel?"

"Tough on my legs up the hills, though I managed to stay up out of the seat as you taught me. Coal did not struggle at all, she is a good girl." He patted the mare's neck affectionately. "Downhill felt wonderful!"

"You leaned back well, coming down that last steep one and kept your balance for Coal. Tie her up over there and we will explore the lake. I am going to tie Perseus here to keep them separate. Otherwise she might be foaling in a year's time!" Davy walked the mare over to the trees slightly apart from those that Nathaniel went to tie Perseus to. Then he joined his father at the side of the lake. They stood together looking out over it, before turning to walk along its edge.

"Are we going to swim?"

Nathaniel ruffled his son's hair. "Not today. We will have to ask the freak about the reeds and fish in here first. I wonder if he has a boat?"

"I do not like Mr. Horncastle either, Father. You are right, he is a freak!" Nathaniel looked shocked towards his son. Being a father held a lot more responsibility than he imagined it would. He realised quickly that Davy loved to emulate him and it pleased Nathaniel. He endeavoured to be the kind of man he hoped his sons would be, but to have his vitriol repeated back to him and with such venom shamed him.

He still did not like Horncastle, but leave Harriet alone with him? Could the man protect her? Could he help her with running this enormous estate? Two key staff already left. The stable, that Nathaniel took in with a quick glance before riding off, needed taking in hand judging by the disarray.

"Davy," he began, shaking his head and wondering how to berate his son for repeating what his father just said? "I should not have used that word with Mr. Horncastle, I do not want to hear you repeat it."

"I am sorry, but I still do not like him."

"Do not be sorry, hearing you say it made me realise that we are better men than that. You may still not like him, I have my own reservations, but we have not even known him a day yet. Perhaps we should give him more time."

"Issie thinks he is wonderful. She plans to feature a fr… small man in a story."

Isabella's affection for the shorter man, obviously displeased Davy and Nathaniel smiled.

"Maybe she will write that a dragon eats him, though he should not make much of a meal." They laughed together at that.

"Why are Mother and Issie so accepting of people?"

"We should be glad that they are, as they both accepted us into their lives did they not?" Davy grinned up at him. "Let us return and see what they have cooked up without us. I have an idea for the stable, but I need to speak to Mickleson first."

Chapter Four

That evening, James assisted the colonel quickly with his dress. The man did indeed go riding and that boot and his leg needed cleaning. Thankfully, his spare straight leg did not need his attention and the colonel wore trousers rather than breeches with it. James could clean everything else later ready for the morrow.

Leaving the colonel waiting for his wife to emerge from her rooms, James hurried down the corridor where Mr. Mckinnon indicated Mr. Horncastle's rooms could be found. Unsure, he paused at several doors listening for any activity, until he heard a groan coming from the room behind the door nearest the end of the corridor. He knocked tentatively.

"Come!" a voice barked from within. James entered promptly, expecting the man to be almost completely dressed, but he found him in his dressing gown, lying on the hard floor.

"Are you well, sir? Have you fallen? How can I aid you?" He hurried to him, dropping to one knee and reaching his hands out to assist him.

"Do not touch me!"

"I apologise, sir," then under his breath, "this is not a good beginning."

"Not a good beginning to what?" Mr. Horncastle looked up at James, seemingly noticing him properly for the first time.

"Our relationship." James blurted it out in his frustration over the inauspicious first impression he must have made.

"Are we to have a relationship?" The man seemed amused despite his obvious pain and James smiled.

"I hoped to make a good impression, to encourage you to realise that it might be time for you to consider hiring a valet of your own."

"How would you be impressing me?"

"I expected you to be mostly dressed by now, sir. I hoped to tie your cravat for you. I am rather good with some stylish knots. Why are you lying on the floor?" James looked around for some evidence of a fall.

"I experience some back pain now and again, a side effect of my short stature. Your colonel has tensed me more than I should like. The thought of another round with him at dinner the final straw. What are you doing?"

James moved to slide his hand under Mr. Horncastle's lower back where his spine curved and did not touch the floor.

"See if you can tilt your lower half, sir, and get your back to touch my hand. It might take a few tries to stretch it, but when I have been on my feet all day, I find it helps my back." An idea occurred to him, and he moved the man's hand to replace his under his back and then stood and moved away quickly.

"Where are you going?"

"Keep trying that, sir. I will be back momentarily."

"If we are to have a relationship, you should tell me your name!"

"James, sir!"

He returned with a small jar and found Bertram Horncastle on his feet.

"What is that?"

"Mrs. Hopkins' miracle cream." He smiled down at the man. "It is the colonel's, but I have more and will write to Mrs. Hopkins for a supply if you find it suits you. If you could disrobe and lie on the bed, I will apply some to your back."

"Leave it with me, I will apply it myself."

"If you try to do that, you will only tense your back again, sir. I have applied this to the colonel's leg stump in the past. I am sure if I can do that, I can manage the sight of your bare back."

"It is not my back I am worried about. I do not have anything on under here."

"I am sure I can cope. If you wish to be modest, tie it low around your hips." James turned away and perused the rest of the room while he waited. When he first walked in, he took in the rich woods of the panelling and the furniture. As he glanced around now he could see the tasteful additions of colour and texture. It added some softness to the room, but it remained masculine overall.

He heard the movement of the bed, gave it a moment and turned back. Two things struck him directly as he looked down at the prone form of the man. Firstly, his exceptionally muscular physique surprised James. The only man who compared, the colonel, only became so since he lost a leg. Secondly, the assortment of scars across his back. He said nothing of them, but quickly warmed some cream by rubbing it between his hands then applying it, concentrating on the lower back and moving in circular motions with firm pressure.

"Thank you."

"Not at all, sir. May I assist you with your dress now?" He walked to the dressing room to allow Mr. Horncastle the opportunity to cover himself again, and found some clothes already laid out. "Black again, sir?"

"Yes, black. Always black," the voice at the dressing room door snapped, so James said nothing further and helped him.

Bertram enjoyed the lively conversation between Helena, Harriet and himself at dinner that evening. The ladies talked of him riding, but he noticed the colonel rolling his eyes which made him wonder if it could be truly possible.

Then the man announced his own idea of Mickleson being the stable manager, saying he spoke to him about it on his return from his ride. Bertram felt that the colonel hoped for the attention and praise to be all upon him at the declaration, but Harriet glared at him.

"Nathaniel! Why would you presume to ask Mr. Mickleson to be *my* stable manager? It is not your place to talk to Mickleson of that before mentioning it to me! I agree it should be an excellent idea if he is willing to stay and Redway is willing to release him, but I would like to run these kinds of ideas past Mr. Horncastle and speak to Mickleson myself before coming to my final decision."

Bertram hurriedly hid his smirk as she turned to him expectantly awaiting his response. He thought her simply marvellous! She wanted his opinion, when it meant nothing legally. He liked that she put the colonel in his place and could see the man's earlier improved temperament sinking again, which gave him a perverse pleasure.

"I thank you for asking me, Miss Wyndham. Of course the final decision is yours. If Colonel and Mrs. Ackley value him, I am sure we should be lucky to have him."

"Thank you, sir. I will talk to Mickleson myself tomorrow, when we all go out to ride in the morning. Helena, I suggest we withdraw." Mrs. Ackley agreed and Bertram stood with the colonel, feeling the loss of the buffer between him and the man who held him in such disdain.

Mckinnon poured some port and lit cigars, as the colonel stared at Horncastle across the table. When the butler moved to stand sentry by the door as usual, Bertram jerked his head at him, indicating he should leave them. After watching the door close, he looked back at the stony faced soldier, waiting.

"This is hardly port and cigars with the *men*, is it? Perhaps you should have withdrawn with the ladies, Horncastle."

"Are we to get our members out to compare the length and determine who is the better man? I assure you I have never lost that competition." Bertram kept his temper, he found he enjoyed riling this man who did not restrain in showing his contempt once finally alone. The more reasonable and calm he remained, the angrier he made his opponent.

"Neither have I." Nathaniel scoffed.

"So, is it only to be the height of the man that determines if he is indeed a man? Not perhaps the number of limbs? At least both of my legs are the same length."

"You would disparage a man who lost a limb fighting for England? That is not a wise idea."

"You think you are the only one who has faced hardship? You have only dealt with that affliction for two years, I fought all my life. Not even my family wanted me and threw me out as soon as they realised I would not grow normally. I understand from your wife that you help those who have fought and lost a limb, learn to ride and fight again. You accept them as men. Why am I any different?"

"It is no fault of theirs to be injured in battle. They fought bravely and deserve respect for risking their lives for our country." Bertram conceded that well-made point with a curt nod of his head, but it occurred to him in that moment that this explained the colonel's behaviour toward him. Had the colonel observed disrespect of a disfigured soldier or possibly even experienced it himself? Surely many in society would find such a man abhorrent without consideration for his service to his country?

"I was born this way, it is no fault of mine. I know why you dislike me, Colonel. I am just wondering if you have discovered the reason for yourself yet."

"You want to prove to me you are a man? That you can protect Harriet if we leave her here with you? Let us fight. Swords, in the morning after breakfast. If you can beat me, I will teach you to ride." Obviously a command, *Colonel* Ackley did not wait for an answer. He threw his cigar into his glass, pushed back on his chair so hard he toppled it over, and stormed out of the door that opened when Mckinnon burst in to check on the noise.

Clearly he lost the taste for the cigar and the port after their exchange, but Bertram smiled and raised his own glass towards the man's retreating back, before supping upon it and following it with an enjoyable puff of his own cigar.

Helena wondered whether she should be surprised when Mr. Horncastle arrived in the drawing room without her husband. She looked questioningly at the little man, but he divulged nothing other than the colonel left his company abruptly. Covering her continued befuddlement over Nathaniel's manner, Helena commented on Mr. Horncastle's cravat.

"I see that James Dawley has made himself useful to you, Mr. Horncastle. Your cravat looks very befitting."

"A very competent, young man, madam. He found me flat on the floor unable to move. His techniques and a cream from a Mrs. Hopkirk eased my back pain and allowed me to make it to the dinner table."

"Mrs. Hopkins," Harriet corrected him, still very loyal to the Eastease housekeeper whose cream helped her many times.

Mr. Horncastle smiled at Helena, giving her the impression he got the name wrong on purpose and she gave him a small smile in return.

"If it is of interest to you, James is an excellent valet. The colonel has not really needed one at Redway, where we are less formal, but James has always served him excellently at Eastease."

"Excuse me, Mrs. Ackley," the ever present Mckinnon unusually interjected into the conversation, "I understand from James that he served you in some capacity at Eastease a few years back, and in return you assisted his muther considerably. Though James did nae divulge the details, I think Mr. Horncastle might be interested in hearing about the lad's loyalty. If I'm nae too bold as to suggest you talk of it."

"Am I to understand you are in favour of James, Mr. Mckinnon? A good valet could take over the responsibility of the upstairs staff, relieving you of some of that burden." Mrs. Ackley regarded the butler shrewdly. She felt him a very useful man, the like of which she would have chosen for a butler at Redway, if they ever felt the need for one. She felt torn in telling her story, between being of assistance to James and not wishing to make herself out to have performed any exceptional duty. She would also be revealing a secret kept from Harriet by her guardians and disparaging a man who recently improved in his character.

"I never did learn what happened that night, Helena," Harriet quickly worked out it must have been the evening of the dinner at Eastease when Nathaniel and Helena first met.

"Oh-ho! A story of intrigue or a secret rendezvous? What is it to be?" A weariness seemed to have lifted from the shoulders of Mr. Horncastle, his exuberant side returning swiftly.

Helena waved his question away. "Before I tell you of that, I must start with three caveats. Firstly, Harriet, if your guardians kept this from you, it must have been with good reason. As the most likely of those is your age at the time, I feel it is acceptable for you to hear it now. However, I will deny ever telling you, if either of those men find out! Secondly, it is true that James' actions that night did prompt me to seek out his mother's living situation and, finding it appalling, I moved her to one of my cottages. However, I have been the one to gain the most from that seemingly charitable deed. Mrs. Dawley has done exceptional work sewing, mending and washing for Redway and me personally. Since she joined forces with Enid Smithson, they have provided their services to many houses in the area."

"You mentioned a third caveat, Mrs. Ackley?" Mr. Horncastle prompted when she paused, the excitement of hearing of some hidden story of Eastease showing in his eyes.

"Yes. Thirdly, the man whom the light of this story shines least favourably upon is much improved in recent years, and I should hate anyone here," she glanced at Mckinnon who nodded, "to repeat it. I only wish to tell you of it, Mr. Horncastle, as James Dawley is a most trust-worthy, honourable and loyal servant. He is intelligent and works well in directing other staff, a fact that I have only recently learned on our journey here. I am sure it should have taken us two more days at least, had it not been for James."

"Let me start the story, Helena." Harriet's excitement at hearing a closely held secret evident in her voice. Helena nodded resignedly. "I will begin with what I know... At the end of August in 1813, the colonel returned to us after being injured in battle, I hear the scar from it slices right across his chest!"

Helena nodded again.

"Lady Aysthill, the colonel's mother mollycoddled him for weeks, but he finally escaped and came to us. That Lady, however, wished to see him well cared for at Eastease and so we agreed there should be a dinner with several guests including Helena and Mr. Brooks. All guests planned to stay overnight. I practised an aria with Helena a few times and persuaded her to sing it."

"Marvellous!" exclaimed Mr. Horncastle. "Would you honour me with your singing while you are at Wyndham House, Mrs. Ackley?"

"We will have to wait and see, sir. You are forgetting to tell of your mischievousness in getting Nathaniel to play while I sang two other songs later in the evening, Harriet!" Helena did not forget any of the details of that evening, so hesitant she felt back then at being distinguished by the playful Colonel. He exuded power and strength and reminded her of a stallion, and she noticed moments of caring and gentleness that people never knew stallions possessed, too. Despite the changes in his physical appearance, she saw little change in him regarding any of those extremes. How could it be possible that such a timid mare as she, attracted such a man? She could hardly recognize that mare in herself now.

She smiled bringing her thoughts back to the room where Harriet told how Nathaniel took over the piano playing, all planned when Harriet saw him looking often at herself. Bertram Horncastle looked at Helena intently and she blushed as if he could read where her thoughts wandered. Harriet finished her part of the story telling how she and Helena assisted a very large and tired Gennie up to her bed. The first of the Harkers' children arrived only a week later. The younger woman looked expectantly at Helena who began her story.

"I readied for bed, then opened the curtains in my room next to Harriet's to ensure the sun should wake me early. I looked down at light in a window in the opposite wing and saw the rest of the party playing cards. Nathaniel won often. Then most of the party left, leaving only him, his brother and his father, Lord Aysthill."

"Did the colonel spot you at the window?" Horncastle asked. Helena noted the sparkle still in his eyes.

"Yes, yes, he did, but I blew out the candle and continued to watch him. He did not give anything away to his father and brother. Oh, his father! Lord Aysthill and I locked horns over horses. He wanted me to sell to him and I refused. I heard of his beating his animals and none of my beasts should end up in his hands if I could help it.

I fell asleep on that window seat and woke to the door handle rattling. I locked my door, just a precaution, but my instincts proved correct. Moving to the door, I listened and could hear Nathaniel telling his father to leave, which the man did. I risked a look out to the corridor and saw Nathaniel move to sit on the couch lining the opposite wall. He planned to sleep there and ensure his father did not come back."

Harriet sighed, "that is romantic."

"I took a pillow and coverlet out to him and asked how he knew what his father planned. He told me that James returned to him after being dismissed because he saw Lord Aysthill heading to the corridor that led only to the rooms Harriet and I slept in. The servants knew of that man's proclivities, servants always know, do they not, Mckinnon?" Her eyes slid towards the butler who returned to his usual position by the door and he gave a small smile, but said nothing.

"But, madam, you locked your door, you said. That should have been the end of it whether the colonel arrived or not, surely? Neither he nor James saved you from any real danger." Bertram questioned her.

"Ah, a sitting room adjoined my room and Harriet's and I forgot to lock the outer door to that, or the door from that room to mine. I am sure he would have tried that door next. He planned to *'teach me a lesson'*. It is a phrase, Nathaniel has told me since, that his father often used with any woman who refused him anything or he felt impertinent towards him. So, you can see how James' vigilance saved me that night and such a good deed should be repaid."

"The earl did not make any further attempt to compromise you?"

"No, the following day, so I have been given to understand by Mr. Harker, Nathaniel threatened to kill his father, if he ever stepped a foot on Redway property or tried to touch me."

"My word, Helena, I had no idea!" Harriet looked aghast at her friend since she mentioned the rattle of the door handle.

"But you mentioned Lord Aysthill's character has improved?" Bertram looked as if he wanted to ask several questions, but she would have none of it.

"That is a story for another day," she told them all as she rose. "I think I need to find the soldier who helped me that night and thank him once more." She walked to the door and smiled at Mckinnon.

"I believe the colonel went to the stable, Mrs. Ackley."

"Thank you, Mckinnon. Very discreet of James not to give you those details, do you not think?"

"Aye, ma'am." He smiled warmly.

"Is there a blanket I can take with me to the stable to keep warm?"

He directed her in finding one, as she insisted he need not disturb a servant to fetch it and bid them all goodnight before leaving.

Helena found Nathaniel feeding the last of some carrots to Perseus. She draped the blanket over his shoulders and then ducked underneath his arms to stand between him and the stall door, looking in at the grey stallion. He wrapped the blanket around them both as his arms came around her.

"I am trying, Helena." Glumly, he rested his chin on her shoulder.

"Not hard enough, evidently." She said it gently, as the glow of recalling that first evening they met still warmed her.

"I cannot explain it, just to look at him gets my goat. He says he knows why, but did not tell me."

"It is not how you usually are with people, my love. Is your leg causing you pain? I know you can be unhappier when that is the case."

"Nothing exceptional. Thank you for coming out here to find me."

"I know this is where you feel more at peace, as do I. Why do we not make our way to one of the wonderful bedrooms we have been given?" She leaned back against his hard chest as he straightened and his arms pulled her more tightly against him. The man exuded heat and pulled the passion from within her like no other man.

"Why do we not make our way to this wonderful pile of straw I noticed in one of the empty stalls here? I am thinking of it as an *'option of our sleeping locations.'*" He turned her to him and brushed his lips gently over hers before roaming kisses down her neck, picking her up and walking with her to the stall. She recalled a duet they performed at an Eastease dinner and started to sing in a quiet voice…

"Daylight may do for the gay,
The thoughtless, the heartless, the free,
But there's something about the moon's sky,
That is sweeter to you and to me…"

While her parents lay entwined within a blanket on a pile of straw, Isabella slept peacefully in her comfortable bed. Her room, though positioned next to Davy's the same as at home, seemed so far away with these rooms so big. She woke suddenly hearing loud screaming coming from Davy's room and ran out into the corridor, surprised she did not see her mother, already reaching him.

She entered her brother's room quickly after lighting a candle from the lamp in the hallway and saw Davy sitting up in bed, his eyes open, but seeing nothing in the room, his mind elsewhere. She vaguely recalled these screaming nightmares when he first came to Redway, but they waned quickly. Recently, after the death of Maria Brooks, they started again, Isabella thought it at least a month since the last one.

Their mother always spoke to him in a soothing, but firm voice so she tried to do the same. She felt a little scared, but confident that if she did the same as her mother he would come out of it soon. "Davy, you are safe. It is Issie, you are safe with me." She clambered into the bed, but kept an arm's length away from him. Touching or holding him always made it worse. He still screamed, but she carried on. "Davy, it is Issie. You are safe. We are at Wyndham House with Harry. Coal is here, tucked up nicely in her stall, she enjoyed her ride with you today, I could tell." She continued to talk as if telling one of her stories. Davy always enjoyed her stories.

James put his head in the room. "Miss Isabella, do you need my aid?"

"He is not as loud now, so I think it is almost over. Thank you." The valet disappeared again.

"Issie?" Davy's voice croaked and he looked at her properly for the first time. He told her once that the nightmares felt so real, but faded quickly. Often after he cried in their mother's arms and she noticed tears welling in his eyes. He turned his head away from her, he would not want her to see them.

"I do not mind if you cry. You have seen me cry many times."

"You are a girl, it is different."

"I think you are brave and resilient."

"Resilient?"

"It is my new word." She smiled at him and blew out the candle, so he could cry if he wanted to. Then she got under the covers with him and settled down.

"You want to stay here tonight?"

"Yes, these rooms are so big. I feel safer here closer to you." She put her arms around him and hugged him and he did the same. He should never admit it, but it comforted to him to have her there, Surprised he did not find his mother there when he came out of the nightmare.

He lay in the dark looking up at the tall ceiling. "Issie, why do you want to be the same height as Mr. Horncastle?"

"I know I will not, Mother and Father are both tall, so I suppose I will be, too, but he liked it when I said so. I like having an adult around that I do not have to look up at and he is funny and friendly."

"I am the same height as you, though I want to be as tall as Father one day. Do you like Mr. Horncastle more than me because one day I will be taller than you?"

"No, silly, who should I possibly like more than you? You and Little Nate of course. I wonder how tall he will be when we get back. I miss him."

"Me, too. I told Father that your plan to write a story with Mr. Horncastle in it. He said you should make a dragon eat him, but that he should not make much of a meal!"

"Goodnight, Davy." She giggled into the darkness and he smiled. He loved to hear her giggles.

"Goodnight, Issie. Thank you for coming in here tonight."

After ensuring Isabella and Davy did not need his aid, James headed back across the corridor to the colonel's dressing room. He hoped the colonel should not be much longer in getting to bed. The small form of Mr. Horncastle appear at the top of the stairs. Seeing James, the man smiled.

"Bring your ointment, James. I need your help."

"But, the colonel?" He began to follow Mr. Horncastle, glancing back towards Colonel Ackley's rooms as he spoke.

"He is out in the stable with his wife, I believe they may be some time as she took a blanket with her." Rolling his eyes at that information, James ran to get Mrs. Hopkins' cream and caught up to Mr. Horncastle quickly, he continued talking, "I am going to need a supple back if I am to fight the colonel tomorrow, James!"

Chapter Five

The sun struggled over the horizon and the dim light outside began to brighten when Helena woke, with her husband's arms wrapped around her, in an empty stall of the Wyndham stable. She extricated herself with an exclamation, waking Nathaniel.

"My goodness, it is so late! Well early I suppose. We should get back to our rooms, what will the servants think of us sleeping out here? There are bound to be some awake already."

"They will think I am a very lucky man. Come back here woman, I am not done with you yet."

"You will have to be, Nathaniel. I must check on the children and change." He grabbed at her leg pulling her down to him and she laughed. "You have been insatiable since we left Redway. If I knew you should have been this way, I would have insisted on a trip sooner."

"I have not been working hard in the stable as we have been away from it, though that may change if we are to make this place look its best."

She kissed him affectionately, glad that he intended to help with the stable, it should be fun to see it improved. "You are coming around to Mr. Horncastle then?"

"I will do it for Harriet, not for him. I agreed to teach him to ride if he can best me in a swordfight this morning."

"Nathaniel! Why is a fight the only way to prove yourself a man in your opinion?"

"It is not the only way," he said and ran a cold hand up her skirts.

Helena shrieked, then heard a clearing of a throat in the stable corridor. Someone else entered the stable. Hurriedly, she pulled away from Nathaniel again and standing came face to face with a red-faced Benjamin over the stall door.

"I am sorry, ma'am. I wanted to get an early start on clearing out the stalls."

"I am sorry... I mean I did not intend... Go about your business Benjamin, pretend you never saw us."

"Yes, ma'am." She watched him scurry away gratefully, as Nathaniel lay in the straw laughing. Before he could grab her again, she exited and made her way to the back of the house.

"Mrs. Ackley!" Helena closed the door quietly, but turned at the surprised voice seeing a young woman dressed as a servant in the doorway to what smelled like the kitchen. She bobbed quickly. "I am sorry, ma'am. You startled me. Can I aid you?"

Flustered, Helena tried to regain some respectability in the eyes of the servant, but realised the futility of it with a smile. "Miss? Mrs.? This blanket needs to go to the laundry."

"Let me take that, the laundry is just through here." She crossed the corridor to the opposite door and threw the blanket within the room. I am Miss Cadman. The cook."

"Well then, please allow me to commend you for dinner last night. You have a definite skill in the kitchen, Miss Cadman. Excuse me, I must change."

"Thank you, ma'am." The woman bobbed again with a definite smirk on her face. Helena wondered if the woman saw straw in her hair. She did not doubt the whole house would know that Colonel and Mrs. Ackley slept in the stable like a pair of animals. Nothing, however, could dim the glow of Nathaniel's gentle loving of the night before.

Helena smiled as she looked in Davy's room and found her two children in the large bed there. She missed her youngest son, however, and felt a tug at her gut just thinking about him. Mr. Brooks and those at Redway would provide him with excellent care, and Genevieve at Eastease only a few miles away if they needed more help, with Amelia at Bernier House. Little Nate would not have enjoyed the long journey and she could not have felt the independence she did now, with him here. She could ride off with Nathaniel if they wanted to, safe in the knowledge that Davy and Isabella could take care of themselves and each other. She hoped that Nathaniel would be willing to explore the different landscape here with her, and perhaps they might find some secluded spot to enjoy together.

He seemed in a better mood this morning. Though some of that might be because he planned to fight Mr. Horncastle. The little man did not seemed perturbed at the possibility of being challenged and she wondered if, despite his height, the little man's strength would serve him well. She stopped suddenly as she walked into her dressing room and discovered James asleep on the little bunk there. Quietly she started to look for the items she should need to change into, but not enough as the young man jumped to his feet not properly awake.

"Mrs. Ackley, ma'am. I apologise."

"For sleeping at night? No, I do not accept that apology as it is not necessary. Lie down again, James or at least sit down, you look exhausted. Do I smell Mrs. Hopkins' miracle cream?"

"Mr. Horncastle's back needed it to aid his bad back, I applied it for him. He said he is to fight the colonel today."

"So I have been given to understand, though why Nathaniel thinks it is necessary is beyond my comprehension."

"Mr. Horncastle is rather more muscular than his short stature may lead you to believe."

"Yes, I suspected as much." She could tell the strength and muscle covered by a coat, as much in a man as in a horse.

"Should I warn the colonel?"

"No. He will discover it for himself in due course. What of your endeavour to find work here, James?" The young man looked surprised at her. "Your mother told me of it and asked me to take care of you." He bristled at that, she could tell.

"You have not mentioned it to the colonel?"

"It is more than my life is worth to do so."

"Mr. Horncastle does not have a valet currently, I am hoping to show him that he should."

"And that it should be you, of course."

"Yes."

"He could not do better. Let me know if I can be of any assistance, and James…"

"Yes, ma'am?"

"Be assured that all of us at Redway will look out for your mother."

"Thank you, Mrs. Ackley. Should I fetch Rebecca to aid you in dressing?"

"It is early and I can manage it. Let her sleep."

After breakfast, Bertram Horncastle waited patiently for his opponent on the manicured lawn. He talked to Miss Wyndham whilst young Master Davy regaled him cheerfully with gruesome descriptions of what his father should be doing to him. He laughed the boy's goading off amiably. Mickleson sat on a low wall to the side of them, looking disinterested. Horncastle felt Mrs. Ackley possibly asked him to be there in case he needed to intervene.

The colonel, purposefully late, appeared dressed in his redcoat with his sword sheathed at his side.

"Your tactics are not working, Colonel," Horncastle greeted him. "Your wife, daughter and cousin have provided me ample amusement while I wait, as have Master Davy's tall stories. My courage rises with every attempt to intimidate me. What use to me is a redcoat, when I wear my armour of black to honour my dearest friend?"

"Enough talk, freak. First blood?"

"If you insist on spilling some, Colonel." Bertram picked up his sword and bowed. The colonel unsheathed his and bowed, too.

Bertram moved fast. A sword, not as light as an epee, the colonel might have expected him to struggle with, but he did not. Soon the man moved to a back foot, defending the smaller man's attack. Still, the colonel surprised him, gathering himself to launch an attack of his own. Bertram, however, parried him away easily and noticed his opponent tighten his grip on the hilt to avoid being disarmed. Moments later, Bertram managed a hit to the hand as Colonel Ackley's glove split open.

He glanced at it. "No blood, Horncastle. Try again."

Bertram raised his eyebrows at the colonel using his last name, rather than calling him a freak. Could his point be penetrating the man's thick skull? He hated to shame him in front of his family, particularly his son.

"If you wish, Colonel!" They fought again and after two short attacks, the man held his hand to his jawline, where a thin graze bled. No worse than a shaving cut, but surely he would concede?

"I win, then. You have to teach me to ride, per the agreement, unless you wish to wrestle?"

Throwing his sword to the ground, Colonel Ackley ripped off his redcoat. "Challenge accepted, freak."

Bertram rued his choice of words when goading the man, as he seemed to have returned to throwing insults his way. "Are you keeping that leg on, stumpy?"

"So it would seem." The colonel growled it as he took his stance, but Bertram simply shrugged.

He knew that his only hope would be to get the taller man to the ground, so the moment the fight started he attacked the colonel's good leg and easily unbalanced him. They fell to the ground and scrambled, but the wooden leg impeded the colonel's movement. Before he recovered himself enough to do anything about it, Bertram used his strength to turn him onto his stomach, sat on his shoulders and pulled an arm back. Colonel Ackley roared with the pain and quickly conceded as he lay face down on the ground. Bertram knew the man's shoulder close to dislocating, so he released him.

"If you have quite finished with your foolish games, we will head to the stable." She shooed Davy and Isabella ahead of her with a backwards glance at Bertram. He admired the woman for perhaps the hundredth time since first meeting her only the day before. No doubt she knew the humble pie would stick in her husband's throat enough without them all watching.

Harriet hesitated and looked at the Redway stableman, Mickleson. "I wonder if I might have a word with you privately?"

"Of course, Miss. There is an office in the stable we could use." He stood quickly and gestured deferentially for her to walk ahead of him. When they reached the office, she sat in the only chair in the room at the small battered desk, he stood just inside the doorway, leaving the door ajar. Harriet looked around the room, the bunk only other place he could sit, but when she glanced at it, he said, "I am happy to stand, Miss."

"Then I will, too, I will break my neck trying to look up at you from here." She stood near the desk and looked at the man. She knew him well, as he moved to Redway nearly two years prior, after the death of Genevieve's father, Mr. Hopwood. Mickleson held the position of stable manager at Thornbane, the Hopwoods' home, but did not wish to work for the new master who purchased it. Alexander Harker bid him to ride to Redway as, with an apprenticeship at a blacksmith, he would be useful there. Helena mentioned often how much they valued him.

He took off his cap, his black hair rather wild and unruly. He ran a large hand through it trying unsuccessfully to tame it. Several days beard growth showed on his face and his almost black eyes looked intently at Harriet, waiting for her to speak.

"Mr. Mickleson, I understand that the colonel spoke to you yesterday about the possibility of being stable manager here."

"Yes, Miss, though I know it is your decision. He only mentioned he should talk to you of it." It would seem Nathaniel did not act quite so heavy handed as she accused him of the evening before.

"I have discussed it with Mr. Horncastle, and the colonel and Mrs. Ackley have agreed, though they will miss you at Redway, to you taking the position here. That is, of course, assuming you wish to."

"Of course I wish to! Thank you, Miss Wyndham. I will not let you down. I have learned a considerable amount during my two years at Redway. We will have this stable running smoothly, very quickly."

"We can discuss more particulars as they arise, but I think the first might be for you to get a better set up in this office. Something less battered and at least two chairs! That bunk has seen better days, too. I will mention it to Mckinnon, so be sure to speak to him of it."

"Thank you, Miss. I should like to ask your permission to take the current stablemen in hand."

"Benjamin Bramley? I thought he seemed very knowledgeable and willing."

"Oh, the lad? He is very good and I can teach him a lot more. However, I meant the other men."

"We have other men? I have seen nothing of them."

"There are four others, but since the stable manager left, they made Bramley do all the work. It has taken all his time to care for the horses, that is why the stable is not looking all it could., I plan to make those four work doubly hard for a while to earn the money they still collected all these months."

"I trust your judgement in handling that situation. You can tell them they will not be paid further if they are not working to the standard you require."

"I may have to get a little rough with them, Miss."

She considered him; a big man, tall and broad, his muscles in his arms and across his back and chest strained the shirt fabric that contained them and formed a triangle with his slim waist.

"I doubt that will be a problem for you, Mickleson."

"Not at all, Miss, but will it be a problem for you?"

Suddenly, she realised that her position allowed her to decide how *she* wished her household should be kept. Not simply run it how anyone else did theirs. She wanted to ensure her household reflected the kind of mistress she wished to be.

"I understand that for some men, you need to prove yourself in order for them to respect you." She thought of the display her cousin just put on with Mr. Horncastle. That man allowed Nathaniel every opportunity to be reasonable and despite his revealed superior strength and fighting ability, he did not threaten violence. As much as she respected the colonel, she preferred Mr. Horncastle's approach. "If it comes to that, do the minimum you need to do to gain their respect."

"And if no respect is forthcoming?"

"They are free to leave. I hope you would agree that it should be more beneficial to have to train new men than to work with men that refuse to respect you."

The big man nodded. Though he spoke well, which she knew to be the doing of her friend Amelia Hopwood who taught him in exchange for riding lessons, he would not use more words than needed.

"One final point, Mr. Mickleson. I will not have Mr. Horncastle's size mocked by anyone in this household. I think he has just proven to us what a capable man he is. If you have any questions regarding managing the men, you could do no better than to ask him."

"Yes, Miss."

"Let us go and tell everyone our happy news then!" She led the way out into the stable.

"They have all gone, Colonel."

Nathaniel looked up and saw Bertram Horncastle leaning on his sword. "I underestimated you." He sat up and flexed his arm and shoulder, testing it.

"Yes, you did. I have fought people like you all my life. I have used my arms more to pull myself up, much in the same way you have to now you have lost a leg. However, I have been doing it a lifetime, not just for two years."

"You mentioned nothing of this before."

"Why should I give away my advantage? I hoped we might reach a mutual respect via discussion and not resort to this. I did not know how skilled you are. Considerably skilled is the answer to that. Most men I have cut or disarmed within seconds."

"I thought you would not be able to defend Harriet, if the need arose. I thought that you could not be trusted to assist her in keeping this household, despite the fact that you have done so satisfactorily by yourself for the past seven months. Even through your grief over the loss of Phillip. Helena pointed that one out to me."

"Your wife and your ward are very capable women. But these are not the reasons you have detested my presence here the past day, these are excuses."

"I do not think so, Horncastle. I listed all these grievances to Helena yesterday."

"Yes, but search your heart again, Colonel. You do not believe I belong here now, any more than you did yesterday."

Nathaniel looked the man up and down. "No, I do not."

"Where do you think I belong? You are the son of an Earl, I should imagine that, at a young age, you learned the place of people. The common man, your servant or a foot soldier; the worker, in the fields or the mines; the educated man, in trade via an apprenticeship and the gentleman's son in finance or law, or an officer, like yourself. Only those firstborn to anything higher should inherit. Where does that leave a 'freak' like me? An amusement, on display on stage or in a circus; no matter my birthright?"

"You seem to have fallen on your feet here."

"I am not complaining about my lot, but we are talking of you, not me. So, we have established how your upbringing should lead you to believe I do not belong here. People of your social standing see me as a freak because of my physique. What remains to be established is what people of your social standing make of *your* physicality? My presence here irks you because your own belief must be turned back on yourself. Despite your every effort to fight and ride as the man you used to be, your peers see you as much of a freak as I am. Until you accept that, you will continue to dislike me."

"That is ridiculous, that is... it is not..."

"Do not be concerned, I believe there is hope for you. I understand from your wife that you do challenge your beliefs and society's prejudices. You only need to decide if this is an additional one you are willing to take on. Now I suggest you fix your leg and you honour your word to teach me to ride! What do you say?"

"I say my word is my bond."

When Nathaniel arrived at the stable with Horncastle, Harriet and Mickleson emerged from the stable manager's office. Both of them smiled.

"It would seem we have ourselves a stable manager, Mr. Horncastle."

"Excellent, Miss Wyndham. Welcome to the family of Wyndham House, Mr. Mickleson."

"Thank you, sir."

"Nathaniel, I know you have some ideas for the stable, as does Mickleson." Harriet continued, "there is a lot of work to be done and I would be grateful for your assistance. Yours, too, Helena. Especially when it comes to purchasing more horses."

"We are all at your service, Harriet," Nathaniel confirmed, proud of his cousin. "However, my first duty is to teach Mr. Horncastle to ride, as promised. As Davy and I went for a ride yesterday, I suggest it is the turn of the ladies today. My dear, would you and Isabella like to join Harriet? Davy can stay here. You ride well, Davy. You will be a good example for Mr. Horncastle."

Davy did not look pleased at the situation, but given his son's ill opinion of the little man Nathaniel wanted him to witness his own better treatment of Horncastle.

While Mickleson instructed the men to join him tacking up horses for Helena, Harriet and Issie, Benjamin and Mr. Horncastle expressed their surprise at the ladies riding astride and wearing breeches under their gowns.

Nathaniel instructed Davy to make a start with Coal and turned his own attention to tacking up the gelding, Theo, for Horncastle. As his hands followed the familiar work with practised care. He allowed his mind to consider what Horncastle said of his reasons for disliking the little man. Could he be right?

Nathaniel went to London twice since losing his leg, neither time did he did he make his presence known in society. Even when younger, he held no interest in being seen at the right places or being considered marriage material for the parade of perfectly turned out women. However, he always felt that choice to be his, and he should be welcomed into that life any time he wished. He knew Horncastle to be right, the society that would have accepted him when whole of body, would think *him* a freak now. He did not want or need that acceptance, but the fact that the choice no longer belonged to him irked anyway.

Everyone at Redway, Eastease and even his family home of Aysthill accepted and respected him. When men in the village taunted him, he easily put them in their place, by fighting them. Not so with Horncastle, although he taunted the little man, not the other way round.

Nathaniel felt himself not only a different man from the one who went to war with two good legs, but also a different man from the one who did not know Helena. Could this be another change, accepting who himself, finally? A different man. He rebelled against his father and his upbringing and made something of himself in the army, and now in the horse business with Helena by his side. He liked the man he became because of this and he did not liked his reaction to Horncastle. He would find a common ground with the little man, though he could not quite determine how. Perhaps teaching the man to ride would be a good start. If he did not like the man who treated Horncastle in such a way the past two days, he should change. He did not mind being a different man, providing his wife and children accepted him.

Before mounting Henry, Helena peeked her head over the stall door. She still took his breath away with the way she looked at him. He hoped he could never be such an imbecile that it would cause her change that.

"If you wrap the stirrup leathers around the stirrup, you can shorten them sufficiently for Mr. Horncastle."

"Yes, madam, I considered doing the same, no need to be concerned."

"If the horse does not like the higher leg position..."

"He can use the long crop to tap where a leg should usually be. I do know what I am doing."

She smiled sweetly at him and spoke quietly, "I do love you, Nathaniel."

He looked at her intently. "Even if I am a freak?" He gestured to his wooden leg.

"Even more so because of that. I am proud of you for all that you do, despite it, and I admire the same trait in Mr. Horncastle."

"But you do not love him," he teased and she smiled at him.

"I do not think that I would appeal to him!"

That afternoon, Nathaniel declared himself in need of some physical work. He headed out to the stable taking Davy and Bertram Horncastle with him. An hour later with their sleeves rolled up, they continued to clean or polish tack, wood and brass fittings. The mix of Redway and Wyndham stablemen, Jacky, Benjamin and Peter, with Charlie Mickleson, cleaned out old straw from the empty stalls and allowed the floors to air. With this part of the stable being furthest from the house they decided to house the older horses and the visiting Redway animals there. On the morrow, they should clean up the remaining stalls ready for those they intended to purchase at the fair the day after.

When the stablemen heard the call to the kitchen for their meal, the colonel and Horncastle remained alone. They planned to finish polishing the wood of the last stall before cleaning up for their own dinner that evening. Bertram moved over to Nathaniel who crouched down applying some polish to the last panel of wood, his ball-jointed wooden leg bent. He pointed to thirty-five scars that lined his left forearm.

"Those are very deliberate, Colonel. How did you come by them?"

"I do not know you well enough to tell you that story."

"Then allow me to help you know me better."

Nathaniel started as he pulled his shirt out of the waist of his trousers and turned his back. Horncastle lifted the back of his shirt to show him the variety of scars there.

"You have been whipped," Nathaniel said it matter-of-factly, showing no emotion, knowing the man should not appreciate it.

"Ah, yes, as a soldier, I am sure you are familiar with such scars. Whipping as form of discipline. My father threw me out of his house when my physicality became clear. My mother took me to a farm and the family there raised me. If life could be as a novel, I am sure I would have been raised by kind people, that did not happen. They took me in for the money my mother gave them and when old enough to work, I worked long hours doing laborious, tedious work. This is nothing to it." He gestured around to the work they completed that day.

"How did you end up here?"

"Your turn, Colonel." Again, the little man pointed at the scars on his forearm.

Nathaniel rubbed his finger across them thoughtfully. "During a battle the French captured my regiment and imprisoned us. The man in charge, Arbour, liked to be … cruel. He killed my men in front of me, one each day and marked my arm for each death. I look at these and try to remember them, without seeing their deaths. The only one I truly remember is Duarte."

"What happened to Duarte?"

Nathaniel looked at Horncastle. "Your turn."

"I ran away. Found a show and worked there for quite a while. Phillip saw me there when we visited this area. He came back several times and we struck up a friendship. He saw something in me."

"What do you think he saw?"

"Duarte?"

"The capitão of the Portuguese regiment I commanded. Arbour gave me a pistol to kill him, but I would not. I put the pistol to my own head and pulled the trigger… nothing. I saw him load a pistol, but he switched them. He killed Duarte with the other one." Nathaniel slumped over in recollection, but the shorter man's next statement made him sit straight again and staring at him.

"I am the firstborn son of the Earl of Lorlake."

Chapter Six

The first day of Charlie Mickleson's tenure as stable manager to the enormous estate of Wyndham House started before dawn. He, Jacky, Peter and Benjamin worked hard with the colonel, Davy and Mr. Horncastle, cleaning and polishing the day before. He slept like a log on the old bunk in his stable manager's office, waking as the dark night began to give way to bluer hues.

The young lad, Benjamin, informed Charlie that when the previous stable manager left several months ago, these men saw fit to leave the care of the old horses that remained at the stable to him. He did his best and his hard work earned him the respect of his new stable manager, for at least keeping the animals healthy.

Mr. Horncastle did not appoint a new manager. Consequently, these men felt it acceptable that they continue to be paid and fed for doing very little at all. Things would be changing. Miss Wyndham said she trusted his judgement to deal with the men as he saw fit, that she requested any violence be a last resort suited him. Though a big man, Charlie Mickleson preferred not to fight unless it could not be avoided. During his blacksmith apprenticeship, the master's wife taught him to read and write and he continued to read as much as he could since. If he could use his mind to solve a disagreement rather than his muscle, more the better.

To his mind the best way to shock these men should be waking them early. All four of them and Benjamin slept in an outbuilding with a room for beds and another for storage. Mickleson arranged with Mckinnon for Benjamin and Peter to sleep in the servants' quarters in the house for that night, so they could get a well-earned rest. Mickleson entered the outbuilding's sleeping area carrying two long crops and left the door open, the burgeoning dawn light sufficient to see.

"Wake up you bloody, blaggards," he bellowed, rapping the ends of each bunk with a crop as he passed them.

"Are you a mad man? Leave over and let us be," complained one man.

"Your new stable manager wants you up and working in ten minutes or you will be out of work and out on your ears."

"What bleedin' stable manager?" another man managed to say before pulling his blankets up over his head.

"Me!" Mickleson stuck the crop under his blankets and yanked them away from the prone form of the man. "Get up, you useless pieces of shit and get into the stable. You have work to do."

"Bramley is the man you want for the work at this time of day." The man's arm flung out to try and retrieve the covers, but Mickleson pulled them out of his reach and on to the floor.

"Bramley worked his fingers to the bone yesterday and we saw nothing of you. You have months of pay to earn by my reckoning, as you made that boy do everything. Now move them bleedin' arses before I make them bleed with the crop I have here. Do not test me."

"You wouldn't dare." The man whose covers he removed stood to make his point aggressively, but Charlie towered over him, the muscles in his arms bunched. "There's four of us!"

He turned his back on Mickleson looking for support from his comrades, but they still lay in their beds, the crop swiped at his behind, enough to sting, but no more than that. The enraged man lost all his trepidation in confronting the bigger man by himself. Mickleson easily avoided the punch that came his way and punched the man squarely in the jaw, he dropped back onto his bed and stayed there, stunned.

"You can collect your things and leave. NOW!" Still swaying slightly, the man stood and picked up his clothes before exiting the building.

"There are three of you left; who else wants to try his hand?" Two men who sat up to watch the ruckus, clambered quickly out of bed and pulled on their breeches and shirts, hurrying out to the stable. The third still lay covered by his blankets.

"Get up, man, or leave with that other bastard." Mickleson rapped his behind with a crop, and the man uttered a dark curse getting up quickly and trying to pull on his breeches. Mickleson rapped him again. "Get out to the stable now! Get the Wyndham horses out into the paddock and start mucking out those stalls. I will be there shortly and will expect to see you all working hard."

Shaking his head, Mickleson strode to the house to ask Mckinnon to be sure that the other man left the grounds.

The butler laughed heartily at the story Mickleson told, and assured him he would ensure the man left. Mickleson headed back to the stable to get the other three men working. He planned that they should be the ones polishing the remaining stalls. Two days remained to get it done as they would be going to the fair tomorrow and should need the stalls ready when they returned with the horses they purchased.

When Helena woke that morning, she lay for a few moments, comfortable in the arms of her husband. Everyone enjoyed dinner the night before, as Nathaniel and Mr. Horncastle seem to have found a mutual respect for each other, although she could not as yet term it a friendship. An exhausted Nathaniel fell asleep in her bed quickly. Later in the dark in the middle of the night he reached out for her, caressing her awake and loving her tenderly.

Getting out of the bed without waking him, she wrapped herself in her dressing gown and stepped into the dressing room. James neatly set out the colonel's clothes while a young girl looked through Helena's wardrobe.

"Good morning, James."

"Good morning, Mrs. Ackley. This is Nora Smith, she is a maid here at Wyndham House and has offered to dress you for today, ma'am."

"Is there something wrong with Rebecca?" fear tickled her throat and she swallowed it hard.

"She is unwell and is in bed."

"Is Jacky with her?" If Rebecca suffered the blow she suspected, he should be with his wife.

"Said he must work in the stable, but should get back to her as soon as possible."

"Nonsense, what of the Wyndham stablemen? They cannot handle a few extra horses?"

"Mckinnon told us Mickleson is whipping them into shape. From what I heard at breakfast this morning, with a couple of men he literally did so."

"Please get word to Jacky that he need not work today and must attend his wife as soon as possible. I am going to her now and want to see him there. Nora, I am thankful you are willing to dress me, but it will have to wait until after I see Rebecca. I shall return shortly." With that, she walked quickly out of the room wondering which way to turn to get to the servants' quarters. James dashed ahead of her to find Mckinnon and get word out to the stable, so she could not ask him.

Helena stood there a moment before hearing a polite cough behind her, turning she saw the small form of Nora. As with Harriet's maid, the small girl with brown hair neatly tied back and an orderly maid uniform, looked strong.

"I can show you to Rebecca, ma'am, if you wish?" Nora offered, her brown eyes questioning.

"Yes, lead the way, thank you." Helena gave the girl a quick nod, grateful for her competence in aiding her.

Helena knocked and entered the darkened bedroom, "Rebecca, it is me."

"Ma'am, Nora planned to help you today. I have given her instructions, is there a problem?" Rebecca made to sit up in the bed.

"Do not concern yourself with me. Nora seems very able, but what of you, my dear? Is it the baby?" Helena quickly moved to the bed and pressed the girl back onto the pillows. Then perched on the edge of the bed and picked up a pale hand from the counterpane.

"Yes, it is gone." The young woman's voice sounded flat with resignation.

"Do you need the doctor? We should fetch one for you."

"I don't think so, unless the bleeding does not stop."

"I am so sorry, Rebecca." Helena reached over and stroked the thick chestnut hair, then rubbed her back as the young woman broke into sobs. Rebecca never knew her own parents and the tender glances she gave Helena's baby showed her how much she longed for a family of her own. Since her marriage to Jacky two years ago, Rebecca lost more than this child.

Helena's own tears pricked at her eyes. She desperately wanted to give Nathaniel another child, but since the infection after the birth of Little Nate, she could no longer conceive. Still, she should be grateful for her three children. Davy, though not from her womb, she considered her son and loved him as much as she loved Isabella and Little Nate.

"Have you considered taking a child in, Rebecca?"

"Jacky should want his own child."

"Are you sure? Have you asked him? The colonel considers Davy his son, as do I."

"But he is at least related to him."

"We did not know that until after he brought Davy to me and proposed. He asked to be Davy's father. I do not think it should have made any difference to him. Still, this is perhaps not the time to discuss it. Wait a while until the pain of this loss has moved on a little, for we both know it never leaves us completely." Her own thoughts swallowed her for a moment.

"I will be able to attend you tomorrow, ma'am."

Helena straightened in surprise. "You most certainly will not! I will not have it and if you do I will have Jacky carry you back to this bed. Nora can attend me for a week and then you and I will discuss it again. If the bleeding does not at least taper off over the coming days, you must get word to me and we will fetch a doctor." Her 'mistress of Redway' tone slipped out easily and the urge to confront Jacky Robertson about abandoning his wife at such a time as this rose.

"Perhaps it should be better if I died, Jacky could marry someone who could give him a family."

Helena's mouth hung open at the declaration and she hastily closed it. How could this sweet girl consider such a thing? "Do not think that, never think that! Jacky loves you and would be distraught if you died. He may not find someone else and could spend the rest of his life alone and miserable. Is that what you would wish for him?"

"No, of course not."

"I have sent for him and he is to attend to you today and all week. They have plenty of hands in the stable and you know the colonel will be out there, too, he cannot resist it. Rest, my dear. Do not be concerned about me or Jacky or anyone other than yourself. You will find your way, I know it. Ah, here he is, let me have a word with him outside in the corridor. I will be by to check on you later today."

"Thank you, ma'am."

"You are loved and valued here, Rebecca. It would not only be Jacky's heart that would be broken if you left us. One way or another, I am sure you will be a mother someday."

When Jacky's head popped around the door, Mrs. Ackley pointed into the corridor, indicating he should wait out there. He paced up and down, hating how dreadful and helpless the loss of another baby and all Rebecca suffered made him feel. He wanted to make it better, but what could he do? As Rebecca's door opened, he came to a stop in front of it. Mrs. Ackley, in her dressing gown no less, exited and began laying into him without preamble causing him to take a step back.

"What on earth do you think you are doing out at the stable, Jacky Robinson?"

"Mickleson needed me..." He paused when she held up a hand.

"Last time I checked, you work at Redway for the colonel and I, not for Mickleson. There are ample stablemen here and if he needs more then it is incumbent upon Miss Wyndham to ensure take care of that. Rebecca is your wife and she has suffered a traumatic loss in both mind and body. Your place is here, and here is where you must insist you stay. Would I demand you work after such an event as this? Have I before?"

"No." He managed one word before she struck verbally again.

"No, I have not. That poor girl is in tears and you leave her up here alone to deal with it?"

"I did not think? She said I should go."

"Of course she said so, she just told me she should be serving me tomorrow, which of course I put paid to straightaway. You are both to rest for a week."

"A week? I will go out of my mind cooped up in here for a week, thinking of what has happened."

"What of her mind? She cannot walk away from it as you can. She cannot go to the stable and work it off. Yet you expect her to lay here alone and contemplate what has happened?"

His face must have shown his realisation of the situation he left Rebecca in as he felt his mistress spoke a little kindlier, though her words cut straight to his heart. "She thinks you should be better off without her. If she died."

"My God, no!" He lunged for the door, but Mrs. Ackley blocked his way. "There has only ever been her, could only ever be her."

"I told her as much, Jacky. Remember, your mother is not only my housekeeper, but has been a mother to me, which makes you a brother, and I feel this as keenly for you and Rebecca as I should if we were truly so related. As your 'older sister', I insist you remain with Rebecca while she rests for a week. She is not to get out of that bed, or perhaps sitting in a chair until the bleeding has slowed. You must fetch and carry everything for her, food, chamber pots, cloths for the bleeding..."

He wrinkled his nose.

"Jacky Robertson!" she admonished him easily. "You have cared for foaling horses, all kinds of animals and their injuries, I am sure you can cope. I do not think Rebecca will appreciate having a strange maid assisting her, do you?"

"No, she would not." This he could do for her, he decided. Perhaps he would feel less helpless if he could help her in some way?

Mrs. Ackley continued, "you must carry in the water the laundry staff will need for the soaking of those cloths. You can read to her, or play your fiddle, but most of all, you must hold her and talk to her of your feelings about all of this. You need to get those feelings out and she needs to hear them. Then she will trust you and talk to you of hers. Will you do all of that for the only woman you profess you will ever love?"

"Yes, ma'am. Thank you." He watched her walk away thoughtfully.

Could she be right? Would Rebecca share her feelings with him if he did so first?

As Bertram walked through the house he felt a sombreness subdued the excitement of the first few days of their visitors. According to the report of Mckinnon, their new stable manager reportedly woke the lazy stablemen at dawn with a crop in his hands. They should now be working doubly hard to repay the money they collected, but did not earn.

At his instruction, Mckinnon started the indoor staff working on dusting and cleaning the dark wood panelled music room, and moving the parlour furniture that Harriet indicated to the new parlour. The newly cleaned instruments would then to be moved into their new location. The pianoforte tuner should be there at his work when they visited the horse fair the following day.

Miss Isabella wanted to work on her new story and Bertram directed her out of the way of these goings on to the study that should now be considered Harriet's. She settled herself at the large desk with her papers, ink and quills when he entered.

"Miss Isabella, I apologise. I did not wish to disturb you."

"You are not disturbing me, sir. I have been thinking about you. I am writing a new story and a man the same as you will be in it."

"I am going to be in one of your stories? I am honoured."

"The man will not be called Mr. Horncastle, but he will look as you do. I do not know how to describe him. I want to add him to my dragon slayer stories." She held up her little pamphlet book of her stories that their neighbour at Redway, Dowager Alcott, paid to have made.

"May I read it?" She held it out to him and he took it to the comfortable love seat to peruse. As he read, he laughed enjoying the simply told stories. "When did you write these?"

"When I was little."

He pulled out some loose pages tucked into the back. As he read about the dragon slayer and the preacher taking on the devil's man, his eyebrows raised as he could see the improvement in the story telling. "At what age did you write this?"

"Seven." She looked a little sad when she said it. "Papa hurt his head, writing the story helped and as I wrote he got better. I thought if I wrote a good ending he should get completely better."

"So the dragon slayer is based upon your father I take it?"

She smiled at him. "I thought that he used fight dragons when he went to war. He once teased me about the dragon of Lincolnshire living on top of a hill near us. I know it is not true, but I should like to go up there one day, to see for myself."

Bertram let out a loud guffaw. "I think you should call my character a dwarf?" She frowned at him, so he continued. "A dwarf is a being from mythology that is short and dwells in the earth. It is associated with wisdom and mining."

"What did you say to my father to get him to like you?"

"There are things that men discuss between themselves that they do not tell other people. We call that a gentleman's agreement. However, I can tell you I pointed out to your father that we are not quite so different as he may think."

"Because he lost his leg."

"Yes."

"He does not let it stop him doing everything he always did before. You do the same as any other man, too."

"I try to."

"I like you, Mr. Horncastle. You can call me Issie."

"I like you, too, Issie. You can call me Bertie. My friend Phillip used to call me Bertie, but perhaps we should only do so when we are alone?"

At that moment, Harriet walked into the room and Bertram turned his smiling face toward her.

"That's how it started off with Harry, but everyone calls her that now!" Isabella giggled.

Jacky Robertson sat in the worn armchair in his room with Rebecca and watched his wife sleep. After Mrs. Ackley told him what he must do and what Rebecca said about him being better off without her, he came into the room and held her. She cried once again and he told her, with a fierceness in his voice that neither of them ever knew him to possess before, that he loved her. He never knew the touch or kiss of another woman, he only ever wanted her and would always consider the day she became his wife as the happiest day of his life and it always would be.

"I want to give you a child," she said to him through her sobs.

"I want us to have a child, too, but there cannot be a child unless there is an 'us'. You and I come first until we bring a child into the world. If there is not to be a child, then we will still have each other and it will be enough. We will make it enough."

He laid her down and stroked her hair until she slept. Then he sat watching her and thinking of what he needed to say.

When she woke he helped her change the cloths between her legs. He put them in a pail and headed down to the laundry rooms with them. After bringing in some water to help with the soaking and being given more cloths, he retrieved a luncheon tray from the cook, Miss Cadman, and returned to Rebecca.

Once they finished eating, he cleared his throat, ready to share his feelings with her and make amends. "I am sorry, Rebecca."

"This is not your fault." She pressed at her stomach.

"I know. I mean I am sorry for leaving you earlier."

"You have to work, Jacky. We both have to work. I must aid Mrs. Ackley soon."

"No. She is right about that, you must rest. I am sorry for leaving because I did not have to work. There are men enough to get the work done, and we know that Mrs. Ackley has never asked me to work when this has happened before. I wanted to forget, to block it from my mind and the only way I felt I could do that would be to put my back into some work. I did not consider that you could not block it from your mind, you could do nothing but lie here and face it, and I should have been with you. I am sorry for being so selfish. You did not even have Mother nearby to come and check on you as we have in the past."

"There is no need, you are here now."

"Yes, there is need, please forgive me."

"I do forgive you. Always." She gave him a weak smile and he felt grateful. His beautiful wife, with the long limbs and the soft, chestnut hair. He moved to lie on the bed next to her. He needed to tell her some things and felt he should hold her in his arms while he did, to give him strength. Pulling her to him and resting her head on his chest, he talked.

"I feel so helpless, Rebecca. I do not understand why God sees fit to do this to us when I know what a wonderful mother you would be. To never start the process is one thing, but the punishment of starting to grow a child, only for it to be taken away before it can live seems so harsh. I want to make it happen, for you, for us, but I am powerless.

I promise you this. I will be here for you. No matter what happens, no matter how many times. I will fetch and carry. I will clean, I will love. I am not powerless there. And we must talk. We must share our feelings, if only between the two of us. We can be honest between the two of us."

"Yes, Jacky, we can be honest between the two of us." She lay with her head on his chest. Could she hear his heart beat slow? It beat so fast when he started talking, but as he said what he needed to, it slowed. He grasped her wrist and felt her pulse fast under his touch. She moved her body closer to him and wrapped her arms around his waist. Though tall and slim, he was strong and hoped she pulled strength from him as she said in the past.

"Be honest with me, Rebecca." He kept his tone soft and encouraging.

"I feel, I have felt, so much hope each time I believe the process has started within me. The sickness, my breasts swelling, the roundness of my stomach, even early on I can feel that kernel of hope within me. Then, at some point I can feel my body let go, to expel, to release. It is nothing I do and I try to tell myself to hold on, hold on, but I have no control over it.

Then the sadness, a heavy sadness, that, even more than the pain of it coming out, more than seeing the shape of what could be a baby in the pail. That sadness engulfs me and the ideas of dying come. That you might find someone else to love and have many children with, and you should be happy. That dying might be preferable to suffering through this one more time, preferable to hoping, only to have it all ripped away from me again. Dying might be preferable to thinking I am not good enough for you, because I cannot give you a child.

I do not choose to think these ideas and any other day when I am strong and feel loved and wanted, they do not come, but the sadness brings them, unbidden to my mind."

"Then, from now on I will be strong for you. You tell me when the sadness comes and I will be strong. I will be here and show you that you are loved and you are wanted. You may still feel it, but I will be here until it is gone." He put his hand under her chin and gently lifted her face so he could look at her and she at him. "Never think you are not good enough for me. I wonder every day how I managed to convince you to marry me and I will continue to wonder every day until I die. I love you, Rebecca. I have only ever loved you and I will never love another."

He kissed her forehead and she rested her head back onto his chest feeling her heartbeat slowing to match a pace with his own. Drained, they fell asleep in each other's arms.

By the early afternoon, the weather turned sombre, too. The rain that threatened began to drizzle when Charlie Mickleson exited the storage building to head back to the barn. He saw Annie Brown walk quickly to the far end of the stable closest to the house.

He entered the building at the other end and scowled at the three remaining stablemen, as they scurried back to their work at the sight of him. As he turned the corner, he heard Bramley talking.

"He just popped out this minute, Miss. Can I help you with anything?" Charlie could see the back of the lad, but the diminutive Miss Brown could not be seen behind him. He felt a growl in his throat thinking the lad would be smiling widely at her upturned face.

"I have a message for him from Miss Wyndham."

"I can give it to him. I am second in command now because these bl... men do not work as hard as me." He gestured to the other side of the stable and stopped dead at the sight Charlie bearing down on him. Miss Brown laughed nervously at him almost calling the men *'blaggards'*.

"Have I not given you sufficient work today?" Charlie growled it at the lad, who laughed amiably, and nodded. He put his back into the work of moving supplies, first taking those Charlie brought in with him.

Miss Brown stopped laughing the moment she saw Charlie.

"What can I do for you, Miss?" He gestured to the office behind her and stepped around her toward it, but she did not move.

"I have a message from Miss Wyndham. She wanted you to know they would not be riding today, so could you manage the horses as you think best?"

Having turned back, he nodded curtly and notice her look to the ground, wringing her hands. Was she summoning her courage? She seemed truly scared of him. Then she looked up, her blue eyes challenging.

"I wanted to thank you, Mr. Mickleson, for putting those men in their place for treating Mr. Bramley so meanly."

Charlie looked her up and down, pressed his mouth into a thin line and nodded again. He felt his disappointment keenly, she obviously felt for Bramley being treated badly by these men.

Charlie felt happy at being included in the party travelling here as he liked Annie Brown. spotted her in the village and at church a few times in Eastcambe and found he liked to look at her. She smiled at him a few times when she caught him looking. He hoped, with a few weeks in closer proximity, he might determine if she liked him, too, and managed to talk to her a few times on the journey here. When Miss Wyndham offered him the position of stable manager, he could not refuse it, regardless of her feelings. Now it should seem she favoured the lad. It would be a shame, though of a similar age, her intelligence outweighed his. His good looks must have caught her eye.

Before he could overcome his struggle to find something to say, she turned on her heel and headed down the corridor he came from moments ago. He shook his head upon hearing some rather unsavoury suggestions from the men working there and walked toward them, resigning himself to berating them for such talk, when he heard a more threatening voice and realised he did not hear the door close after her exiting.

"Now Miss, there be no need to stomp off in a huff. We was only having a bit o' fun."

The blood boiled in Charlie's body as he turned the corner to see Miss Brown trapped between the three men who advanced upon her. He could see she did not looked cowed though as she straightened her back and seemed about to set them down.

He put a large hand at either side of the heads of the two men in front of him and clashed them together. Then he grasped their collars and threw them into the nearest stall where they sprawled in the straw and the mess they failed to clean.

She stood frozen staring at him, but he looked beyond her, all his attention upon the man there. Reaching out a big hand, he pulled her to safety behind him in one swift move, holding her there against his back. The other man picked up a pitchfork for his own protection, brandishing it weakly toward him. He easily batted aside with a thick arm.

"Get out," he growled the words, surprised by the urge to pummel this man into unconsciousness for his treatment of Miss Brown. If the man did not leave directly, he might not stop himself.

"You cannot dismiss us just for having a bit o' fun."

Mickleson barely managed to hold himself back as he considered Miss Wyndham's instruction of violence as a last resort. "You are forgetting who has been paying you. Miss Wyndham would not appreciate your intimidation of her maid on her property and the lewd suggestions you made to her. I have no doubt she will be supportive of me and we will find plenty of other harder working men to take your places. Now get out! Get your things and get off this property. You should hurry as the rain has already started."

The man turned on his heel and left without a backward glance to see how his two friends fared. Charlie turned to the stall where the men began getting up from the piles of horseshit they failed to clean. His arm still holding Miss Brown at his back as he turned, to keep her protected.

"You two can get out as well, I have seen Mrs. Ackley be quicker at cleaning a horse stall than either of you." The men left. Mickleson blew out a breath to disperse his anger before turning back to Miss Brown.

She stood, frozen and trembling with fear. He scared the life out of her. Not the impression he hoped to make.

"I am sorry!" she squeaked, turning on her heel and running out of the door to the house.

"Damn it all to hell." Mickleson ran his hand through his thick black hair before turning around to Benjamin, who watched the events with amusement. "We should get to work lad. Go get Peter Robinson first."

Annie ran in to the Wyndham kitchen with her hand across her mouth, still shaking. Miss Cadman, the Wyndham cook looked up from the sauce she stirred, took one look at her and shouted to one of the kitchen maids to run and fetch the housekeeper.

"Sit yourself down there, Miss Annie, and we'll get a cup of tea into you in a moment." Annie slumped into a chair near the fire and watched the cook stir the milk into the saucepan to make her sauce. When she finished she set it aside and picked up the steaming kettle, adding the boiling water to a nearby pot. The normalcy and fluidity of the cook's actions soothed Annie.

Mortified by her actions causing Mr. Mickleson so much trouble and losing him three more men, Annie could do nothing but continue to hold her hand to her mouth and sit there doubled over. More so, the shock of her physical reaction at being held firmly against his back as he protected her radiated through her.

By the time Mrs. Thurston arrived in the kitchen, Annie sat sipping a cup of tea, but started again when Mr. Mckinnon burst in after Mrs. Thurston with a look of surprise and relief at Miss Cadman.

"Miss Cadman, are you well?" Annie forgot her own distress for a moment recognising his concern for the cook and wondered if the woman knew.

"It is Miss Annie, sir. She came in from the stable in quite a panic. I have made her some tea."

"What is distressing ya then lass?" the butler asked kindly.

They listened patiently while Annie told them what happened with the three men and how Mr. Mickleson threw them all out.

"I have never seen him so angry and no wonder. Now what will he do to get those stables cleaned and all the wood polished? It is entirely my fault for walking past those men, instead of going the other way. I will have to help him, but I have so much to do for Miss Wyndham."

"He is a good 'un that Mickleson." Mrs. Thurston looked at Mckinnon with a keen eye.

"Aye, that he is, Missus. We can see who we can spare in the house and who is willing to help out. I am sure Mickleson will be able to find some good hands at the fair tomorrow, as well as horses. I have to say I am glad to see the back of those men. I did nae trust any of them."

"Miss Annie," Miss Cadman interjected, "this is not your fault. I am sure Mr. Mickleson is not angry with you. Those men did not have the right to treating you that way and we all appreciate him stepping up and taking on all three of them. I only wish I could have seen it. Now you run along to aid Miss Wyndham, Mr. Mckinnon has it all in hand."

Back in the stable Charlie, Benjamin and Peter made a start cleaning out the stalls, when a number of indoor staff come in through the door armed with polish and cloths. Astonished, the new stable manager directed everyone in their tasks. Mckinnon stood holding the door, as more men arrived carrying a much better bunk, desk and two chairs for the stable office.

Mckinnon nodded to Mickleson. "We take care of our own here at Wyndham House, Mr. Mickleson, just as you did for Miss Brown. Welcome to the family."

Chapter Seven

The day of the fair dawned dry and bright. Harriet rode in the Wyndham carriage for the first time, but with the much younger Redway horses pulling it. Bertram, Davy and Isabella sat with her and Mickleson drove. Nathaniel rode Perseus and Helena rode Henry using a sidesaddle. Several staff members wished to attend, too, so they took the cart with Colossus pulling it and Peter Robinson driving. Mckinnon sat on the driving seat with him and the staff sat in the back with two sets of spare tack.

As they drove through Bath, Harriet found herself as excited as the children as they all craned their necks out of the carriage windows to get the best views of the town, emerging on the other side to the amazing sight of the fair stretched across two grassy fields in the distance. There were all kinds of farm animals and stalls of wares everywhere, as well as all the horses. Many colourful gipsy vehicles could be seen and numerous tents had been erected.

Before their vehicles came to a stop, Mr. Horncastle turned to Harriet. "Miss Wyndham, if you would permit it, I suggest you allow me to perform any negotiations. I am very familiar with folk of this kind and they often hide their best beasts. Could you provide me with one or two things you might say when looking for a horse you wish to purchase." Harriet imparted a few terms to him.

Harriet asked Mckinnon to remain with their vehicles and mounts while they perused the various stalls and sellers. A rather unhappy Peter accepted Nathaniel's instruction to remain with the Scot. Wyndham's servants dispersed into the throng in their own groups, and Davy and Issie ran off, their mother shouting after them that they must stay together and meet them back at the cart.

Harriet smiled as the rest of them walked amongst the sellers looking for the horses they wanted for Wyndham House. In every direction she saw people bustling and talking. Senses became bombarded with the various smells, both pleasant and foul; the colours of the gypsy carts and the attire of the folk who wandered around enjoying the fair as she did. Calls came from all directions, those drawing attention to their wares and those haggling with their customers over prices.

The men found one particular seller they thought reputable. Helena and Harriet stood waiting and looking around, while the men looked over his animals. The horses looked in good condition. They had obviously been cared for and were well groomed.

"These six should be useful for pulling the Wyndham carriages, however, Harriet really needs eight." Nathaniel spoke quietly to Bertram, not wishing to alert the seller to their interest.

Mickleson agreed. "All six are short-coupled which should be better for driving, but these mares are old and past their prime for foaling."

As the colonel took a step toward the seller, Bertram held up a hand to say him and turned to the man himself. He looked rather pleased at the interest this odd party showed in his horses and turned a smile to the little man approaching him.

"How much for these six? They have strong and muscular quarters and shoulders, but are nothing special," Bertram began with disinterest in his tone. Out of the corner of his eye he noticed the colonel cover his grin with his hand. Bertram liked nothing more than an audience and looked forward to entertaining the man who seemed to be becoming friendlier every day. The owner stated his price, so Bertram said nothing, simply shook his head and walked away.

"That's a reasonable price and ya know it!" the man called after them. Horncastle ignored him and continued to walk, using his arms to usher Nathaniel and Mickleson in joining him in moving away.

"That is a reasonable price, Mr. Horncastle," Mickleson muttered it under his breath, but Bertram winked at him, so he followed.

"There is another seller yonder, sir," said Nathaniel, "I like the look of his horses." Bertram looked up at the man and winked, doing his best to keep his face straight. He missed having this kind of fun.

"Wait!" called the seller, "ya'll find no better animals than mine."

Bertram turned and gave the man a look, waiting, but not moving. When the seller dropped his price by a significant margin, suggesting that it meant they purchase all six, Bertram walked back towards him.

"Let us see your other animals."

"What others? These are all I have," the man protested.

"This is a two-day fair, I am sure the dozen here are not all you have. Let us see the rest."

The man resignedly walked them around a large sheeted wall behind his selling patch. Many horses stood tethered to posts hammered into the ground. Bertram, not particularly a horse man, suddenly came nose to nose with a large Friesian. It was jet black from head to toe with a long flowing mane and tail. He wanted it, as he seldom wanted anything in his life, but he wondered would it be too big a mount for him?

The colonel and Mickleson started to walk around the other horses, but the colonel backtracked to him and the black stallion. He gave Bertram a quick wink and nod, while Mickleson asked the seller a question about one of the horses.

"Close your mouth and stop staring at him. We will get him for you, stay focused on your negotiations. We need some mares, too, and I do not see any more here. He is keeping them for breeding I expect."

Regaining his senses, Bertram marched up to the man again and looked up at him, speaking dismissively. "Nothing of interest here, we are leaving." Again, he gestured to Colonel Ackley and Mickleson to leave, but the man put a hand out to grasp his upper arm. Bertram flexed his bicep, letting the man know not to tangle with him and he quickly released him.

"What are ya looking for, I can get it for ya."

"Where are your mares?"

The man jerked his head towards a covered tent and they walked towards it. Here the horses seemed more spaced out. Mickleson walked straight to a couple of smaller horses and inspected them. Bertram could tell the others there would be foaling soon.

Nathaniel distracted the owner with a question his own regarding the age and foaling of a couple of the mares, while Horncastle moved over to Mickleson.

"We want these two, sir," Wyndham House's new stable manager told him. "They are yearlings. Very young and not with foal, which is good. They should be more likely to grow to full size if they have not foaled so young. He'll want a lot of money for them. Whatever he asks for, they are probably worth it."

Bertram nodded and looked to the colonel. The seller, who answered all his questions, turned towards Bertram again and behind his back the colonel indicated two of the dams and held up two fingers.

Bertram smiled at the man coming towards him. "I think we can do some business today. What do you want for the yearlings?"

The seller stated his price, and again, behind the man's back, Nathaniel nodded. It went against every fibre in Bertram's being not to barter with him, but he aimed to take him for as much as possible with the rest of the deal, so it made sense to sweeten the man first with an agreement. "Accepted, but I want these two that my man is standing next to for a lot less," he pointed to Nathaniel. "Then we will take the six at the front, but I want two geldings that this man," he jerked a thumb behind him at Mickleson, "will pick out from your horses at the back for the same price."

The man sucked in a breath at that, but Bertram knew his type. This deal would make him the money he hoped for over the whole two days, in the first afternoon.

After his confidence in the deal for the mares and the geldings, Bertram felt his throat constrict and could only look pleadingly at Colone Ackley. It would seem where that stallion was concerned he dared not open his mouth.

"We could use that stallion, too, sir. The Friesian."

Grateful the colonel gave him the opening he needed, Bertram croaked out some words. "I do not think I need it." He tried to sound disinterested. His throat felt dry just thinking of the beast, even if he could never ride it.

"I do not see the point in all these mares, sir, unless you get another stallion. Moses is getting on in years and we could do with the fresh blood." With that, the colonel established to the seller that without a deal on the stallion, they may not want the mares and that included the seller's top price on the yearlings. He would not want to lose that. Bertram readied himself to bring the deal home and claim the most handsome horse he ever laid eyes upon.

"Hmmm, I do not know then. I did not consider adding a stallion into the price." He looked up at the seller again, barely showing the eagerness in his face or his tone. "How much?"

"Seven hundred and fifty guineas?" The question in the offer allowed Bertram the courage to push the man once more. He rocked back on his heels, blew out a breath and took a step towards the exit.

"Six hundred and fifty?" another step, "six hundred!"

Smiling again Bertram, held out a hand and they shook. Parting with the money they untied all the mares and made their way through to the front. Mickleson picked out the two geldings at the back he wanted and the seller told a couple of lads working with him to grab the two boys he saw earlier looking for work and walk those and the other six to their carriage. Bertram proudly led the Friesian with him.

Once out at the front, Bertram noted Miss Wyndham and Mrs. Ackley seemed not to have waited for them. The colonel looked unworried, so he decided he should not concern himself, but he could not help looking around for them as he led his stallion back to the carriage and cart. Perhaps Mrs. Ackley saw something to her liking, but he decided they should endeavour to find them after depositing the horses back at the carriages.

Mickleson talked to the two lads who Bertram assumed must have been managing the horses well. Apparently, they lived locally and were getting work at the fair while it was in town. Mickleson instructed them to report at Wyndham House stable when the fair finished, if they were interested in more permanent work. Providing they were willing to work hard, they should be paid well.

"We can work hard, too, Mister!" The older of the two boys they also used to help lead their horses spoke up. Bertram smiled as Mickleson simply nodded an agreement. Bertram thought to advise him that if they did turn up he could at least get each of them a good meal and a bath. They were far too young to be able to work much.

Helena's tasked herself with finding a suitable mount for Isabella. After Nathaniel disappeared behind the wall of sheeting with Charlie and Mr. Horncastle, Helena turned and looked towards another seller. The white coat of a stallion caught her attention. She walked over to it and Harriet followed her. Harriet gasped at the sight of the horse when she saw him and Helena hushed her. She did not want a seller to know they thought him exceptional. She approached the horse cautiously, offering him her shoulder first so he could get a good sniff at her. Harriet stood behind her. He allowed Helena to rub his nose and as she did so she noticed the greyer skin beneath the white hair. Not a true white, but a very light grey.

She thought him beautiful and, so far, well behaved. The term her grandfather always used *a kind eye* came to mind. She could almost hear his deep voice beside her. *You can always tell if a horse is a wrong 'un, as it will look straight through you.* She felt the stallion might be good for Isabella. As he allowed her further liberties with her stroking, she ran her hands down his neck and over his shoulders, then down his legs, which were straight with good feet. Sound, but thin summed him up.

Helena could smell the seller before she saw him. As she finished checking the grey's legs, he came up to them reeking of old sweat and old ale. "Him's a white one, rare they are. Five hundred guineas to you, Miss."

"Mrs. or ma'am. He is not a true white, as well you know and he is not in good condition, but he seems to like me, so I will give you two hundred for him." She straightened as she spoke and looked the man in the eyes. Barely taller than her and filthy from head to toe. His eyes dark and mean. *I expect he is mean with his horses, too.* This thought made her even more determined than ever to get the grey from him, but still she would not overpay if she could avoid it.

"Tha's as if ya are stealin' off me, ma'am! I could go down to three hundred, but tha's all I can do for ya."

"My limit now seems to be one hundred and seventy-five and you will be glad to take it. You know full well you should be lucky to trick someone into giving you one hundred and fifty, the state of him."

When he agreed, she fished out the money, happy with the purchase and caught sight of one of the Wyndham House footmen nearby. On her signal, he took the lead rope for the horse and headed off to the carriage with him. As he left, she noticed Nathaniel and the other men walking towards the carriage, too, leading several animals.

After smiling at Harriet, Helena turned to where the seller went to hide his profits. She saw another man go to him and whisper in his ear and heard him reply. "We'll 'ave ta shoot her. The foal must be dead." Then he picked up a pistol and started priming it as he walked towards a shabby looking tent.

Without thinking further, Helena raised her hand. "Wait!" She ran to the tent and followed them in. A true white dam lay on the ground in the throes of foaling. Obviously in distress, with the foal still within her. To Helena's eye, she did not look big enough for the foal to be ready, but all the signs were there. What struck Helena, in the same way as the stallion she purchased from the man, the mare looked underfed and not cared for well. He probably bred her many years in a row and whilst for a healthy mare that should not usually be a problem, for this mare, it had taken its toll.

"Do not shoot her, I will buy her. How much?"

"Twenty pounds."

"I will give you ten, it would cost you ten to get her to the knacker's yard after shooting her."

"Ten then."

She paid him and got on her knees at the rear of the dam. She pushed Harriet over to the horse's head. The younger woman instantly dropped to her own knees and stroked the dam, speaking to her in soothing tones. Helena moved to reach into the mare. Normally she might be concerned about it kicking her but this one was far too exhausted. She felt the hooves of the foal positioned correctly, so not the problem. The dam must be too tired to push it out. Had the foal died within? Regardless, she could still save the dam. Grasping hold of the legs as firmly as she could, she pulled. Glad she was strong, Helena gained some ground and managed to get a knee to the dam's rear flank and pull again, with some leverage this time. The two men stood there watching. The foal started to emerge and she got a foot in place of her knee now and pulled some more. Finally, the foal came out, a pure white filly the same as its mother and, though small, certainly alive. Helena's purchase thrilled her.

"Thank ya for ya help, ma'am. Here is ya tenner back. It'll be a hundred for the dam if you want her, but that foal is mine."

"You were about to shoot her, you would have lost both. Take the ten and be glad you have that. They are both mine." She stood her ground, but the man moved quickly and grabbed Harriet around the waist pulling her to her feet while his friend grabbed hold of Helena from behind.

"Tell ya what we will do. We will keep the tenner, the dam *and* the foal and take some pleasure with you two fillies into the bargain. What do ya think ta that idea?"

Drummond Mckinnon stood on the back of the cart, shading his eyes, as Nathaniel, Mickleson and Bertram arrived with their purchases. He watched his new mistress' direction when she first headed into the crowds. Her blue gown bright enough to stand out in the throng. Once the other men disappeared behind a sheet, Miss Wyndham and her friend stood looking around, Drum did not take his eyes off the ladies.

He scowled as they headed to a seller's patch, close to the one where the men disappeared. The tent looked shabby in comparison to its neighbours and the man who approached Mrs. Ackley looked rough.

Drum continued to watch as the colonel, Mr. Horncastle and Mickleson came back into view with many horses, heading his way. As they arrived, Mrs. Ackley disappeared into that shabby tent with Miss Wyndham following closely behind.

"What is it, Mckinnon?" demanded the colonel. He evidently picked up on Drum's concerned expression.

"Damn it all!" he leapt down from the cart and started to run. "Mrs. Ackley and Miss Wyndham entered the tent of a rough looking seller."

Drum glimpsed Mickleson throwing his ropes to Peter Robinson and heard the man's clipped order to tie up the horses, before heard heavy footfalls behind him,

Within the tent, fear gave Harriet's face a tautness Helena never saw before. What on earth had she done? In her fear for the animal about to be shot, Helena did not consider her or Harriet's safety. For the third time in her life, she found herself in a position to be attacked and this time it was completely her own fault!

"We are protected here, you will regret it when my husband gets his hands on you."

"He don' know ya 'ere does 'e?" He laughed at her as she realised the truth in his word, but then determination set her mouth in a thin line. She watched Nathaniel fight with the men he taught often enough to know what she could do. *I'll be damned if I just let them take me!*

She stomped down hard on the foot of the man holding her and jolted her elbow back into his stomach so he released her and doubled over.

"Stop it woman, or I slice her." Helena froze. The man with Harriet pulled out a knife and held it to her throat. The man she fought straightened and started to reach for her again when to her greatest relief Mckinnon burst into the tent. He turned to that man and butted his head at the nose. He crumpled to the ground, blood pouring across his face.

"I *will* slice her!" the other man almost screamed.

"Let her go, man," Mckinnon's soft, Scottish burr was soothing as he pulled Helena behind him.

"These are my horses." The man gestured wildly with the knife.

"Yes, they are yours. We are leaving and taking the Miss with us. You can keep the horses." Mckinnon pointed to Harriet.

The man released her and she ran to Helena, who embraced her and quickly exited the tent. Mckinnon backed out behind her and they found themselves, and Charlie Mickleson, surrounded.

A crowd of seller and gipsy folk upon hearing a commotion or seeing people running, gathered around them. Helena saw Nathaniel squeezed through the throng, upon seeing the scared look that must have shown on her face he pushed towards the entrance of the tent, Mickleson held him back.

"Let me at him," Nathaniel growled, but another voice stopped him. Bertram Horncastle stood between his people and the growing, unruly crowd.

"We have to leave, Colonel. I know these people remember, they will defend their own, no matter how wrong they are."

"But he is keeping my horses *and* my money, and he threatened Harriet and I," Helena added, loud enough for the closest in the crowd to hear her. They did not seem interested in her protestations.

"Regardless, we must leave now. If we do, we can leave peaceably, if not we will be lucky to leave with the horses that brought us here."

Despite his small stature, Mr. Horncastle's words gave Helena a sense of protection. He instructed Mickleson and the colonel to make a way through the crowd and back towards the carriage, cart and horses. The women walked closely behind them. Mckinnon followed them equally closely, walking backward. Helena glanced back at him occasionally, noting he looked for the faces of the Wyndham House staff in the crowd and signalled to them to get back to the cart.

"Mrs. Ackley," he said in an undertone. "I see Master Davy and Miss Isabella running towards the cart." She blew out a breath of relief. Behind them she could hear Mr. Horncastle's clear voice, still speaking calmly.

"We are leaving, peaceably," he repeated often.

When they reached their cart, all the servants were already sitting in it. Mckinnon joined Peter Robinson who held the reins of Colossus. The children were inside the carriage and Harriet quickly joined them. Helena moved to ride Henry, but Nathaniel stopped her.

"Get in the carriage, woman." It was a rough command.

"No, I rode here I can..." she stopped as she looked into her husband's eyes that were so fixed on hers with an expression of such frustration and anger, that she obeyed him.

She watched out of the carriage window as Nathaniel checked the horses tied to the cart. Then he affixed a lead rope to Henry and mounted Perseus. The carriage rocked as Charlie hoisted himself up on the carriage driver's seat, leaving Mr. Horncastle the only one on the ground.

He bowed extravagantly and aimed a quick, "Thank you for your hospitality!" at the crowd. They dispersed as he got into the carriage and they headed back to the road through Bath.

Within the carriage, Helena told the story of what happened, leaving out that the men threatened Harriet and herself with Davy and Isabella present. Davy was indignant that they did not get the horses after she saved them both, but Mr. Horncastle calmed him.

"We will get those horses, young man, have no fear of that, but we could not do so with such a big crowd, they should have objected to any move we made against those men, even though they were wrong. I must talk to the colonel, Mickleson and Mckinnon; we are far enough away from the fair now." He rapped loudly on the roof of the carriage and Mickleson brought it to a standstill.

Bertram stood on the carriage runner and pulled himself up and out of sight, joining Charlie on the driver's seat. Nathaniel rode up on Perseus without a glance inside the carriage at her and Helena saw him signal McKinnon to join them. That man pulled himself up on the runner of the carriage. Helena strained her ears to try and hear what the men were saying but could only hear their deep muffled voices.

Nathaniel remained on Perseus and instructed Mickleson to switch Helena's sidesaddle on Henry for one of the others they brought with them and tack up the Friesian.

"I can do it," she offered, but he ignored her. Riding away from the carriage.

Mr. Horncastle appeared back in the carriage. "Mrs. Ackley, I am informed you can drive the carriage and suggest Master Davy rides with you. Peter will drive the cart behind you, but take it slowly. She nodded, unable to speak after Nathaniel's dismissal of her, and noted a look of sympathy in Mr. Horncastle's eyes.

Mckinnon boosted Helena up onto the step to the driver's seat and she took up the reins and whip easily. Davy arrived beside her. As they headed off, she saw Mickleson boost Mckinnon onto Henry's back, before hoisting himself up onto the black stallion. As she drove past Nathaniel, with Mr. Horncastle now sitting in front of him on a blanket, he turned Perseus away. If she did not need to see clearly to drive the carriage she would have burst into tears.

They made their slow, tired way back to Wyndham House and upon arrival, the servants went into the house, while Helena, Harriet, Davy and Isabella helped Peter and a surprised Benjamin in taking care of all the horses. As they worked Peter and Davy imparted the whole story to Benjamin and then all three lads started to speculate on what the other men were doing to get the whites back.

Harriet and Isabella dealt with the yearlings, while Helena settled the white-grey stallion and the mares that were close to foaling. She did not expect either one to foal that night, but decided to instruct Benjamin to sleep in the stable manager's office and get word to her if there were any problems. Lastly, she, Harriet and Issie managed the eight geldings, they were so tired, they could not really appreciate them fully.

As they passed through the kitchen, Harriet instructed the cook to prepare dinner for them and the children and get a good meal into Peter Robinson. If the other four men needed food upon their return, perhaps she could leave them something cold. Before Harriet made to go to Annie and get her clothes changed, Helena stopped her and asked for a quiet word. They walked to Harriet's study and sat together on the love seat in that room. Helena grasped the younger woman's hands in hers.

"Harriet, I am so sorry. I feel sick to my stomach when I think of what could have happened to you today. Thank goodness Mckinnon kept watch and thought to be so vigilant."

"And of what could have happened to you, Helena! You must think of yourself, too. All that you have been through and we ended up in that position. I still think you marvellous for saving that dam and foal, but those men were not nice and you cannot put your own safety above that of a horse."

"I know Harriet, I know, and I do not know what to say to make it up to you."

"You do not need to say anything. You mean so much to me, you are my family, as you know I consider Nathaniel as a father. I would follow you into the gates of hell for a worthy reason. As much as I love horses, I am afraid it is not enough of a reason to walk into the gates of hell for either of us. If you refuse to think of your own safety, you must think of Nathaniel, of Davy and Isabella. For heaven's sake Helena, you must think of Little Nate!" Helena felt equal parts chastised and proud of her friend who sounded completely the part of the mistress of this house.

"And I must think of you and your safety, too."

"What do I matter compared to your children, Helena?"

"You matter a great deal to a lot of people. Many of those are right here in this house, who seem to hold you in high regard after only a handful of days. Mr. Horncastle as much, if not more, than any of them."

"I should imagine you should thank Mr. Horncastle and Mckinnon when they return. I certainly will. I fear Nathaniel will have more to say to you than I have."

"I fear you may be right."

Chapter Eight

Horncastle directed the colonel, Mckinnon and Mickleson to ride to a nearby tavern. They went inside and ordered some ale and food, occupying a table in a quiet corner.

"Why are we here, sir?" asked Mckinnon, taking a sip of his ale in between forkfuls of his stew.

"We are waiting for our informants."

"You are a sly one, Horncastle," said the colonel. "I was not aware we had informants."

"I recruited them hastily, so I am not sure they are going to arrive. They are the boys you suggested come to Wyndham House after the fair, Mickleson."

"If they still want work with us, they had better turn up soon!" Mickleson added.

"Not the bigger lads, Mickleson, the boys. I needed informants that could get in and out of meetings unseen."

"While we wait, I suggest you tell us what you saw in that tent, Mckinnon." The colonel spoke tersely. His anger over Helena's behaviour had not waned.

"As I entered, Mrs. Ackley was elbowing one of the men in the gut, but she froze as the other man drew a knife and held it to Miss Wyndham's throat." He paused as Nathaniel hissed in a breath. "The one she had elbowed lunged for Mrs. Ackley again, so I butted him."

"Nice," Mickleson interjected.

"The man went down easily, but the other still had Miss Wyndham and a knife."

"What did you do?" Horncastle asked.

"Well, he said the horses were his, so I calmly agreed and said all I wanted was to leave with Miss Wyndham and Mrs. Ackley. He let her go and we left. You saw the rest."

"Welching on a deal and an attack on well-to-do ladies, should not be tolerated by the clan running this fair, despite their solidarity against us. I believe the men will be on the road tonight and that should give us our opportunity. Ah, and here are our informants ready to let us know the situation."

Two boys walked into the tavern and viewed its patrons before seeing Horncastle and Mickleson, and heading over to stand in front of the table. The older boy had brown hair and brown eyes that were old beyond his years, the younger was blond with green eyes that still held a naivety right for his age. Mickleson did not think they were brothers, but they knew each other well. The older one spoke for both.

"Hello, Mister. We did as ya said. Those men were thrown out and are headin' south. They packed up and started off half an hour ago."

"Good work, young fellows. Just two men?"

"Yes, sir!"

"Here you go, as promised." Horncastle handed over half a crown for each. Mickleson's eyes were wide.

"For that much money, you had better turn up at the house the day after the fair and do some work to earn it, boys."

"We thought we should like to come wi' ya now, ya might need our help. We know the south road. We could come back to the house wi' ya after that. Ya did buy a whole lot of horses today. Ya need us!"

Mickleson looked to the colonel and then Horncastle, they both shrugged. It was up to him and they would be his responsibility. He pointed to each of them. "You keep quiet, not a peep, you hear? Do what you are told when you are told. Agree and we will take you with us."

"Yes, sir!" they said it in unison.

They finished their meal, providing some for the boys, too, then mounted their horses. Mickleson and Mckinnon each put a boy in front of them and Bertram resumed his position in front of Nathaniel. The older boy pointed in the right direction and they took that road south skirting around and beyond the town of Bath. Convinced they should soon catch up to the men, who should be moving slower with their cart and horses, they turned each corner cautiously. Finally, they came to a corner where they could see the cart ahead of them, and stopped.

"I can run the hedgerows, sir," whispered the boy with Mickleson. I can signal when they have moved on and then continue to the next corner.

"What is your name, boy?" he whispered back.

"Richie and tha's Arnie." He jerked his thumb at the smaller boy riding with Mckinnon.

Mickleson quietly addressed the rest of the men. "This boy is going to run the hedgerows and signal when they turn the corner. Arnie here can wait at this corner and look for the signal. Keep low boys, and quiet." They both nodded and Mickleson grasped the boy in front of him by the shirt front, lifting him off his horse and onto the bank of the high hedgerow with one strong arm. Richie wriggled through the base of it and they heard his feet as he set off at a run. Mckinnon did the same with Arnie and the younger boy wriggled through the bushes the same way.

"Richie is waving you on, I can see 'im clear as day," the boy's voice came from the other side of the bushes.

"It is day, Numskull," Mickleson shot back and the boy giggled.

"He's runnin' on, I'm going to run to the next corner so I can see 'im." They heard more running feet and started their horses around the corner. As they approached the next bend, Arnie's voice came to them. "You can keep going, mister!" then more running. It continued in this vein for about an hour. The evening started to dim and the running feet they heard became wearier. They knew they were closing in as they had to wait longer and longer at each corner.

Thought not a full moon, there was plenty to see by to keep the horses on the road, Mickleson led the way on the tall, black Friesian.

They approached the next corner, but heard no small voice urging them on.

"Numskull!" Mickleson said in a loud whisper.

They heard a yawn and a voice. "It's too dark to see 'im." An owl hooted in the distance. Arnie piped up again, "an 'oot is good, you can move on. If he does a screech tha's bad."

"You might as well ride with me, Numskull. We can hear him ourselves." There was some scrabbling and the smaller boy appeared from under the hedges. Mickleson's strong hand grabbed his shirt front and pulled him onto the horse. Nathaniel smiled on hearing Mickleson's gruff voice. It was tinged with an affection that he may not have realised it held. Nathaniel was reminded of the first time he had met Davy.

After hoots at the next few corners, they finally heard an owl's screech, and brought their horses to a standstill before turning the next corner. Nathaniel was unsurprised. Those men should not risk their horses and cart in the darkening sky much longer and at the last few turns there had been only trees. Now there were fields in sight, places where the men could stop for the night.

More rustling was heard then a voice piped up beside Mickleson. Richie stood on the high bank of the hedgerow.

"Mister, they are making a camp around the next corner in a field. Your whites don't look good, they put the foal up on the cart and the Mum's hooves dragged, and she's still bleeding."

"Dam," Mickleson corrected him.

"Sorry, Mister. I am just sayin' what I saw."

"The mother of a foal is called a dam." He smiled as the boy snorted a laugh. "It is spelt differently."

"Well I cannot spell it either way, so it don' matter to me."

"We need a plan, men," Horncastle piped up. No one said anything, but he felt all eyes upon him in the darkness. He was surprised they were looking to him, particularly the colonel. He felt that was a good thing, however, as the man bristled with barely controlled anger. "One of us should stay with the horses. I should suggest you as the obvious choice, Colonel, but I know you wish these men bodily harm and I think your rage could be handy when we are ready for that."

"I will stay with the horses and the boys, Numskull is asleep on me already."

"I can stay with the horses instead if you like, Mister." Richie was eager to please this big man who could lift him easily with a single fist. Mickleson reached over and tousled his hair where he stood on the tall bank of the hedgerow.

"You can help me, Richie."

"Ain't ya goin' ta call me a numskull?" The boy sounded disappointed.

"I will think of another name for you, Little Owl."

"Sounds as if you have to me," Mckinnon laughed.

"This is not getting our plan put to action, men!" Horncastle admonished them. "Mckinnon, the colonel and I will make our way quietly over to their camp. One of them will be on watch while the other sleeps, but I should not be surprised if they both fell asleep. Then we will creep up on them and pounce."

"Are you going to rob 'em?" With the action almost upon them, Richie wondered if what they were doing was right.

"No, they robbed... they stole from us. Mrs. Ackley bought the white dam and foal fair and square, but after she got the foal out, saving them both, the men welched on the deal."

"They said they have not seen a woman do such a thing before."

"Who said?" Nathaniel was surprised by this statement, this boy had been with Peter Robinson at the cart when they ran to the tent with Helena in it, how could he know what happened?

"I snuck into the clan group when they were talking about what to do and there was a boy there who told them what had happened. He had been under some blankets when the women came in, he saw the red one put her hands in the horse and pull the foal out. He told them the men had tried to give her money back, but she wanted the horses. Then the Scot came in and took the women."

"What happened to the boy?" Nathaniel hardly dare ask it, a sick knot was forming in his stomach.

"He is in the cart, of course. He did not want to go, but the man said he was his son." He was talking to empty air, as Nathaniel had disappeared around the corner legging Perseus on quickly. He doubted that man even had a son, but chances were he was taking out his frustration on the lad even now.

"Colonel, this is not the plan!" Horncastle shouted at him as he hung on to Perseus' mane for dear life.

"We are standing around talking and he is probably beating that boy as we speak." He heard hooves behind him as Mckinnon and Mickleson followed. Mickleson had handed Arnie down to Richie and told them to wait for his holler.

As they approached the camp there was one man outside the covered cart and he stood with a shout. Nathaniel and Horncastle thundered towards him on Perseus' back.

"Get near and I will tackle him, Colonel."

Nathaniel did not need telling twice. He moved Perseus to ride alongside the man and Horncastle threw himself at him, timing his leap from the stallion perfectly. He knocked him over, his momentum causing Horncastle to roll past him and allowing him to get straight back to his feet. He turned the man onto his back and got him into a choke hold. Up close he could see the bruised nose and swollen eyes from the head butt he had received from Mckinnon. When he kicked his legs, and pulled at Horncastle's arms, the smaller man tapped him on the nose and he roared with pain.

Meanwhile, Nathaniel reined Perseus to a stop outside the covered cart, and dismounted. The second man appeared at the rear of it and before he could say anything, Nathaniel had grasped him by the shirt and the belt and hurled him out of the cart. He turned in midair and lay stunned on the ground. Nathaniel straddled and pummelled him, his gloved fists cracking onto flesh and bone.

"I think he has had enough, Colonel." Mickleson put a firm hand on his shoulder.

The man groaned. "Why?" he said through swollen lips. Nathaniel put his mouth to the man's ear.

"You cannot put a knife to my cousin's neck and threaten my wife without repercussions, these are yours. Be grateful I am not alone or I would murder you and no one would ever find your body. I am going to take what my wife paid for, the white dam and foal." The man nodded, realising the red-headed bitch had been right, he did regret tangling with her. "Now tell me, is the boy truthfully your son? Is he?"

"No."

"Then I am taking him, too."

"What should we do with this one, Colonel?" Bertram asked, still holding the subdued man in the headlock. The colonel stood again and walked over to them.

"This is the one that had his hands on my wife?"

"No! No! Not me." Having seen what had become of his comrade, the man looked panicked. Mckinnon dismounted and walked over to Mr. Horncastle.

"Yes, it was him," he pointed to his face. "He is the one I butted."

"Get up!" Nathaniel commanded. Horncastle released him and he stood, but not for long. Nathaniel drew back his fist and punched him so hard he fell backward again, narrowly missing Horncastle who had rolled quickly out of the way. He lay there motionless and unconscious for the second time that day. Nathaniel huffed out a breath and walked towards the cart to climb in.

There was a lamp in the cart, but all he saw was a bundle of blankets. He got one hip up and his left leg, then hoisted his wooden leg up. It landed with a heavy thump. He leaned his back against one side as he sat in the entrance with his legs out in front of him.

"He cannot hurt you anymore. None of us will hurt you. You have my word. Will you come with us? We can take care of you."

"They said that at the other place when they made me tell what had happened and then they gave me back to him because he said I was his son."

"You are not his son."

"I do not want to be."

"He just confessed to me that you are not. Do you not remember where you are from?"

"No."

"The woman in the tent who saved the foal, she is my wife. I can take you to her, she will take care of you."

"The red woman?"

"Yes."

"What about the white woman?" Nathaniel assumed he meant Harriet.

"She is my cousin. They are both very kind women. Or you can stay here and wait for these two to wake up?"

"No." The boy moved out from under the blankets warily and as he did so Nathaniel could see how dirty he was, by the light of the lamp. There was blood on the back of his breeches, too. He would not be comfortable riding astride a horse all the way back to Wyndham House. He took one of the blankets and tied it around his shoulder and ribs forming a sling, as he had seen Helena do for Little Nate. The boy was so tiny he fit inside it and curled against Nathaniel's chest. He scooted out of the cart and over to Perseus.

"I have him." He tapped the sling gently. "How are the whites?"

"The mare is tired, but I think she can make it. I had some sugar in my pocket for her and she has perked up some. The foal cannot walk," Mickleson answered quickly.

Nathaniel pondered. Would Perseus tolerate the foal over his shoulders? With the boy in the sling he could manage them both, that would leave the other two boys with Mickleson and Horncastle riding with Mckinnon if he was willing. As he thought of them, the two boys came running up to them, exclaiming over the two men passed out in the grass.

Perseus was cooperative and they all managed to get back to Wyndham House. Mckinnon knew of an alternate route around the other side of the town which made much quicker work of it than retracing their steps. When they finally returned, exhausted, Nathaniel left Mickleson to deal with the horses. The two boys slept on the bunk in Mickleson's office, while he worked, and he regretfully woke Benjamin and Peter. Promising them all the details the next day if they would brush all the animals down now. He could not sleep until the white dam was producing milk for the foal and he set about getting water and food into her where she had collapsed on the straw in a stall. He laid the pitiful foal close to its mother's teats, ready.

The other boy, who was asleep in the sling, Nathaniel left in the care of Mckinnon, and he headed to his own bed. The ride back had not been good for his own mind. They had ridden in silence as they were all so tired, but his anger with Helena, that had dispersed somewhat when he had beaten the men and talked to the boy, resurfaced. In her concern for the white horse, she had endangered herself and Harriet, and he would have been faced with the possibility of having let them both down again.

He could not face her with this mood upon him. He had to stay away from her or risk hurting her in his anger.

Helena had not been able to get to sleep and was, therefore, awake when Nathaniel came into the dressing room. She heard the anger in his voice still as he hurried James, but she did not move from her bed. He should come to her, he would be angry, she would apologise sincerely and promise never to do anything so rash again. He should forgive her and then he would love her. She would pour all her gratefulness for him and his forgiveness, into loving him. But he did not appear!

After five minutes of silence she wondered if he was waiting for her in her dressing room or perhaps thought her asleep, but he had always shared her bed and they had never slept on anger. She got out of bed and padded to the dressing room, but it was dark and empty. With the moonlight coming through the windows, she lit a candle and walked over to the opposite door to the room he had been assigned, but not used. She tried the handle, it was locked. Her heart sank and nausea rose up in her throat. He was obviously far angrier than she expected.

"Nathaniel," she whispered it, but did not know why, no one was around to hear her other than him. "Nathaniel!" She rattled the door handle.

"Go to bed, Helena," his angry retort seemed to reach through the door and slap her. She stepped back in response, but then rattled the handle again.

"No, Nathaniel. We must talk of this. There is no point waiting until the morning. I must apologise. I was foolish and we were lucky Mckinnon was so vigilant. Lucky that Mr. Horncastle got us all away from there safely. Nathaniel!"

"I do not want to speak to you now. Go to bed."

"No, Nathaniel. Open this door!"

"Goodnight, Helena."

A sob caught in her throat at being dismissed by him so callously. She knew what she had done had been wrong. She had not needed Harriet to tell her that, although the young woman had certainly done a good job of it. But she did not need to be punished in this way, without even having a chance of apologising. She ran around to the door to his room that led directly into the hallway and tried that, but he had remembered to lock it, too. She did not want to be seen begging at her husband's door to be allowed admittance and so returned to her own bed and sobbed.

The sleep that came to her was disjointed and full of horrible nightmarish scenarios. The worst of them was where the man who had held Harriet had slit her throat. In the one that had woken her Nathaniel had assumed she had chosen the man and had left her with him. Relief had flooded through her when she realised that she was at Wyndham House, before the despair of Nathaniel not wanting to discuss it with her, hit her once more.

Lying there, looking at the ceiling trying to calm her heart, she heard James come in to the dressing room and then another door open. He must have a key! She leapt out of her bed, and was through her door and across the dressing room in moments. Still in her nightgown, her hair wild around her head and shoulders, she stood in the doorway of his room.

"Get out, woman!" he shouted at her from his position in the bed. James had stopped what he was saying and made to leave. "You stay, James. You leave!" He pointed at her.

"I will not. James, please leave us alone." Unsure what to do, James decided to retreat.

"I do not want to talk to you, Helena. I made myself clear last night. I am afraid if I do I will lose my control. I am so angry with you."

"Of course you are, you are right to be. But shutting me out is not getting this worked out. I have not slept, you have not slept. This is the first night we have spent apart when we have not had to. We must discuss this."

"If I had gotten into bed with you last night I might have hurt you. It is taking all my control not to 'teach you a lesson' right now. That is how my father would have termed it and I hate even saying it. Feeling it is even worse, so get out of my sight!" At that she wanted to turn and leave with some dignity, but the knowledge that she had driven him to this, that she had been wrong and made him feel this way, made a sob escape her and tears to overflow her eyes.

She ran from the room and made to do the only thing that could help her get away from her swirling thoughts of despair. She ripped off her nightgown, right in front of an astonished James, who turned away quickly, and she pulled on her riding habit with the separate legs that allowed her to ride astride. It buttoned in the front, so she did not need help in putting it on. Then she pulled on her riding boots and left without even pinning her hair or finding a bonnet.

Nathaniel slumped back into the pillows, she had left the room, which is what he had wanted, but he did not feel any better for it. Some of the anger in him that had only built during the night when she had begged to come into the room, dissipated. James reappeared at the door.

"Tell her to come back in, James. She is right of course, we should discuss it."

"She is not here, sir."

"Knock on her door and tell her to come in here. I should myself, but it would be quicker for her to come to me."

"I cannot, sir. She is not in there. She left."

"Left? But she is not even dressed. Nora is not there, is she?"

"No, Mrs. Ackley... ah... dressed herself."

"Right in front of you?" He laughed a little at that.

"I apologise, sir. I did not see her intention until it was too late, but I turned my back directly."

"Do not be concerned, James. I think she is safe from you."

"Yes, sir."

"Did she put on her riding habit?"

"Yes, sir, but she did not even pin up her hair."

"Oh, this I have to see." He moved himself to the edge of the bed and James rushed to him with a robe and crutch. Nathaniel walked to the window and looked out to the riding stables. "Damn it, it is going to rain shortly, she should not ride these hills in the rain. Especially when she is upset. Get my riding clothes ready, James. I will be out there shortly." James left and Nathaniel continued to look out of the window. After a while, he saw Helena riding out to the hills beyond the stable. She was riding Henry and her hair was flying behind her, showing him how fast she was going.

As Nathaniel exited the stable and mounted Perseus the rain started to pour. Grimly he turned Perseus to the hills, confident of his mount's surefootedness. Still, he rode with caution, watching out for slippery mud, particularly going downhill. As he approached the last hill before the lake, which was the steepest one, he turned Perseus towards one side of it rather than over its pinnacle, to avoid the steep run the other side. As they came around it, his heart caught in his throat. Helena lay curled into a ball at the base of the hill. Henry marched around seemingly unhurt a short distance away from her. Looking at the steep ground of the hill, he could see grooves in the mud where Henry's hooves had obviously slid.

"Helena!" he called, but she did not move. Her shoulders seemed to be shaking, but she did not lift her head or acknowledge him in any way. He rode Perseus over to her and slid off the saddle, dropping to the ground beside her. He put a hand carefully on a shoulder.

"Helena, are you well? Did you fall? Have you hurt yourself?"

Between the sobbing she managed only single words. "Fell... unhurt... heart... heart..."

"What is it, Helena?"

"Heartbroken."

"No, Helena, no!" He stood and shouted at her now, his relief that she was not hurt mixing with his earlier anger. "That is not fair. Am I not allowed to be angry with you? What you did was beyond foolish. You risked yourself and Harriet for a horse! I did not know where you were, I could not have saved you. I was not able to save either of you from Davenport and could not have saved you yesterday. Thank goodness for Mckinnon and Horncastle."

She had pushed her shoulders up from the ground and swiped at the mucus that had flown freely from her nose and mouth as she sobbed. Her eyes were wet and red as she gasped in more air, holding it to stop her sobbing, before shouting back at him in return.

"You have every right to be angry, of course it is allowed, but you do not have the right to shut me out, to punish me more than my mind is already doing over my stupidity and what could have happened. The dreams... nightmares I had last night..." She shuddered. "I could not relieve my mind of those ideas because I could not talk to you of it."

"I could have hurt you, Helena. I still feel it, every time I think of us not reaching you in time and of the danger you put Harriet it."

"I feel it, too. So angry with myself, but I would have preferred your violence of my body than that you inflicted on my mind, that you inflicted on my heart." She looked up at him from the ground.

"I would not have been able to forgive myself for hurting you, if I had," he said it rather than shouting, but the anger still bubbled within him and the falling rain did not dampen it as it soaked them.

"You did hurt me, Nathaniel. I know I hurt you, I made you feel this anger, but you did not give me the chance to apologise, to say I was wrong. I have never done that to you and goodness knows you have been wrong."

"Are we to talk of my decision regarding my leg again? Do you never tire of bringing that up? I apologised for that long ago."

"And I accepted that apology straightaway, I only bring it up to point that out to you. I accepted you back into my life, even though you had been determined to leave it and I would do so again and again, because you apologised, because you said you were wrong."

He paced away from her and then paced back and looked at her expectantly.

"What?" she asked, exasperated, waiting for his angry retort.

"I am waiting. You said I have not given you the chance, you did not actually say the words." He was calmer.

"I am sorry, Nathaniel. I am sorry for putting myself, and especially Harriet, in danger. I have already apologised to her. I am sorry for making you so angry, justifiably so. I will be more careful in future, you cannot know how awful it was to see the look on Harriet's face when he held that knife to her throat. I do not think it will ever leave me. I am sorry. I was wrong."

He held out a hand to her and when she took it, he pulled her to her feet. Then he pulled her with him to the trees a short distance away to shelter them somewhat from the rain, before looking down at her. "Say it again."

"Which part?"

"The last six words."

"I am sorry. I was wrong."

"I do not think I have heard you say so before, so I am making the most of it. I thought you always in the right!"

"Do not get used to it. Mostly I am right!" She laughed a moment. "Please forgive me, Nathaniel. I love you so much, my heart hurt for what I know I put you through. How scared I made you. You cannot know."

He held her to him then, tight to his chest. She was right about that, he had been scared.

"I do know, it was how I felt after my leg was removed and I was stuck at Aysthill House, while your fever raged after having Little Nate. I blame myself for that. You would not have been in that carriage had you not come to visit me, and you should not have needed to visit me if I had not been so stubborn about having my leg removed. I had to wait a week before I knew you would be well again and that was how I felt the whole time. I needed you to forgive me, but you could not."

"I could have ended up with an infection had I been at Redway, there is no way to know if it was because I was in the carriage. He would have been the wrong way around no matter where I gave birth to him. I do not see that as your fault, but yes, I understand how you would have felt. You do not need forgiveness for that. I am still waiting for yours though. Can you forgive me and know that I will never be so rash again?"

"Yes, Helena, I forgive you. I love that you are an independent woman, but that comes with responsibility. You must think ahead." He bent his head to kiss her and as he did so the rain stopped and the sun came out, shining upon them.

"Nathaniel, look." She pointed through the trees behind him and he turned.

The sun dappled through the leaves and shone on a grassy bank at the side of an inlet of the lake. It was protected on three sides by the wood and to the fourth side the gleaming water of the lake shone in the sun. They should not have noticed it but for the exact spot they stood upon and the sun shining in that moment. A wide smile spread itself across his face.

After tying up their horses, they made their way through the trees towards it. Nathaniel had checked with Horncastle, who had indeed assured him it was a pleasant lake to swim in.

When they reached it, Helena turned back to Nathaniel as he stepped out of the trees, pulling off his gloves, "I completely forgot to ask you, were you able to get the whites?"

"I wondered how long it would take you to ask me that. Did you not see them in the stable?"

"You got them?" She flung her arms around him.

"Of course we got them. Did you doubt me?" He took her face in his hands and kissed her. As his hands moved away she saw the raw bruises there and took them gently into her own.

"I did not doubt you. Thank you." She kissed the bruises.

"I have to say my intention was to sell them. I did not think you deserved them." She opened her mouth to protest, to say that she had paid fairly for them and then saved them, but his look stopped her. "You could earn them back."

"You want to buy my favour with horses, sir?" she said playfully.

"Yes, I do." He growled it in her ear.

"Well you know how highly I value horses and we are talking about two true whites. Very valuable indeed. I should have to do a lot to earn them back."

"Indeed you would. We should make a start." He began unbuttoning her riding habit and realised very quickly that she wore nothing underneath it. "Helena, you changed into this right in front of James! No wonder he was so flustered."

"I did? Poor James. I was so upset I was not thinking straight."

He looked at her intently and kissed each of her eyelids that were still puffy and red from her crying.

"I love you, Helena." He slipped the riding habit off her shoulders and it slid down her back and over her hips. She stood only in her ankle riding boots. He adjusted his wooden leg so it would bend and he could kiss his way down her body. His lips ran over her breasts and stomach and into that soft triangle of hair as he moved lower to unlace her boots. She pulled his shirt out of his breeches and slipped it up and off him as he bent. Her boots undone, she stepped lightly on the mossy ground. Protected by trees as it was, it was barely damp from the rain. When he stood again, he rubbed his muscular chest, with the fading scar that sliced across it, against her body.

"Nathaniel," she murmured his name on a gasp as he had stopped and taken a breast in his mouth, sucking on the nipple. "Anything we do together is never in exchange for payment of any kind. I give my body freely to you to do with as you will, safe in the knowledge that you will never hurt me and that you will always endeavour to provide me with as much pleasure as I give to you."

Raising his head, he looked into her eyes. "I give you those horses freely and anything else it is in my capability to provide you with, as I know it gives you as much pleasure, albeit of a different kind, to care for horses. I cannot live without you, Wife."

"I do not want to live without you either, Husband." At that he caught her lips in his, as he pulled her naked body against him and wrapped his arms around her, his lips became more demanding and his tongue slid between hers. Her arms wrapped up and around his neck, her hands in his hair, she was so grateful that they had made things well between them again. She had not cared about their shouting, she much preferred that to the silence and rejection of the night before.

"Make me a very happy man and help me live out a fantasy that I have had since I saw you swimming naked in the stream at Redway, when you were only fifteen years old."

She could think of no better way to make amends for causing so much anger within him and, as she knew it was now, making him so scared. She walked naked over to a large flat rock that hung over the deeper part of their little inlet and dove into its depths as he watched. The deep water was cool on her eyelids, that were still swollen from her crying. She surfaced with her red hair slicked back and spouted a tall fountain of the lake's water. He had taken off his leg, boot and breeches and laid back on his elbows on the grassy bank. She swam back to the large rock and noticed there were several smaller ones under the water that formed wide steps up to it. Was it manmade or a happy circumstance? Walking up them she climbed the rock again and stood looking at him. Her creamy skin glistened and her long hair was plastered down her back and over her rear. She looked as if she was a Greek statue, all smooth, white and curved. Evidently, from how erect he was, he enjoyed the sight.

"Are you joining me?"

"In a moment." She dived in again and when she surfaced she saw him balanced on the rock and watched him dive in easily. As he surfaced he wrapped his arms around her and pulled one of her legs over his hip as he kissed her. Then he licked and sucked on the wet skin of her breasts, shoulders and neck. Out of their depth, he could not hope to enter her and he felt frustrated. Maybe it was the way of things, that fantasies should never be allowed to come true, as the reality was never as satisfying.

"Come over here." Helena pulled him to the 'steps' and made him sit upon one, his foot resting on the lower one. With him there, she could wrap her legs around him. As he kissed her again, she delved a hand between them, into the warmer shallow water, and positioned him to enter her. Grasping her hips, he pulled her down upon him slowly and then released her allowing her to float upward with the natural buoyancy of the water. He smiled and repeated the process. Laughing, she lay backward, allowing her hair to float around her head in the water and her breasts, that now only skimmed the water's surface, to bob there for him to feast upon.

She held onto his arms as they found their rhythm, then she leaned forward to kiss him again and her breasts slapped pleasingly against his chest. As the passion built in them both, she lay back again. Taking a wet nipple in his mouth once more, his desire overcame him and he peaked within her. "Helena," he moaned as he pushed one final time inside her warmth.

For a moment, she lay back in the water panting, waiting. He released her hips and they floated up to him as she unwrapped her legs from behind him. Her red curly hair sprang to life as her pubis surfaced, the folds of her glistened in front of him and his seed spilled from within her into the water. Putting his face between her legs and with his hands supporting her buttocks, he licked.

She gasped, it was glorious to lay on the surface of the water, the sun shining on her, warming her skin, as the water lapped over her. She had just given her husband the reality of a long-held fantasy and now he proceeded to pleasure her with his tongue. The contrast of the heat of him and the cool of the water added to her pleasure as the peak built within her. Differing from the time they had enjoyed in the carriage on the journey to Bath, here in the seclusion of their little inlet, she could moan and scream as much as she liked, as she knew he liked her to do.

When they finally got out of the water and dressed, they agreed this little slice of green grass should be a location they would visit again.

Chapter Nine

The night before, Mckinnon had taken the sleeping child in the blanket sling from the colonel. No one was awake in the kitchens, so he had taken him to his own sitting room where he had a bunk and laid him upon it, still within the blanket. The boy did not stir. Exhausted, Mckinnon stretched out in an armchair and fell asleep, too.

He awoke with a start early in the morning, to see the bunk empty. As he moved he groaned, his back was stiff and his legs locked as he had slept with them stretched out and his ankles crossed. The door was still closed, so he guessed the boy was still in the room somewhere. After rubbing his eyes, he looked again to the bunk and noted the ratty blanket was there, but one of his own had disappeared, as had his pillow. Then below the bunk he saw a corner of that blanket sticking out. As he reached for it, it disappeared under the bunk.

"No one will hurt you here. Will you come out?" There was no response. "Would you like some food?" Nothing. "Stay here, I'm getting some food."

He left, leaving his door closed. His sitting room was off the staff

Trish Butler

dining room and that was joined to the kitchen. He found the cook there as expected and stood in the doorway watching her pleasing figure for a moment or two before addressing her. "Miss Cadman, I wonder if I could trouble you for a plate of food for a hungry young boy."

"Well, Mr. Mckinnon, you should not be hungry if you had been back in time for dinner last night and I doubt anyone has called you a boy for many years!" She laughed as she looked back at him, she did like to look at him and his soft accent melted her knees when he talked to her sometimes. She was surprised when she took in his crumpled appearance and sombre demeanour. "Mr. Mckinnon, you do not usually sleep in your clothes, although I have to say you look as if you have not slept at all. What is wrong?"

"We rescued two horses and a very put upon young boy last night. Mr. Mickleson is caring for the animals and at least he has some information of what he is doing. The boy was left in my care and in the night, he moved from sleeping on the bunk in my sitting room to hiding underneath it. He will not speak or come out."

"You are a big man, Mr. Mckinnon. Can you not simply reach under and pull him out or move the bunk even?"

"I fear he has been abused, in his mind and his body. I should hate to scare him more and have him run away. I have no experience in this kind of thing. How am I supposed to know what to do?"

"I will get you a plate and you had better give him a chamber pot, you do not want those kinds of accidents in your room. Perhaps as he learns he will be well cared for, he will trust us and come out?"

As he carried the plain food and a drink back to his sitting room, Drummond Mckinnon wondered what to do to coax the boy out. He would also need some clothes. As he approached, his heart jumped into his mouth, the door was open halfway. From the distance he stood at, he could see beneath a third of the bunk and a pair of eyes peeking out from under it, that disappeared as soon as his own locked on them. By the time he reached the door, he could no longer see under the bunk.

He placed the plate and cup on the floor nearby, but nothing happened. He took two steps back, keeping his boots visible to the boy, waiting. A hand came out and grabbed the bread. It was a test, Drum knew that, it was quicker to grab one big thing than the whole plate. He took another step back and the hand came out and took the plate and cup. Turning to the cupboard to the side, he fished underneath it for the chamber pot and placed it near the bunk, too.

"You need to do any business, boy, do it in there, not on my floor." He said firmly, letting the boy know that he would not tolerate a mess. He stood back again, but the chamber pot did not move. "I mean piss or the other, if you need to shite, lad. Make sure it goes in there." The pot disappeared and he thought to give him some privacy. "I will be eating in the next room." He stepped out of the room, leaving the door ajar as the boy had done before.

Miss Cadman was walking towards him with a tray. "Would you like yours in your room Mr. Mckinnon, or will you sit out here?"

"I will give him some privacy." He sat at the head of the large table and she served him his breakfast from the tray. "And you? Have you eaten?"

"The house staff had theirs and are in the process of setting fires and cleaning rooms. I am grabbing a bite before the stablemen come in after finishing with the horses this morning."

"There are a good many more horses now, they may be longer than expected. Would you join me for breakfast?"

"Yes, sir."

"It is a request, Miss Cadman. You do not have an obligation to sit with me."

"I would like to, sir." She returned to the kitchen for a tea tray and her own food, then poured their tea and sat next to him. He enjoyed talking to her and told her of the previous evening's events, leaving out the state the men were in when the colonel had finished with them.

"That sounds as if it was an exciting adventure! I did not know you could ride, Mr. Mckinnon."

"It has been a while, but I did enjoy it. Have you ever had the opportunity to ride, Miss Cadman?"

"I was brought up on a farm, sir. I rode every day. I miss it."

"I am sure, with the new horses, there should be opportunity to ride if they needed exercise. I could ask Mickleson."

"I do not think I should want to ride alone, Mr. Mckinnon." She looked at him expectantly. She had seen him glance at her often and they had shared a joke or two, many times. He seemed to enjoy her teasing of him, and this was not the first time he had singled her out to share a meal with him. It seemed, however, that he was not as interested as she had hoped, as he did not offer to ride with her and said nothing further. His eyes, that often looked at her with interest, took on a faraway look, as if he was remembering something.

She stood, embarrassed, when he did not respond and worried she had perhaps been too forward. "I had better prepare some more food, you have just informed me we have two new mouths to feed and young boys at that. You know they are bottomless pits."

"Thank you for your company, Miss Cadman." She barely nodded and quickly cleared her own tray. He wondered at her sudden formality when they had been talking of going riding. Had he been inappropriate? Had he said something amiss? He went over the conversation in his head until he came to the point when she had mentioned not wishing to ride alone. He had thought of them both riding out on a picnic. He could talk to her of his feelings without the fear of someone bursting in on them and ruining the moment. Then an image of a wild, Scottish girl riding bareback on a large stallion came into his mind and guilt prevented him from saying anything further. Miss Cadman must have taken it as a rebuff.

She returned with a slice of cake on a small plate. He smiled at her, thinking she must not have been too upset if she was bringing cake to him, but she did not return his smile.

"For the boy," she said simply and his face fell as she picked up his tray and walked efficiently back to the kitchen.

He reentered his room. The breakfast plate was on the floor, empty and the pot was full. He put the cake down, resignedly and picked up the plate and pot. The hand shot out for the cake before he moved away, which he took as a small accomplishment.

Charlie Mickleson woke up in the stall of the white dam and foal. Late into the night he had still been coaxing the dam to eat and drink, until finally he saw her teats beginning to produce the thick starting milk. The foal he had lain in the straw next to her must have scented food as its tongue licked out at the teats as soon as the thick creamy substance was excreted. Once the filly started suckling, he had lain in the bank of straw to the side watching the sight; tired, but happy. He planned to make sure the activity continued then he would force the two boys on the bunk in his office to budge over and give him some room.

He had woken because he had been licked in the face. He looked right into the beautiful pink nose and white face of the filly. She was on her feet and peering down at him. He smiled and sat up slowly, where he could see the dam was on her feet, too. A few days rest and they should be doing well. He rubbed at his grimy face.

"You are awake then, Mister?" A little voice came from the other side of the stall. Mickleson looked up to see an angelic little face looking at him.

"Numskull! You are awake. You slept the whole way home." 'Numskull' smiled at the word 'home' and Mickleson grinned back, realising what it meant to both of them. "What have you been doing?"

"Mr. Bramley said to leave you to sleep and we should work for our breakfast. We have done enough to earn it now, he said, and told me to see if you were awake."

"I could eat." He was impressed that Benjamin had been getting them to work and wondered how much they had accomplished. He got up and had a quick look around the stable. A lot of work had been completed already. Benjamin came around the corner with Richie. "Nice work Mr. Bramley. Ah, here is Little Owl, I hope he has not been any trouble."

"Not too much, sir!" said Benjamin, pleased with his compliment. This man was not free with them, which made you want to earn them more and made them more valuable when you got them. "Mrs. Ackley was in here early, she looked a little wild and took Henry out. It is lookin' t' rain, and I almost woke you, but the colonel arrived a little after and took Perseus to ride after her. He said not to be concerned and he had it all in hand."

Mickleson nodded, but wondered at that. He knew Mrs. Ackley to be a very independent and opinionated woman. At Redway she always said she was in charge and it was not unusual for her and the colonel to disagree. John Robertson, Jacky's father, who owned ten percent of Redway, was always the one to decide whose decision they should follow. This was different though. He knew the colonel was angry about what had occurred yesterday. Actually, if he thought about it and imagined Annie Brown in the place of Mrs. Ackley, he would have termed the colonel's emotion as scared.

"Mr. Bramley said it is time for breakfast, are you coming, Mister?" Richie, who was keen to talk to the big man, pulled him out of his thoughts. "Can you carry us with one fist as you did last night?" He grasped his own shirt at the front as Mickleson had done when lifting him off and on the horse the night before.

"Your clothes will not last the day if I keep doing that. Here, lace your fingers." Both boys copied his action of locking his fingers together as if praying. "Keep them locked tight, boys!" Mickleson put a big fist up into the pocket each formed with their hands and hoisted them in the air, keeping his arms bent and his biceps flexed. The boys dangled there and loved it.

They entered the kitchen in a similar fashion. "I have a couple of hungry animals for you here, Miss Cadman!" Mickleson bellowed, laughing as he entered. The boys were swinging and laughing, too. "Miss Brown!" he exclaimed as he saw Annie Brown in the kitchen talking to Miss Cadman. He unceremoniously dropped the two boys. They laughed as they fell to the ground, unhurt.

"Mr. Mickleson, I wanted to say… oh, Mr. Bramley!" Whatever she had wanted to say, she forgot when she saw Benjamin. Her eyes darted to the younger man. "It is nice to see you again."

"You, too, Miss. It is a nice day."

"It is raining!"

"Oh well, I had not noticed." They laughed and Mickleson could not stop the low growl in his throat.

"You are hungry, I am sorry, I shall not keep you. Thank you for the powder, Miss Cadman. It will work a treat." With that she turned and left.

"She is pretty," Arnie piped up.

"You are too young for her!" Charlie swiped playfully at an ear.

"Are you washed up?" Miss Cadman asked them.

"Yes, Miss." They all answered and sat down at the table while she served them their meal. As she had predicted, they were bottomless pits and even after all their breakfast, the two youngsters found room for some cake.

Mckinnon had gone to look for the colonel to find out if he had plans for the boy, but had discovered both Colonel and Mrs. Ackley had gone riding. He had raised his eyebrows at James when he had informed him of it. James had said it was not his place to talk of it. Mckinnon suspected that the colonel was still angry with his wife and was pleased with James' discretion. He should need it if he were to work at Wyndham House for Mr. Horncastle.

On his way back to check on the boy in his room, he had met Jacky Robertson coming down the stairs, he was collecting a breakfast tray for his wife and had answered Mckinnon's polite inquiry with the news that Rebecca was improving. She was worrying that she was causing so much trouble, but Mckinnon put a hand on the lean man's shoulder and confirmed to him that she must not. They all understood it was a hard time.

Jacky stood in the dining room while he waited for the tray and looked at the two new boys interacting with Mickleson. They were taking turns telling Jacky of the previous night's events and laughing. Jacky happened to glance towards the open door of Mckinnon's sitting room and though he did not show it, was surprised to see a face under the bunk. He winked in the direction of the face and then looked to Mckinnon.

"Rats are pretty large in this house, sir. You seem to have a big one under your bunk." He jerked his head towards the room.

"It is the boy from last night. Will not talk and will not come out. I put food down for him and it disappears under there and the empty plate pops back out." Miss Cadman walked in with the tray for Jacky and Mckinnon nodded approvingly. Jacky left them to it.

"Mickleson," Drum addressed the man, "you seem to have a way with these two, do you think you could talk to the boy?"

"I do not think he will want to be called a numskull."

"You can't call 'im Numskull. Tha's my name!" Arnie looked mortified at the suggestion.

"Nor Little Owl." Richie obviously did not want his special name used for anyone else either.

"What about you boys?" Mckinnon looked to them hopefully.

"Well I could tell him that it's alright here." Richie seemed confident.

He walked in and stood by the bed. "You can come out, you know. The folks here are good people. They won't hurt ya. Food is good and they are friendly, ya know." He walked right back out and announced, "he won't come out."

"As long as you put some effort into it." Mickleson ruffled his hair and then wiped his hand on his breeches. "You need a wash, I'll put you under the water pump."

"You will do no such thing, Mr. Mickleson!" Miss Cadman shouted from the kitchen. "Finish your work with them and I will make sure we set out some tubs in the bathing room this afternoon. Are you in need of a bath, Mr. Mckinnon?"

"I think she is saying you smell, Drum!" Mickleson chortled.

"Get back to your stable and stop stinking up my dining room," Drum ordered with a laugh.

Jacky Robertson took the breakfast tray to Rebecca and told her the story he had heard of the previous day's events. She had been shocked to hear of the danger her mistress and Miss Wyndham had been in and doubly shocked to hear about the gaunt face Jacky had seen under the bunk. Her mothering instinct had kicked in straightaway and she had exclaimed *'poor bairn'* many times as he told her of the state he had been in when they found him.

"You must keep going downstairs and see how he is faring. I think you might be able to help him."

"Me? What can I do? Mckinnon could not get him out. As I left the kitchen I heard him ask one of the other boys with Mickleson to try."

"You must take our breakfast tray down and see if they were successful." She rushed to finish eating and Jacky did not complain about the task she had set him as it was so good to see her eat so much, but he doubted her wisdom in thinking he could do any better than anyone else in this household. When he voiced that opinion, she smiled serenely.

"I remember the day I fell in love with you, Jacky Robertson. I had made an excuse to come to Redway on my day off from Eastease and walked across the fields. Molly had seen me coming and ran over to me. She was full of news of puppies that had been born to that old, barn dog and the poor Mummy had passed away with the effort. You had made a smaller version of the leather sack used to feed orphaned foals and filled it with goat's milk. Molly had wanted to feed the puppies, but they would not let her hold them and feed them. She was unhappy that they would not let her help them, but she was young and had no patience to let them do it in their own time. She said you were going to try it and pulled me over to the stable to watch.

There you sat in a stall amongst the straw with those puppies. Your long legs stretched out in front of you, just talking to them about some nonsense. You didn't even see me there, so intent you were on helping those puppies. You sat so still and let them come to you. They sought the warmth of their mother, but in her absence, they honed in on the warmest thing there, you. Once they were all snuggling against your thigh, but shaking with hunger, you did not try to pick them up, but moved that leather sack of goat's milk to their mouths for them to suckle upon.

How they fought for the teat of that sack, but you made sure each of them got some milk and gradually they settled and when they did, they let you touch and stroke them. You soothed them and managed to move each one into your lap. How ever many were there? Perhaps six or more? Then you brought each to your chest and allowed it to suckle until full and falling asleep. You did not care if milk spilled on you or if they peed on you. You sat there and let them sleep.

I must have stood watching you for an hour. When you finally noticed me, and looked up with that long, lazy smile you have, I knew. I knew I loved you. I would never love another. I knew that you would be a wonderful and patient husband, lover and father."

Moved, he removed the tray from the bed and laid next to her, allowing her to come to him. She nuzzled at his neck and smelled that familiar man smell of him with a sigh, then she looked up at him. "See what I mean?" She smiled and he lowered his lips upon hers kissing her long and tenderly. Then he looked into her eyes and she could see the teasing in them.

"I cannot believe, Mrs. Robertson, that you took so long to fall in love with me! You had my heart the moment I laid my eyes upon you." She laughed at that and his heart sang again. He was still not convinced he had it in him to help the boy under the bunk, but if she thought he did, then he should give it his best shot.

Word got around that there was a small boy hiding under Mr. Mckinnon's bunk and one by one various servants tried to talk the boy out. It got to the point where Drum decided it must be overwhelming for him, particularly when Mrs. Thurston arrived in his room with her broom which she was about to stick, none too gently, under the bunk. He grabbed the broom from her and ordered her out with a short word about her insensitivity. She complained that no one had time for all this nonsense.

Jacky Robertson had ventured back into the kitchen and staff dining room several times, he helped with any chores Miss Cadman needed and fetched plenty of water for her, then he headed back upstairs sometimes with a tray or a pail. As he worked or waited, he would look in and see the boy looking at him from his hideaway. He would wave or give him a wink and carry on with his task. He hoped he might be piquing the boy's interest.

"Take your recorder and play him a tune. He will love it." Rebecca insisted when he told her how he was not pressing the boy, letting him set the pace. He picked up the recorder and turned it over in his hands. It could not hurt to try and it should please Rebecca, so he would do it.

He stopped in the dining room and crouched low so he could see the boy, then he put the recorder to his lips and played a quick tune, moving his long fingers quickly over the holes. He could see the boy's fingers moving as he lay on his back under the bunk and an idea suddenly struck him. He walked into the room and dropped the recorder on the floor near the bunk, before gently kicking it underneath and stepping away. He heard a couple of squeaky notes before he walked away with a small smile on his face. When he reached the room he shared with Rebecca, he was grinning ear to ear.

"Did it work?" She was eager to hear what had happened the moment he crossed the threshold.

"Well, he liked it and I could see his fingers moving as if he had a recorder, so..."

"You gave it to him! What a marvellous idea. What did he do?"

"He tried to play it. Of course the notes squeaked, but it was music to me."

She held out a hand and he came to her and sat on the edge of the bed. "What? What is it?"

"How would you feel about taking a child in? Not necessarily this child, but another. The colonel and Mrs. Ackley took in Davy and look how happy they are with that decision, all three of them."

"I have thought about it. I did not want to say because I did not want you to think I had abandoned all hope, but we could do both, could we not? Take in a child and yet still hope to have another in the usual way? Why not this child?"

"We do not know his situation yet, if his father was not the horse seller, then who is his father? Who is his mother? Where are they and are they looking for him? Is his mother crying herself to sleep every night with worry? I know I would."

The next time Jacky arrived in the dining room he called to Mr. Mckinnon who was sitting in his room. "I asked James for some of Davy's old clothes, Mr. Mckinnon. They will likely be too big, but you could roll up the sleeves and the breeches and it should work for now. If we can get some idea of his size, Rebecca could alter the length of the other set I have. Of course, he would need a bath first and I think Miss Cadman said she had some baths going later today." He walked away, talked a moment to Miss Cadman, and before leaving he turned at the point where he could see under the bunk and gave another wave.

At luncheon time, Mckinnon came out of his room to ask for a luncheon plate for the boy. He was thinking they might never get him out of there and would have to resort to Mrs. Thurston's tactics. Jacky was in the kitchen waiting for the plate ahead of him. He had asked Miss Cadman to let him know when it was ready.

"Mr. Mckinnon, I think you deserve a break. I will watch the lad for you." He took two plates from the cook and after making sure the boy saw it was him, he marched into the sitting room.

He sat on the floor with his back against the wall about four feet from the bunk and stretched his long legs out in front of him, putting the two plates of food by his side out of reach of the bunk. He smiled and thought about puppies, then he heard a couple of squeaky notes from the recorder. "I can teach you how to play that and get a good tune from it." There were a couple more notes. "Is there a mouse under there, with a cold?" He heard two more notes with a laugh at the same time and laughed a little, too.

"My name is Jacky. What is your name?"

"Boy."

Jacky broke off a piece of bread and held it out with his fingertips. The boy's fingers were as fast as lightning grabbing it and disappearing again.

"Boy is not a name."

"He just called me boy." Another piece of bread. Jacky was thrilled.

"What did your mother name you?"

"I don't remember." Tears formed a lump in Jacky's throat as he handed the boy a piece of cheese. He swallowed them down as he noticed the boy's face appear just under the bunk. Pale blue eyes ringed in dark circles looked at him and he gave him a small smile, but did not move from his seated position.

"What name would you like to be called?" he addressed the face.

"Jacky."

"Do you want cheese or bread?"

"Cheese." He handed it to him. Thinking.

"You know, I am named Jacky after my father, he is an excellent man. His name is John. What do you think to that? Shall we call you John until you remember your name? That way we will not get confused."

"John. Yes. Bread." He handed it over.

"Is it dusty under there, John?"

"Yes!" Again he was rewarded with a little laugh.

"Mrs. Thurston left her broom here, should I hand it to you and you can at least clean up while you are under there. It would only be good breeding." Jacky helped himself to bread and cheese on the other plate and munched on it, saying nothing more, but offering no more food.

"Where do you go with the trays?"

He handed the boy some of the ham from the plate and ate a bit more food himself. "My wife is ill, I am taking food to her. Everyone is being very kind. Everyone here is very kind."

"What is wrong with her?"

"She was going to have a baby, but it came out too soon and died. She has to rest to get her strength back and make sure she is going to be well again." He had not offered any food, he had completely forgotten as he talked of Rebecca, but the hand came out to him this time and he popped some bread into the palm.

"Will she be well?"

"I think so, at least her body will be, but she is very sad. I am sad."

"Do you have any children already?"

"No."

"Will you have another baby?"

"We will try, but this is not the first time this has happened." It had not been his intention to talk so much of Rebecca, but the boy seemed curious and Jacky wanted to keep him talking. He hoped he should be able to get him out from under the bunk at least.

John looked out from his hideaway at the man who had been catching his attention all morning. He was long and lean and moved fluidly, calmly. He differed from everyone else and had not stood by the bunk, a pair of feet speaking to him, telling him what to do. When he did come to talk to him he sat down and talked. He liked Jacky and wondered what his wife was like. The cook lady appeared at the door and he pulled his head back out of sight.

"I have the cake for you, Mr. Robertson. The other is ready, too, when you are, and I can have Mrs. Robertson's tray ready in five minutes once you give me the nod."

"Thank you, Miss." He stood to relieve her of the smaller plates and winked at her shocked expression. She rushed off, no doubt to tell Mckinnon of his success with the boy so far, but he was not done yet. He looked at the cake and smiled as an idea came to him. While his back was turned the rascal had snuck out far enough to get both plates of remaining food. He did not admonish him, but simply sat back down again.

He broke off a piece of cake from one plate and started eating it. He made a few noises of approval as he ate and then took another piece. The empty plates were pushed out from under the bed and the hand reached out for the cake. He moved the plate further away.

"Cake." He put his palm up.

"This is good cake. For good cake, you really have to be out from under the bunk."

"No."

"More for me then." He took the last piece from his own plate and then piled all the plates up, the topmost one holding the last piece of cake. He reached for it to break a piece off.

"Wait." Slowly and with a wary eye on Jacky, he emerged from under the bunk. Jacky dared not move a muscle. John looked at the cake and then back under the bunk. Realising his intention of grabbing the cake and scooting back under the bunk, Jacky slowly shifted away another foot or two and pulled the plates with him. He held his hand out, palm up, for the recorder that the boy still clutched.

"It's yours, but while you sit there and eat the cake I will show you how to play it." He made to push the cake towards John while holding his hand out for the recorder. John moved towards him more and quickly made the switch without touching him. He was interested enough in the recorder to stay where he was munching the cake. He watched the man's long fingers move easily over the holes while he played a lovely tune.

"Why does it not work for me?"

"When you play, you have to press your fingers down hard on the holes to cover them completely so the air cannot come out, look." Slowly he held out his hand to the boy and let him see the circles the holes in the recorder had pressed into his fingers. Curious, John ran a small fingertip over them. Then looked up at Jacky and they exchanged a smile.

"Can I see your wife?" John was suddenly aware that the man was going to go away to see her again in a moment and he did not want to be left alone. He did not want to go back under the bed either as he felt that Jacky might be upset by it and he liked him.

"Well now. You know how women want things to be clean." John nodded, he did not really know, but he thought it probably right. "And if you look at yourself and your clothes, you are not very clean. These clothes I got from a lad staying here. He is a bit bigger than you, but it is all we have. If you want to take a bath and put on these clothes, then you can see my wife." Jacky gestured towards the pile of Davy's old clothes on Mckinnon's couch.

"I do not want anyone to see me."

"In the bathtub? I will stand in the doorway and keep guard. Will that be alright?" John nodded and together they walked across the kitchens and to the bathing room where a nice hot bath and a good deal of soap awaited him.

Chapter Ten

Helena's hair had dried on the ride back to the house, she tucked it into her riding habit once they dismounted to appear at least a little more respectable to anyone she ran into as she went to find Nora. Nathaniel took the reins of both horses and walked them into the stable. The men were obviously eating their breakfast and the two boys Mickleson had brought back with him, too. He put each animal in its stall and then started untacking Perseus. He was grateful when Peter and Benjamin appeared and took over with both horses, as he was exhausted.

Nora was shocked at Mrs. Ackley wearing nothing under her riding habit and for going out without her hair pinned up or with a bonnet. She covered it well and quickly had her dressed acceptably for breakfast, her hair took a lot longer to get under control. Once it was detangled it was at least clean from the lake and with additional brushing it gleamed. To show it off to its best, she looped it up loosely.

At breakfast, Helena thanked Mr. Horncastle for his part in getting them safely away from the fair and the retrieval of the two white horses, and apologised for her actions that had made it necessary. Davy had demanded to hear how they managed to get the whites back and that story was duly told. Having inspected Nathaniel's bruises, Helena was sure her husband down played how much injury he inflicted on the men, but mentioned nothing of it.

After they had eaten, Nathaniel and Helena headed out to the stable to see the whites. He had not allowed her to enter the stable to see them directly on their return from the lake and she had accepted his ruling. Anything to do with these horses, she should have to rely on his decisions. She felt it a fair price to pay to have them at Redway.

She was pleased to see how healthy the dam and foal looked. They were both on their feet, the foal suckling at the mother, who was obviously providing a good amount of milk after her ordeal. Mickleson appeared around the corner and seemed to have two shadows with him. Their own shadows, Davy and Isabella, eyed them warily.

Helena talked to Mickleson about the dam and his endeavours in the night, and she had been impressed. She took the trouble to thank him for his assistance at the fair and with Nathaniel that night. He looked at her directly, seeing her sincerity but also some humility which was something he had rarely seen in her since he had joined Redway two years ago after the death of Mr. Hopwood. He had thought that he knew all there was to know of horses, but had been surprised to learn from both Colonel and Mrs. Ackley. They both had, what he had termed 'a feel' for horses, but Mrs. Ackley had almost an affinity, as if she thought as a horse did or could even communicate with them. The colonel held that more for people and Mickleson had often felt that the man read his mind.

Richie, Mickleson had determined over breakfast, was almost the same age as Davy, Arnie was a little younger than Isabella. Both of the Ackley children could ride exceptionally well for their ages. Davy had learned very quickly after joining the family four years prior, but Isabella had been riding since before she was four years old. He decided he should have to teach these two boys to ride and aimed to talk to Miss Wyndham of his ideas about apprenticeships for them, including some learning as he had established that Richie could not spell, and he doubted his ability to read or write.

"I am Richie and this is Arnie." Richie looked mainly at Isabella when he spoke. She looked coyly back at him.

136

"I am Miss Isabella Ackley, this is Davy Ackley."

"You can call me, My Lord. My grandfather is the Earl of Aysthill."

"Davy," Nathaniel said with a warning tone.

"Master Davy will do, or sir?" he directed the question towards his father who nodded.

"Miss Isabella, Master Davy." The older boy of the two pulled on his forelock as he had seen Mickleson do. Arnie did the same. "Can I get the stool for you, Miss? So you can see the whites?"

"Yes please, Richie." She smiled at him and he ran off to find the stool, returning quickly despite its weight. She stepped up on it. He stood to her side and looked over with her, talking about their adventure the night before and how when it was too dark he had made owl noises. Then he loudly demonstrated the noises which was followed by several whinnies around the stable. Mickleson glared at him.

"Sorry, sir."

Davy who had immediately moved protectively to the other side of Issie, had stood sullenly during the telling of a story that he had no part in. He harrumphed when the boy had to apologise to Mickleson.

"You know these are whites, because of the pink skin on the nose," Richie knowledgeably imparted the information he had only learned that morning. It made Mickleson smile when he heard it with half an ear, while he talked to Mrs. Ackley.

"Everyone knows that," Davy retorted, although he had not known it and was annoyed this boy knew more than him.

"I did not know it! How did you know?" Isabella questioned Davy which was not appreciated, though Richie grinned.

"I read it." The other boy's face fell and Davy sneered, realising that Richie could not read. Isabella was too intent on the whites to notice.

"Sometimes you think a horse is a white, but the skin is grey, so it is actually a grey. The stallion you got yesterday is a white-grey." Richie continued knowledgeably.

"We did? It is?" Davy's interest in an almost white grey overtook his need to seem more knowledgeable than the other boy. Helena had also lent half an amused ear to the boys, Davy had inherited his father's competitiveness, and she jumped into the conversation at that.

"Yes, we did! It was too late last night to look at him. Isabella, I believe I have found you a horse, but he is a little thin, so you will have to wait to ride him, if you want him. Let us go and see what you think." In all what had followed that purchase, Helena had almost forgotten about the stallion that she got from the same seller as the whites. "I suspect that he may be from this white mare, if she was mated with a grey."

Mickleson led them to a stall around the corner from the dam and foal and Helena moved to open the door.

"Allow me, madam." Nathaniel stepped in front of her and entered the stall instead.

"Of course, sir." She gave him a small smile and he nodded with a smile of his own. He allowed the grey to sniff at his pocket which held an apple. He pulled it out for him and offered it in his palm. Rubbing the horse as it chomped on the fruit. It seemed even tempered and well treated, if a little thin, but they could soon take care of that. He was sound and his frame should hold his bulk well once they built him up. He should imagine Issie would be able to ride him before they left for Redway.

"What did you pay for him?" He looked back at Helena who was smiling, she loved watching his way with horses.

"One hundred and seventy-five."

"Really? No wonder he did not appreciate you getting the dam from him for a song as well."

"He tried to tell me it was a white, but I told him he could not fool anyone with that. It would seem even young Richie here would not fall for that!" she smiled at the youngster and her son scowled at her.

Nathaniel encouraged the horse towards Isabella who was standing on the stool Richie had carried for her again and she stroked his nose. "Does he have a name?"

"Not that I know of," her mother answered. "It is up to you."

"Snow."

Davy harrumphed. Helena rolled her eyes, it was a prerequisite that he should scoff at the name Issie chose.

"I think it is perfect, Miss." Richie took his opportunity to get on the good side of the pretty girl.

"Thank you." She did reward him with her sweet smile. Helena was distracted and looking over at a stall further down the line.

"Who purchased the Friesian?" Helena had forgotten all about the horse Mickleson had ridden the night before.

"Horncastle! My God he was almost salivating at seeing it." Nathaniel laughed and they moved down to that stall.

"He is handsome."

"Smart and sensitive horses are Friesians," Mickleson mused. "You do not hit them if they do the wrong thing, you simply ask the question a different way."

Helena looked into the face of the man whose way with horses most reminded her of her grandfather. For a big man, he could be a real sap, and she was going to miss working with him. "I think that is true of all horses and wish that more people would hold that opinion!" She turned back to the animal. "He must have paid a fortune for it."

Mickleson and Nathaniel exchanged a look at that and smirked at each other. "He is a master negotiator, Helena. I think I might have to have a poker game against him, but I will have to be prepared to lose more hands than I usually should." They proceeded to tell her all the details of their negotiations, showing her all the other horses they bought, some of which she had groomed quickly the night before. She was very impressed, especially with the yearlings.

"I wonder if Harriet will want to keep them both?"

"I am sorry, Mrs. Ackley. I will certainly be informing my new mistress that the best course of action will be to keep them both."

"Her best decision was taking you on here, Mickleson. We will sorely miss you at Redway, but we understand your best option is to stay here." She turned to her husband. "How on earth are we to get the carriage Charlie drove, back to Lincolnshire?"

"I had thought of that," he informed her, "either I will drive it or we will have to leave the Eastease one here for the time being. Harker can spare it."

While the others were in the stable, Harriet went to check on the changes in the house that had been finalised while they were at the fair. She had been so tired the night before she had forgotten all about it and had gone straight from dining to her rooms. Firstly, she entered the new parlour. It was a beautiful room, in more blue and green hues than the golden ones of the other room. As the day was now fine, after the earlier rain, she opened the French doors and walked out onto the courtyard. The views from there were less restricted than within the room. She turned back to see Bertram standing in the frame of the open doors, with the balcony to her rooms above them.

"What do you think, Mr. Horncastle? Are you disappointed?"

"Not at all, I assure you. If the weather is fine this afternoon, we should have tea out here, it should be easy enough to bring out that smaller round table and a few chairs."

"An excellent idea!" She smiled and spun a circle in delight, which made him laugh.

"Now, Miss Wyndham. I must show you to your new music room. Mrs. Thurston confirmed that the pianoforte tuner visited yesterday. He checked over all the instruments, we hope he has met your requirements." He offered her his arm as she stepped back into the parlour and she found she could tuck her hand around his bicep without having to stoop at all.

As they entered she gasped, everything gleamed. The windows had been cleaned and the view sparkled in the sunlight, the instruments had been polished to a high shine and her suggested arrangement of everything was followed to the letter. It all looked magnificent. She moved swiftly to the piano and ran her fingers over all the keys, the sound was excellent. The man had done good work, she hoped they paid him well and then realised it was up to her!

"He did a good job, we should make sure to pay him something extra."

"I can let Mckinnon know if you wish." She nodded.

She looked through the music in front of her and realised it was her own, with her own notes upon some of the pages. She smiled, Annie had obviously brought it down from her rooms. Shaking out her fingers to loosen them, she began the top piece, which Annie knew to be her favourite, completely forgetting the presence of Mr. Horncastle.

When she finished, he clapped enthusiastically, and it gave her a jolt. "I apologise Mr. Horncastle, I forgot you were there." She looked apologetically at him sitting on the armchair that he had requested be moved to that exact spot so he could see her as she played.

"Evidently, but it is of no matter, it was beautiful to watch and listen to as I could tell you were as lost in it as I. How do you feel about playing another? I think I could listen to you quite happily all day. You are very accomplished. I have heard nothing that compares at any of the concerts I attended with Phillip."

She blushed pleasingly at that. She had worked hard at her music at first to be as accomplished as her sister, so she could emulate her. They had both learned to play at a young age, but it was her twin who had more patience for truly mastering the instrument. Harriet found as her playing improved she enjoyed it more and when ideas of Mr. Davenport entered into her mind, it had been her place of escape. She was thrilled that Mr. Horncastle might think her talented enough to play in public, though of course it was unheard of for a woman to do so.

"How do you feel about a dinner party, Mr. Horncastle? In a few weeks, before Helena and the colonel leave us."

"It has been a while, of course, with Phillip, but despite my own feelings, a house cannot remain in mourning forever."

"Thank you, Mr. Horncastle." She turned back to the pianoforte and began another piece. He smiled as he watched her.

After luncheon, Harriet and the children decided they wished to ride. Isabella would borrow the thoroughbred she rode before, until Snow was strong enough for her. Nathaniel and Horncastle went with them to the stable so Mr. Horncastle could become acquainted with his new black stallion. His heart beat fast and his hands shook in anticipation.

Helena decided a ride was not the ideal occupation for her, after her tumble earlier in the day. Her shoulders ached from landing on them as she had curled up and rolled with the fall to avoid as much injury as possible. She had been lucky that she had not broken her neck in her foolishness, but thankfully Nathaniel had not reprimanded her for it. Possibly because he felt he had driven her to it by upsetting her so much.

Instead, she walked towards the kitchens and sought out Mr. Mckinnon in his sitting room. She had heard of the boy hiding under the bunk and looked towards it when she entered. Mckinnon was sitting behind his desk and stood quickly when she knocked on the door. Looking at him, she noticed the dark circles under his eyes, he must be exhausted. She should have to insist he lay down on that bunk, that afternoon or he would be dead on his feet when dinner was served later.

Trish Butler

"Please sit, Mr. Mckinnon. You look exhausted. May I have a quick word?"

"Mrs. Ackley, please come in, of course you may." He gestured to the armchair he had fallen asleep in the night before and she sat in it. He waited until she was seated, then sat back in the chair behind the desk.

"Do you still have a guest under there?" She gestured to the bunk.

"No, Jacky Robertson tempted him out with food and a recorder. Then the boy asked to see Mrs. Robertson, but Jacky told him she liked things to be clean and so the boy took a bath!"

"Really? We have a Pied Piper in our midst?" She laughed and wondered at the child going to Rebecca. If the boy was an orphan perhaps she and Jacky would take him in.

"Mr. Mckinnon. I really must thank you for your vigilance and quick action at the fair yesterday."

"There is no need, madam. I was doing my duty for my mistress and her friend." He gestured towards her.

"No, sir. I feel I must! I was foolish in going in that tent and doubly so for taking Harriet into possible danger. I feel nauseous thinking about it even now. I can be headstrong and I love horses so much, I hate to see any beast mistreated and in this case shot, when it is unnecessary. I let my concern for the horse override what should have been my first priority and that was the safety of Harriet and myself. I did not consider where we were and the type of people we were dealing with."

"I am sure your mind has punished you enough over that. I suggest you set it aside, safe in the knowledge that we all came out of it unscathed, including the horses. You will know better another time, as we all learn from our mistakes."

"That is very kind of you to say, Mr. Mckinnon. I have set myself the task of apologising to and thanking all of you who helped us leave the fair safely and then retrieved the horses as well. I have done so to Charlie and Mr. Horncastle, but saved you for last as you were the one stopping them from hurting either myself or Harriet. It was over and above your duty. I apologise that I put you in the position to risk yourself to defend us and thank you for all that you did." Tears had sprung to her eyes at that and he aimed to relieve the moment, although he was grateful that she took the trouble.

142

"I am a Scot, Mrs. Ackley, and there is not much a Scot likes more than a bit of a brawl. I do not get much opportunity for one in my role here at Wyndham House. I should thank you."

She laughed and then looked to him again. "Mr. Mckinnon, I wish to assure you that should you ever find yourself in need of anything in the future, I am at your service, as is my husband and anyone associated with Redway and Eastease. We all value Harriet very highly. She is the last of the Wyndhams and we hope to see her live a long and happy life. Many of her younger years were marred by the loss of her parents and stepfather and of course just a few months ago her twin sister."

Mckinnon nodded, much of the information Mrs. Ackley had imparted to him was contained in the letters Mr. Horncastle had received from Eastease after Phillip Wyndham's death, and he had shared them with him. He looked towards his open door and through the staff dining room, to the kitchen where he could see the shapely form of Miss Cadman moving around, he came to a decision.

"Mrs. Ackley, I wonder if I could impose on you and ask you a personal question."

"Of course, anything."

"I understand that you were married before, that your husband died fighting in France."

"Yes, that is correct."

"How soon after that did you feel able to let someone into your heart again?"

"I am afraid I cannot be as helpful to you as I wish. I was never in love with him. My parents arranged the marriage, but I refused as he was much older and cruel. Due to my mother's encouragement, my father insisted. Shortly after that, he died. I had never had an interest in men, despite those that came because of my dowry. I loved horses. I loved Redway, where my grandfather lived. Once I was widowed I moved there to raise Isabella. It was not until she was nearly five years old that I met Colonel Ackley at Eastease. He is an exceptional man and the only one who has ever held my interest and my heart. If anything were to happen to him, I cannot imagine a scenario where I should find anyone to capture my interest in the same way."

"I see."

"Were you married before then?"

"Yes… no, she died before we managed that, but in my heart, aye."

"I understand that better than you might think, Mr. Mckinnon."

"It has been many years. I walked away from Scotland, walked away and never returned. I worked here and there as I decided what I wanted to do. I was in Bath when I found out that they needed a butler here. So I applied. I do not know if Mr. Horncastle picked me because I was the only one who was interested or if he wanted me regardless. I hope both, perhaps. I thought I could never let anyone else into my heart, but it would seem there is room, and lately I have not been able to think for long of much else." His gaze was drawn to the kitchen again. Helena did not even need to know who he looked to, she had guessed.

"Cook does seem very capable. Handsome, too?"

"Aye."

"I do not think that anyone should capture my interest as Nathaniel does, but if I were in your position and someone did? I hope that I should be bold enough to do something about it. Love ebbs and flows, anyone who marries should know that. If I died I would hope that Nathaniel should find someone who loves him."

"You think my wife would look down from heaven and approve?"

"You are once again asking the wrong person. I am not a believer, Mr. Mckinnon, though goodness knows Nathaniel drags me to church whenever he can. I have many disagreements with our local clergyman over his interpretation of the bible. What I do believe, however, is that we carry those who have passed, within us. We talk of them, we share stories, we cry because we miss them, but they do not live on in some place up in the clouds, they live on in our hearts and in the hearts of those with whom we share our memories of them. Any spouse who would not wish their husband or wife to find love again, did not truly love them."

"Thank you, Mrs. Ackley."

"I am not sure I was much help, but my offer stands and will forever more. You need only ask."

"Mrs. Ackley?"

"Yes?"

"Have you considered that if events had not played out as they did yesterday, the little boy who had been so badly mistreated by those men, would not have been hiding safely, though rather inconveniently, under my bed this morning?"

She looked at him sincerely. "Regardless of whether you were Mr. Horncastle's only choice for butler, he could have done no better."

Rebecca Robertson would forever remember the moment that her husband, Jacky, walked into their room with the small boy who had chosen to be called John. He had pale blue eyes and his hair had been discovered as fair once the filth had been washed off it. Jacky had ended up having to scrub it with soap to clean his scalp, but John had trusted him enough to do it and, upon seeing the bruises that covered the small body, Jacky was as gentle as he could be.

As John stepped into the room, with Jacky behind him, he looked at the young woman who was sitting up in bed. She was beautiful to his eyes. Her chestnut hair was loose and hung over her shoulders and down over her chest. Her eyes were brown and her face touched with freckles. She wore a sleeveless, white nightgown and her arms were pale. He could tell she was tall by how far her legs stretched down the bed. She smiled at him, taking in his cleanliness, soapy smell and rolled up sleeves and breeches.

"Hello. I have a visitor! That is a pleasant change."

"I am John." She glanced up at her husband at the name and smiled fondly.

"That is a strong name. Would you like to come in and talk to me?" He nodded, there was only one chair, but Jacky gestured to it for him to sit on. Jacky rounded the bed and sat on the other side of it. He left the door to the room open a little to put the boy at ease.

"Are you feeling better?" John had asked what he should say to Jacky's wife as they traipsed up the stairs and that was one of the questions Jacky had told him to ask.

"Yes, I am getting better. I have to take my time or I could get worse again. Everyone here is being very nice. How are you feeling?"

"Dunno." He blinked back the tears and looked down at his hands which held the recorder Jacky had given him. Seeing it helped him recover. "If I could play this better, I could play you a tune. Mister Jacky said he would teach me."

"Play it anyway, then after Jacky teaches you I will be able to tell how much you have improved." He put the recorder to his lips and tried his hardest. He desperately wanted to please her. He managed a few notes without squeaks and she clapped as all three of them laughed. "I feel better already!"

"Mister Jacky plays it better."

"Well he has practised for many years and can play the fiddle, too." She pointed at the chest in the corner where the fiddle and bow lay on top of it. "John, Strong John, do you think you can tell me how you came to be with those bad men?"

"I don't want to talk about it."

"I understand. Do you remember anything before you were taken by these men?"

"No, it was a long time ago."

"Do you remember how long? How many winters have there been?"

"Two." He remembered the winters, as she had suspected he might. He had gotten so cold that he had contemplated curling up near one of the men for warmth, but thought he should rather freeze than risk their hands on him again.

"Do you know how old you are?" She felt she was peppering him with questions, but she said them kindly and smiled at all his replies, despite how frustrating it was that he had no idea who he was.

"I remember the last birthday I had, I was three."

"Well you are older than three now."

"I do not think so, no one said I had a birthday."

"Just because no one said, does not mean you did not have it. Your birthday happens every year, so I should imagine you are five or possibly six."

"How old are you?"

"Twenty. I have had my birthday this year already. Jacky is twenty as well, but his birthday is in December, so he will be one-and-twenty this year."

"Do you live here?"

"We live in Lincolnshire at a place called Redway Acres, our Master is Colonel Ackley who brought you home last night. Jacky is a stableman there and I am lady's maid to Miss Isabella Ackley. On this trip, I am maid to Mrs. Ackley, too. Or I will be once I am well again. She is the lady who pulled the foal out of the horse, I am told you saw her do it."

"Is it nice there?"

"It is and Jacky's family is there, but we are happy wherever we have each other." She turned that beautiful smile to Jacky and patted his hand that rested near her on the bed.

"Where is your family?"

"I don't have any family. They all died. I'm part of Jacky's family, now." He was silent, thinking, wondering whether there was a family he would become part of and wishing he could remember who his family were from his first three years. Did they miss him? Did they want him back? Maybe they were glad he had gone or they gave him away? Tears formed again, but there was a knock at the door and he wiped them away.

"Rebecca, Mr. Horncastle suggested I bring my book for you to read to... for you to read." A pretty girl with red hair stood in the doorway. John thought she was probably the daughter of the woman who had helped the horse. She smiled at him. "Hello, I'm Issie."

"I'm John."

"Oh, that is the name of our stable manager at Redway." He did not say more, so she shrugged and gave the book to Rebecca. "I hope you are feeling better, Rebecca."

"I am, Miss. Thank you and thank you for this, I love your stories." Issie smiled, ran back to the door and was gone. John looked at the small book that Rebecca had placed in her lap and put her hands upon.

"What are the stories about?"

"A dragon slayer." His eyebrows shot up, he did not think that a girl should write about a dragon slayer. "Would you like me to read one?" He nodded.

"Come and lean on me while we listen," suggested Jacky, "that way if we fall asleep, we will be comfortable." He moved a pillow to his side for the boy to lean against, as aside from allowing him to help with his bathing, John had avoided touching him.

"I'll sit here." John moved and sat on the end of the bed. Rebecca nodded and began the first story about the dragon of Lincolnshire. By the time the story had come to an end, the boy had worked his way slowly between them and up the bed. Neither of them had dared to move. She began the second story of how the dragon slayer had rescued a chimney boy and by the time it finished and she looked over to John again, he was asleep.

"Now what do we do?" She looked fondly at her husband as she asked the question.

"Do not move and let him sleep. See what happens when he wakes up?" she nodded.

That evening at dinner, Harriet and Bertram talked of the possibility of a dinner party before Nathaniel and Helena left. Receiving an enthusiastic agreement from them, there was a discussion around whom to invite, as they knew no one other than Bertram. Harriet also expressed a concern, mainly towards Nathaniel, regarding the mourning period for her sister, which still had two months remaining.

"Harriet, my dear, you have put so many years of your life on hold for your sister, since her elopement when you were sixteen. Do you think she would want you to continue to do so now you are at the beginning of this exciting venture? Alexander and I agreed, when you first mentioned coming here two months ago, that it made sense to make the journey in the warmer weather and not wait until next year. Now you are here, you should take every opportunity to forge your new life."

With that settled, Bertram said he had an idea about meeting some people he knew. "If we were in the middle of the season, I should suggest going to a performance at the Theatre Royal in town. Phillip and I attended many times. The last, if I remember correctly was Shakespeare's 'Much Ado About Nothing.'"

"*I do love nothing in the world so well as you: is not that strange?*" Nathaniel turned to Helena as he spoke and picked up her hand that rested on the table.

"*I love you with so much of my heart that none is left to protest.*" She smiled at him as she quoted a reply, her lips parting as he brought her hand to his lips and kissed her palm.

"Ah, our very own Beatrice and Benedict! Yes, those characters suit the two of you very much indeed, both fierce *and* passionate. However, I suggest we make our way to the grand concert and fireworks to be held in a few days to celebrate the Prince Regent's birthday. I am sure to be able to introduce you to a great many people there. What say you?"

Exclamations of what a marvellous idea that was and how exciting such an event might be were forthcoming from all at the table. Helena was thankful that Davy and Issie were not dining with them that night. She felt they would not sleep for the remaining three nights before that event in their excitement and made everyone present agree not to tell them until the day was upon them.

"The person I need to introduce you to, Miss Wyndham, is Baroness Freyley. The Freyleys live just south of here, their land is the other side of the Bath Road to the entrance to Wyndham House. Their house is about five miles away by road."

"Baron Freyley is the magistrate for these parts, is that not correct?" The colonel looked to Mr. Horncastle.

"Yes, and an avid horse man. I am sure he will be interested in making your acquaintance, Colonel, if he accompanies his wife. I am certain at least that *she* will be at this event and that she will have quite a crowd of people around her with whom you could become acquainted. Would you do me the honour of accompanying me, Miss Wyndham?"

"Mr. Horncastle, I thank you and would be very happy to accompany you." Harriet smiled widely at him and he met her smile and the excitement in her eyes with his own.

Chapter Eleven

Over the next two days the rain poured heavily and relentlessly. The expected journey to Wyndham church for the service on Sunday was abandoned and they entertained themselves within the confines of the house. Helena was relieved, as Nathaniel had been making noises to the effect that she should attend church with them. She had feared her continued efforts to obey him as much as possible, after their argument in the rain the day before, was going to be tested only a day later.

Nathaniel sought out Bertram to play cards and as he suspected, he found they were evenly matched. When they finished, and he had won the most hands, he suggested payment should be Horncastle teaching him some of his fighting moves. They ended up in the massive ballroom and while they fought, Harriet fended off the wooden swords of Davy and Isabella quite deftly with her own, much to the amusement and admiration of Bertram.

Helena made her way out to the stable. She was keen to check on her whites again and to talk further to Mickleson about the plans to improve Issie's grey stallion, Snow. She found the big man in his office with his two boys. He was painstakingly trying to teach them the alphabet, but they were whining about it being too dull.

"I could never teach Issie to read or write, Mr. Mickleson. It is why parents get other people to teach their children."

"Well, they are not my children, Mrs. Ackley." He stood quickly when he spotted her in the doorway looking affectionately at the scene in front of her. She only smiled at his comment, thinking of Nathaniel and Davy and noticing the disappointed looks in the boys' faces at his statement. "You taught Miss Isabella to ride."

"Yes, but I cannot take all the credit for that. My grandfather was the one to instill the love of horses in both Issie and I, but he never managed it with his own daughter. My mother."

"Was there something you needed help with, ma'am?" he looked almost hopeful.

"It can wait. May I?" She gestured to the desk with the quill, ink and paper and he held out the chair for her. The boys had squeezed themselves upon the other chair. She looked at them and smiled, then picked up the quill and filled it full of ink, speaking as she wrote.

"A is for apple, we like to feed a horse,
B is for bridle, for its head of course,
C is for colt, the four-legged boy,
D is for dam, its mother, what a joy,
E is for eating, what horses love to do,
F is for foal, who can eat enough for two…"

She continued in this vein with the boys laughing at various points, especially when she mentioned G is for gelding and what it was missing! At the end, she had written that A is for Arnie and R is for Richie. They had liked that. To see their names written down. She stood and smiled at Mickleson again.

"You are a natural, Mrs. Ackley."

"As I said before, it is easier when they are not your own children." When he opened his mouth to protest the comment again, she shook her head slightly and moved her eyes to the boys, who were once again looking up at him. He looked into their faces and swallowed hard.

"Come on, boys! Let's look at the horses with Mrs. Ackley. We know that is what she loves to do best and we should always endeavour to do what a lady likes best. It shows good breeding."

As they stepped out into the stable, two young men that were unfamiliar to Helena stepped in. Mickleson immediately moved forward in an action that was protective of his former mistress, before he recognised the lads. They were the two locals who had been serving the seller with whom Mr. Horncastle had bartered. They were bedraggled and soaked through to the skin, they also looked a little worse for wear. Mickleson suspected they had drunk much of their earnings from the previous two days.

"The barkeep must have seen you two coming. Did you save anything from the past two days?"

"Not much."

"Not much, sir," he corrected them.

"Not much, sir."

"What do you know of horses, then? Let us find out." He started to question them.

"Mr. Mickleson, I do not think it is acceptable to question them in this state. Look, they are shivering. Get them warm and dry at least."

"Yes, ma'am. Well you heard her did you not? Or are your ears full of water, too?" He marched them towards the kitchens. Helena smiled at his gruffness. She had heard John Robertson speak to their younger stablemen in this manner quite often and it reminded her of him. She felt a sudden pang for the man she considered more of a father than her own had ever been.

"It is you and me then, boys," she turned to Richie and Arnie, "let me talk to you of my plans for the white-grey stallion and we will write it down for Mr. Mickleson. What say you?" With laughter and much jumping around, they agreed. Charlie Mickleson was going to have his hands full.

Rebecca Robertson felt that the little boy, John, and herself just needed some time to heal. Neither of them set foot outside the little bedroom she shared with Jacky for the rest of Saturday and Sunday morning. After falling asleep leaning against Jacky that first day, and waking in the same position with no one hurting him, he was more reassured that he was safe. He opened his eyes and looked at the beautiful woman who was watching him intently.

He had insisted she read more of the stories, and after hearing them twice more he almost knew them by heart. She had explained how Colonel Ackley was Isabella's father and the man she based the dragon slayer upon. John fully believed that the man he had seen beating the two men, who had been dragons to him, would be capable of defeating an actual dragon.

Jacky had started to teach him to play the recorder and had played the fiddle for both of them. When Helena had come to visit Rebecca on Sunday afternoon, she had smiled outside the door to hear all three of them laughing. Jacky had suggested that he and John should take their luncheon trays back to the kitchen and leave the ladies to talk.

"How are you, Rebecca?" Helena asked the moment the door had closed. "Is the bleeding slowing down?"

"Yes, ma'am. I am feeling much better, each day it is less. I hope to serve you perhaps tomorrow, or Tuesday."

"Nora is doing a fine job. Do not concern yourself with that. I do not think I want you serving both Issie and I on this trip, even if you are up to it. So perhaps just Isabella, but we will worry about that once you are up and about again. What of the boy? It was good to hear you all laughing a moment ago."

"He is looking so much better already. He eats so much, it is as if he fears that it might stop being given to him if he does not eat it."

"Has he spoken of his treatment at the hands of those monsters?"

"No, but I hope he will trust me enough soon."

"It might not be pleasant to hear."

"I am willing to hear it, if it will help heal his mind. He has to know that it is not his fault."

"Perhaps he needs to be told that."

"Why should he think it is?"

"We forget what it is to think as a child does. I remember how Davy felt he earned the beatings he received from the Bainbridge butler."

"I will try telling him that then and see if he will tell me."

"Has he remembered anything of his past?"

"Nothing. Nor how he came to be with these men."

"I wonder if his family gave him away, or even sold him."

Rebecca gasped at that. "Who should do such a thing to a wonderful child?"

"Not all parents are as loving as you."

"I am not a parent."

"I beg to differ, Rebecca."

The following day, Harriet and Mr. Horncastle met with Charlie Mickleson. They discussed the two lads that arrived at Wyndham House the day before Mickleson recommended they give them a try. They could be paid for a fortnight and if he was satisfied with their work, and if she agreed, then they could take them on permanently. They had local families, so could stay in the outbuilding with Benjamin and return to visit their families on their day off. She agreed after a look at Mr. Horncastle who was nodding.

"Mr. Mickleson, I am sure if you are satisfied with their work and their character, then I will be, too."

"I would like to ask you about the two boys who helped us when we went to get the whites back, Miss Wyndham. As far as I can ascertain from them, Richie is nine and Arnie thinks he is six or possibly seven. Their parents are dead."

"Are they brothers?" Mr. Horncastle interjected.

"No, well not by blood, but Richie is protective of Arnie as if he were. I think they have been living rough for a while and found each other that way. Honestly, if it were not for Richie, I do not think Arnie would have survived. He still has an innocence about him."

"What would you like to do with them, Mr. Mickleson?" Harriet asked gently. It would seem he had struck up a close relationship with them.

"I should like to give them each an apprenticeship in the stable. They would learn about horses and do some work. They could not do the work of men, but it should build up their strength to do some tasks, and teach them to read and write. If you were willing to continue to provide them with food and shelter, I should be happy to pay them a little money out of my own pocket, for the little work they would be doing. A man should be paid for the work he does, I believe."

Harriet looked at the man in front of her and considered. It had cost him a lot to ask her for this. He clasped his large hands so tightly together the skin was turning white, and the earnestness in his dark eyes showed her how quickly he learned to care for these two boys. She had been silent for a few moments and Mickleson had said nothing. He simply waited her out, it was part of what made him a good horse man, he was patient. Mr. Horncastle, thinking she was unsure, made to speak, but she held up a hand to stop him.

"Mr. Mickleson, you are right. Every man or woman should be paid for their work. If these boys are to be apprentices at Wyndham House, then Wyndham House should pay them. I do not want them working excessively hard, and I am pleased that you agree with me on that. They are boys and should have some fun and some learning. Certainly, you are in charge of ensuring that all the Wyndham House stable hands can ride and drive satisfactorily, but leave their education to me. I am working on a plan, but it is not finalised in my mind yet."

"Thank you, Miss. I am very grateful."

"I think we will wait and see how grateful you are when your hands are full with these boys!" Mr. Horncastle laughed as he spoke.

"As they are boys, where should they sleep?" Harriet wondered, "is the outbuilding with the other men appropriate? We must find more hands for you. Once the colonel leaves you will need more help. The outbuilding will be more crowded."

"They have been sleeping on my bunk in the stable office, Miss. It does not leave much room for me, but I know where they are."

"That is not satisfactory in the long term either. I will consider it further, and Mr. Mickleson?"

"Yes, Miss?"

"I value your work and ideas. Never hesitate to come to me."

On the day of the fireworks, Helena excitedly told Davy and Issie about the evening to come. No sooner had she spoken, than word got to them that the rain, now in its third day, had caused the event to be postponed a day.

Helena groaned, and the children wailed. They were faced with another long, wet day with no governess. Nathaniel had already escaped to the stable and Helena had hoped to do the same. She wanted to groom the whites thoroughly herself, so she could learn their characters and preferences.

"I want to go out to the stable, you had better come with me."

"I have finished my story, I will bring it with me and I can read it to you, Davy."

"I do not want to hear another of your stories, Issie. I want to go riding and then go out tonight and see the fireworks. I have never seen them before. Three days of rain is making me itch all over, I want to go outside. It is dull in here listening to you! Dull! Dull!"

"Davy Beckett Ackley, I will not have you talk to your sister that way. Mr. Mickleson is short some hands and you will go out to the stable and do whatever work he needs doing. That way you will be where I or your father can keep an eye on you. Go! Now!"

She turned to her daughter who was pouting and had tears silently falling from her eyes. "He hates my stories, that is the same as hating me," Issie spoke quietly after Davy had left the room.

"He does not hate you or your stories, sweet girl. He is frustrated with the rain, we all are, but today he is the one feeling it the most and he lashed out at you. He will realise how nasty he was and will feel bad about it. Then he will apologise. Will you forgive him?"

"Yes, Mama, but first I will make him act out the stories with me. That is always fun."

"He enjoys doing that, whatever he may say. Why not bring your new story out to the stable with you? Richie or Arnie might like to hear it and then we can groom Snow together." Happier, Isabella ran to her room for the story and went out to the stable with her mother.

Richie and Arnie were working hard. They had let some of the horses out into the nearest paddocks to give them some exercise, despite the rain. Helena understood what Davy had said about feeling itchy and expected the animals had probably felt the same way. When the horses were brought in again, they were rubbed down well and the boys were learning how to do that. Mickleson had Davy doing the same work, while Nathaniel was standing with his arms folded watching his son with a grim face. Knowing his mother should tell him anyway, Davy had confessed to his father what he had said.

Seeing his daughter come in and look at Davy in the same way he had seen his wife do to many a man who crossed her, brought a smile to Nathaniel's face. "Here is my sweet girl." He walked to them both and spoke quietly to Helena. "We will work off his mood."

"If there is anyone who understands him, it is you!"

"I wanted to read my story to Richie and Arnie," Issie spoke up.

"I will give them a break when they have finished these horses, Miss Isabella."

"Thank you, Mr. Mickleson." She walked with her mother to the little office and sat on a chair to wait for the boys. She sniffed a bit, thinking again of Davy saying her stories were dull and worried that these boys might think so, too.

Richie and Arnie raced into the room and threw themselves onto the bunk, jostling each other to sit closest to Issie. "Are you going to read us a story, Miss Isabella? Is it from a book?"

"No, it is a story I have written, about a dragon slayer. Would you like me to read it?" They both nodded eagerly. Pleased, she began the tale. It was a story of a one-legged dragon slayer who was following a particularly nasty dragon. He had tracked him across many lands to some large mountains where he entered a maze of caves that tunnelled deep underground. There he met a dwarf who lived in the tunnels and mined them with his family. The dwarf was angry, as he felt the dragon slayer had lured the dragon to their home, but the dragon slayer explained he had followed it there. They fought, but were so evenly matched, there was no winner. They heard the dragon roar and the dwarf said he should fight it if the dragon slayer got his family to safety. The dragon slayer had replied that the dwarf was too small to make a good meal for the dragon, so they made a gentleman's agreement to join forces and fight the dragon together. Together they defeated it.

Isabella had been pleased as she read it. Richie and Arnie had been captivated and laughed when she told the part about the dragon eating the dwarf.

"It is the colonel and Mr. Horncastle!" Richie had said, and she had blushed, "it was a really good story."

"Davy should have liked to hear it, I know it," she sniffed again, a tear trickling down her cheek. Richie put a hand on her shoulder to squeeze gently and comfort her. He hated to see her cry.

"Get your damn hands off her!" Davy shouted as he came barrelling into the room and grabbed Richie's arm, pulling his hand away from Issie.

"Davy, he was not hurting me. I was upset."

"You were the one who hurt her, not me! I never would."

"I will not give you the chance." As Davy's blow connected to Richie's mouth he was pleased to see it bleed. The two boys rolled on the bunk, where Davy pinned Richie down and pummelled him. Davy's fists were flying, but ineffectual, and when Richie heard his breathing labour from behind his arms that were covering his face, he acted. He pushed Davy over and landed a hard punch to his stomach, then he rolled him over and pushed his face in the bedding, holding him there for a moment, "Tha's for makin' her cry."

Isabella had stood to get out of the way and her chair toppled over. The noise brought Nathaniel to the door and he pulled Issie out of the room, as he watched the boys tussle with a smile on his face.

"No fighting in the stable!" Mickleson squeezed past the colonel with a scowl and grabbed Richie around the waist to lift him out of the way, leaving Davy on the bunk for his father to deal with. "I have a couple of stalls left that need cleaning, mares in them, too, so you will soon learn how messy they can be." He had already moved the mares and threw Richie into a messy stall, handing him the smallest pitchfork they had.

"He started it, I only squeezed her shoulder. He made her cry, not me."

"I do not want to hear it. You keep your hands to yourself with Miss Isabella and Master Davy, and no fighting in my stable, with anyone." He moved to tousle the boy's hair, but Richie flinched. "I will never hit you Richie, no matter how angry you make me."

Nathaniel stood at the office door looking at his son, but listening to Mickleson. So much about this man and boy reminded him of himself with Davy. His son looked up at him, rubbing his gut.

"He got you good."

"I split his lip. He was touching Issie."

"I approve of you being protective of her, but he was not hurting her. She was crying because of you. You know that and that is why you fought with him. Now get out there and help him clean those stalls and think about who you need to apologise to."

"I am not going to apologise to him."

"You have more in common than you realise." Davy got to his feet and, hunched over, he headed out of the door to the stalls. As he passed him, Nathaniel reached out a hand and tousled his hair. He looked up and saw Mickleson watching him. The two fathers nodded to each other.

They worked side by side in neighbouring stalls, Mr. Mickleson had been right Davy thought, mares were messy, you had to watch your footing all around. He eyed Richie occasionally and finally broke the silence.

"I will apologise to her, but you should not touch her."

"If ya hadn' bin an idiot, I wouldn' 'ave ta. You have to be kind to younger kids and girls."

"Was it a good story?"

"It was exciting. There was a dragon slayer and a dwarf and they fought."

"Do not tell me! I want to hear it from her, if I can get her to read it to me. She has written a lot of stories about a dragon slayer."

"If I promise not to touch her, can you get her to read more to us?"

"Yes! I act them out sometimes, we could all act them out."

"What, be the people in the stories?" His eyes were wide as Davy nodded. "I wish I had a sister who wrote stories. You can hear her stories anytime."

"We could put them in a letter to you."

"I cannot read, ya know that."

"Well then learn, I only did three years ago." Richie looked at the boy sharply, was he laughing at him? He did not think so.

"Why did ya not learn sooner?"

"No one taught me where I was. Mother and Father took me in. Then I learned at Redway."

"Does it have to be a mother and a father for you to be taken in?"

"No. It was Mother who took me in at first, then she married Father. He asked to be a father to Issie and me."

"Could it..." Richie stopped his work and looked over the stall at Davy. "Could it be just a father who takes you in?"

"I suppose so." Davy looked up from shovelling the horseshit and recognised the expression on Richie's face. He realised now what his father had meant about what they had in common. They had both had it tough early in life and they both hoped for adults they could trust, to love them. They also both cared for Issie and loved her stories. His father was friends with Tommy, who was a miner's son, they had bonded in battle. Perhaps he and Richie could be friends who bonded in a different shared experience. He held out his hand.

That evening, Davy laid in his bed looking at the ceiling. He had apologised to everyone, Mr. Mickleson, his father, his mother and of course Issie. She had forgiven him, but she would not read her story to him. He deserved that he supposed, but he really wanted to know what was in it now. He would have to give her something, something of value to her, but what could that be? Knowing the only thing that he could give her that she truly wanted, he pulled back the covers and headed to her room.

"Issie." Though she lay in bed with her eyes closed, the candle still burned on the small table by her bed. "I know you are not asleep, your candle is alight."

She refused to open her eyes, so he moved to that side of the bed and sat beside her. He looked over at the papers on the table, assuming they were her story and moved a hand towards them.

"Do not touch my story Davy Ackley!"

He smiled into her green eyes that were so familiar to him now. "Issie, if you will read me your story, I promise to take you to the top of the hill of the Dragon of Lincolnshire when we get home."

"It is too far for us to go alone, Father would not permit it."

"Then I will persuade him to take us and if he refuses, I promise I will take you there when we are old enough to go alone. I will write it down and sign it, as a legal letter."

"I will read it to you in the morning."

"No, it has to be now, I cannot get to sleep without knowing the story."

"Then get into bed, silly, and I will read it."

He lay beside her with his arms above his head and she rested her head on his chest, while she held the pages and read it to him. Then she blew out the candle and settled beside him to sleep.

"It is a really good story, Issie."

Charlie Mickleson was exhausted when he entered his office in the stable that night. He thought it good that he was, as sharing his bed with two small boys was not very comfortable. When he looked to the bunk, he was surprised to see Richie sitting up with his legs crossed and his back against the wall. Arnie was curled lower down the bunk fast asleep. Charlie sat on the bunk to take off his boots before laying down on the bunk and looking up at the boy.

"What is it?" Richie pointed to the lamp by the bed and Charlie snuffed it out. It was going to be serious if the boy did not want to talk with it lit.

"Master Davy was taken in by Mrs. Ackley before she married the colonel."

"I did not know that; did he tell you that?"

"Yes. So one person can take a child or children in... if they wanted to?"

"Yes, that is true." Charlie felt a tug in his chest. He cared a lot about both these boys. Cared enough that he had secured their future at Wyndham House. They should be fed and learn a trade, and would not be abused, he would see to that. But what could he offer them? He had no cottage. He was in the same situation as they were, except he earned more money. Perhaps he could find out if he could rent a cottage, but if it were not on Wyndham land, it would be a long walk to work every day for them all, before they even started the day's work. In the winter, they should have to walk it in the dark and cold.

He did not have a wife, they would not have a mother. Richie was right, he could take them in himself, but what woman should want to take on a man with two boys? Would Annie Brown? There was no point him wondering about her, she was too busy looking at Benjamin. Even if he was wrong about that, she was lady's maid to the mistress of this enormous estate, no rough stableman for her, even if he was the manager. Choosing these boys could mean the loss of any opportunity for a wife.

Richie sniffed a bit and said no more. He curled up with his back pressed against Charlie's side and the big man could feel his small body shake with tears. He doubted the boy had cried in a long time. Tears pricked his own eyes. He had not answered the boy and he realised, as his heart broke, that there was only one answer.

162

"I do not have a place for us to live, but I will find something so we can be a family. Can you be patient, Little Owl? I will make it work. I promise." Richie turned to him and wrapped his arms around him, fresh tears soaking Charlie's shirt, but he did not care. His own tears slid down the sides of his face and onto the pillow as he held the boy tight to him.

Chapter Twelve

The following evening, Mickleson drove their carriage with the two boys beside him. Bertram had looked up at the large figure of Mickleson in his Sunday best and declared that they really should get a uniform for him, at least for events such as this. Mickleson did not look happy at that and suggested they look for a driver who should find more pleasure in this kind of occupation than himself. A stable manager had far more important tasks to be taking care of in the stable. Harriet nodded her agreement.

They pulled up near the Sydney Hotel, where a throng of people and carriages were gathered. Access to the gardens beyond was through that building. Mickleson pulled the carriage to a stop close by which allowed their descent, before he planned to turn the carriage around and wait at a point where he hoped the boys might catch a glimpse of the fireworks. Mr. Horncastle had made a couple of suggestions to him.

Nathaniel stepped down easily and bent to fix the knee joint of his wooden leg. It could move if loosened to allow him to bend his leg when riding or sitting in the carriage, but to walk, it needed to be rigid and had to be tightened. Then he turned and offered his arm to aid his wife's descent.

He was surprised to notice Helena look rather scared. It was an expression he rarely saw on her face. He had not considered that she had possibly never been to London, or even a town the size of Bath. To her a crowd this large, which he estimated was close to a thousand, was probably quite daunting.

"I will not lose you, Helena, just keep a tight hold onto me." She squeezed his arm tighter and it pleased him that she needed him in this way.

Bertram, despite his height, seemed undaunted by the throng. He jumped down easily from the carriage, avoiding the horse dung piles nicely, and offered his arm to Harriet when she followed him, smiling widely up at her. Harriet had been to large events when she was younger, with Harker and her sister most often. Still, it had been sometime since she had wanted to leave Eastease and it took her some moments to adjust to the noise and the bustle.

The children requested to go ahead and explore. They had been given strict instructions regarding their manner and if they did not adhere to those, they should find themselves back inside the carriage waiting for everyone to return. After his fight the day before, Davy was determined to win back the good favour of his parents and listened intently when Mr. Horncastle told him where they were to meet them for their supper.

Once Harriet had grasped his proffered arm, Bertram turned to Nathaniel. "With your permission, Colonel, I will lead the way. Ah, I see Baroness Freyley." He led them towards a large group, with a large woman heading it, she was dressed in very fine clothes and a large headwrap adorned with similarly large feathers. Approaching them from the side, he was able to head her off. As he was easy to notice once in front of you, she did indeed spot Bertram and step towards him.

"Mr. Horncastle, a pleasure to see you, how are you faring? I see you are still dressed in black, such respect for your friend."

"The pleasure is all mine, I assure you, My Lady. I thank you for your concern. May I have the honour of introducing you to Miss Harriet Wyndham? Miss Wyndham recently arrived at Wyndham House, which of course she inherited from dear Phillip. Miss Wyndham, this is Baroness Freyley."

"Miss Wyndham? Mr. Horncastle, you must correct your address. This is of course, Lady Harriet Wyndham, great-granddaughter of the previous Lord Aysthill. I am pleased to meet you, Lady Harriet." The woman looked expectantly at Harriet and then towards Nathaniel and Helena.

"Thank you, My Lady. I assure you I do not use that title as, I am sure you know, my mother married Lieutenant Wyndham when I was a year old. May I introduce my cousin, Colonel Nathaniel Ackley and his wife Mrs. Helena Ackley of Redway Acres?"

"Ah, Colonel Ackley," she said in a tone that was familiar, "it has been many years since we have seen you in these parts."

"Of course, My Lady. An honour to meet you again, it has been too long."

"I should offer that you should sit near me and we could become reacquainted, Colonel. However, as you see, I did bring rather a large number of people with me tonight and my supper box is full. Would you visit me for tea tomorrow, Miss Wyndham?"

"I thank you, yes."

"And bring your quiet friend," she looked at Helena, who groaned internally. Visiting people in this way simply reminded her of her mother. She would do it for Harriet, of course.

Mr. Horncastle moved his company aside, to allow the baroness to continue towards the entrance. He stopped a few more times, introducing Harriet and the Ackleys to more people. Some greeted him in a friendly manner. Others rather more formally and in several cases, reluctantly. However, having seen Baroness Freyley allow an introduction, they had little choice in the matter, which was exactly his plan.

Harriet enjoyed the view, despite the light rain that had begun to fall. There were thousands of lamps lighting the gardens beyond the hotel, and Mr. Horncastle enjoyed imparting nuggets of information about the park as they wandered towards their own supper box. He talked of the Kennet and Avon Canal, that connected those two rivers. It allowed greater quantities of goods to be transported from east to west at much less cost than by horse drawn cart and he pointed to the other end of the park where that canal cut through.

The curved rows of supper boxes extended from the back of the building and they could see the musicians on the Orchestra above the loggia at the back. Harriet felt sorry for the performers exposed to the rain, light though it was.

Their supper box was only a short distance away from that of the baroness, and as Harriet sat, she perused the gathering of people the baroness had around her. Some of them Mr. Horncastle had already introduced her to, but she noticed a man arriving late and bowing low in front of Baroness Freyley, obviously making his apology. As he rose, he caught her looking his way and nodded his head. Turning her head away quickly, she focused on what was going on around her. She felt a blush rise to her cheeks and was determined not to look back at him, however, after a minute her curiosity got the better of her and she looked towards Baroness Freyley's box searching for him.

He sat straight in his chair and looked to be half a head taller than anyone else in the group. He was slimly built with fair hair and, she imagined, blue eyes. He was well dressed, too, she was impressed with that. He smiled, though he was looking ahead of him, did he know she was taking in his appearance? Still smiling, he turned his head. Sensation from his look seemed to run down her throat, across her chest and did a somersault in her stomach.

"If it is of interest to you, Miss Wyndham, that is Mr. Joseph Collingworth. His property is not far from the estate of the baroness, both are south of Wyndham House." If Bertram Horncastle's voice held some bitterness, she did not notice it.

"He is a gentleman then?"

"Yes," he confirmed, but added unheard in a low voice, "in the social standing meaning of the word, at least."

"Perhaps you could introduce us when there is opportunity, Mr. Horncastle. Then I should be able to invite him to our dinner party." Bertram sighed his consent, but as it worked out, he did not have to make that introduction.

As soon as their supper was complete, and people began to mill around, the baroness sought them out as it would seem that Mr.

Collingworth had requested to be introduced to *'the handsome creature sitting with Mr. Horncastle'*, she informed them with a laugh. Harriet consented to the introduction and it was duly made.

"Lady Harriet, I am honoured." He bowed low and she gave a demure curtsey.

"As I explained to Baroness Freyley, I do not use any official title, I prefer *'Miss Wyndham'*."

"So she advised me, but if one is so ennobled, why should you not have people refer to you thus, in order to ensure the required deference and respect due to you?"

"Mr. Collingworth, I assure you that I do not need a title to ensure the required *'deference and respect'*. If people are to respect me, then it can be for myself, my actions and manner, not because my great-grandfather was an earl. I should hope that anyone informed of my preference, should offer me sufficient deference and not question it."

There was a moment of silence in which Mr. Collingworth looked to Bertram Horncastle and noted the barely concealed glee on the little man's face, then he, too, smiled. "Quite right, *Miss Wyndham*, quite right, and eloquently put, if I may say so."

She smiled widely. "Thank you, Mr. Collingworth. I believe you are acquainted with Mr. Horncastle. May I be allowed to introduce my cousin?" He nodded eagerly and she introduced Colonel and Mrs. Ackley.

Talk moved on to the shooting season. It had started the day before, but so much rain had curtailed the gentlemen's activity. Harriet and Helena were called over to the baroness to be introduced to more acquaintances. Upon their return, they were informed that it had been agreed that Mr. Collingworth and a few other men she had already been introduced to, would visit Wyndham House in the morning to shoot while she was visiting Lady Freyley. They should be back from their shoot in time to join her for lunch.

"And what if I wished to shoot, Cousin?" Harriet demanded of Nathaniel. "I believe it is my land."

Helena smiled at that, she would much prefer to shoot than sit in a stuffy parlour with Lady Freyley.

"I apologise, Miss Wyndham. The fault is entirely mine," Mr. Collingworth said. "You see I have a prior engagement to shoot the day following tomorrow and desired not to wait too long to see you again."

"Apology accepted, sir. I hope to hear of your many shooting successes at lunch." She blushed.

Mr. Horncastle had seen more people to whom he wished to introduce them, in the opposite direction to that of Lady Freyley. As he called her away, Mr. Collingworth bowed graciously. She looked back occasionally and was pleased when she caught Mr. Collingworth looking in her direction.

By the time the music had finished, and the fireworks were arranged, Isabella was asleep on her father's shoulder. No amount of cajoling from Davy could rouse her. He would have to remember them in detail, as she should be sure to want him to describe them to her the next day.

Unknown to Davy, Arnie had fallen asleep on Mr. Mickleson's lap. Richie, assuring the big man he would not be caught, descended the carriage and disappeared into the shadows to get a better look at the fireworks.

The eyes of both boys, in their differing locations, shone with delight and awe watching the fireworks. Bright lights spat and roared in their canisters, before rockets soared into the air with a screech louder than Richie's owl, and a deafening bang. Sparks seemed to rain down upon them but burned out without reaching the ground. Several small, wheeled fireworks turned together and spun out their fire in bright colours, until finally, a large, single spiral-wheel richly illuminated the darkness then it changed to a cascade of golden rain.

Harriet and Helena had already left in the carriage by the time Mr. Collingworth and several other men arrived to shoot with the colonel and Mr. Horncastle. The Wyndham House gamekeeper kept numerous healthy covvies to provide the men with plenty of game. They enjoyed a good couple of hours of it. Mr. Collingworth was an excellent shot and was more successful than any man in his grouping. Nathaniel did wish his wife there. Helena could have matched Collingworth, he was sure.

While the men were shooting, Mickleson decided on a riding lesson for Richie and Arnie. Davy and Isabella wanted to ride, but had to agree not to ride on the land while the men were shooting. Therefore, they were asked to ride close to the house with Richie and Arnie and show them how it was done.

Davy and Richie continued to be competitive, but in a friendlier way. Mickleson did not mind it providing they were not silly with the horses. Richie should feel it more than Davy the next day, when muscles he never knew he had would ache. Isabella was very accommodating in demonstrating correct posture, and hand and leg positioning. She was patient with Arnie, which garnered more respect for her from Richie.

As the day was a fine one and Rebecca continued to improve, Jacky Robertson suggested she take a walk with him and John. The boy seemed keen and they set out in the opposite direction from the men shooting. Rebecca walked slowly and watched her husband and the small boy run around in the long grass. She had done as Helena suggested and assured John that anything that had happened to him at the hands of those horrible men was not his fault. That he could tell her and she would still think the same of him.

All of the things that she could imagine in the darkest recesses of her mind that an evil man would be capable of doing to a small boy had been done to him. He had told her everything and had cried. She had opened up her arms and, as she now admitted to herself as she watched him run and laugh, she had opened up her heart. He had finally allowed her to hold him close and tight to her while he cried and the tears had fallen silently down her cheeks.

When his tears had stopped, she had sung him a lullaby and he had fallen asleep. Jacky had walked into the room and seen her tear stained face. He had silently handed her a handkerchief and looked down at John. He had asked her two questions, both of which she had answered with a nod. Had John told her what had happened and was it as bad as it could possibly be? She had seen a fury in her husband's face and she knew in that moment that he was a father, for who but a father could look capable of murder after hearing what had been inflicted upon his son?

They passed the backs of a few cottages, that Rebecca assumed housed some of the married servants in the house, and then she looked beyond them and frowned. She could see several rooftops and chimneys beyond some large trees. As they got closer she could see it was a house similar in size to Bernier House, opposite Redway, at home. They walked through the trees and came out on an overgrown lawn. The garden was less formal than some of those she had seen at Wyndham House and everything needed attention. They had not wandered so far that they were off Wyndham land, so what was this place?

They called out, so as not to startle anyone, but there was no response. They found the kitchen entrance and knocked on the door, but there was no answer, so they walked around the front of the house. There was a smart plaque on the house that read *'Wyndham Lodge'*. There was no answer at the front when they knocked there, too. Rebecca stepped back and looked up at the house, an idea was forming in her mind and her heart skipped a beat. She turned her shining eyes to Jacky.

"What is it?"

"I have an idea." She grinned at him and it was a welcome sight. The exercise had put a colour into her cheeks that had been lacking since she lost the baby.

"Well? What is the idea?"

"Let us walk back to the house and I will tell you." Jacky picked John up and put him on his shoulders. The boy pulled the little recorder out from his pocket and tried playing it. He bounced up and down with Jacky's long gait, so the sound was wobbly, but he did not care. He thought that if he had died at the hands of those men and gone to heaven, it could not be any better than this moment.

Rebecca talked to Jacky of a conversation she had overheard between Miss Wyndham and Mrs. Ackley in the confines of the carriage on the journey here. Miss Wyndham had been talking of doing some kind of charitable venture along the lines of the Harker Academy school that Mrs. Harker had started at Eastease, but she did not want a school.

"If no one maintains that lodge, I wonder if she should be amenable to us doing it? We could take in orphans, there must be hundreds of them in Bath."

"What is an orphan?" John was curious.

"A child who does not have any parents."

"Like me?"

"Like you, as far as we know," Jacky confirmed.

"We could teach them to work. Cook, serve, be a maid or a valet. Was there a stable?"

"I think I saw something that could have been one, just big enough for a few horses and one vehicle I think," Jacky was looking at his wife and smiling. He liked the idea of it. It would be hard work though. Some of the children would be rough and need some taking in hand. Some would have had experiences the same as John.

"You could teach them to care for horses."

"And to play the recorder!" John chimed in from above Jacky's head.

"Who should they be serving? Who would live in the main house, not the servants' quarters? It is doubtful Miss Wyndham would want orphans roaming what I am sure must be handsome rooms."

"It should be ready for guests I suppose, but there is so much room at Wyndham House, when would they need it?" Her face fell then and she looked up at her husband. "It is no use Jacky, it would mean leaving Redway! Leaving your parents."

"If it is what would make you happy, Rebecca, we can move here. Firstly, we have to find out if Miss Wyndham should want to do it. One step at a time." They had reached the outbuildings of Wyndham House. "How are you feeling? Would you like to look in at the stables? Mrs. Ackley purchased two whites at the fair and the foal is adorable." She nodded, so they headed towards the stable. John felt he had an affinity with those horses as they had all been rescued by the colonel and could start new and happy lives.

As the carriage drove up to the large house of Baroness Freyley, Helena experienced a sinking feeling in her stomach. She remembered it of old when she should have to visit houses of her mother's friends. She pulled a tendril of her hair from her bonnet and twisted it around a finger. It would drive her mother mad when she did that and she smiled at the fact that she had done it without thinking. Harriet frowned at her.

They were shown into a bright parlour, within which sat the flamboyant Baroness Freyley. She welcomed them enthusiastically and asked them about their first week at Wyndham House. Harriet spoke about her changes with the music room and the new location for their main parlour. Baroness Freyley hoped she might soon hear Harriet's playing and was, of course, duly invited to return their visit.

Harriet talked of her recent decision to provide two stable apprenticeships to the two boys they had acquired from the horse fair.

Both boys were orphans and had formed a relationship with her new stable manager who also wanted them to learn to read and write.

"Surely you will not allow the stable manager to act as a governess? Although I have to admit, I should not mind seeing it!" The baroness laughed at that.

"Mr. Mickleson is a very capable and intelligent man, My Lady," Helena defended her prior stableman.

"I mean no offence, Mrs. Ackley. I simply mean seeing a man more used to stable work teaching young boys, should be amusing." Helena had to laugh at that, given his first attempt that she had witnessed.

"I am mulling over another idea, but it has not fully formed yet, so I hesitate to speak of it. I would rather have Mr. Mickleson concentrate on the stable, which has been neglected of late." Harriet confirmed to the two ladies, but refused to give away anything further on her thoughts when they pressed her.

"I understand that you had an interesting trip to the horse fair last week?" Lady Freyley's sharp eyes easily spotted the look exchanged between Helena and Harriet and she would not let go of a juicy subject once she had her teeth into it. "I heard, Mrs. Ackley, that you were cheated out of two horses and that very handsome butler of yours, Miss Wyndham, caused some bodily harm when you were threatened."

"I should rather not think of it again, My Lady," Helena jumped in quickly. "We were very lucky Mr. Mckinnon arrived when he did."

"I doubt that husband of yours would have allowed an incident of that kind to pass. I remember Colonel Ackley from his younger days and he still seems very active, despite his loss of a limb. Something I know should have sat down many a man."

"We have been lucky to have a friend who makes legs for men who have lost a limb and he made that very useful one with a knee specifically for the colonel. You are correct, he did set out with Mr. Horncastle, Mickleson and Mckinnon to retrieve the horses for us."

"I saw the way he looks at you, Mrs. Ackley. He would have done more than just retrieve horses!" Her eyes gleamed at the thought. "He is still a very physical man, too?"

Harriet looked shocked at the older woman for asking such a thing. Helena blushed slightly, as thoughts of their behaviour in the lake came into her mind, she could not help but smile. It probably was not an appropriate discussion to have in front of Harriet, but the young woman was not entirely naïve.

"Oh, do not look at me in that way, Miss Wyndham. The colonel was always a favourite for me to set my eyes upon, even as a young man. His injury has not diminished his allure. I assume from your blush, Mrs. Ackley, that I have hit the nail on the head."

"Yes!" Helena said on a laugh, "he is *physical*."

"I hope that he is attentive to your own needs, too? Forgive me, that is a personal question, but in these matters, I am afraid I must live vicariously. The baron is more interested in his shooting and his horses than attending other... matters, but he was a considerate lover when we were younger."

"Yes, My Lady," Helena leaned forward conspiratorially, "he is most considerate and takes pleasure in doing so, which does add to the experience. He also prefers outside locations."

"Oh, my word!" Lady Freyley fanned herself. "Now that does give me something to consider."

"Tell me," Helena exacted her price for her information, "is your husband interested enough in horses that you have a considerable stable here?" Lady Freyley laughed, confirming that they did and all three women agreed to leave the parlour and take a tour around it.

When they returned to Wyndham House, Helena sat happy on her seat in the carriage having enjoyed the visit with the baroness much more than she had thought she would. Harriet sat opposite her, much less relaxed and looking often out of the carriage window for a glimpse of her new home. She hoped that they should arrive before the men returned from shooting so that she would have time to change her clothes and refresh herself. Helena admonished her for her tapping foot and shifting in her seat.

"I wish to change for lunch, I am sure I smell of horse."

"I always smell of horse, I do not see what is wrong with that. Mr. Collingworth will be smelling of gunpowder. I am sure he will not notice the smell of you."

"I will notice it." Harriet blushed at Helena perceiving her preference. She had decided to be a little more reserved than she had the last time she had felt an interest in a new acquaintance. She did not want everyone suspecting her preference of this distinguished looking man. She had to find out a lot more about him before she should determine if her initial ideas of him were to be built upon.

She need not have worried; the men did not appear for over an hour after she and Helena had returned. For the first fifteen minutes after changing, she alternated between sitting and pacing in her new parlour. Giving a frustrated groan, she marched off to her music room. Helena smiled and followed her, listening to the stormy piece her friend performed, before it turned much more melodic and soft as her frustration died within her at the release the music provided.

"I have not heard that before, Harriet. Who is it by?"

"Me I suppose, I was just playing whatever came into my mind. Feeling more really."

"You must write it down. It was wonderful. Harriet, you composed a piece of music of your own! I loved it."

"No, I cannot. Ladies do not compose music."

"Well you just did!"

"I was only playing out my mood."

"Can you remember it?" Harriet nodded. "Then write it down before you forget it. Even if only to play again for yourself."

"No, it is not proper. I am sure any composer should laugh at it."

"Then write it down for me. Give it to me as a gift, I will not laugh at it. It sounded as I feel at times when I get angry and then it soothes the anger as it moves on. I can get Isabella to play it for me when I need soothing!" She picked up a piece of paper from the piles on the piano and handed it to Harriet.

The rest of the time before the gentlemen returned passed very quickly for Harriet who was furiously scribbling and then playing a piece and scribbling again. When she handed three pages to Helena, her friend glanced at it reading the title she had given it and smiled. *'Helena's Moods'.*

In addition to Mr. Collingworth, Mr. Horncastle and the colonel, there were five other men. Mr. Horncastle introduced them all to Harriet and Helena as they entered the dining room for luncheon. Mr. Ashman and Mr. Milford they had met the night before, Mr. Chapple, Mr. Holder and Mr. Leake those gentlemen had brought with them at the insistence of Horncastle. Mr. Ashman and Mr. Milford were both married, and Harriet remembered meeting their wives at Sydney Gardens. They were pleasant women, though a little older than her, and had not attended the shooting at Wyndham House that morning.

As those men stepped aside, Mr. Collingworth stepped up. "Miss Wyndham, a pleasure to see you again. I trust you are well and you enjoyed your visit with the baroness?"

"I am, sir, and I did. Thank you. You look as though the exertion of shooting has agreed with you, I take it you were successful?" The trays of luncheon food had been set out on the sideboards and she walked with him to fill a plate each. He talked of the shooting and how they had enjoyed a gentlemanly wager. They had divided into two groups and those in the group that bagged the most grouse took the winnings. His grouping with Mr. Chapple, Mr. Leake and Mr. Milford had won.

She walked with him to the table and he moved his free hand to pull out a chair for her to the right of the head of it. Harriet placed her plate at the setting at the head of the table and looked at him. He obligingly pulled out that chair for her, having placed his own plate at the setting to her right.

They talked pleasantly about her visit with the baroness, how she was finding Wyndham House and she asked him of his home. He dismissed it rather quickly, saying it was nothing compared to her property.

"It was rather daunting to see the size of it when we arrived. Of course, I was used to Eastease, but this house is at least twice its size and with much more acreage. I need not have feared, however, as I have found that the secret to running this household is to surround myself with the right people to advise you and make happen whatever decisions you make." She looked up at Mr. Horncastle at the other end of the table as she said this and caught his eye. She smiled, and he raised his eyebrows at her, wondering of what they were talking.

Mr. Horncastle and Colonel Ackley were none too happy about losing the shooting bet to Collingworth. Both had outshot him, but Mr. Ashman and Mr. Holder were not good sportsmen at all. Bertram knew that Collingworth knew this and had ensured he had both the better shooters with him. He scowled at the man who was occupying all of Miss Wyndham's attention.

However, Harriet was no longer distinguishing Mr. Collingworth. Not that she did not find him pleasant, but because her stomach was turning circles in the excitement of having written her first piece of music. It had flowed out of her and she had been able to remember every note of it. She had created her own music before, many times, but she had never done it with such a purpose as she had earlier with Helena. Was it not odd, she thought, that the one person she wanted to share it with, who she felt would appreciate it most and should not mock a lady for composing, was Mr. Bertram Horncastle.

"If you were to marry, Miss Wyndham, then you should have a husband to take care of the running of the estate and need not concern yourself over it. That is something to consider, is it not?"

"Hmmm, I bed your pardon, Mr. Collingworth? What were you saying? Marriage? I should hope that whomever I did marry, would discuss all the particulars of decisions with me. I like to think that I have some ideas of my own and that I should learn much before that would take place." After that exchange, Harriet had joined into some of the other general conversation around the table as the men told their shooting stories. After everyone had left, Mckinnon spoke quietly to Miss Wyndham, informing her that Jacky and Rebecca Robertson wondered if she could spare them a few minutes and she agreed, asking him to show them into her study.

At dinner that night with just the four of them, Harriet asked to talk of a subject she had discussed with Rebeca and Jacky Robertson. They had talked of her wanting to find some purpose while at Wyndham House, although she had not wanted a school as they had at Eastease. Then they had suggested a home for orphans, a safe place for these children where they could be cared for, fed and grow. Where they could play, but also learn. Learn to be house or lady's maids, butlers, footmen, valets or cooks. They could be gardeners or gamekeepers or stablemen.

"That sounds admirable, but where should they live?" Nathaniel looked questioningly at her.

"They were out on a walk this morning and found a house. It seemed unlived in, but large. Apparently, it is called Wyndham Lodge. Do you know of it Mr. Horncastle?"

"Yes, Phillip liked to go there on occasion. When he felt this house was too big for his mood. It would make sense to put it to use. I take it the Robertsons are suggesting that they should run it?"

"They are very capable," Helena interjected. "What are your ideas about it, Harriet?"

"It is the kind of thing I had been looking for... just... I am not sure it feels exactly what I wanted."

"What did you want, Miss Wyndham?" Horncastle asked with a gentle tone.

"I do not know exactly, and that idea could be part of it, but not the whole. I had thought it might be something where I could somehow help young girls, ladies, as Maria and I had been. If we had not had Alexander and Nathaniel. If we had no family, what would have become of us? What of young ladies who have been compromised and their families were not understanding? Or perhaps if they were going to be made to marry where they did not want to? Their only alternative would be to run away. Where should they go? Where *do* they go?"

"Well, it would seem to me, that you have two pieces of the puzzle that should fit together very nicely." Horncastle looked up at the expectant faces. "The children can work the house, learning what each servant should do, with the aid of an adult in various places or in the garden or the stable. They will be loved and cared for by the Robertsons I am sure. Any young ladies, could live in the house and grow up to behave as ladies, sewing, music and such with a governess, perhaps two, overseeing them. They could become governesses themselves and even teach the orphans to read and write, did you not say that Mickleson was frustrated in his attempts to teach those two boys himself? The governesses in training could teach any staff who needed it."

Harriet had looked at him then, just looked and gradually as it all started to sink in, she felt the idea swim around in her head and down her neck and realised that this was it. This was what she wanted. "Mr. Horncastle, do you think you would ride with me to Wyndham Lodge tomorrow and show me inside it? I think we might have a plan!"

"It would be my honour, Miss Wyndham."

"Now, if you two gentlemen would not tarry too long with your cigars, I have a new piece of music I would like to play for you. Perhaps you could meet Helena and I in the music room?"

"Who is it by?"

"I will leave it to you to guess!"

Chapter Thirteen

Before Harriet set out with Mr. Horncastle to see Wyndham Lodge, Nathaniel asked to talk with her. He was taking Helena, Davy and Issie out for a ride and they should swim in the lake if the sun stayed out. He assured her that should she wish to go ahead with the plan once she saw the Lodge, he and Helena had agreed that they should manage getting at least one carriage back with them and the cart. They would also explain to John and Ruth in person why their son did not return to them, but felt sure that they should understand.

He suggested, if she was thinking as approvingly of Mr. Horncastle as she seemed to be, that she make him an offer. If he planned to stay at Wyndham House, as Phillip wished, it made sense to make the situation more formal.

It was a pleasant, sunny morning when Harriet mounted Hudson and Mr. Horncastle mounted his black Friesian. He had decided to name him Duke. They walked the horses along the lane within the grounds of Wyndham House, planning to give them more of a run in the fields on their return journey. There were several cottages dotted along the lane and Mr. Horncastle told her who lived in each. The housekeeper, Mrs. Thurston lived in one with her husband, the gamekeeper. Their children were grown and worked elsewhere.

They followed the curve of the lane and then saw Wyndham Lodge up ahead of them. It was a house similar in size to Bernier House near Redway, Harriet thought. However, whereas that house was more of a box shape, Wyndham Lodge had different height thatched roofs and some of the third-floor windows poked out from under the low eaves. As they entered the garden, Harriet could see that, although the house looked sound enough, the garden needed plenty of care.

They dismounted and Mr. Horncastle fished into his pocket for a key. They tied up the horses and entered. Harriet wrinkled her nose a little. There was a musty smell as the house had not been looked into for at least the eight months since her Uncle Phillip had passed away. Inside was pleasing to the eye as the outside, if a little dusty. There was dark panelling and bright wall coverings. Comfortable furniture, much of it old but nothing too worn. She declared she should go and look at the bedrooms and headed to the wide dark wood stairs. He confirmed he would look in at Phillip's study. It would be good to check if he had left any papers there.

As he entered the big room with the enormous desk dominating its interior, Bertram Horncastle was taken back to a time when Phillip had wanted to stay at the Lodge and never go back to the main house. He had railed at him from behind that desk and Bertram had listened, because that was what a friend would do.

Sadness welled in his throat, but he swallowed it back. There should be time enough to grieve for his friend again, when he was in the privacy of his own rooms. He walked around the desk and opened each drawer in turn, his movements causing the dust to rise up and dance in the sunlight. There were pieces of blank paper and quills in one, and some bottles of drying ink and Phillip's knife for sharpening the quills in another. Bertram ran a finger tenderly over its hilt.

In a third, he spotted Phillip's address book and lifted it out. It slipped out of his grasp a moment and as he grabbed for it his finger slid between the cover and the paper stuck to it on the inside. More carefully, he put the book on the desk and climbed up onto the chair. Opening the cover, he tried to press the paper back into its proper place, but he had wrinkled it too much. As he lifted it to crease it in the opposite direction and try again to lay it flat, he noticed the corner of a single page of paper that had been folded once, tucked inside. Carefully sliding his finger into the gap between cover and paper, he pulled it out and opened it.

As he read the words upon it, the tears poured down his face. At that moment, Harriet walked in gaily declaring the place to be perfect, all it needed was some care and cleaning. She stopped halfway to reaching him and looked at the small man that she had come to consider a friend, companion even. When Nathaniel and Helena returned to Redway, there would just be the two of them. He sat at the desk with a book and a single piece of paper in front of him, his head was in his hands and he was trying to compose himself.

"Grief is a funny thing, Mr. Horncastle. You think you are past it and it comes right back full force, with a room or a smell or an item of clothing. It must be so hard for you to work through your grief over my uncle when you cannot truly show the emotion you felt. You loved him."

Horncastle looked up sharply at that, swiping at his tears, "Phillip and I were friends. I suppose you could say that, as friends can, we cared a lot for each other."

"I understand. You need not confirm or deny anything. It is not a concept I am unfamiliar with. I think if anyone can find love, the kind of love you obviously held for Uncle Phillip, they can count themselves lucky."

"I found this note in the cover of this book. I have read it. I think you should." He held it out for her to take and read. There was a dusty loveseat opposite the desk, so she swiped her handkerchief over it and then sat down to read.

I am sick. I know I do not have long to live. The doctors I have seen all seem to think it is a sickness within my stomach. I cough up blood and it gets harder and harder to eat anything. Bertram of course fusses over me and sometimes I admit I take out my frustration and angst on him. I do not know why he has stayed with me all this time.

I hope this note will never be found, but if it is, that someone is discreet enough to burn it. I feel I need to write this down, to get it off my chest, if you will. It took me a while but I have finally forgiven you for your marriage. I understand why you did it. You hurt me so much and made me so angry. All you wanted was Wyndham House and so I changed my will so you should never get it.

I do not know why you do not understand that if the law allowed it, I would give you everything. You already have my heart. No matter what you do, it seems I cannot get it back from you. If we could marry as man and wife... and yet I know that goes against God's instruction. I am what I am, what God made me and I cannot change it. It is the same for you, though you try harder to disguise it.

I offered you the Lodge once. To live here for the rest of your life, but you laughed at me. I know you never cared for me, but something kept bringing you back to me. Was it only the money?

Regardless, you will always have my heart and I will always love you. Only you. Forever.

Pip

"It is not written for you, as you are mentioned within it," tears of sympathy were in Harriet's eyes.

"There was only one man that ever called him *'Pip'.*"

"Who?"

"Robert Davenport."

Harriet must have sat for a full minute with her mouth open, her eyes, unblinking, on Mr. Horncastle. Though she sat quite still, her mind was racing with ideas. *"Am I never to be free of this man? Will he follow me everywhere I go?"*

"That man, if he can be called thus, is dead."

"Killed, I heard, by your Colonel."

"No. Davenport tried to take Nathaniel with him, after declaring that he had always loved him." Mr. Horncastle, to Harriet's surprise began laughing at that. Fresh tears rolled down his face, but these were in amusement, not the despair he had felt moments ago when he had read what he had always known. Harriet looked at him confused and between his laughing he explained.

"I loved Phillip, but he did not return that love. He was desperately in love with Davenport, but that was not returned, either, and Davenport was in love with the colonel? He had no hope. I almost feel sorry for him."

"Never feel the slightest sympathy for that man, you know what he did to my sister, what he did to me?"

"I only know some, but I would be willing to listen and will take it to my grave, if you wish to confide in me." So they sat there in that musty room and she told him everything that had happened with Robert Davenport, including revealing that she was originally Maria Wyndham. He listened and at the point where she talked of her sister he moved to sit next to her and covered her hand that was on the seat, with his own.

When she finished, he still sat holding her hand, she looked at them clasped together on the loveseat cushion, "I care for you very deeply, Mr. Horncastle, and I did think that we could have married. We could have had a companionable relationship." He did not directly drop her hand as she thought he might, but he looked intently at her. "I think, however, that it would not work given what we have just talked of and I do believe we both deserve to be loved and to love in return. We should at least hope."

"I doubt a lady such as yourself should ever consider me marriageable."

"If you are referring to your height, Mr. Horncastle, I think I need to tell you the same thing I have told all the staff at Wyndham House. I value you and I will not tolerate anyone calling you a freak or mocking your stature in any way. You are to be treated with as much respect as I expect for myself. Anyone who cannot do so, or is heard doing otherwise, will be dismissed on the spot. I only wish I could have said as much to your valet before he left."

"Ah, do not concern yourself with regard to Smith. He did not leave of his own accord, as I led you to believe. I must be honest and confess to something that may change your opinion of me. Mr. Davenport visited Wyndham House after Phillip passed. He expressed a wish to pay his respects, but he was not respectful in any way and as usual demanded money. I refused and threw him out, however, it was not before Smith had informed him that the property now belonged to you and your sister. Later, when word reached us of Davenport's actions, I confronted Smith and he confessed he had told him, saying he would rather work for Mr. Davenport. I informed him that he had better leave and do just that. Of course by that time, Davenport was dead. I am sorry that what he learned here, caused him to return to Lincolnshire."

"Do not blame yourself, Mr. Horncastle. Helena has told us all many times that what Mr. Davenport did, and what befell him, was all his own doing and responsibility. We all did our best to prevent him, including yourself."

"I should have written to Mr. Harker and the colonel of it. They should have been more on their guard."

"No one knew what Mr. Davenport was capable of, not even Nathaniel, and he had known him all his life."

"I will have to confess it to the colonel. It has weighed on me since you arrived, but with his attitude towards me at the beginning, I felt I should not add to his dislike of me. Since then I have been enjoying his improved opinion."

"We need not disclose any of this discussion, Mr. Horncastle." She handed the note back to him. "I suggest you do as my uncle wished and burn this. I will leave it to you to decide if you want to talk to the colonel of Smith, but I hold you no ill will and I hope that you will not continue to burden yourself with any blame."

"Thank you, Miss Wyndham. You are, as always, considerate and discreet. So, you like this house for your venture? I only wish to check with you because if you do decide to marry at some point you, and especially your husband, may not wish to have me lurking in the shadows. You could move me out here."

"Would you want that, Mr. Horncastle? Given that Uncle Phillip offered it to Davenport?"

"No, but for your happiness, I would move gladly."

"Nathaniel has actually given me an idea that would make me very happy. I wonder if you might consider a title such as Estate Manager? You have done an admirable job maintaining things this year so far. I need help to learn all there is to learn about Wyndham House and someone who will allow me to make my own decisions, while giving me sound advice. It would be a lifetime position, unless you change your mind. You would be paid handsomely and provided with your accommodations at Wyndham House as already arranged. I would make it legal, make it so that if I ever marry, my husband could not change a thing, though I have to say I hope I should choose wisely enough that it should not matter. You would be comfortably situated for the rest of your life, Mr. Horncastle. What do you say?"

"The colonel suggested it?" He was incredulous, so she nodded with a smile. "I say yes and thank you, Miss Wyndham. I am honoured."

"I am honoured, Mr. Horncastle. Wyndham House is your home, you must always consider it thus."

"My first recommendation, Miss Wyndham, is for us to take a ride across the grounds back to the house. Let us blow all these old memories away. We do not need them as we start anew. Here is to the success of Wyndham House, the Lodge and our continued endeavour to find the love we deserve."

They did, indeed, enjoy a freeing ride back to Wyndham House. Bertram was becoming a very accomplished rider. His talent for learning quickly, stemming from his younger days. He loved his black Friesian as much, if not more than, the day he first set eyes on him and he was often spotted in the stable taking the horse a treat. Harriet still had to rein in her speed to accommodate that of Mr. Horncastle, but she felt that soon she should not have to and it would be fun for them to ride out together often in the future.

When she had enjoyed a moment to herself that afternoon, Harriet once again walked to the pianoforte and started composing a piece that had come into her mind that morning as she had seen Mr. Horncastle crying over the letter. This piece was more subdued than her first had been. The notes were in a minor key and told of grief and despair, as well as sadness, but as she worked through her own grief, there stemmed from it love. Deeper notes that resonated and built as she moved to the higher register and the notes became lighter and happier. She called the piece 'The Lodge'. She knew, that after their exchange at that building, Mr. Horncastle should recognise and understand its meaning, but she could say it was because the children that were helped there would be in despair before hopefully meeting a happier time in their lives.

As had become usual, when Bertram was pulling on his shirt that evening, James knocked and came into the room to tie his cravat for him. The young man did do a much better job than Bertram could ever manage.

He had wondered, of course, from the first moment they had met and he properly took in the sight of James through his pain, as he had lain on his back on the floor. Wondered if James' preferences matched his own. He had chosen to ignore the touches that lingered a moment longer than necessary, the times their eyes had locked before James looked away with a blush, but he had enjoyed it.

The handsome man was at least five years his junior and it was flattering that such a man might show an interest in him, but he had no intention of anything further. He had loved Phillip and had vowed on that man's deathbed that he would keep his memory alive in his heart.

After reading Phillip's letter to Davenport, he had been upset. He did not know why it had affected him so. Perhaps because it was a final rejection. Each time Davenport had visited Wyndham House Phillip had rejected Bertram in favour of that man. Each time he left, Bertram would hold Phillip as he cried, and he would forgive him. When Phillip had died in his arms, he had felt as though the man he loved could never reject him again, but there it had been, in black and white on that piece of paper that he had burned in the first fire he found back at the house.

What he had vowed in his heart to Phillip, he thought of now as a waste of the rest of his life. Why should he not enjoy the comfort of another? Phillip had done so, with Bertram alive and in a room down the hall from him. Bertram was nearly twenty years younger than Phillip, who had been nearly fifty when he passed. The thought of a younger, firmer body under his hands suddenly appealed to him.

He stepped up on the window seat as James approached him and he watched the man's easy gait as he walked.

"Good evening, sir. I take it you are ready for me to tie your cravat? I thought I should try a different knot, but it is a little complicated if you can be patient with me."

"Certainly, James. I am in your hands." As James stepped close to him, to start the first knot, he studied the younger face. He was clean shaven, well-groomed and kept himself clean; Bertram could smell soap on him. In the past, he had always stared at one spot on the far wall while his cravat was tied, but this time he allowed his eyes to follow that face. He enjoyed watching those brown eyes so intent on their task, unaware of the admiration being bestowed upon them and the thick lashes that surrounded them.

Suddenly aware that the air felt a little different around him and that Mr. Horncastle was breathing a little faster than usual, James chanced a look away from his creation into those deep, blue eyes. Though he had not moved his head, Bertram was looking directly at him and smiled a warm, slow smile as James held his gaze, for a heartbeat, two. Then he looked quickly back at his task.

"You seem rather more content this evening, if I may say so, sir. You enjoyed your ride this morning?" some of the staff had commented on Miss Wyndham riding out with Mr. Horncastle. That she had insisted all staff showed the little man respect or be dismissed, added fuel to their ideas and raised eyebrows. James wondered if his own opinion about the intensity of Mr. Horncastle's grief for Mr. Phillip Wyndham had been wrong. The older man had never married and that was why the enormous house and estate now belonged to Miss Wyndham and Mr. Brooks.

"Yes, you are correct on both counts, James." The younger man chanced another look and sure enough, Mr. Horncastle was still looking at him and this time he smiled in return, his heart beating faster. In a low voice that was almost a whisper, Bertram spoke, "if this is a complicated knot, you had better be sure to be here and help me untie it before I get undressed for bed."

"Yes, sir." His throat felt dry as he uttered the words. Bertram said no more until James made to leave the room.

"James, bring some of your miracle cream with you?"

"Yes, sir."

Dinner that evening was spent pleasantly talking of Wyndham Lodge and Harriet's plans for it, as well as the position of Estate Manager she intended to bestow upon Mr. Horncastle. She had spoken to Jacky and Rebecca Robertson that afternoon, and they had started their planning of what should be done. She would go with them to the lodge one day and they could make more plans then.

After dinner, Bertram Horncastle and Nathaniel sat enjoying their cigars in a much more amiable atmosphere than that of barely a week or so ago. Bertram had decided he must confess to this man how Robert

Davenport had become aware that the woman who had been Davenport's wife, had inherited half of Wyndham House.

"Robert visited here on his own?" Nathaniel had given Wyndham House little thought after Mark Wyndham had died, but he had visited this house on occasion when he was younger and he recalled a couple of times when Robert had come with him. They had all known what Phillip Wyndham was, but it was something that was not discussed. If it was ignored then it was not happening.

"Many times, over the years. Phillip... well he loved him." Nathaniel looked over his shoulder at the butler who stood impassively at the door. "Drum knows all of these particulars, Colonel, but he can leave us if you would rather." Nathaniel shrugged and Bertram smiled at the action because it was a movement he had seen Davy do often. He looked up at Drummond Mckinnon.

"I can stay if you wish, sir, but I do have several things I need to attend to, if you can spare me." Horncastle waved him away. "I will return in twenty minutes, sir." He left, and Bertram looked again at the colonel, who was rubbing his face with his hand.

"Did you kill him, Colonel? Did you kill Davenport?"

"No." He relayed to Bertram what had happened on the clifftop at Botany Bay. "He said he loved me. He knew I would never love him, not in the way he wanted. Instead of wanting me to be happy, he chose to try and ruin everything I love, even Helena. I do not understand that kind of love. Oh, do not look at me that way Horncastle! I mean the kind of love that twists everything up and makes it into something it is not supposed to be. That's not real love. Real love is selflessness, giving anything to the other person for their care and happiness. If the other person does not return it, then it can be painful. If they do and are equally selfless, then it is the most wonderful thing."

"It is a crime for one man to love another." Bertram said, cautiously.

"No, the crime is what they do about it. I have given it more thought since last April on that clifftop. It is as if the law thinks a man has a choice about who he loves. If that were true, why would a man love another? Knowing the act of showing that love could see him strung up at the end of a rope. He would not, it is not logical. Therefore, the assumption must be made that it is not a choice and that is how some men are made. If loving Helena was a crime, I do not think it could stop me."

"Most do not think that way. Well, most do not think at all. Thank you, Colonel."

"I did want to advise you that you could do no better than James," he paused deliberately, enjoying the surprised look on Horncastle's face, "as a valet. He is very loyal and trustworthy."

Bertram cleared his throat. "Ah, thank you. Your wife has already extolled his virtues. She seemed to think you were unaware of James' wishes."

"Oh, they think, as a man, I cannot see the difference between the tears of a mother when her son is leaving for a month, or leaving for good."

"Colonel, I am sorry that I did not inform you that Davenport had been here and possibly knew of your wards' inheritance. I did not think he would act in the way he did."

"None of us did, Horncastle. You are not to blame!"

"So I have been told by a very gracious Miss Wyndham."

Later, Bertram sat in his room thinking of what Colonel Ackley had said to him. Certainly, if his mind and body could let him choose, Miss Harriet Wyndham should be a perfect choice for him to marry. He certainly cared for and liked her enough. He enjoyed her company and her piano playing was exceptional. She had written a second piece and had played it for them that night. It had reminded him of how he had felt earlier in the day, then it finished light and hopeful, which had made him think of James.

As he sat there he wondered where the man was? Had he scared him away? He had begun to think that James may not be experienced in any of the things he was, and that both excited and alarmed him. He would have to take things slowly, let him be sure of what he wanted. Standing he removed his coat and waistcoat, and moved to the mirror to poke at the cravat. It might take him all night to get it off his own neck. He pulled at one end tentatively, but it seemed to tighten it.

The door opened and James walked in. "Sorry, sir, I wanted to see to the colonel first, so I could give you my undivided attention." He placed the jar of cream on a chest of drawers and looked at Bertram who stood still in front of the mirror with his mouth open and one end of the cravat between his thumb and forefinger.

"James."

"Yes, sir. Let me help you with that, sir." He bent to start untying the knots, but Bertram took hold of his hand and pulled him over to the window seat where he could stand and be on a level height with him once again.

"I am all yours, James." He said it with a smile, but with a serious look in his eyes as James' eyes fell upon his. Bertram had regained his composure upon seeing him again. He had thought he would not come back and it had saddened him. James looked away quickly and started to tackle the knots on the cravat, but could not resist looking often into those dazzling, blue eyes.

"Are you teasing me, sir?"

"No, James, I am not teasing you."

"You like to say things that have two meanings. I worry I might be taking your meaning incorrectly."

"I apologise and no, you are not taking my meaning incorrectly, because I mean both things."

The cravat knot came loose under James' expert fingers and he held both sides of it near Bertram's neck. He let it slide through his hands, his knuckles running gently over the ridges of Bertram's chest and stomach, through the thin material of his shirt.

They were standing so close and looking into each other's eyes. James licked his lips and in the next moment they were caught in Bertram's, he could not believe it was happening at last. The man clasped the back of James' head as he feasted upon his lips. He could do nothing but return the kiss with as much passion as he was being given. Bertram's tongue slid into his mouth, he groaned at the sensation and pulled him against him. Their bodies, of similar length, meshed together and he could feel Bertram's arousal pushed up against his own.

Fear slid over him as if a bucket of cold water had been thrown over him and he stopped the kiss, trying to pull away, but Bertram was stronger. "Wait!" he managed to say, to stop James from running out of the room. He gasped in air trying to steady his breathing, while James stared at him. His eyes were so damn innocent and fearful, his hair ruffled from where he had held him. "Wait a moment, give me a moment." Bertram closed his eyes and pulled their foreheads together.

"I should leave, I should not have come."

"You did come. Of course you should have. I wanted you to. You wanted to. Now you are unsure and that is allowed. I will not force you, but do not leave, not yet. Let me speak." Slowly he released James, when he was confident he would hear him out, he dropped his hands to his sides.

"I am sorry, sir."

"No, no need. God damn it, James, I want you so much. I had not realised it fully until a moment ago. I will wait. I will wait until you are ready. I want you to know that I will not act upon my wishes until you show me you are ready. We should continue as we have been, as I do enjoy our moments together. Please do not be afraid to come to me, for goodness knows I need your aid with my cravat and of course, my back. Can you promise me that?"

"Yes, sir."

"And James...?"

"Yes, sir?"

"Be bloody obvious about it when you are ready, so I know for certain. I never want to put that fear in your eyes again."

Chapter Fourteen

Harriet was busy over the next three weeks. She was learning all she could about Wyndham House and the running of it from her new Estate Manager, Mr. Horncastle. Additionally, the two of them were planning a dinner en that was to take place prior to Colonel and Mrs. Ackley returning to Redway.

Rebecca and Jacky Robertson were thrilled about the opportunity Miss Wyndham was giving them with regard to Wyndham Lodge, and they talked at length, together and with her, of their plans. Harriet had also considered that it might be worth asking other wealthy families in the area to contribute to the Lodge, in particular Baroness Freyley. That Lady had returned the visit Harriet and Helena had made to her and was brought into the details of the plans for the Lodge. She felt it a wonderful scheme, agreed she should contribute and that she had connexions she could inform that they would be assisting young ladies who found themselves orphaned or in difficult situations.

Almost every day one combination of them or another went riding when the weather permitted. Sometimes only Helena and the colonel, sometimes the whole Ackley family. There had been one occasion when they had all ridden out and picnicked near the lake before taking a swim, and several others when Harriet and Mr. Horncastle had ridden together. towards the end of those three weeks, Isabella was finally able to ride her white-grey stallion, Snow.

Finally, one day, the saddle Harriet and Helena had ordered for Mr. Horncastle was delivered by the saddler. As directed, the saddle flaps had been shortened and there were shorter stirrup leathers to avoid having to wrap them around twice. The girth straps had been lengthened to ensure their buckles were not under his feet when he rode. The seat of the saddle was made narrower than a regular seat and it made him feel more secure on the Friesian, but the panels that rested on the horse's back were the same to ensure Duke's comfort. It made a tremendous difference to Bertram's confidence in riding his stallion.

Within all of these activities, Harriet managed somehow to eke out some time to attend to her music. She played often for everyone after dinner and had even managed to persuade Nathaniel to play for Helena. The children were allowed to dine with them occasionally and at those times Isabella also performed. However, it was the times when Harriet found an hour or two to herself, that she had the opportunity to work on the two pieces she had composed. She had decided to write the accompanying instruments' music for those pieces, and as she worked she became more confident that the pieces were good. In her daydreams, she imagined playing them in front of an audience at the kind of recital Mr. Horncastle had said he had attended with her uncle. Then she would shake herself at how ridiculous she was being. It would never be permitted.

Bertram had been relieved that James had returned to aid him the morning after they had kissed. He had felt sure that James had wanted to be kissed by him, but had not been ready for anything further. His promise not to rush him was difficult to keep, but it would be worth it, of that he was sure. Instead, he had lain in his bed that night thinking of the things they should do together when James was ready. He had not slept very much.

James had slept fitfully, too. He groaned into his pillow at his foolish action in stopping the kiss. He wanted Mr. Horncastle, had waited so long to let anyone touch him. He had never wanted a woman, and although his mother had suggested one or two village girls who had shown an interest in him, he had done nothing about it. She had asked him once if she should stop hoping for grandbabies and he had apologised to her. He said he did not have an interest in women that way and she had nodded. She confirmed that she would always love him and only wished for his happiness.

When he was not berating himself over leaving the room, he was reliving that kiss. It had been more than he had hoped for. He had met another man with the same preferences before, but that man had not appealed to him. No man had, until he laid his eyes upon Mr. Horncastle. That he was considerably shorter than him, was not a concern. He had been attracted to his face and those beautiful blue eyes. The man was so muscular, and yet had obviously been hurt judging by the scars on his back. James wanted to kiss those scars and take the hurt away.

The kiss had been passionate and when James had tried to pull away, Mr. Horncastle had held him fast, trying to regain his control. That he had managed to bring that desire out in the other man had made James feel powerful and attractive. It had taken all his courage to go back to that room the following morning, but he felt the alternative was not acceptable. The man had said he would wait until he was ready, and though he was not sure when that should be, he knew he would never find out if he did not go back to him.

They had grinned at each other when James had entered the room. They held a secret between them and it was bittersweet, but for now, it was enough. Each man looked at the other and thought the same, *It is enough... for now.*

Since Drummond Mckinnon's discussion with Mrs. Ackley about moving on with his life after the death of his wife, he had manoeuvred his mealtimes, whenever possible to coincide with those of Miss Cadman. As she was often the last to eat the meals that she prepared with the aid of the kitchen staff, it was usually the two of them at one end of the large table, and the four young kitchen maids with their heads together at the other end.

The kitchens had been particularly busy over the past week, as the date for the dinner planned by Miss Wyndham and Mr. Horncastle approached. Finally, Drum had managed to arrange his day off to the same day as Miss Cadman and he had talked to Mickleson about the possibility of them taking out two horses if the weather was fine. Then he had asked the most senior of Miss Cadman's assistants to arrange for saddlebags of supplies, before approaching the woman herself and asking her to ride out with him for a picnic. She agreed very happily.

As they mounted their horses, with the aid of two of the newly appointed stablemen, Charlie Mickleson watched with what he acknowledged was a little envy. He wondered if Annie Brown could ride and looked up at the window he knew to be the dressing room of Miss Wyndham, where Miss Brown did most of her work. He had seen her open that window and shake out a blanket once. There was a balcony that stretched across what he assumed were rooms either side of the dressing room. He had not seen her at that window again, but he looked often from his vantage point to the side of the house, when he stepped outside of the stable.

Drum did not know if the Ackleys would be riding out later that day, but he knew their favourite place was the large lake, so he chose to ride with Miss Cadman further east and to a picturesque pond. At this time of year, it was thick with lilies and the flowers were wide open. He laid out the blanket he had brought with him and then laid their packs upon it. While he tied the horses to nearby trees, she laid out their picnic.

He watched her as he approached the blanket again. Her usual practical movements were slower and graceful. On her day off, though she was still serving food, she did not have to rush it. She smiled as she opened a package.

"This is for you I believe, sir. Katie knows your preferences." He bent to look in the package and smiled at the generous portion of porkpie. As he sat down opposite her and took the pie, he grasped one of her hands and then kept hold of it as he looked at her.

She wore a pretty flowered, if somewhat worn, gown and a small jacket covering the top part. Her hair had been covered by a bonnet, but she had removed it to eat. She had pinned it up in a softer, looser style than she usually wore when working in the kitchen. Her hair was brown as were her soft eyes and a few freckles dotted her nose and cheeks. She was very different from his wife, who had been tall and slim with shocking red hair, but the heart wanted what it wanted and his, he had found, wanted her.

"Do you think, as we are alone, you could call me Drum?" he looked in her eyes as he still held her hand and saw the amusement there.

"And with my name being Fiona, do you think they might be calling us 'fife and drum'?" He laughed and it pleased her to hear it. He was often serious as required for the office he held at such a large house.

"I should be honoured to call you Fiona, or perhaps Fi? Would you allow it?"

"As we are alone, I find either one acceptable. However, I think I would prefer to call you Drummond." He twitched his nose at that. "What is wrong with that? It is your name."

"It is not my name that is the issue. It is a perfectly acceptable name. It is your pronunciation of it. You should roll the 'r' and pronounce the 'u' as an 'o'. Drrrommond." She tried it and he smiled.

"Well then, Drrrommond, you must let go of my hand or I will not be able to enjoy our picnic." He did as bid, with slight regret, but looked forward to the opportunity to hold it again as soon as they finished eating. While they enjoyed their food, he asked after her family. He knew her parents were in service together at a local farm and still had three children at their small home with them. She was one of eight and her two older brothers had gone into the army. Her older and younger sister were cook and cook's assistant at other houses nearby. Unfortunately, or fortunately, none of them had the same day off as her this week, which allowed her to come with him on this picnic. She was very happy he had invited her.

Tentatively, she had asked about his family and what had brought him south of the border. He told her how his family had a long-standing feud with the Dalgleish family, who lived on neighbouring land. The feud had gone on for generations and no one could tell you why it started, but the Mckinnons hated the Dalgleish and they, in turn, hated the Mckinnons. At a fair one summer day when he was sixteen, he had met and fell in love with Senga and she had fallen in love with him. They had agreed to meet again, but when he went home and talked of her to his mother, she had told him that Senga was a Dalgleish and he should forget her.

He went to the meeting place that she had arranged. Checking first that there was no Dalgleish ambush waiting for him. She had cried in his arms as she had come to realise, that he was a Mckinnon and they would never be accepted by their families. They agreed to wait a fortnight, when they would meet again at the same place, if they still felt the same, then they would leave together on his horse and travel south. If either had changed their mind, they need not come to the meeting. He had waited over an hour for her. Each minute adding to the pit of despair in his stomach. She was not coming.

He had finally given up and was about to mount his horse when she came running towards him. He had never felt so happy! They embraced and kissed, and then got on his horse and rode away. They stayed at inns and in barns, wherever they could find shelter as they travelled. When they arrived at Gretna Green they should marry and cross the border to England to find work.

One night he laid in a pile of straw in a barn with her in his arms when the door to the barn was smashed open and in strode Senga's three brothers. He stood to retrieve his sword, but her eldest brother had a pistol and aimed it at him. Senga launched herself at him to push him out of the way and the shot had hit her in the chest instead. He had gathered her to him and she died in his arms, love was the last word on her lips. He had not cared what happened to him in his grief, he did not pick up his sword to fight, there was no fight left in him. He was prepared to die. Then his father, an uncle and his brother had entered the building, they had been following the Dalgleishes who had been following his trail. They dispatched them quickly and bloodily with their swords.

His father had stood over him, with no pity in his voice. He said they had saved him some effort for he should have killed her if he had found them first. He would not have the Mckinnon line sullied with Dalgleish blood. Then he disowned him and told him to leave Scotland. If he ever returned he would kill him. So he had journeyed south, finding work here and there and learning as he travelled. Finally, he settled here after nearly ten years.

"You were so young. You had not actually married?" Fiona hated herself for feeling a little glad of that.

"Not by law, but in my heart, and I should have felt no differently if we had made it a legality."

"Why did you choose to stay here, at Wyndham House?" They had finished eating as he told his tale and she had packed away the empty packages. He looked at her, into those sweet eyes he had come to love, the smile that had first caught his attention and started a crack around the stone that had covered his heart for so long.

"This is my first go at being a butler, I thought I should start low and move up. I mean to be at Buckingham Palace before long." She laughed and he moved towards her a little. She sat with her legs tucked under her and leaned on one arm. He mirrored her pose, with his legs out to the opposite side. "I liked Mr. Horncastle the moment I met him. In England, I am different. I stick out because of my accent. He sticks out rather more obviously, but I suppose you could say we had a meeting of minds, seeing as we are both different." He moved a little closer.

"Then I noticed as I sat in my office with the door open, so I could see straight through to the kitchen, that I enjoyed watching a beautiful woman at her work. She would bring me a tea tray with some cake and that cake was very good. One day she brought in some oat cakes, and those oat cakes looked the same as my mother used to make. One bite and I had fallen in love." His face was inches away from her as he had moved closer and closer while he spoke. He still looked into her eyes as he moved, but when he mentioned falling in love, she turned her head away, embarrassed.

"You are teasing me, sir!" He picked up her hand and put it to his lips, she turned back and looked at him. "Drrromond."

"I do love you, Fi. Please will you marry me?" she hesitated. "I promise you that my father would never set one foot in England. He detests the whole country."

"My poor Drrromond. How I feel for the boy you were then, and the man you are now. You have no family in effect, but we will make our own family and be very happy. Yes, I will marry you."

"May I kiss you then, Mrs. Mckinnon-to-be?"

"Yes, you may. I love you, Drum." He leaned in tentatively as she lifted her face to his. Then he brushed his lips gently over hers and wondered if she had ever been kissed before, because she did not move her lips at all and kept them pressed closed.

Stopping, he pulled his lips away but kept his forehead resting on hers as he looked in her eyes. "Is that the first time you have been kissed?"

"Did I do it wrong? I did not know what to do. Do not be upset with me, sir. I can learn fast." Colour rushed up her cheeks as she pulled away. Surely, he did not expect her to know what to do? He was the first man she had ever let kiss her.

His heart did a somersault of joy. She was only a year or two younger than him and he had wondered if there had been other suitors before him. "Do I look upset?"

"No, actually you look rather smug, if I were to put a name to it!" she hit his arm none too gently and pushed him away. She made to stand, but he laughingly pulled her into his lap and allowed his thick Scottish brogue out.

"Get yourself used to that look, lass. I am going to be a very smug husband because I will be the only man to have ever touched you. It is as well that you are a fast learner, because I have a lot to teach you and we will both enjoy it. Your first lesson will be in kissing. Make your lips soft, be willing to part them and follow my lead. Oh, and do not be surprised if you feel my tongue."

She struggled to get off his lap, what was he thinking of with his talk of tongues? She should have none of that, she was sure. Laughing he grasped her wrists and held her in place. "I will try it then, sir, but I do not think I will like it!"

Her lips were softer this time and he slid his over hers, slowly deepening the kiss. He released her wrists as she wrapped her arms around his shoulders. Her hands were in his hair with the passion he was bringing out in her, then he ran his tongue over her top lip. It was warm and wet and the moisture allowed their lips to move more fluidly. A sensation pulsed through her and she pushed her breasts against his hard chest. When his tongue moved again, she found hers met his and slid along it, there was a groan, but it was not hers.

Drum was groaning, her hands in his hair and her breasts pressed up against him. It was sending all his blood to one place on his body and if he were not going to teach her all her lessons at once by the side of this pond, then he would have to stop kissing her. Regretfully he pulled away and gently placed her back on the blanket before getting up and pacing away from her, running his hands through his hair where hers had been moments ago. She said nothing, but watched him, perplexed. Had she done it wrong again? As he returned, he did not look angry, so she smiled.

"Aye, lass, you were right. You are a very fast learner. I think we should be getting back to the house and perhaps keep this news to ourselves for today. We can talk to Miss Wyndham and Mr. Horncastle tomorrow and then make our plans."

Drum had agreed with Mrs. Thurston that while he was out for his day off, she could have the maids give his office a thorough clean. Despite the lack of smell, she was not convinced that little rascal who had hidden under his bunk, had not left some of his business under there, so she instructed the maids to pull the whole bunk out of the alcove it was set in and she inspected the floor herself. She pursed her lips, dissatisfied in herself that she had been wrong, but relieved not to have discovered anything untoward. She snapped her fingers for the broom the maid was holding and swept around the edges of the wall and floor. Then she heard a little metallic noise on the floorboard as she dislodged a small round item from a crack in the corner where the walls met.

Thinking it was a coin, she bent to pick it up, but turning it over she found it was some kind of medallion with a crest on one side. It had a hole at the top where a chain could be fed through, so it could be worn around the neck. Assuming it was Mr. Mckinnon's, though he had never mentioned losing it, she placed it on his desk.

When he returned, Drum sat at his desk very happy, tomorrow he should tell Miss Wyndham he wanted to marry Fiona Cadman. She surely should have no objection to it. Service staff married each other often. The rest of the day, they should be busy with the dinner that had been planned meticulously for a month at least. After that, he hoped to sit down with Fiona and they could discuss when their wedding should take place. In his opinion, the earlier the better after that kiss by the pond.

Shaking himself from all of these ideas, he noticed the medallion on his desk. Picking it up he turned it over in his hand. He would have to ask

Mrs. Thurston how it came to be there and whose it was. He put it to the back of his desk, giving it no more thought until James came into his office.

He had obviously finished serving the colonel and Mr. Horncastle dress for dinner. The footmen were attending its service as it was Drum's day off. He had trained them well enough not to be concerned. James was carrying a dark blue suit. Was Mr. Horncastle finally ready to wear something other than black? Drum suspected James had something to do with that.

"Mr. Mckinnon, I know it is your day off, but I was looking for one of the laundry women and saw you in here. Can I leave this with you to get it freshened up in time for the dinner tomorrow night?"

"Certainly, I am pleased to see he is finally able to switch from his usual black. Put it on the couch there." Drum looked at James who was staring intently at the medallion on his desk. "Will there be anything else, James?" He looked up at Mckinnon from the medallion and shook his head, throwing the suit to the couch as he left.

Bertram had enjoyed dinner, then he had listened to Miss Wyndham performing again and Mrs. Ackley sang an aria. She was going to sing it at the dinner the following evening and wanted to practise it. Her voice was astonishing and he had seen the love his friend, as he now felt he could call Colonel Ackley, held for the lady as he watched her. This was the aria she had sung the first evening they had met. Miss Wyndham had been correct, they both deserved to have somebody look at them the way Colonel Ackley did his wife.

After everyone retired for the night, Bertram roamed the music room and the new parlour. He looked in at the old music room that had become his study, it was across the hall from what had been Phillip's study, that Miss Wyndham now used. The thoughtful, young woman had offered the use of that room for him instead, but he declined. He had taken all the good memories he had of Phillip and locked them away in a corner of his mind and heart. All the bad memories, he was working through one by one and hoped never to revisit them. There had not been many, but there had been times when Phillip had hurt him.

His thoughts then turned to James. After that first heady kiss, they had returned to their roles of gentleman and valet. He had, however, endeavoured to put James more at ease, asking him about his mother and how she felt about him not returning. That was the first time he had confirmed that he should like to keep James as his valet. He had mentioned it to Miss Wyndham and offered to pay him from his own stipend that he should get for being Estate Manager, but she refused, saying James would be working at Wyndham House.

There had been that one night that he was in so much pain with his back, that James had aided him. He had thought of asking him before, even though he had not been in pain, just to enjoy James' hands upon him again, but he had felt that it would not be fair. When James had attended him that night, he had noticed him grimace and commented upon it. He had been incredulous that Bertram might have considered not asking him to help him and could not stop himself berating him for it. Bertram smiled at the recollection.

When James had returned with the cream, Bertram still stood on the window seat. Efficiently, but with trembling hands, James had unbuttoned and removed his shirt, after looking into his eyes and then down at his ridged and hairy chest, he had bitten his lower lip. Bertram remembered he had whimpered, but had not moved towards James. Instead, he had turned and walked haltingly to the bed laying down for the cream to be applied. Even if James had wanted him to, he did not think his back would have allowed him to act the way he wished.

As he rubbed the cream onto his back, James asked him where he had got the scars. As Bertram had told him, leaving out who his family was, James had bent to him and gently kissed each one. He recalled how that action had brought tears to his eyes, Phillip had never even questioned him about them, much less endeavoured to remove the emotional hurt of them with a simple, tender kiss.

James continued to tie, and untie, his cravat each evening, and he stood on the window seat as he had before. James was always slow and deliberate, and as frustrating as that could be, Bertram would not change it as he felt one day they should kiss again. He felt he had gauged sufficient time for James to have seen to the colonel's needs and walked to his rooms with anticipation.

James was waiting impatiently in Mr. Horncastle's rooms. The dinner and evening entertainment seemed to have gone on forever to his mind, since he had seen the medallion in Mr. Mckinnon's office. When the colonel had entered his dressing room he had rushed so much that the man had admonished him, something the colonel had never had to do in all the time he had known James. He had unbuckled the wooden leg and then pulled it roughly from his stump. The buckle caught on the stump as he pulled it away quickly.

He had apologised to the colonel and applied some of the miracle cream to it. It was already sore as the colonel had worn it a lot recently and he advised him to leave it off most of the day tomorrow, that way he should be able to tolerate it for the evening.

James had been surprised when he entered Bertram's rooms not to find the man there and had paced around the room while he waited. When Bertram finally did come in, he had a bounce in his step that made James scowl. Not noticing the man's mood when he entered, Bertram directly walked to the window seat and stood upon it.

"As always, I am in your hands, James!" he declared with his arms as wide as his handsome smile. James glared at him and then rather unceremoniously started to tug none too gently at the cravat. It pulled upon Bertram's neck and he was startled enough to finally notice James' mood. Grasping his hands, he stopped him from causing his neck any further damage. "What is wrong?"

"Where is your medallion, let me see it?"

"Why?"

"Show it to me, now!"

"Do not use that tone with me, James. I have done nothing wrong. I will show it to you, after you have explained yourself."

"I saw your medallion on Mckinnon's desk while you were at dinner. How did he get it? Did it fall off when you were in there with him? Did you bang the Drum?" James was so overcome with his jealousy the he lost all his sense of deference towards Bertram, but Bertram did not notice. He was dealing with his own emotions, how did Drummond Mckinnon happen to have a medallion the same as the one around his own neck? He pulled it out of his shirt despite the cravat still hanging half undone and thrust it under James' nose.

"A medallion the same as this? Exactly? Look, James. Was it exactly the same as this with this crest upon it?"

"Yes, that is the medallion. Did you go and see him tonight after dinner? Is that why you were not here when I had finished with the colonel? You cannot fool me. Do the two of you..."

"Show me! Show me now! Where in Mckinnon's office was it?" James had stopped mid-sentence, his mouth open as he took in Bertram's countenance. He looked almost panicked.

"It was not yours?"

"No, you fool. It was not mine. You must show me. Let us go." He began to walk to the door and James followed miserably behind him. When they came to Mckinnon's office they found the door locked, though curiously they could see some candlelight coming through from under it.

"Mckinnon!" Bertram shouted and banged on the door, "open this damned door, man. This is urgent." Mckinnon appeared at the door, rather dishevelled with his hair ruffled, but he did not open it for Mr. Horncastle to come in.

"Sir, how can I aid you? What is the urgency?"

"I must come in there."

"You cannot at this moment, sir. I apologise. If you can wait a minute, please?"

"Why? Do you have a woman in there, Drum?"

"Um," he looked back into the room, "aye, actually. Miss Cadman has just this afternoon agreed to be my wife. I was going to inform you tomorrow."

"Congratulations, you sly dog, I am happy for you. However, James said he saw a medallion on your desk the same as this one. He held it up to show Mckinnon. I would like to see it. Bring it out here, let us not embarrass the lady any further, but Drum, if you cannot keep it in your breeches, I suggest you had better marry her sooner rather than later."

Moments later, Mckinnon returned and handed the medallion to Bertram. Bertram took it to the candle that was lighted on the table and stared at it, turning it over twice. "Where did you get it?"

"Mrs. Thurston cleaned my room today while I was out and said she found it under the bunk, where the boy had hidden, I can only assume it was his. It was hidden in a crack in the corner of the wall."

"It is the same, sir. Is it not?" James was peering at it with Bertram and then looking at the one hanging next to his half-undone cravat. Bertram did not need to see his own, he had looked at it often enough.

"I will have to speak to the boy in the morning. Has he continued to talk, to improve, Drum?"

"Yes he has, with the help of Jacky and Rebecca Robertson. I think they plan to take him in as their own."

"I fear they may be out of luck. I believe I know who his parents are." He looked from Mckinnon to James, and both men knew him well enough not to ask, as he wore a pained expression.

"May I suggest then, sir, that you speak to the Robertsons before you speak to the boy. It will be a shock, to Mrs. Robertson in particular."

"Yes, I will see them directly after breakfast, if someone can take care of the boy while I do."

"I will, sir." Mckinnon confirmed before they left. Then he turned and entered his office again. Fiona Cadman sat on his couch looking sheepishly up at him. "Miss Cadman, you tempt me far too much. I believe Mr. Horncastle is correct and we had better marry as soon as possible."

As they reached the top of the stairs, Bertram told James to leave him and said goodnight. "I should still help you with your dress, sir."

"No, I will manage," his tone was dismissive.

"I am sorry, Bertram."

"As you should be. I am not angry, but you should trust me. I do not want to talk of it now." He looked down at the medallion in his hand. "I have too much on my mind." He walked away leaving James standing and watching him, wondering what had come over him that he had behaved in such a way towards Mr. Horncastle?

Chapter Fifteen

James knocked tentatively on Bertram's door in the morning. It was early, but he felt the man should want to be awake early after what had occurred the night before. Bertram was already awake, had dressed himself in his trousers, had just put his shirt over his head and was tucking it in.

"James, come in. I want to talk to you."

"Let me help you with that, sir." He moved to straighten the shirt, but Bertram slapped at his hand impatiently.

"No, James. Sit down." Used to always standing in front of gentlemen, James found it unusual to sit on the ottoman at the end of Bertram's bed. Instead of sitting on the armchair opposite or perhaps on the window seat as James thought he might. Bertram lifted himself up easily onto the ottoman next to James and carefully took his hand in his own. He was gratified when James smiled at him for doing so.

"James, my real name is Bertram Frammington. I believe it is a well-known name in Lincolnshire." James' eyes widened, and his mouth fell open. "I am the first-born son of the Earl of Lorlake. I wanted to tell you of it before you heard speculation through the staff news, everything moves at light speed there! Given our... *relationship*, I did not want you to wonder what was going on."

"My Lord?" James wondered if he needed to change his address of the man then put his hands up to his lips as he realised he had kissed the son of an earl! Bertram smiled at the reaction.

"No. This is not something that will become public information. The heir to the earldom will remain my younger brother, Joshua. My father will see to that and I am happy. In fact, I find that I am happier now than I have ever been in my life. This medallion is all I have from my early years and, as you discovered with me last night, the boy we rescued after the fair last month has one the same. Assuming he did not acquire it somewhere, he must be my nephew." At this declaration, Bertram's shoulders started to shake and he bent his head as the tears started to fall. He had thought about it all night, but to finally say it out loud broke down his defences. To have a connexion to his family after more than twenty years. Did they ever think about him? Did they ever wonder what had become of him?

James hesitated only a moment before putting his arms around Bertram. He leaned his shoulder lower so the man could rest his head upon it as his tears fell. He was astonished at how much comfort he gained in trying to comfort Bertram, and pulled him closer. Gratefully, Bertram accepted the embrace, he could not remember any other time he had felt another's arms around him in comfort.

"Thank you for telling me, sir. After my behaviour last night I would not have blamed you for being angry with me."

Pulling himself together, Bertram lifted his head and looked at James. "Yes, but you apologised and I am grateful for that. You must trust me. If there is to be something between us, which you know to be my wish, then you must know that there will not be anyone else. I would want the same from you."

"Yes, sir."

"And James, I did like it when you called me Bertram last night, do you think you could do that when we are alone? Bertram, or Bertie."

"Which did Phillip Wyndham call you?"

"Bertie."

"Then I will, with your permission, call you Bertram." James smiled a small smile at him, cupped his face in his hands and wiped the tears away with his thumbs. Leaning in, he brushed a quick, gentle kiss across Bertram's lips, then released him and stood up quickly.

"I should finish dressing you, if you are to talk to the Robertsons about John."

Bertram moved to the window seat with a spring in his step, happy that James had kissed him again. He did not think it was the sign that James was ready, but it was a start. He had told the man to be obvious, a quick kiss after comforting him was not obvious. James started to tie his cravat for him and suddenly his head shot up from his task and he looked at Bertram in horror.

"What? What is it?"

"Rebecca Robertson will be devastated. Many of the women staff were saying how much she perked up after John arrived and Jacky coaxed him out from under that bunk. They thought the couple were thinking of taking him in, as their own."

"They cannot, he will have to return to his family in Horncastle." James looked confused at that and Bertram realised why. "It is the town closest to my family's home, that is why I chose it as my last name. It is about a day's ride northeast of Eastease."

"Perhaps Mrs. Ackley should be with Rebecca when you talk to her? She took Davy in, she will understand how Rebecca feels about it." He returned his attention to the cravat.

"Yes, very astute, James. Do you think you could ask her to meet me in the breakfast room? Is she awake?"

"She was not when I looked into the dressing room. Nora was there waiting for her. She should want to be woken for this I believe. She is close to Rebecca, because she is very close to Jacky's mother, Ruth Robertson. She is Mrs. Ackley's housekeeper." The cravat was finished and he held up Bertram's waistcoat and then coat.

"Thank you, James." With a quick, cheeky smile, James pecked him on the cheek and walked quickly out of the room and back to the Ackleys.

Mr. Horncastle had apprised Mrs. Ackley of the circumstances regarding the medallion over breakfast, and now they sat in his study waiting for Jacky and Rebecca Robertson to attend them there. Mr. Horncastle sat behind the desk and Mrs. Ackley on a chair to the side. The couple entered, Rebecca with rather more trepidation than her husband. She had wondered if they were angry with her for doing so little over the last few weeks. She had returned to work as Isabella's lady's maid, but at the request of Mrs. Ackley, had not continued in her aid as Nora was doing well with the work. The rest of her time was spent planning how to move forward with Wyndham Lodge and caring for John, for he would rarely let either herself or Jacky leave him. He was only allowing it now as Mr. Mckinnon whom he also trusted and Miss Cadman the friendly cook had promised him more cake.

Surprisingly, Mr. Horncastle indicated that they should sit on the chairs on the opposite side of the desk to him and as Rebecca sat in the one nearest Mrs. Ackley, that lady shifted her chair towards her slightly.

"I am sure you are wondering why I asked to speak with you both this morning," the little man began. Although he did not smile, his face was open and friendly, which put Rebecca at her ease a little. "I wanted to show you this." He placed the medallion that had been found under Mckinnon's bunk onto the desk and pushed it towards them with his finger, nodding at Jacky when he moved to pick it up. As the younger man looked at it his eyes widened in surprise and he looked at Mrs. Ackley.

"I have seen this crest before. It was on a carriage that came to Redway a year or so ago, they bought a set of new carriage horses. Do you remember it, Mrs. Ackley?"

"No, but I do recall the horses." He smiled at her, of course she would pay more attention to the horses.

"It is the crest of the Earl of Lorlake, that family's estate is near Horncastle, in Lincolnshire."

"Horncastle!" Jacky looked to the man astonished, "do you know of that family then, sir?" Mr. Horncastle did not reply straightaway and in his pause the quiet almost resigned voice of Rebecca was heard.

"Where did you find it, sir?"

"That is the more pressing question, is it not, my dear?" Helena could see that Rebecca had worked out why they were the ones being made privy to this information.

"It was found under the bunk in Mr. Mckinnon's office." A single sob escaped Rebecca as Mr. Horncastle said these words. "It is believed that it belongs to the boy."

"To John?" Jacky was incredulous.

"We need to ask him where he got it. If it belongs to him. I need to ask him." As he said the last part, Mr. Horncastle reached between his neck and collar and pulled out a chain. He lifted it over his head and held the medallion out in his palm for them both to see.

"If it is his, then this is his family and he must return to them." Mrs. Ackley said it gently as she placed a hand on Rebecca's arm. Her tears were running freely down her face and she pulled a handkerchief from her sleeve to dab at them. "Jacky, perhaps if you could get the boy? And Mr. Horncastle if you could give Rebecca and I a moment alone?"

"Certainly, we will return in ten minutes."

As soon as the door was closed Helena pulled Rebecca to her feet and over to the couch that lined the far wall. Once seated together she put her arms around her and pulled her head to her shoulder. Rebecca sobbed and through the tears gave way to the grief she was feeling once again.

"It is so unfair! I am to have another baby torn away from me. How many? How many before I can be a mother? I love him, Helena. I love him with all of my heart, I do not know how I can part with him and live. Why should this happen to me?"

Helena allowed her to cry and have her moment of wailing at life for its injustices, for goodness knows she had done so herself many a time. It was best to get it out there, shout out how unfair life is, and then realise that you know what you have to do to move on and love again, try again and hope again. Once the tears had subsided a little, she spoke.

"It is unfair, Rebecca. We have seen what a wonderful mother you have been to John over the past few weeks. How improved he is from the scared, rag-covered creature that hid under that bunk. That is the work and love of you and Jacky. You will both be doing a lot of this with the kind of work you will do at Wyndham House. John has helped you realise how equipped you are to accomplish it. If he is who we suspect he is, then he has a mother who misses him. She has been without him for two or three years and does not even know if he is alive or dead. He was so young he had forgotten her, but he will *never* forget you."

"Maybe she never loved him. What if she gave him to those men?"

"Mr. Horncastle does not think so and you know I would not have sold horses to people who would give over a child to such men." She smiled down at the woman who was resting her head on her shoulder.

"His mother must feel sick to her stomach every day. I know I should. I am sure I shall!"

"You will miss him, but you will know that he is safe with them. She does not know he is safe."

"He was not safe before!"

"They will be ever more vigilant do you not think? And he is older. Now dry your eyes and be strong for him, although it is the hardest thing you will ever do. It is what we mothers do."

Mr. Horncastle entered the room first followed by Jacky who was holding tight to the hand of John. Seeing Rebecca's tearstained face, the little boy slipped his hand out of Jacky's grasp and ran to her. He grasped her face in his hands. "You've been crying, what's wrong? You will not send me back! Don't send me back!" He made to bolt for the door, but Jacky had closed it and stood firm in front of it.

"Do not take on so, John. We would never do that." Jacky spoke in his soft voice, calmly and kindly. John grabbed the man's leg and calmed down as a large hand came down onto his head to ruffle his hair. Then Jacky grasped his shoulders and pushed him gently back, so he could crouch down and look into John's face as he talked to him. "Please listen to what Mr. Horncastle has to say and answer his questions as best as you can." John returned to the couch and sat as close to Rebecca as he could. She clasped his hand in hers and squeezed reassuringly.

Seeing everyone was staying on the couch, Bertram Horncastle walked back around his desk and pulled up one of the chairs to sit facing them. Jacky did the same with the other chair. Bertram looked at the boy properly for the first time and was surprised to notice the fair hair and blue eyes, that matched his own.

"John," he began gently, "I want to ask you about this." He held out the medallion in the palm of his hand. John reached out and snatched it from him, holding it tightly in his fist without looking at it first. It was obviously his but Mr. Horncastle asked him anyway.

"Does that belong to you?"

"Yes, it is mine, you cannot have it. I hid it, why did you take it?"

"The maids were cleaning under the bunk and found it. I do not want it, as you can see, I have my own." Again, he pulled his own medallion out from his collar, and the boy studied it. He then opened his fist to check what was there was his.

"It is the same."

"Yes, it is. How did you come by yours?"

"It is mine. I did not want the man to take it, so I hid it. Where did you get yours?"

"It was given to me when I was a baby, as yours should have been given to you. I suspect I might be your uncle."

"If you were my family, you should know me. You do not know me."

"My father, your grandfather, was ashamed of me and sent me away."

"Because you are little?"

"Yes."

"I am little."

"You are supposed to be little, you are a boy. I should imagine your mother is very worried about you and wonders if she will ever see you again." John looked at Rebecca at the word mother and she smiled at him, trying hard not to break down into tears again. She had to think of his mother who must have worried and thought about him every day.

"What if she sent me away, if she does not want me? What if I do not want to stay?"

"If she does not want you, then you will always have a home here, with Jacky and me."

"What is your name? Is my name the same?"

"I do not use my family's name, which is Frammington. Does that sound familiar?" John shook his head. "My name is Bertram Horncastle."

"Bertie!"

"Yes, I am sometimes known as Bertie."

"My name is Bertie. I remember it now." He stole another look at Rebecca who smiled, "I did like being called John though."

"It can be our secret name for you then, but we should call you Bertie if that is acceptable to you." Rebecca was looking at the boy and did not see Helena move to put out a hand to Bertram, who had put his face in his hand and was rubbing his thumb and forefinger over his eyes. She squeezed his other hand and he looked towards her, his tears visible.

"My brother remembered me."

"Yes, he did, and he thought enough of you to name his son after you."

"That must have upset my father." He gave a little chuckle at that and got himself under control again. "The question is, what to do next? I suggest I write to my brother advising him we have John, I mean Bertie. Then I recommend we travel back to Lincolnshire with you and your husband tomorrow, Mrs. Ackley." Everyone agreed, though the boy looked to Jacky first before nodding.

The rest of the day was busy as they prepared for their guests. Harriet and Bertram would be the hosts, and of course Nathaniel and Helena would attend, too. The Baron and Baroness Freyley were their distinguished guests and were bringing Mr. Collingworth and his sister with them. They were the first to arrive and were shown into the new parlour. As the evening was warm, refreshments were served outside in the courtyard before dinner. Baroness Freyley approved greatly as did her husband who much preferred to be outside.

The other guests joined them as they arrived. This time Mr. Ashman and Mr. Milford brought their wives with them. Mr. Chapple brought his sister and Mr. Holder and Mr. Leake arrived on their horses. Everyone planned to stay the night at Wyndham House.

Baron Freyley was very interested to learn about the stable that the Ackleys ran in Lincolnshire. As he discussed it with the colonel, Helena sat with them and added her comments to the conversation whenever possible. The baron was thrilled at this handsome lady knowing so much about horses and very happy to discover himself seated next to her at the dining table.

To the baron's other side, Harriet sat at the head of the table. Bertram sat opposite her at the other end and they exchanged looks and smiles often, as the conversation was lively and amiable. Harriet had ensured that Mr. Collingworth was seated at her other side. Since their meeting at the fireworks, and after his shooting with Nathaniel and Mr. Horncastle, they had seen each other only a handful of times more.

He had visited alone and gone shooting again with Nathaniel and Bertram. He had also arrived impromptu one morning when she was at her pianoforte, he had apologised for interrupting her, but had declined to listen to her efforts, instead he had accepted the offer of refreshments. She had danced with him at a local assembly, but not before she had raised many eyebrows as she danced gracefully with Mr. Horncastle, and Helena had danced with Nathaniel. Men with missing limbs dancing at events at Eastease or Bernier House was not considered unusual, but it had not been seen in this society.

She found Mr. Collingworth amusing and was certainly aware that he was interested in her, which she found flattering. She felt that her life in Lincolnshire had been somewhat sheltered, which was of her own choosing. Along with the attentions of Luke Parker, she had never wanted for a dance partner at Eastease's balls. At the last of those the previous Christmas, she had danced with several soldiers with wooden legs, including Nathaniel, although some of those men seemed to have an interest in her, she felt they did not pursue it as they were unsure of her regard given their altered physicality.

Since her mistake with Robert Davenport, she had decided that she may never marry. However, if she were to, then it would have to be a man who understood exactly who and what she was, as well as a man who should share Wyndham House with her, not take it over. In the few short weeks they had been there, she had come to love it and considered it her home. That man should also have to be accepting of Bertram Horncastle, because she had come to care for the little man as much as any family member.

"Mr. Horncastle looks to you often, Miss Wyndham. Am I to think there is an understanding between you?" Mr. Collingworth had noticed the looks exchanged between them.

"Only in that he is now Wyndham House's Estate Manager and advises me in all things to do with it."

"Well until you marry at least, I imagine your husband should not feel the need of his services."

"Why not? Mr. Horncastle has lived here many years and kindly took care of this place quite admirably after my uncle's death. Regardless, if I were to marry, my husband could not dismiss him. I have made it legally impossible. Wyndham House is Bertram Horncastle's home for the rest of his life." Mr. Collingworth looked astonished, but said nothing. Instead he changed the subject.

"I heard that Wyndham Lodge has had a lot of attention paid to it lately. Will Mr. Horncastle be moving there?"

"No, not at all. It will be used for orphans to be cared for and to learn to become servants in houses such as this. Also, young ladies who are in dire situations will live there. They can teach the children to read and write, and the children can practise their service skills on the ladies. It is all rather exciting. Several families have committed to provide payment to assist the venture, including the baron here." She gestured to her left.

"Why on earth would you house such a place so close to Wyndham House and on your own land? Why not give the money you are spending to the poor houses and keep them off your property?"

"My sister and I were motherless by the time we were six and orphans when we were nine. Were it not for the dedication of Mr. Harker and Colonel Ackley as our guardians, we would have had nowhere to go and no one to love us. This will provide a place for girls in the same situation as we were. At the same time, it will give hope to children who are homeless. I am surprised that you think it not a good undertaking."

"You are quite right, Miss Wyndham. It is very altruistic of you. I assure you I was thinking of nothing more than your safety and peace of mind." She smiled at him.

The ladies awaited the gentlemen in the new music room. All of the ladies had exclaimed at how pretty it was and when the gentlemen entered, Mr. Leake and Mr. Holder were nodding to each other and Mr. Chapple had exclaimed, "At last, Miss Wyndham. I had admonished Phillip often of his choice of that other room for his instruments."

"This room is much better as a parlour as it was before, is it not? The view is superior to the other room we were in earlier," Mr. Collingworth added his opinion.

"I found, Mr. Collingworth, that the sound quality in this room is *far* superior to any other room in the house and selfishly chose it as my own." She moved to the pianoforte and played the first two measures of the piece she was planning to perform.

"My word, Miss Wyndham, you are quite correct, I had never noticed." Mr. Chapple walked towards her. "May I?" He tinkled a few notes and continued to nod. Then he spied the music she had been playing and picked up the pages. "Who wrote this? It is nothing I have seen before."

"I... um," Harriet looked towards Mr. Horncastle, unsure what to say. These men would never believe it if she said she had done it.

"Her brother sent her the pages," Bertram spoke up seeing the uneasiness in her expression. "He travels abroad and has not been back in England in years. Sent these pages from America I believe."

"But it is titled *'Helena's moods'*, does he know Mrs. Ackley?"

"She heard me playing it and said she felt it an angry mood that was washed away and replaced with sunshine. He had not titled it, so I did it for him."

"Would you play it for us?" She nodded and held her hand out for the pages. Mr. Chapple had continued to review them and handed her only the piano piece, keeping the pages for the other instruments.

"He sent me those pieces, too, saying he had toyed with adding other instruments to it. I do not think it is finished."

"Perhaps you would allow me and my fellows here to review them? We play in our own group, during the season we get many offers for performances in town." She nodded, embarrassed, but shook herself. Everyone sat in the chairs and on couches arranged in the room and she started to play. Bertram sat in his usual chair and smiled as she lost her inhibitions and lost herself in the piece. Nathaniel, who had not known the name of the piece when he had heard it before, looked to his wife, who smiled at him as the music seemed to wind around them. The morning of their argument came into his mind with the fast pace and loud notes. He imagined Helena riding over the wet fields and falling off the horse, only to lie sobbing into the ground. There was a back and forth in the piece as notes were repeated, loud and angry then soft and appealing, until the soft and appealing won.

At that point in the piece, Mr. Chapple, who had walked over to where a violin and bow were set on a stand and picked them up, and Mr. Holder, who had picked up the flute, started playing from the pages Mr. Chapple had been reviewing. Their music soared and complemented the pianoforte, the flute with some light and bright tones, while the violin added to the poignancy of the piece after the stormy beginning.

Harriet did not look up or falter in her playing, in her mind she heard the pieces she had written for the violin and the flute as clearly as if they had been played in the room and so as she played the last few notes, she started at seeing the two men standing and playing. Her heart leapt at how perfect the piece had sounded with the added instruments. In that moment, she could not have been happier.

"Your brother is a most talented man, Miss Wyndham. What a shame he is travelling, we need a pianist for our group. If he were to write more pieces, we could play them. They, and consequently we, should be very popular I am sure."

With his words, her heart and spirits plummeted to the floor and it felt as if he were stamping upon them. Bertram saw it in her countenance as if she had told him, but the other man had no idea his words hurt her. Why should he? "Excuse me My Lord, My Lady, ladies, gentlemen, I feel a little queasy. I will return shortly." Harriet rushed out of the room and Helena hurried after her, putting her hands out to both her husband and Mr. Horncastle to stay them as she passed.

She caught up to Harriet in the corridor and hurried her to the farthest point and into Harriet's study. "Harriet, your music is truly wonderful. How thrilled you must have been to have those two gentlemen play it with you."

"I was, until I was not."

"Mr. Chapple's comments about wanting your 'brother' to play with them hurt, when you wanted to be the one asked to play. They will never ask you."

"I know, but why did Mr. Horncastle say I had a brother?"

"I expect he knew they would not really listen to the piece if they thought you had written it, nor would they have played it with you. They may have even thought you were lying."

"Oh why is it so unfair on women? Why do they think I cannot compose, when I certainly can? Why am I not allowed to perform in public with their group? You heard how good it sounded. It is so easy for you, because Nathaniel accepts you for who you are. He respects your opinion on horses and allows you to do as you please."

"Do not say it is easy for me, Harriet. That is not fair. Living with Nathaniel is often not easy at all, and I am sure he would say the same of me. It took a lot for me to earn the respect and trust of that man. I still have to tolerate men always talking to him about the stable and only deigning to allow me into the conversation once I have proved my knowledge several times. Look at Lord Freyley tonight, he still looks at my breasts rather than my face when he talks to me, even though he has established how knowledgeable I am. I think he hopes they might actually reply!"

Harriet let out a laugh at that. "I am sorry, Helena. I was so frustrated, I spoke without thinking. You are such a good example for me. I love you so much and am so happy you are in my life."

"I am very proud of you, Harriet. Look at how much you are doing and achieving here. Mr. Brooks is very satisfied with everything you are doing and Mr. Horncastle is very supportive. Now, you must continue to make me proud and get back in that room with your spine of steel in place. Show everyone why you are in charge of this estate."

"Are you ready to sing, Helena?"

"Yes, we will let Leonore inspire us, shall we? We had better hurry or Nathaniel will have them all singing, *'Oh No, John'*!"

Chapter Sixteen

It had been a most pleasant evening. After everyone had left to go to their own beds, Bertram had gone to his study to think the day through. It had begun with his conversation with little Bertie, and his discovery that his own brother had named his son after him. He had written his letter to the Viscount shortly after that, but had advised he should not reply. He had stressed that they should not travel to Bath, as he was leaving for Lincolnshire with friends the next day and would bring Bertie with him.

He had known, when he had said it, that Harriet Wyndham was not happy about her made up brother, but he had known the men should dismiss Harriet's composition if she declared it her own. At least this way they had accepted it, embraced it even. If she were a man, there would have been no question. He might have even desired her as a man, but no, James came into his mind at that moment and he realised there was only one man in this household he wanted.

At the thought of James, he pushed himself to his feet. He wondered how long it would be before James was ready, but regardless, he wanted to see him again. He had kissed him once more prior to dinner. It had been a little more ardent than the kisses that morning, but not quite the same as that first passionate kiss.

He opened his door and came to an abrupt halt at the sight that greeted him. The feeling inside him was as he had felt when he had first come nose to nose with his black Friesian, Duke. He wanted. Differing from his first sight of the horse, however, this want was physical as well. He wanted in such a primal way, he was surprised he did not growl and leap across the room to devour. Deliberately, and in an effort to control his desire, he turned and locked the door.

James stood in the room near the foot of the bed. He was barefooted and bare-chested. His only clothing the black trousers that were part of his uniform. The muscles in his arms and across his chest were smooth and his stomach gently ridged. His body tapered to the waist and his trousers lay flat on his stomach.

"James," Bertram whispered.

"Is this obvious enough?"

"Yes, yes, it is," but Bertram could still do nothing but stand there and drink in the sight.

"Is there something wrong? I can leave if..."

"No, James, I do not want you to leave, but are you sure? If I come over there, I want you to be sure."

"I am sure, Bertram."

He walked over to him then and put a hand flat on his chest, which was at his head height. The man's flesh quivered under his touch. James put his own hand over Bertram's and made to pull him to the window seat. "No, sit here." Bertram pushed him onto the ottoman at the end of the bed and stood between his legs. He grasped his face between his hands and started kissing him. The feel of the man's rough skin, with a day's beard growth, against his own thrilled him and he moved his hands from James' face and into his hair as the kiss built in his hunger.

Bertram moved the kisses down James neck, nipping as he progressed towards his collarbone and shoulders. He felt greedy, he wanted all of this man at once, everything, but he kept his control. He did not want to frighten him away again. His hands had moved with him out of James' hair and onto his chest and round his back.

"Let me see you." James busied his capable hands and quickly stripped off Bertram's coat, waistcoat and cravat. Then he undid the top buttons of his shirt and started pulling it out of his trousers before Bertram stopped him.

The ottoman was lower than the bed and he pushed James back so he rested his elbows on the counterpane spread across its foot.

"You are beautiful." With that, Bertram laid his body along James' and set his mouth to work on the smooth almost hairless skin of his chest. His groin pushed up against James' as he rubbed himself against the man's hardness. He groaned as he moved, enjoying the moans of desire he brought out in James, too.

He unbuttoned James trousers and tugged at them as he released him, then he stepped back as he pulled them off his legs. He stood a pace or two away, with the trousers in one hand and stared at the man. His appreciation must have shown in his face, as James, who still laid back with his legs outstretched, had a smile on his handsome face. He appreciated his own view of a dishevelled and captivated Bertram. The shorter man's hair was ruffled where James had run his hands through it, the buttons of his shirt were undone, and it hung half out of his trousers. James could see the man's more considerable chest hair protruding from the gaping neck of the fabric.

Dropping the trousers on the floor, Bertram walked slowly towards James and stood between his legs again. Keeping eye contact with him, he reached down to stroke the long length of him, before wrapping his hand around him and moving it firmly, but tantalisingly slowly. James closed his eyes, feeling sensations run over him as Bertram leaned forward and started kissing his chest and running his tongue over that smooth skin and down James' stomach. Bending down onto one knee, Bertram took him into his mouth. He licked and sucked him, allowing his lips and teeth to rub gently against him each time he took him in.

James groaned and Bertram looked up from his vocation, enjoying the pleasure on the face of this innocent man, knowing that this was something he never felt before. When James was spent, Bertram kissed and licked over his quivering body, before allowing him to recover somewhat while he stripped off his own remaining clothes. James watched him, smiling at Bertram fumbling a little, as the humour of the situation appeased his nerves over what was to come.

They climbed onto the bed, arms wrapping around bodies as their lips sought each other again. James enjoyed the smoky taste of Bertram after his cigar that evening, and Bertram the soapy smell of James that had become so familiar. James ran a hand from Bertram's back, down his side and between them, he looked into Bertram's beautiful eyes as he took him into his hand to return some of the pleasure he had been given.

Bertram relished the feeling of another's hands over his body, it had been too long since he had experienced it. James had a deft touch, but he wanted more from him. Sensing Bertram's desire increasing, James turned his back, he knew what Bertram wanted. He was not sure how much he should enjoy it, but he wanted to be taken, to give himself to him.

Bertram reached over him to the small table near the bed where there was a small jar of the miracle cream, scooping out a finger of it, he applied it between James' buttocks before positioning himself to enter him.

James tensed. "Relax James, it will be more enjoyable." Bertram leaned forward and bit James on the shoulder, just enough of a nip to distract him. He pushed himself into him and moved gently, allowing him to get used to the sensation. When he heard James' groans of pleasure, he thrust into him more. His own pleasure mounting quickly as he had waited these past weeks for James and finally was permitted to take him. As he peaked he groaned his name.

They lay together in the bed. The sheets barely covering them. Their legs entwined, enjoying the feel of their naked bodies lying together. The night before, when Bertram had interrupted them, Drum had considered himself a fortunate man. His control in his 'lessons' to Fiona Cadman was slipping and he had been sure, if the knock on the door had not come, he would have taken her before she became his wife. What was wrong with him?

Now he lay with a naked Fi in his arms and decided there was nothing wrong with him. He loved her, she loved him, and they were to be married. She had been willing, though he knew he had used his skills to make her receptive to him. He had given her a choice before he had penetrated her, but he knew he had brought her to the point of such pleasure that she could not refuse him.

She was so different from what he remembered Senga being. She had been a wild animal he was taming, whereas Fiona was a virgin he was teaching. She was not a virgin any longer, but he still had plenty to teach her. That thought had him hardening again and he wondered how she would feel about a repeat performance. He pulled her on top of him and started kissing her again.

James lay in Bertram's embrace, his head on his chest. He could not believe how his life had turned out since leaving Eastease. He had found a man he cared for deeply, loved, probably, and that man cared for him it would seem. Cared enough to want him to stay at Wyndham House with him. Cared enough to tell him about his past before he told anyone else. Cared enough to take his time showing him what they had just experienced together.

"Why did you decide to come to Wyndham House and stay here, James? You said you told your mother not to expect you to return with the colonel."

"It was a man named Mr. Robert Davenport. I think you might know him."

Bertram closed his eyes at the mention of this man again. Even in death he haunted him. Then his eyes snapped open and he grasped James hair in a tight fist, pulling the man's head off his chest. It was a visceral reaction to the thought that had crossed his mind and put fear in his heart. He looked into those surprised brown eyes and found a demand cross his lips in a tone he did not expect.

"What is he to you? What did that man do to you? Did he touch you?"

James smiled at him, looking at the anger and jealousy clear on Bertram's face and recognising it as the same as his own the other night. "No, he is nothing, he did nothing. Are you jealous?"

Bertram still held his hair and harrumphed. "No, of course not!" He was relieved beyond measure and pulled James' head down to him and kissed him hard, possessively. Then he released him and conceded. "Possibly. No more than you. *'Bang the Drum'* indeed!"

James smiled a little sheepishly, but remained with his head up above the other man resting his elbows either side of him effectively trapping him there. Unconcerned, Bertram put his arms above his head and listened as James told him of his interaction with Robert Davenport.

227

It was in April of 1812 when Robert Davenport had arrived at Eastease. The twins, Harriet and Maria Wyndham, had turned sixteen that day and the ball to celebrate their birthday was to be the coming weekend. An invitation to the ball was extended to Mr. Davenport, which he duly accepted and he was permitted to stay at Eastease during that time. He had been to Eastease many times, as his father lived in a manor house nearby and he had grown up friends with Mr. Harker and the colonel.

The colonel had arrived that night and the following day, wishing to wash off the dirt of the road, he took a bath. James was attending his needs while he was in the bathtub, when a rather dishevelled and irate Davenport had burst into the room...

"I cannot believe it, Ackers! Did you know? Tell me you did not know." The colonel did not react directly, but when he saw the distraught look on his friend's face, he stood to get out of the tub.

"What is it, Robert?"

"No, nothing, Nathaniel. I did not know you were taking a bath, forgive me." James had been startled by the look he saw in Davenport's face when his anger had subsided as he took in the dripping-wet form of a naked Nathaniel Ackley. If he had attempted to put words to that look, he should have said it was a mix of lust and desperation. Averting his eyes, Davenport saw James looking at him and sneered, before making a quick excuse and leaving the room.

When James had dressed the colonel, he headed down to the far end of the east wing where the narrow servant's staircase was hidden. To get to it he had to pass the doors to several rooms, including that of Davenport who was leaning in the doorway with his back up against the door to keep it open and his feet up against the opposite side.

"Dawley, is it not?" James stopped and looked at him.

"Yes, sir." As quick as lightening Robert Davenport's hand shot out and grabbed James by his collar, pulling him into the room and closing the door. He turned him and pushed him up against the wall, pressing his own body along James back with his groin up against his behind.

"Whatever you think you saw, you did not. Understand?"

"Yes, sir. I saw nothing."

"If you say anything I will deny it and say you propositioned me.

They will believe me before they believe you. Then I will come to your room and put a pillow over your face while you are sleeping. Do you understand?" To demonstrate his ability to overpower James, he pushed his elbow between James' shoulder blades and pressed him hard into the wall. It became hard for him to draw a breath and he was starting to panic when the pressure was released. He gratefully took in a breath.

"Yes, sir," he croaked. Davenport released him, and he turned to look at the man. He wanted to run away, but was afraid he might provoke another attack. Davenport looked him up and down and then gave him a sneering smile.

"Have you ever been touched, Dawley?" James' eyes widened, but he said nothing. "A good friend of mine at Wyndham House near Bath should pay good money for an innocent. Here is my card, contact me if you should wish to travel. I can introduce you and make sure you get a good piece of that money."

"I don't think I would be interested, sir. Thank you."

"You should reconsider. Who will you meet in this backend of nothing? My friend has a lot of friends. I could introduce you." He laughed then, and James ran out of that room and down the stairs.

After that confrontation, he kept his distance from Robert Davenport. Mostly he kept to the colonel's rooms and slept in the dressing room that adjoined his room, making sure the door was locked. When he did have to go downstairs, he used the main stairs, even though it was not permitted. A reprimand from Watkins, the butler, was preferable to another confrontation with Davenport.

"I am sorry, Bertram, but just because Davenport said your friend would have wanted me, doesn't mean it is true."

"No, he was right. Phillip was a man of many appetites and I was not enough for him. I loved him, though he loved Davenport."

"And Davenport loved the colonel."

"So I have been given to understand. If that man was not dead, I would kill him myself for what he did to you."

James smiled. "I love you for saying so." Bertram did not say anything, so he continued. "Had he not spoken to me of Wyndham House, I should not have known to come here or set my mind to staying, hoping I might meet someone who understood me."

Knowing he had disappointed James by not saying he loved something about him, too, Bertram aimed to keep favour with him. "I will be travelling to Lincolnshire with the Ackleys tomorrow. Will you come with me? I will be seeing my family again and I feel I will need your support and comfort."

"Yes, of course. Do I ask too much to introduce you to my mother? She knows what I am, but we do not speak of it. I would not tell her directly what we are to each other, but she is astute and will know. She only wishes for me to be happy."

"I would be honoured to meet her. We already have something in common." James raised questioning eyebrows at that. "I only wish for you to be happy."

"Then would you permit me to take you, as you just took me?"

"It is not my preference, but I think you should experience it. Firstly, tell me this. How well does the colonel look dripping-wet and naked?" James slapped at Bertram's chest for that and he laughed.

"He never appealed to me as he did to Robert Davenport."

"And why is that?"

"He is too tall."

In the morning, final preparations were in full swing to organise travel back to Lincolnshire. With Charlie Mickleson and Jacky Robertson both planning to stay at Wyndham House, Nathaniel and Helena had wondered how they should transport all their belongings, two carriages, the cart and all their horses, including the newly acquired ones, back with them. However, with the discovery of the young Bertie Frammington's identity, and his attachment to them, Jacky and Rebecca Robertson had asked to travel with him and return with Mr. Horncastle and James, so they could continue with their plans for Wyndham Lodge.

The two carriages they had arrived with were from Redway and Eastease. The cart that had been driven by Peter Robinson and pulled by Colossus their Shire, was also from Redway. There were enough of them now to get all three vehicles back to Lincolnshire, but Mr. Horncastle would need a carriage for the return journey. Mickleson suggested to Miss Wyndham that they buy the cart from the Ackleys and they could take three carriages instead, bringing the Wyndham carriage back with

Mr. Horncastle. They needed a new cart anyway, as he had discovered in his inventory of the stable. He suggested, hopeful, that they leave the Shire in his care as well, as he loved to ride that magnificent beast, but Helena would not part with him. Miss Wyndham promised him if they could find another Shire, she would buy it for him.

Peter Robinson surprisingly requested an audience with Miss Wyndham and Colonel Ackley and they met with him that morning shortly after all these decisions had been made. He entered Miss Wyndham's study with his cap in his hands and politely asked if Nora Smith might be joining the Ackleys now that Miss Isabella needed a new lady's maid. Nathaniel had said he assumed Mrs. Ackley should search for one upon their return when Rebecca Robertson returned with Mr. Horncastle.

Peter explained how he and Nora had been talking and as she had no other family, she wished to travel with him back to his home. He wanted to introduce her to his family, but she did not want to leave without work to go to. He wanted to ask if they should consider her for Miss Isabella's ladies maid, if Miss Wyndham would be willing to part with her.

Additionally, he asked, if the colonel was pleased with his work on this trip, whether he could be considered for work at Redway, now that Mr. Mickleson planned to stay at Wyndham House.

Miss Wyndham agreed that if Nora Smith wished to travel back to Lincolnshire, she would certainly be willing to part with her and she left the other decisions to the colonel. Nathaniel had said that he should talk to his wife and let Peter know. Harriet had smiled a little at that. She had been free to make the decision straightaway, but Nathaniel was not!

When Peter had left them alone, Harriet broached a subject with Nathaniel of which she was unsure. "What do you make of Mr. Collingworth, Nathaniel?" She had wondered what he thought of the man because she had felt that he had an interest in her and she was unsure of her feelings. She easily recalled how she had been deceived by Robert Davenport and did not wish to be so again by another man.

"Why do you ask me, Harriet? I do not know what a woman looks for in a man."

"No, but you can tell me if you think him trustworthy. Do you think he would be the kind of man who should allow me to make decisions? I see you and Helena together and you discuss the business of Redway Acres, you value her opinions and listen to her. I wonder if Mr. Collingworth is that kind of man. I have expressed my opinions with him and even disagreed with him on occasion and he has tolerated it well, but I wonder if he would be the kind of man who should continue to do so if he were married."

"I was a very different man when I first met Helena. I did not behave in the way I do now, not even after we were first married, but she has worked on me and pointed out things to me in the way that only Helena can. She has changed me for the better, but I was only willing to change because I love her. I love her so much that I would do anything for her, I would die for her. I do like to think that I have changed her, too. Her behaviour at the fair here is an example of how I have changed her. She will never be so reckless again and I am thankful, but the process of change is painful and you both have to be willing.

If you think that a man loves you so much that he would be willing to die for you. Then I believe that he should be willing to change for you."

"How would I know that though?"

"Think of your deepest secret, if you feel able to share that with a man and that he would take that secret to the grave with him, then you can trust him. If you cannot share that with him, he is not the man for you. Do you trust Bertram Horncastle?"

"Yes, in fact, I have already told him about Maria."

"So, you have learned to trust a man other than me and Harker. That is a good start. Ask Bertram about Mr. Collingworth, or any other man that might be interested in you. You have an awful lot to offer someone and I do not only mean Wyndham House, but *you*. Make sure any man you decide to marry is interested in you, not only what you own." He pulled her to him and kissed her forehead, blinking away a tear or two.

Finally, they were ready. They had been at Wyndham House for six weeks and much had occurred. The people and horses that had travelled together had changed considerably more than they had expected. Three carriages with their horses lined the driveway of the enormous house, one each from Redway, Eastease and Wyndham House. Peter Robinson sat atop the one from Redway with Nora Smith sitting at his side. That carriage was packed with all their supplies and luggage. Jacky Robinson and James sat atop the one from Wyndham House. Their passengers were Bertram Horncastle, the young Bertie Frammington and Rebecca Robertson. Nathaniel drove the Eastease carriage, with Helena and the children as his passengers.

Tethered to the carriages were their various horses, Pegasus, Colossus and Coal, that they had brought with them. In addition, were the two whites and Isabella's white-grey. With so many additional animals, Helena had decided to give Henry, Maria Wyndham's horse who was so similar to Harriet's own Hudson, to Harriet. Mr. Brooks had left him in the care of Redway, asking only for a horse in return when Maria's son was old enough to ride. With tears in her eyes, Harriet had accepted gratefully. It should be a slow journey, especially with the foal not being able to travel such long distances as the older horses, but they should reach their destination eventually.

Helena had said a heartfelt goodbye to Charlie Mickleson. He would be sorely missed at Redway Acres, but Harriet Wyndham had gained a considerable asset in hiring him. She had also wished Drummond Mckinnon and his new wife-to-be all the best things in their new life together and had reminded him that if he was ever in need, he had only to reach out to her and he would receive all the help she could give him.

Harriet had said tearful goodbyes to everyone, embracing them all. Especially her guardian, Nathaniel, who had insisted on telling Mckinnon and Mickleson in no uncertain terms that he would hold them responsible if anything were to happen to her before Mr. Horncastle returned. She had thanked Helena and that woman had held her and told her to believe in herself and her capability to keep this household. Davy had not cried of course, but Helena had seen his lip wobble a little. Harriet was a favourite at Redway. Isabella had cried copiously and had promised to write a story about Henry and Hudson that she would send to Harriet.

Lastly, Harriet had turned to Bertram Horncastle. "Will you write to me, Bertram?" He had been surprised but pleased at her use of his given name, and took the liberty implied and did the same.

"Of course I will, Harriet. I will miss Wyndham House, but more so because you are in it than I should have if I had left before. I will inform the Harkers and Mr. Brooks of all your success here, and will promise to them that I will do all that is in my power to help you. I am sorry to have to leave you, but I must see young Bertie into the hands of my brother personally."

"I wish you all the luck in the world in returning to your home."

"Wyndham House is my home, you have made it so and I am eternally grateful to you."

"Then come home soon, Bertram."

Chapter Seventeen

Harriet had stood watching as the last of the carriages and horses drove down the long Wyndham House driveway and out of sight, then she stood looking at the empty horizon for a full minute more before turning back to the house. Unsurprisingly, Drummond Mckinnon stood at the door waiting for her, as a sentry. She wiped at the tears on her cheeks and smiled at him.

"Well, Mckinnon, I had better make a start!" He smiled and nodded in return.

The first task she had set herself was to look into every room in the house. In each room, she inspected each cupboard and looked at each view. She had drawn herself a map and named each room as she went. Most of the main floor rooms she had looked into already, but with Bertram there, she had felt a little odd about poking around in case he felt she was intruding. She did not enter his personal rooms, but did look in, just to see how they looked. When Mckinnon was not attending her, she noted any questions she had to ask him and intended to make an equally thorough inspection of the outside of her new home.

In addition to this attention to the house, she rode both Hudson and Henry on alternate days and visited the other cottages on her grounds that were occupied by various members of staff. Mckinnon rode with her to those and, where occupants were available, she asked permission to view the inside. All were well maintained on the outside and well kept within. There were two empty cottages and she suggested to Mckinnon that he choose which he should move into with Fiona Cadman after their wedding.

The other available cottage she suggested that Mickleson might want to occupy. She knew that he had taken to the two boys for whom he had asked for apprenticeships and it did not seem appropriate that those boys sleep in the same quarters as the other stablemen and they should soon outgrow fitting onto Mickleson's bunk with him.

"I had thought the boys should join the Robertsons at Wyndham Lodge, Miss," Mckinnon advised her.

"Perhaps it might be an option for them, but offer Mickleson the cottage first, I think he might take the initiative."

On the days with good weather, she had ridden the boundaries of the estate. Some Nathaniel and Mr. Horncastle had ridden with her over the past month, but since their leaving, she had ridden out with Mr. Thurston, her groundskeeper. In the same vein as his wife, he was a practical man who wanted to get a job done, rather than wait, but he did at least have a sense of humour. She had to stop him several times from dismounting and start to mend a piece of fencing or in one instance start to pull branches off a fallen tree. That was not why she was out there.

Only one time did she allow him to distract her and that was when they discovered a young deer that was trapped in a deep gully. It was unable to climb out due to the mud on all sides. Thurston had some rope with him and suggested he would tie one end around a tree and then loop the other around the deer. After which, he could climb out and pull the animal up. Harriet could not see how he would be able to climb out of the gully if the deer was unable to. She could not possibly hope to pull up either the animal or Mr. Thurston. The only solution was for her to take the rope down with her. He could then pull both of them up easily.

Thurston tied a large loop in the rope that he could pull tight once it was over the animal. The important thing was to get it around the deer's middle rather than just its neck. Harriet was glad that she had chosen to ride astride and had breeches underneath her skirts. She held the rope at the loop firmly and Thurston held the other end tight to give her some support as she descended.

She slipped and slid most of the way, but managed to stay mostly upright, her skirts were quickly covered in mud. As she reached the bottom, her feet sank into several inches of mud and she was glad she had worn the taller riding boots, rather than her ankle length ones. She approached the deer cautiously, and tried several times to throw the loop over its head, but missed.

Renewed in its efforts to escape its entrapment by the presence of a human, the deer scrambled again to get up the steep slope, but to no avail. Before it tried again, Harriet flung the large loop in front of its hooves, making a circle on the ground. As it tried again to clamber up the slope, its front hooves landed within the circle, she whipped up the other side of the loop, arcing it over the deer's head. Then she pulled the end of the rope to tighten the loop.

"Well done, Miss," shouted Thurston, as he pulled on the rope. She felt he should have the more difficult task of untying the animal, but he simply pulled on an end of the knot and it unravelled instantly. Throwing the rope back down to her, he pulled her up easily. She leaned against a tree, catching her breath.

"Thank you, Thurston. I think perhaps we should return to the house and continue our survey another day. I will not be comfortable riding for long with all this mud."

Annie Brown was sure she had timed coming down to her luncheon in the staff dining room correctly, the stablemen should all be eating, with them would be Charlie Mickleson and his two shadows, the two boys that followed him everywhere. Miss Harriet had told her that Mr. Mickleson had tried to teach the boys to read and write himself, but that she planned to get a governess at Wyndham Lodge and they could learn from her. That could be weeks away, however, and Annie had decided to suggest to him that she at least start to teach them herself.

She was disappointed when she sat down at the table to see his usual place was empty. She looked at Benjamin Bramley and saw disappointment in his eyes, too. She blushed a little and gave him a sheepish smile.

"Mr. Mickleson is showing the visitor around the stable," he said by way of explanation.

"What visitor?" she asked as Mr. Mckinnon joined them at the table, sitting in Mickleson's usual spot. He had missed his luncheon with his staff due to the arrival of the visitor.

"Mr. Collingworth made an impromptu visit. I explained that Miss Wyndham was out on a ride, but he wanted to wait. I confirmed she may be sometime yet, but after waiting for half an hour he suggested a tour of the stable," the butler explained.

"Miss Harriet should probably prefer to have shown him around the stable herself, as she loves the horses so much," Annie commented.

"I did mention as much to him, but he insisted."

"Probably sizing it all up for himself," Fiona Cadman who was bringing over their trays of food with her staff, could not help saying her piece.

"Miss Cadman, those are comments probably best not mentioned with smaller ears around."

"Who has small ears?" asked Arnie. He and Richie had been sent in for their luncheon by Mickleson, under the supervision of Benjamin.

"You!" Benjamin laughed. "Small ears, but a big nose! Now get eating, you do not have long for it." Arnie laughed as Benjamin swiped at an ear and Annie smiled at Richie.

"You can tell Mr. Mickleson he can come and eat with me and the girls here or I can have a tray sent out to him." Annie did not miss the smile and look that passed between two of the girls who had just set down trays of food and tea. They walked away arguing about who would sit next to him when he did come in for lunch. Miss Cadman scolded them, "no arguing you two, he has two sides, right and left, same as any regular man. If he is fool enough to let you, you can sit either side of him."

Charlie Mickleson was indeed showing Mr. Collingworth around the Wyndham stable, but he took no pleasure in it. He was tired and hungry. He had spent much of the night waking and checking on one of the dams they had bought at the fair. He was sure she was about to foal and he did not want to miss it in case she got into difficulties. In the early hours, she had finally brought a colt into the world without any aid from him. Shortly after that the men had come lumbering into the stable to start the process of cleaning out the stalls before having their breakfast. He had joined in that work and then seen to saddling Miss Wyndham's horse. They still needed a few more hands to be at full complement, but for now they did not have Mr. Horncastle's stallion or the horses that were pulling that Wyndham carriage, so they could manage. The majority of the stalls were cleaned prior to them heading to luncheon.

He had been walking with the men to the kitchen when Mckinnon had arrived at the stable with Mr. Collingworth in tow. He had known there was a visitor as one of the men had been dispatched to take that man's horse from him when he went into the house. That horse, a fine gelding, if a little old, was enjoying a happy stay within the stable. Mckinnon had requested he show the man around the stable and Charlie looked once towards the kitchen and the smell of food, before acquiescing. He was disappointed as Annie Brown had been at mealtimes with them often lately and he did enjoy looking upon her. The two boys liked to talk to her and he wished he could be as free as they were and talk to her himself, but his tongue got all twisted up when he looked at her.

His resentment grew as he showed the man around. He obviously had no understanding of how a stable should be run and criticised much of their arrangements, even when Charlie explained the reasoning behind his decisions and Miss Wyndham's own preferences. He showed him the dam and new foal and Collingworth reached out to stroke the colt.

"I would not do that, sir, if you would not mind. It is best if the dam smells only herself and the colt, so she does not reject him. It is still early in the process for her."

"I fail to see that it should make any difference."

Collingworth's look would have cowed many servants, but Charlie simply placed himself between the man and the stall. If he was honest, he was not sure that what he said was true. He liked to give a dam and foal peace as much as possible for the first two days and let nature take its course, only intervening if necessary.

However, understanding how Miss Wyndham felt about her horses, he felt this man's presence in the stable, without even her knowledge, was an intrusion or even a liberty, and it did not sit well in his gut. He saw indignation cross Collingworth's face as he straightened and rose to his full height, but though he was a little taller than Mickleson, he could not intimidate a man who was twice his breadth. Luckily, there was a commotion heard outside.

Harriet was taken aback by the sight of Mr. Collingworth standing outside her stable as she rode up with Thurston. She was riding astride of course and her face was flushed. She had been thrilled to rescue the deer and could not wait to tell Helena of it in her next letter. Happiness shone out of her, but the disapproval on Collingworth's face dimmed it immediately. As Mickleson approached to take Hudson's reins for her, he thought it was as if a cloud covered the sun.

She threw them to him and dismounted easily, jumping to the ground. Her skirts were thick with drying mud and what he could see of her boots were caked with it, too. Mickleson turned and saw his men exit the kitchens, followed by Annie Brown carrying a luncheon tray that presumably was intended for him. He called out for Roberts, one of his recent additions and a very competent man to come over and hold the horse for him, he would fetch a brush for Miss Wyndham's boots.

"I'll get it," shouted Arnie.

"No, me! I know where it is, Mister!" shouted Richie and the boys both raced in ahead of him.

Annie, had stopped in her tracks at the sight of her mistress in such disarray and in front of a gentleman no less. Then she flew into action pressing the tray into Benjamin's hands and scurrying to Miss Wyndham's side, to brush effectually at the mud with her hands.

"Mr. Collingworth," Harriet managed over this flurry of activity, "I was not expecting to see you until the dinner at Lady Freyley's tomorrow night. I apologise that I am not in any state to receive you correctly."

"So, I see, and you ride astride!" He avoided having to explain his unexpected visit.

"Do I? Thank you for clearing that up for me," she said it with amusement, but his scowl showed her he did not think it at all amusing.

She ignored him instead and moved to the boot scraper outside the door to the stable and began scraping off as much mud as possible.

"Surely your maid can deal with that once you take them off."

"And where do you propose I take them off, sir? In my room once I have traipsed mud through the whole house? My skirts will make enough mess as it is."

"May I, Miss?" Mickleson took the brush Richie had proffered him and made to brush the mud off Harriet's boots, as she lifted her muddy skirts enough to expose the mud on the sides that she could not reach with the scraper.

"You most certainly may not! Know your place." Collingworth snatched the brush from a surprised Mickleson, who had been about to bend down. Instead of brushing off the mud himself, as Harriet had thought, in one thrilling moment, that he might, Collingworth handed the brush roughly to Annie, almost knocking her over. "Aid your mistress this instant, woman!" Mickleson took a step forward.

"Mr. Collingworth!" Harriet's commanding voice stopped them all at once. She stood to her full height and looked directly at him. "Mr. Mickleson is my stable manager. He is completely honourable and shows me nothing but respect. Annie here has been with me for nearly ten years and is perfectly capable in aiding me in everything I require. I surround myself with good, hard-working people and I would appreciate your respecting me and them by never using those kinds of words or that tone at my property again. Now, as I was not expecting you to call upon me today and as I am in no fit state to share tea with you at present, I request you leave and I look forward to seeing you tomorrow at the Freyley's dinner."

"Miss Wyndham, I hardly think it is appropriate..."

"Good day, Mr. Collingworth."

He turned on his heel, collected his horse from the stable and left. Harriet, blew out a breath and looked at each of the stunned faces surrounding her. "Well? Let us take care of this mud shall we or am I to still be caked in it when I see him at dinner tomorrow? What should he think of me then?"

"Yes, Miss." Was the chorus of voices around her, which she felt held some gratitude. She still felt she was right in her admonishment of the gentleman, but there was a knot in the pit of her stomach at the thought that he might not show her the same deference in the future. Nathaniel had said that changing someone was painful, was she beginning to realise just how painful?

Annie managed to return to the stable after seeing to the mud on Miss Wyndham's attire. Miss Cadman had not had a moment to collect Mr. Mickleson's empty luncheon tray, and she had not wanted to send one of the girls working with her as who knew how long they would take while they flirted with the man. Neither had someone from the stable brought the tray back, so Annie offered to collect it herself.

She entered his office and noticed he was laid out on the bunk asleep, she had heard he had been up in the night with a foaling. Looking down at him for a moment, she noticed his handsome face, so often scowling at her, was relaxed in repose. Not wishing to disturb him, she turned her back and walked quietly to the desk to retrieve the tray.

"Does Miss Wyndham have you working in the kitchens now, Miss Brown?" Charlie had not been asleep when someone entered. Fearing it might be one of the girls coming to fetch the tray, he feigned it so he would not have to fend off their attentions. They must be nearly half his age, it was embarrassing and the men in the stable often chortled over it at his expense.

Annie was startled at his voice and dropped the tray loudly back on the desk, relieved not to break anything. She turned back and saw him still lying there with his arms above his head as he watched her. She looked quickly away and he moved to sit up.

"I apologise Mr. Mickleson, I didn't mean to disturb you, but I did promise Miss Cadman I would take the tray back with me as I was coming out here anyway."

"Why were you coming out here anyway?" he rubbed at his face as he asked it quietly, hoping it had not been to see young Bramley.

"I wished to talk to you, actually, but it can wait if you wish to rest." She moved to pick up the tray again, but he had stood and pressed a hand upon it to prevent her moving it and gestured for her to sit down.

"We can talk now. What can I aid you with, Miss Brown?"

"I came to offer my services in teaching the two boys their letters and numbers. That is, at least until Miss Wyndham hires a governess for Wyndham Lodge. If Mr. Mckinnon is amenable, I could stay with them at the dining table after their luncheon each day for a short time."

"I could not impose on your time. I'm sure you have little of it to spare."

"I have enough, and I think it should be a good change for me. I like them, they are sweet boys and I am happy you are giving them a new opportunity in their lives." He looked at her in that intense way of his that made her squirm, and seemed about to speak when running footsteps were heard.

"Perhaps we should ask them?" Richie and Arnie burst into the office, and when asked, they insisted they should like to learn from Miss Annie. It was agreed, and she confirmed she would get the agreement of the butler, too.

After that, Charlie sat the boys down on the edge of the bunk and looked intently at them, "I have a question to ask of you and I want you to think long and hard about it before you answer me."

"Yes, Mister!" they chorused it.

"Miss Wyndham says I can live in the cottage behind the stable, but it is a little big just for one person. I was thinking I might share it."

"With Mr. Bramley?" Richie hardly dared think that he might mean them. It had been a while since he had talked to Mr. Mickleson about taking them in and he wondered if the man had forgotten.

"No, with you two. Though what should possess me to take you both on is beyond me," he spoke with a tease.

"You have a place to live? We can be a family?" the word caught in Richie's mouth and Annie could see him battle back the tears. Arnie had no compunction in showing his and ran to the big man, flinging his arms around him.

"Yes, we can be a family," Charlie finally said the words and lifted Arnie up into his arms moving to sit next to Richie on the bunk. Richie leaned on his other side and when Charlie put his arm around the boy, who had grown considerably these past few weeks with all the good food they were eating, he burrowed his head into the man's side. "I will take that as a yes then."

With tears in her eyes, Annie picked up the tray and left the office quietly, unseen by the newly formed family.

Dinner at Lady Freyley's was a welcome distraction. Harriet had found that she missed Helena and Nathaniel, and of course the children. Wyndham House was large, even when you had guests staying, but with them all gone and Bertram, too, she had been feeling lonely. Lady Freyley introduced her to a few more local families and of course Mr. Chapple, Mr. Leake and Mr. Holder were present, as was Mr. Collingworth and his sister.

Not knowing of their altercation from the day before, Lady Freyley had seated her next to Mr. Collingworth at the dining table. They spoke amiably, she was relieved to note, and neither of them mentioned Harriet's harsh words. He did however, look her up and down and comment that he was pleased to see she had been able to remove all the mud.

Mr. Chapple sat to her other side and asked if she had brought her brother's music with her. He had some ideas to add to the violin piece and if she thought her brother should not mind, he would like to write it down. Mr. Holder, who could also play the clarinet had worked upon some countermelodies for that instrument. Perhaps they could play it that evening? She had nodded enthusiastically.

Lord Freyley had talked unceremoniously across two people, including Mr. Collingworth, to ask Harriet where her red-headed friend was, he had been hoping to discuss horses with her again. She had explained that they had all left nearly a fortnight ago and had arrived safely in Lincolnshire, with all their animals.

"Did she take the whites with her?"

"I am afraid so, My Lord. I did try to persuade her to part with at least one of them."

"Good for you for trying, though I cannot blame her for keeping them, when I would have done the same."

"I have two new foals now, My Lord. The two mares I purchased at the horse fair foaled two nights in a row. My stable manager is exhausted."

"No problems with either I hope?"

"None, sir!"

"But the stable manager stayed up both nights anyway?" She nodded. "He is a good man then! You have done well in choosing him."

Collingworth, harrumphed at that, she gave him a sidelong look and a small smile before answering the baron.

"Indeed he is, sir. I could not have found better. He worked at Redway with the Ackleys, but I managed to poach him because they already have a longstanding stable manager there. It made the sting of Mrs. Ackley taking both whites with her a little less as I know she will miss him. He apprenticed with a blacksmith, too." Lord Freyley nodded at that, impressed, and she invited him to Wyndham House to see their new stock of horses and talk with Mickleson any time he wished.

While they waited for the gentlemen to join them, Harriet informed Lady Freyley that Mr. Chapple was hoping to play her brother's musical composition again and wondered if that should be acceptable. "I know Mr. Horncastle mentioned at your dinner a fortnight past, that your brother composed that music, but I was unaware you had a brother, Miss Wyndham. I thought you and your sister had inherited Wyndham House." Harriet thought quickly. She supposed it was up to her what story she made up for this fictitious brother.

She spoke quietly, "as you know, Lieutenant Mark Wyndham was my stepfather, though he always considered my sister and I as his own. He had loved my mother since he was fourteen years old and when Ernest Eldridge died, he asked the lieutenant to take care of us all. Not knowing my mother should be free to marry, he had been involved with another but broke it off. Later he discovered what had happened and of course he made sure the woman and child were well cared for. When he died, she died of grief as she still cared so much for him. Uncle Phillip ensured the boy, my brother, was educated well and when he was old enough, he chose to travel and has been travelling the world ever since. However, given his birthright, or lack thereof, Uncle Phillip left Wyndham House to me and my sister."

"What is his name?"

"Whose?"

"Your brother's?" the baroness smiled.

"Harry," the name sprung unbidden to her lips without thinking it through. She had been so caught up in her story, but the practicalities such as a name she had not considered.

"Harry! That is unusual do you not think? That the other woman should call her son Harold when his father's legitimate daughter is called Harriet."

"Oh, his name is Henry, but as you know Henrys are often called Harry."

"Especially Kings!" The two ladies laughed together at that. Lady Freyley consented to the playing of the music and once again Harriet found herself lost in it. Mr. Chapple's adjustments had melded well into her own composition for the violin and after a few discussed alterations, the clarinet ornamentation added to the overall whole.

Lady Freyley exclaimed how wonderful it was and how the men should always play with Miss Wyndham, as her playing was exceptional. They agreed that she certainly was talented, but that a woman could not withstand the stresses of a full concert, nor would she have the stamina for it.

"Good Lord!" Lady Freyley exclaimed, "a woman must have double the stamina of a man for childbirth, performing at a concert would be nothing to it. You men have no idea." She rolled her eyes at Harriet, who thought of the two times she had witnessed Genevieve Harker in the throes of her confinement and of all Helena had gone through after the birth of Little Nate. She gave the Lady a small nod and smile in agreement.

"Perhaps, Miss Wyndham, these narrow-minded men should be in luck one day if your brother were to return from his travels and visit Wyndham House!"

Harriet had received several letters from Bertram Horncastle, the latest of which told her they were leaving Lincolnshire the day following the date of the letter and expected to arrive back home six days later. She had sat in her music room reading the short note and felt rather lonely. She wished he were there so she could talk to him of her argument with Mr. Collingworth and the dinner at Lady Freyley's. She had hoped that upon his return she should be able to perform a new composition for him, but nothing had come to her since she had first performed the stormy piece with the other men and they had praised her non-existent brother.

She missed Maria and wondered what she should have made of all of this. The Maria she had become when she fell in love with and married Mr. Brooks, would have laughed gaily and thought it all very amusing. Harriet thought of how wonderful it would have been to compose a piece with Maria. Her sister had been the more talented one on the pianoforte. She had played diligently every day when they were younger, whereas she herself had preferred to go out riding or play chess with Alexander.

Putting the letter down on top of the instrument she sat at, she placed her fingers upon the keys and her forehead next to the letter. She pressed down on the keys wherever her fingers had landed, making a doleful sound. Moving her fingers slightly to the keys she knew so well she pressed down again and the dolefulness had a better sound to it. She continued, letting her feelings of loneliness overcome her as their notes made their way to her fingers. The despair over not being able to play publicly came into her mind, tinging the sound with a harder edge and her mind moved to the brother she and Bertram had created. In her loneliness, she almost wished she had a real brother who could come to visit and play her music with the group. He would take credit for her creations of course, as she could never say they were hers, in the same way of some writers who had been discovered as women after their works had been accepted under a pseudonym.

What had Lady Freyley said? *'They should be in luck one day if your brother were to return from his travels and visit Wyndham House'.* She wondered if she might get someone to pretend to be her brother. That was ridiculous, it would still not be her playing her own music in a concert, which was all she wanted. Bertram had put her in a fix, in the same way she was in a fix now because Nathaniel had wanted her to pretend to be her sister five years ago. That had worked though.

Suddenly her hands thudded carelessly onto the keys as a thought crossed her mind that shocked her. She could not... how could she? Would she dare? The idea took hold of her and felt right. Her mood lifted and she felt energised beyond anything she had felt before. A smile spread across her lips. As she thought it through, she wrote down the notes of the tune she had been playing and titled it *'Loneliness'.*

"Miss, I cannot. Please do not make me do it."

"You must, Annie. I insist."

Harriet sat in front of the mirror at her dressing table. Annie stood behind her with a pair of large shears in her hand. Harriet's fine golden hair was tumbled around her shoulders and she was insisting Annie cut it all off. "You cut James' hair for him all the time and the style of his is very fetching and fashionable. I am sure you can do it, but be sure to keep all the hair safely to take to the wig maker. Mckinnon says he knows of a talented man in town."

"Mckinnon is not pleased with your decision to do this either. He wants you to wait until Mr. Horncastle returns."

"Neither Mckinnon nor Mr. Horncastle are in charge of me. In fact, if I recall correctly, I pay all of you to do my bidding. I am standing firm on this. It is what I want, now cut my damn hair off!"

"Well I see you have been practising your man's language, Miss!" Annie smiled at Harriet's reflection and picked up the first section of hair ready to cut. She opened her mouth to speak once more.

"Do not ask me again, Annie. I am sure."

As Annie worked, Harriet sat still thinking over the past twenty-four hours. After writing down her third piece of music, she called Mckinnon and Annie into her study and told them her plan of pretending to be her own brother that Mr. Horncastle had created. She wanted the men in the group she had played with to accept her as part of that group and she wanted to play publicly. The two people in front of her were astounded. Mckinnon warned that the men would not be appreciative if she was found out and he was not sure he could count on all the staff of Wyndham House, who would have to be in on the duplicity, keeping their mouths shut.

Harriet had suggested they all get a rise in their pay, something she had been considering anyway, if anyone gives the game away, they all lose out, so it should behove everyone to make sure the secret was kept. Her butler had smiled at her ingenuity. He could not deny that this was something she was determined to see through. If Bertram Horncastle disapproved, he had no one but himself to blame.

Starting with the cutting of her hair, so a wig could be made for her to wear when she was Harriet, over the next five days they created Henry 'Harry' Wyndham. Bindings were found to flatten her chest; she already had breeches that she used when riding astride, so more were ordered, as well as shirts, waistcoats and jackets. Mckinnon then taught her daily, to walk, talk and act as a man. She had improved considerably in those days, which only proved to him her determination.

Her first test was going to be Bertram Horncastle and on the day of his arrival she felt the anticipation build up inside her. She had not felt that loneliness, bitterness or despair of the morning of her last composition in all these past days. She was pleased to note that her excitement was not only in Bertram seeing her dressed as a man, but in seeing Bertram himself once again. She really had missed him.

When the Wyndham carriage had been spotted entering the grounds, word was sent to the house ahead of them. She sat in the parlour with her back to the open door and waited for Mckinnon to announce Mr. Horncastle as they had planned. Sitting straight, she tugged at her waistcoat and felt the cravat at her neck was tightening.

"Where is she? I have a surprise for her." Bertram's voice was loud and her anticipation of what he would say built in her as she tried to remember to keep her voice low, bow and not curtsey. Footsteps approached the parlour. "Miss Wyndham, we are returned."

She stood and turned to greet her friend, but the shock of what she saw instead made her forget everything she was supposed to do.

"Mr. Parker!"

"Harriet?"

Chapter Eighteen

The colour rushed to her face in her embarrassment of being dressed as a man in front of Mr. Parker. What must he think of her? She could think of nothing to say to explain her situation. Luke's first thought was that he could not fathom what had got into her dressing that way, but it was quickly overshadowed by the unbidden thought of those slender hips and long legs underneath the form-fitting trousers she wore. He could not help but smile.

Bertram Horncastle let out a long roar of laughter. "Harriet, is that really you? My word, I do not think I should have known you had I not had this lumbering giant with me." She managed a smile and felt the heat recede somewhat.

"Welcome home, Bertram. I have missed you. Welcome to Wyndham House, Mr. Parker."

"Welcome back you mean, Harriet." Bertram corrected her with a slap on Mr. Parker's back, "this is not Parker's first time here."

"I was not aware of that. Then welcome back, Mr. Parker."

"Thank you, Miss Wyndham. I am sorry about my previous greeting, I was shocked. May I ask why you are dressed this way?"

"I know, oh yes, I know!" Bertram was still chortling. "Let us take a seat, Drum is fetching some refreshments for us. So what is your chosen name, Mr. Wyndham?"

"Henry, also known as Harry. Lady Freyley was asking about my 'brother', I cannot be blamed for that." She looked pointedly at Bertram.

"I was not aware you had a brother, Miss Wyndham."

"I am afraid, Parker, that is my doing. Before my trip to Lincolnshire, we had a dinner here and some gentlemen wanted to hear a composition of Harriet's, but I told them her brother had composed it. These gentlemen would not have believed a lady capable."

"Miss Wyndham is more capable than any musician I have heard. I should be honoured to hear anything you have composed."

She smiled at him, of course he would support her. He had always been appreciative of her in her music endeavours. He had learned to read music so that he could always be the one to sit next to her and turn the pages for her. "I did write a piece when I was feeling a little lonely. Right after that I had the idea to be Henry Wyndham."

"I would love to hear it after dinner tonight. Mr. Horncastle has offered me a bed for the night tonight, if that is acceptable to you."

"Of course. You are always welcome here, for as long as you wish." She looked to Mckinnon who had arrived with the refreshments.

"I was thinking the Redway room, sir, and Masters to aid Mr. Parker with his dress?"

"Perfect."

"The Redway room?" Bertram looked questioningly to Drum and then at Harriet.

"I renamed all the rooms with places I love. I hope you do not mind."

"And what did you name my rooms?"

"I did not take that liberty, sir. I had thought Lorlake, but I was waiting to hear from you directly how your visit went." Bertram did not trust his voice, but simply nodded. Luke nodded at Harriet's thoughtfulness.

"I am sure you are eager to hear of Lincolnshire, Mr. Wyndham, but perhaps you could indulge Horncastle and I in your exploits recently? We have bored each other considerably over the past few days of travel. Then we can advise you of news from further north over dinner."

She smiled at him picking up on Mckinnon calling her 'sir' and turned to serve the tea without thinking. Mckinnon, who had returned from issuing instructions regarding Mr. Parker's rooms and valet, coughed. She waved at him nonchalantly. "Would you mind, Mckinnon?"

"Certainly, *sir*." And he poured for the three of them, before leaving them to enjoy their tea.

Harriet regaled them with her tours of the house, the grounds and her rescue of the deer with Mr. Thurston. That story led naturally to Mr. Collingworth and her sending him on his way. Bertram laughed heartily, but Luke seemed less amused. After that she told them the story she had made up to Lady Freyley of her brother Henry and that lady's comment of the possibility of him visiting, giving her the idea of impersonating him.

"Where did you get that wig? It is very snug and realistic." Luke looked at the cap of hair on her head, which matched her own hair colour very well.

"It is my real hair, I cut mine off and had it made into a wig."

"You cut off your beautiful hair!" He was incredulous, and his sudden disapproval brought her protective instinct out.

"Of course! I could never have fitted a wig over all that hair, Annie does a wonderful job with it, you will see for yourself tonight." Luke was fighting with the loss of the hair he had dreamed of running his fingers through and the feeling at seeing her bareheaded with this man's style, similar to his own in fact. It was intoxicating.

Seeing only frustration in Mr. Parker's face, Harriet raised her voice, showing her own frustration. "It will grow back!" Throwing up her hands she unceremoniously left the room.

"She has the rude male withdrawal mastered at least. Let me show you to what I am guessing will be the Redway room."

That evening, the two gentlemen did as they promised and gave her all the information about the goings on in Lincolnshire since she had left. Much of the story of Bertram's return to his childhood home she had learned from his letters, but it was good to hear him tell it in person. Genevieve Harker was growing large with the Harker's third child and her sister, Martha, had announced, just before Bertram returned, that she was expecting her own child in the spring.

After their meal, Harriet played her third composed piece for them, the one she had titled *'Loneliness'*. Bertram had secured his usual seat that provided him with an optimal view of the performer and Luke pulled another chair next to his. By the end of the piece, tears were pouring down Bertram's face, it was such an emotional composition. Luke, who had been imagining how Harriet must have felt alone in this enormous house when she wrote it, had to swallow down a lump and brush at his eyes a little, pretending he needed to cough.

Harriet, as usual, had been lost in playing it, and was astonished when she looked up and saw their reactions. She smiled when Bertram suggested she play *'The Lodge'* piece for Luke to hear. As she started it, Bertram closed his eyes, he knew that he had to play chaperone to this couple, though he desperately wanted to get back to James. They had been very cautious on their trip and had only spent quick moments in each other's embrace and no time together in bed. The beginning of this piece reminded him of the angst he had felt over Phillip's passing. He smiled a little as he realised he had thought that in the past tense. Then it moved on to lighter, livelier music and as it had the first time he heard it, and every time since, it brought James into his mind. As the piece ended he gave a little snort and kept his eyes closed so they could assume he was asleep. He carried on thinking about James and ignored their quiet talking.

"Miss Wyndham, when you said you needed to travel to Bath alone to find your path, I did not know that would include finding a gentleman." Luke leaned forward in his seat, glancing back at the sleeping Bertram.

"I only recently decided to become Henry Wyndham, no one will believe I can compose music as a woman, I have to be a man. They will not allow me to play in public either."

"I do not understand why you should wish to."

"When you have created something that, when performed, can bring people to tears, or give them joy, it is an unexpected gift in return for your work. I would imagine it the same with painting or a novel."

"Then write and claim it as Henry's. Allow others to perform it."

"The men I know that perform in a group, need someone to play the pianoforte and if I allow them to perform 'Henry's' work, they will do it as they please. They would never deign to allow me to direct them."

"We men can be fools. I can truthfully say I have heard nothing comparable to your playing and I have heard your compositions for myself. I am astounded." He looked at her seriously again and Bertram snorted a snore once more. "I will help you pass yourself off as a man. We will work on it over the next few days, and then we will announce the arrival of Henry Wyndham at Wyndham House. What do you say?"

"I say a very grateful, thank you. Would you like me to play something else? You could sit here and turn the pages." She smiled and he willingly sat next to her on the wide stool. The nearness of her after nearly three months without seeing her was heady and her scent was familiar. Why could he not speak to her of his feelings? It was all too mixed up in the events of five years ago and the death of Maria Wyndham earlier this year. He was afraid she would turn him away and he would never see her again. When he had travelled before, he had missed her terribly.

Now she had this absurd plan to pretend to be her brother and he sensed some danger in it. Men could be very proud creatures and if they felt the wool was pulled over their eyes, they could react badly. No, now was not the time to find himself estranged from her.

She was looking through various pieces of music and he leaned over and looked for the quietest, longest piece he knew from her repertoire and pointed to it. He followed it with a quick look at her neck and the rise of her breasts at the neckline of the gown she wore. Looking up again to meet her eyes as she turned slightly to him.

"Pianissimo?" she whispered softly.

"Indeed," he spoke quietly, looking to the sleeping Bertram. She began to play softly and he followed along to turn the pages. Once he knew she was into the piece, he spoke again. "When I spoke of you finding a gentleman, I was referring to Mr. Collingworth. From all you have said, I am wondering if he might be holding an interest in you?"

"He might." She smiled gently.

"And if he did, would you return it?" he held his breath.

"I do not know, mostly I disagree with him. He tolerates it well, but I have yet to discover whether he listens to what I say."

"A man who feels it necessary to demonstrate his superiority over a woman or servants, a man who demands their deference, is a man who is lacking in his own self-worth."

She gave him a sidelong look at that, turning her head away from the music, but not faltering in her playing. Though she did not look at the music he still leaned over and turned the page, and she did not suggest he need not. His face was merely an inch or so away from hers, she drew in a breath and he glanced at her lips as they parted. Then she turned her head back to the music and Bertram gave a stir and opened his eyes.

As the piece came to an end, Bertram suggested they bid each other good night. He had seen through the narrow slit in his eyes as he pretended to sleep that they had almost kissed. He had hoped for it as he liked Luke Parker very much and felt him a good match for Harriet, but when the attempt failed, he intervened to save any further embarrassment for them both. He was done thinking of James and wanted to take action.

After luncheon at the staff dining table the following day, Annie Brown stayed with the two young boys, Richie and Arnie, to work on their reading and writing. She had even added some numbers and counting to their work that they had started a week ago after Mr. Collingworth's visit.

She had the boys working on a surprise for Mr. Mickleson, as they had moved into the cottage behind the stable just this morning. Richie looked up at her and she smiled. "All done?"

"Yes, Miss Annie! Can I go and show him?"

"No, wait for me! Wait for me!"

"Richie will wait, Arnie. Do not rush and spoil it, now." She smiled at Richie, he looked thoughtfully back at her.

"How old will you be when I am sixteen, Miss Annie?"

"I do not know exactly. About thirty I suppose. Why?"

"If you have not married Da by the time I am sixteen, will you marry me?" She laughed her sweet laugh at that.

"I do not think you will still want to marry me when you are sixteen, but that is the best thing anyone has ever asked me."

"Finished!" shouted Arnie and he raced off ahead of his brother, who sat there looking at Annie.

"Go and show him then." She gave him a soft smile and he charged off to catch up to Arnie. She followed quickly. She did not want to miss this.

"Da! Da!" Richie ran through the stable holding his paper aloft, with Arnie running behind him, unable to say anything as he tried to keep up. He had his own page clasped in his fist. At the noise, Charlie Mickleson poked his head out of the stall he was working in. He stared at the boy who was calling him 'Da' for the first time and felt his heart leap at hearing it.

"What is it... son?" he hesitated at using the word, but Richie's broad smile confirmed he was happy he had and the boy who talked non-stop was suddenly speechless. Arnie stepped up instead and handed his paper over.

"We wanted to show you our work, Da!" He copied Richie using the term and looked hopefully.

"Well then son, let us go in the office so I can sit and take a proper look at these." He took both pages and turned the boys toward the office with a tender smile at Annie who had followed the boys at a distance.

"We wrote them ourselves, remembered all the letters and everything." Richie had found his voice. Charlie looked down at the papers, one said Richard Mickleson and the other Arnold Mickleson. He swallowed down the lump he felt in his throat.

"It would seem we have some artwork for our kitchen wall. Thank you, Miss Annie." Annie stood at the doorway and watched him hug the two boys to him and her heart yearned to be part of that embrace. She turned to leave instead. He saw her leave out of the corner of his eye and then saw a young, lean figure follow. "Bramley," the warning voice growled from him, "where do you think you are going?"

"I think if you are dumb enough to let that woman leave, I'll chance my arm."

"You chance your arm with Annie Brown and I'll break it off." He stepped out of the office and grabbed Benjamin by the back of his neck, pulling him into the room.

"Then I'll try with the other." He thought Mickleson a fool to let a woman, who looked at you the way Miss Brown looked at him, go.

"A maid as refined Miss Brown would have nothing to do with the kind of men we are. No rough stableman for her. So forget it."

"I do not see myself as not good enough for her. How I see it, I would go to the ends of the earth for that kind of woman and if a man was willing to do that, how could she want more?"

"We like Miss Annie, Da." Arnie looked up at him. "She would be a good Ma. Richie and me talked of it."

Annie had stopped just outside the stable and turned back. If she wanted to be a part of that embrace. then she was damn well going to go and join in. As she stepped back in, she had seen Benjamin Bramley hauled into the office and walked up to it to listen. When she heard what Mr. Mickleson was saying, her anger rose. Who was Charlie Mickleson that he should decide who was right for her and who was not? She would have to show him she was not a precious doll.

She walked in, stepping between him and Benjamin and placed her hands on her hips. She enjoyed the shocked look on his face. "Who were you calling refined and putting on a pedestal so high even an oaf as big as you cannot reach her? I am no more refined than you, so you can damn well get that idea out of your head!" As she spoke she pushed at his hard chest and was satisfied when he stepped back.

"But you are lady's maid to a fine lady, you should marry a man who is refined, too. I am always scaring you and making you run away."

"You do not scare me, I was worried that I seemed to keep angering *you*. I was her maid at Eastease. Why did you follow me here and accept the situation here if you did not think you had a chance?"

"I hoped, but when I saw this place I knew it was futile."

"So, I am too refined although you know the meaning of futile?"

"Now, I have lumbered myself with these two, how can I expect you to take all of us on?" He smiled at the glimmer of hope in his heart.

"I returned just now because I wanted to be a part of that embrace I witnessed." At that Richie and Arnie jumped up onto the bunk, cheering. "Would you go to the ends of the earth for me, Mr. Mickleson?"

Charlie Mickleson looked down at the petite woman who had just cowed him and took her hands in his. "I would, and back again of course. Miss Annie Brown, do you think you could endure the three of us and marry me?"

"Yes, Charlie, I will marry you. I am sure I can *endure* the three of you! Now for goodness sake kiss me and no gentle brush of the lips. I want one of those that I have seen the colonel give Mrs. Ackley."

His eyes widened at that. He was not the only one to have witnessed the passion between that couple he realised. He was surprised that Miss

Annie wanted that for herself. He did start the kiss with a brush to her lips, just to tease her and himself, but he soon changed it as he moved his lips over hers, firmly and then more demanding as he parted hers with his tongue that he dipped into her mouth. His strong arms wrapped around hers and melded their bodies together as he held her close. Two years of frustration and love were in that first kiss, as that was how long it had been since he first laid eyes on her. Miss Wyndham had been staying at Redway when he had arrived from the Hopwoods to find work.

When finally, they did pull apart, he looked at her face and saw her stunned expression, he felt he had achieved the kind of kiss for which she was hoping.

"Can we call you Ma now, Miss Annie?" Arnie asked.

"You have to wait until we are married," their father told the boys.

"Do they have to?" Annie looked at them tenderly.

"No, I suppose not, if that is what you want."

"Yes, it is what I want." He found it pleasing to give her what she wanted, and as all four of them embraced, and the boys shouted 'Ma!' over and over he whispered in her ear.

"What else can I possibly give you?"

"A daughter."

Harriet was thrilled. First her butler and cook, and now her stable manager and maid were getting married. She had been living there less than two months! Mckinnon's wedding was to be a fortnight after this coming weekend, and as yet, Annie had no idea when she should be marrying Mickleson, but soon she hoped.

This weekend there was to be a big event at Lady Freyley's estate. There should be dancing and Lady Freyley had insisted that Miss Wyndham and the other three men who had played with her before, perform one of her brother's original pieces.

Bertram and Mr. Parker had been working with her on being a man and a gentleman. How she sat, how she walked and talked. What she talked about, speaking first and how to disagree with people. They even talked of the fact that she needed something in the front of her trousers, which caused the two of them to laugh uproariously. At least until she pointedly looked at the front of their trousers and announced Bertram's seemed larger.

Finally, they had agreed that she could, at Lady Freyley's event, announce the arrival of her brother from his travels in a few days. On the night of the baroness' event, Harriet descended the stairs at Wyndham House looking stunning. With her hair now a wig, Annie could spend as long as she liked creating the style for it without an impatient Harriet sitting beneath it and her creation was magnificent. Bertram had brought back with him the gown she had ordered from Martha and her tall figure shimmered in the soft and sheer layers.

Luke looked up at her and took in a quick breath, then he smiled. Bertram had told her to leave her neck and hair unadorned and when she arrived at the bottom of the stairs, Mckinnon, who had been standing silently to the side, stepped forward with a velvet lined box in his hands. Within it shone a diamond tiara and necklace. The Wyndham jewels that had been worn by her grandmother. Luke fixed the necklace in place for her, and Annie, standing on the bottom stair, ensured the tiara was in place in her hair.

"You look absolutely beautiful, Miss Wyndham."

"Thank you, Mr. Parker."

"Do not forget that *I* have the first two dances!" Bertram reminded Luke with a smirk, but Luke did not begrudge his friend.

"I have the second pair *and* the sixth."

"I do have a full card."

"We have not even arrived yet!" Bertram was happy as they made their way to the carriage.

The baron's house was bright with lights when they arrived, and the baroness claimed Harriet the moment she arrived and took her around introducing her to everyone. After this she showed her around the rooms for the dancing and the meal. Harriet was reminded of the balls at Eastease and felt a pang of homesickness. It lifted quickly as she turned to the entrance of the grand room and saw, over the heads of other people, Luke Parker's handsome face. She smiled at him and then quickly noticed from behind him another familiar face.

Mr. Collingworth, though tall, was half a head shorter than Mr.

Parker and though both men were slim, Mr. Parker's shoulders seemed double the breadth of the other man's. She noticed some similarities in them that she had been unaware of before. Both had fair hair, but Mr. Collingworth's was dull compared to the shine of Luke's. They both had blue eyes, too, but Mr. Collingworth's were small, whereas Luke's seemed open and bright with the candlelight flickering on them.

How had she not noticed before? She had obviously been looking for a man similar to Luke Parker and had come across a poor replica. The truth was, she could never find a man comparable to him. Aside from his superior looks and physique, he was kind, considerate, tolerant and loyal. He treated Bertram the way he treated everyone, and she had been able to tell that he was a favourite with the servants from his previous visits and now with Drummond Mckinnon, too.

"With six days of travel between them, it can be harder to tell, but side by side there can be no comparison, can there, my dear?" Lady Freyley had followed her gaze and read her expression. "I do hope you have secured some dances with Mr. Parker. I am looking forward to witnessing the frisson the two of you will conjure."

"My Lady!" Harriet objected.

"I have told you before, my dear, I must live these things vicariously these days. Do not begrudge me."

"The second and sixth pair, assuming your dance continues that long. Though he might have to carry me by then."

"Surely you did not give the first to Collingworth?"

"No, Mr. Horncastle, much to his delight."

"Ah and here comes Mr. Collingworth. He will not be happy with third."

"Oh! Do you think your event will stretch to seven pairs? I have a full card."

"Oh dear, this I must see."

"Lady Freyley, I thank you for the invitation tonight," Mr. Collingworth was gracious. "Miss Wyndham. Could I hope that you might be free for the first pair of dances?"

"I apologise, Mr. Collingworth, but no. Mr. Horncastle asked for that privilege when the invitation arrived."

"Of course he did. I cannot protest to him doing exactly as I would have in his position. The second then?"

"Mr. Parker asked right after Mr. Horncastle. He is staying at Wyndham House at the moment while visiting from Lincolnshire."

"I see, then I will be happy to wait until the third."

"I am sorry, Mr. Collingworth, but Mr. Chapple, Mr. Leake and Mr. Holder were all present when the invitation arrived and… I am afraid my card is full."

"Then I will leave disappointed in this at least, and here is your first partner."

Harriet enjoyed dancing with all her partners. As predicted by Lady Freyley, she did feel a frisson when dancing with Mr. Parker, similar to that she had always felt, but whether it was because she was not at Eastease, or some other reason, she felt it a little more intensely. When the time for the fourth pair arrived, she was surprised to see Mr. Collingworth arrive to offer her his arm. "Mr. Leake has a sore ankle and insisted I step in to ensure you were not disappointed."

"You are too kind, Mr. Collingworth. I would have happily kept him company for the duration of the dances, but I see he is waving us on." The music had started, so she quickly took her place opposite Mr. Collingworth. His dancing was superb, but the frisson was not there. When the dances finished, she thanked him graciously and quickly suggested she see if Mr. Leake was well. Mr. Holder, her next dance partner, was sitting next to him. Mr. Leake was rubbing his left ankle and assured her he should be well with a day or so rest and that if seated while he played his clarinet, he should still be able to perform with them all later.

Mr. Holder offered her his arm and she found herself once more lining up with the dancers. He was a shorter, rounder man, but nimble on his feet and very genial. She smiled at him easily and then started laughing. "Are you well, Miss Wyndham?"

"Perfectly, sir. I am just recalling Mr. Chapple's comment about ladies not having the stamina to perform a whole concert, and yet I have been dancing now for over two hours and will perform with the three of you later, and no one seems concerned!"

"Quite right, Miss Wyndham, quite right!" He laughed with her.

Chapter Nineteen

Joseph Collingworth stood in front of his valet and scowled. "I told you how it looked, this is not even close to it. Try again." He flicked a hand at the side of the head of the man in an action that was more insulting than painful. Bertram Horncastle's cravat had looked exceptional since his new valet started recently, but that would change soon.

Joseph wanted to look his best for the dinner at Wyndham House tonight, as he was going to get Harriet Wyndham's agreement to marry him. He had it planned out. They would have dinner and then when the gentlemen stayed at the table for their port and cigars, he would slip out and request Miss Wyndham have a private word with him. Once she agreed, he would announce it to everyone there. He would have particular pleasure in seeing the faces of Horncastle and the younger Parker as he felt either one of them would want to be in his position.

At this dinner, they should all be meeting the Wyndham brother. Upon hearing of his impending arrival at the Freyley event a fortnight past, Joseph had decided on this course of action. He did not want the brother to stake a claim on the Wyndham estate, though being a bastard, he was not sure he could. Harriet, as he should soon be allowed to call her, was soft and might even be inclined to give her brother a share in it. He must act before that happened.

They should be married quickly and quietly. He did not want to give her friends in Lincolnshire time to travel to Bath. He did not want freaks at his wedding, such as the colonel with his unwieldy wooden leg, and he would get rid of the worst of them all, Bertram Horncastle. He wondered if Harriet had signed the papers she spoke of, making it legally impossible to dismiss the small freak. If not, it would be easy to throw him out. If so, he would have to rethink his plans. He might find a legal loophole, but if that proved impossible, then he should have to be sure the man met with an accident of some kind. Perhaps that horse of his would throw him, though he should be sure not to injure the Friesian. He wanted it for himself, perhaps as much as he wanted Harriet, and of course he would have that man's valet, too.

As he rode through the early evening chill, he was grateful of his greatcoat. There was still sufficient light to see the road by and he would have to spend the night as he would have no carriage lights to see him home. After tonight his plan was to spend most of his nights at Wyndham House. He wondered if he might even be able to get Harriet to allow him into her bed.

When he had heard that the surviving niece of Phillip Wyndham was coming to Bath to take over running the estate, he had decided to marry her. That she was a handsome, graceful and slender woman, was his good fortune. Unfortunately, she was rather opinionated and outspoken, but he would soon cure her of that. Her beauty cushioned the blow of those unladylike traits.

Joseph began to think ahead to more of the changes he would make. The Celt would have to leave, his own butler was much more refined, and the beast in the stable should leave. He would not have that man taking his liberties with Mrs. Collingworth, as Harriet would be. What had possessed Harriet to make him stable manager? That alone proved that a woman is incapable of logical thinking, and she had started this venture with Wyndham Lodge and the two Robertson servants. It beggared belief that she thought it wise to house orphans and disgraced ladies on her property.

As he turned into the long driveway of the estate, he considered the last time he had seen Harriet. He had been disappointed to learn that her dance card was full. With so many people crowding the room, his only chance to talk to her alone had been during a dance. In that he had been thwarted by those musical clowns, Horncastle and this young upstart that Harriet gazed at often, in a way that displeased him. He learned that she had known Parker since she was six years old and decided if he had not taken action to secure her in all that time, either he was a fool or she was not as interested in him as her gaze implied.

However, Joseph Collingworth was not a man to be foiled easily, and he soon found the leverage he needed with the fool Leake. He had to wait for the fourth pair, but he did manage to procure her hand to dance. She was, of course, a superb dancer and did not show him up at all, but afterward he had hoped to take her to the drink table for some refreshment. The soft Harriet insisted on ensuring the health of Leake's fake ankle pain and then danced with the fat Holder.

Later, he had not even been able to sit next to her for the entertainment, as she and the three musicians *were* the entertainment. They played three pieces that were written by her brother and then Lady Freyley took great pleasure in announcing the arrival of that man this week. Everyone was excited by this news and fell over themselves with praise for the pieces, but he did not perceive anything particular about them. One of them was positively maudlin.

He arrived at the house and was shown into the room that Harriet had changed into the parlour, so her musical instruments could take over the much superior room. An indulgence he might let her continue if she made it worth his while. He smiled at that as he entered, looking around the room to see the object of the fantasy he had just been spinning in his mind. He came up short. She was not present. He was sure he had timed his arrival well, to avoid most of the small talk prior to dining. It was not good for a hostess to be last coming down to greet her guests.

"Mr. Collingworth," the Scot announced him with his dreadful accent. Joseph's teeth ground against each other at the sound of it.

"Ah Collingworth," Horncastle greeted him, "so glad you could make it. I believe you know everyone here. Lord and Lady Freyley of course."

"My Lord, My Lady." He bowed formally.

"All the gentlemen you know and thankfully Mr. Chapple brought his sister as we are one short on ladies tonight." He had bowed to the men and the ladies before bringing his eyes sharply back to Horncastle.

"Where is Miss Wyndham?"

"Unfortunately, she has a rather bad cold and insists on staying in her room and resting. This is her brother, Henry Wyndham."

"Mr. Collingworth," Henry Wyndham stood and bowed. Joseph did not take in his appearance much. He was shorter than him and slimly built. He, too, had inherited the fair hair and blue eyes, but other than that he did not stick out particularly. Joseph bowed to him, with no particular deference.

"Mr. Wyndham, I do hope your sister will not be ill for long. Perhaps she could be persuaded to play for us later?"

"Thank you, though I doubt she will feel up to it and will probably be asleep by then. Do not concern yourself. I am a capable player and have been persuaded to play a couple of my own pieces with these gentlemen." Wyndham indicated the other musicians Chapple, Holder and Leake.

"Your playing will be as easy on the ears as your sister's, I do not doubt. The view will not be as easy on the eyes, however." Wyndham's eyes flashed at the comment and he took a step toward the man.

"Come now, Mr. Collingworth, you must save such talk between you men when the ladies leave you at the table. Here we expect the good breeding befitting a gentleman. See, you have made Miss Chapple blush."

"I apologise, My Lady. Miss Chapple."

"Dinner is served, sir." The Scot appeared in time to allow the brother to simmer down, and they all followed Lord and Lady Freyley to the dining room.

The meal was good, he would keep the cook, that was certain. His own overcooked everything. However, as the ladies left to head to the music room, Lady Freyley put a fat hand on the butler's forearm. "Please pass my compliments on the meal to your lady friend, Mckinnon. When do you finally marry her?"

"On Saturday, My Lady. I thank you. I will certainly let her know."

"Congratulations, Mckinnon."

"Thank you, My Lord."

Joseph scowled, what a shame about the cook, but he was not keeping the butler just for some good food. He would find another, maybe even better.

"Good Lord, Collingworth, did you wish to marry the cook yourself? That is such a scowl." Lord Freyley had noticed his countenance, he had to be more careful.

"Not at all, My Lord, though it must take a certain *kind* of woman to settle for Mckinnon."

"Indeed, sir." The jaw muscles moved in the cheeks of the butler as he poured the port, but he kept his tone even. The lack of Miss Wyndham in their evening was causing Joseph to feel belligerent. His plans were being thwarted, as this was the time in the evening that he had decided he should be taking Harriet aside and taking the final step to becoming master of this household.

He took up his port and downed the glass in one, then he tapped the rim of the glass. Mckinnon had only moved two seats away from him and returned quickly to refill it. Collingworth did notice the look he gave to Horncastle first and it annoyed him. He turned that annoyance to the man next to him, "how is your ankle, Leake?"

Leake coloured at that and laughed. The man was a fool. He leaned to his right to reach his ankle and rub it. "It is much improved, thank you, Collingworth."

"I was under the impression, from my sister's tale, that it was your left ankle that bothered you, Leake?" Wyndham shot it at the man from the end of the table. Leake realising his mistake leaned the other way, but it was too late, he was found out.

"Lucky for me this fool owed me some gambling debts. I was able to *encourage* him to relinquish his dance with your sister, in exchange for forgiving the debt." At this, both Parker and Wyndham stood. Wyndham's rage more obvious as his chair fell backward and landed on its back on the floor.

"How DARE you!" the man positively yelled it, but Collingworth just sat there amused. "I will inform my sister of what you think of her, you bastard!"

"I should be careful who you are calling a bastard, Wyndham. I know your history."

"My sister thinks a lot less of my birthright than she will of you paying for her favour. You should not count on being invited back here again, if I have anything to do with it." Realising his mistake by not considering the inference that could be made over buying that dance with Harriet, Collingworth sat up a little straighter.

"I apologise, sir. I meant nothing of the kind that you are implying and would never intentionally demean Miss Wyndham in such a way. I had it within my power to dance with her and could not resist doing anything I could for that opportunity. No money exchanged hands I assure you."

Parker put his hand on the shoulder of the smaller man and nodded. They both returned to their seats, as Mckinnon had picked up that of Mr. Wyndham, though the man continued to glare at Joseph.

Joseph's mind was racing, he should have to make sure he spoke to Harriet before this man had a chance to mention his mistake to her. He did not want anything spoiling her opinion of him. He wondered how early the man awoke. Distractedly, he downed his port and tapped the rim again. Again, Mckinnon looked to Horncastle to get a nod first, then refilled the glass, but Joseph said nothing.

They returned to the ladies and the entertainment ensued. None of it interested Joseph, it all sounded the same as the night at the Freyleys', although everyone praised the superior pianoforte skill of Mr. Wyndham. Mckinnon offered him some coffee, but he preferred to keep drinking the port. He could hold his drink without embarrassing himself. He continued to mull over how to speak to Harriet before her brother in the morning.

Then it struck him. He should go to her tonight. He should be respectful and sit on a chair by her bed. She would be angry with him, but she should forgive him when he gave her the honour of his hand. His mind began to wander at that point. As soon as she agreed, he could move to the bed and kiss her hand. He should be able to tell that she would allow more and he should kiss her lips before standing to leave. She should ask him not to leave of course and he would chide her for her impropriety. The wife of the owner of this estate should have to behave better.

She would beg his forgiveness, moving forward and looking up at him, so he could see the swell of her breasts where her nightgown fell forward. She would gasp as he put his hand down the neck of the garment to fondle her. Anyone would forgive him for what should inevitably happen next and they should be married anyway, they would have to be.

That was it! That would be how he could thwart the brother. He would compromise her tonight and they would have to be married. He should wait for everyone to go to bed and for the house to be quiet, then he could go to her. The remainder of the evening dragged on and he consoled himself with more port.

It was late into the night before Joseph felt he could creep along the corridor unheard by any of the guests. He had known which was Harriet's room from seeing her enter it on a previous stay. She had apparently renamed it the Wyndham Room. Checking he had the right door by its position near the head of the grand stairs, he reached for the handle and turned it. Nothing happened, it was locked. Damn it. He moved to a door further down, which he assumed must be the maid's entrance to the dressing room, there should be an adjoining door to Harriet's bedroom that should not be locked.

He tried the door, but that was locked, too. He stood there considering his options. He would not return to his own room without his prize. No doubt there should be a further room for the husband and both rooms should share the dressing room. How fitting that he should go to her from that room, as would be his right once they were married. He tried the third door and it opened easily. Closing the door behind him he held his candle aloft to view the room. Empty of course, but the door to the dressing room stood to his left. As he had deduced, she had not thought to lock this door and he stepped through it. He could see his destination ahead of him, moonlight shining through the windows to the right added to the light of the candle in his fist. His hand reached out for the handle.

"What are you doing in here, sir? These are Miss Wyndham's private rooms."

"Shut up!" he spat out the words to the maid who was sitting up in the small bunk. He made to reach for the door to Harriet. The maid leapt from the bed and tried to get out to the corridor, no doubt to get help. She had forgotten it was locked however and reached under her pillow for the key. "Not so fast. I will have that." He made to grab the key, but she shrieked and threw it away into the darkness of the room.

He struck her then. His arm flung out and the back of his hand connected with her face. She sprawled across the room a few feet away and toward the windows. He turned and set the candle down on the small table nearby, but noticed the sudden chill and the candle blow out as the window was opened. Putting her head out of the window the woman screamed twice. He pulled her away and struck her again and she fell onto the bed stunned. Once again, he reached for his prize, but that door was locked, too.

"Where is the key?"

"Same, same as I threw." She mumbled it through her swollen lip. He could not hope to find it without the candle and would not have time to light it and search.

"You stupid woman! I will make you pay for this insolence. If it cannot be Harriet, then I will have you."

"No, no!" She screamed it, panicked now, as he approached the end of the bed where she had fallen. She tried to back away, but he was on her so fast. "Charlie! CHARLIE!"

"No one will hear you." He was pinning her down and pushing up her nightgown while she kicked. In her panicked state, she was ineffectual and he manoeuvred himself between her legs. He held her wrists with one hand while quickly undoing his trousers. Positioning himself he pushed to enter her but came up against a barrier, "a virgin! What a treat. Poor Charlie will be disappointed. That's the stable manager is it not? Better and better." Then he thrust into her. She screamed again as he continued to thrust. He imagined it was Harriet, that he had just taken her virginity and he would finally own this house.

Suddenly he felt himself pulled away from the warmth of the woman and he landed hard against the wall below the open window. Light shone upon him as the door of Harriet's room opened. She stood there in her nightgown, her lithe figure silhouetted from the light of several candles shining behind her, her hair cropped short in the style of her brother. That was when it dawned on him that there was no brother, it was her. No doubt in an effort to catch him out in his lie with Leake.

"You...!" but he was unable to say more as a thick pair of hands were laid upon his shirtfront and he was hauled to his feet and turned to the window. Collingworth's only glimpse of his attacker an unruly shock of black hair and bared teeth as the creature growled. The hands were placed on the collar at his neck and the back of his trousers as he was hurled through the window.

He landed on the balcony outside, the rough stone floor of it scraping his cheek, forearms and knees. Before he could stand, the hands were once again upon him as he was half marched and half dragged to the edge where the three-foot-high stone balustrade stretched. "No, no!"

"My Annie told you 'no', you bastard!" the beast growled in his ear. Then he was flying through the air...

Chapter Twenty

Mickleson had been in the stable late that night, one of the mares who had foaled the week prior had an infection around one of her teats. He had been applying a hot compress as much as the mare would allow him and before she went to bed, Mrs. Thurston had brought a poultice out to him. It should not hurt to try it at least he felt.

Late into the night he had sat in his office on the bunk considering closing his eyes for an hour before checking on the horse again. He was so tired that he wondered, when he heard the first scream, if he had imagined it. At the second one, he was out of the stable and into the courtyard looking up at the house within seconds.

The window to Miss Wyndham's dressing room, where Annie was sleeping that night was open. Then he heard her screaming 'No!' and his name. He was frantic, he had to get to her. There was a mounting block by the side of the stable and he picked it up, despite its weight, and carried it to below the balustrade of the balcony in front of those rooms. Standing upon it he tried to clasp the stone floor of the balcony, but he could not reach it. He crouched and jumped. His fingers clutched around a stone balustrade and started to slip and scratch on the rough stone. The thought of Annie needing him, however, made him press his fingertips into the stone and pull himself up enough to get an arm around it. His booted feet scrambled to find purchase.

He hoisted himself over the top, and ran to the window. He felt sick as he looked in and saw a man pinning Annie down on the bed and forcing himself on her. The anger he felt at anyone hurting his Annie in any way, but in such a way, rose up in him. Before he knew where he was, he had pulled him off her and thrown him against the wall.

As he turned back to Annie, she turned her face away from him. Did not even cover herself and he could see blood between her legs. Tenderly, he pulled at the edge of her nightgown and pulled it down over her. She curled up on the bed and her shoulders shook. Then a hand touched his arm and he looked into the face of his mistress, "I have her, Charlie. Throw out this rubbish, please."

With a growl in his throat, he turned to the man and realised it was Collingworth. He dragged him to his feet and threw him headfirst out of the window. The man sprawled on the floor of the balcony and he followed him. The thought of his Annie lying there so quiet and so bloody had him lifting the man up again and marching him to the edge. He threw him over it without a second thought, despite his protests. He watched him fall and land with a crack. The moonlight showed the dark blood seeping from his head and his lifeless eyes looked back up at Charlie.

The anger drained from him and he hung his head as he turned back to the window.

Robert Davenport was kissing her. She wondered why he was there when he was dead. Why was she letting him kiss her again? She did not want to kiss him. His body was on hers and his hands on her breasts. She struggled to get away from him, but he laughed. She screamed, but the scream seemed far away as if it had not come from her, then there was another and she was screaming for Charlie, Charlie... It was Annie!

She woke with that realisation washing over her and scrambled off the bed and to the dressing room door, grateful she had fallen asleep with candles burning. She turned the key in the lock and opened the door to see a figure being thrown across the room and to the floor under and open window. It was Collingworth and she could tell he had realised that she had impersonated her brother, because she did not have her wig on.

Turning she saw Charlie Mickleson pulling down Annie's nightgown and the woman curled up into a ball on the bed. Her heart broke for the woman who was as much a friend as a servant. Having just woken from a dream of Davenport, she easily recalled that feeling of being worthless, nothing, something a man could take at a whim. What whim had brought Collingworth to her rooms?

"I have her, Charlie. Throw out this rubbish, please." She did not know what the man would do with him, she did not care. She watched Mickleson bodily lift the smaller man and throw him headfirst out of the window, then she sat on the edge of the bed and looked at Annie. She rubbed her back and let her cry.

A banging was heard at the dressing room door, "Harriet, Harriet! It is Bertram, I heard a scream. Are you well?" Lighting a nearby candle, Harriet looked for the key to the door, but could not find it.

"I am well, Bertram. I cannot find the key. Can you come in through the other room?" She realised this was how Collingworth had gotten in. She had told Annie to lock the dressing room door when she recalled Helena's story about Lord Aysthill, but neither of them had considered the other door. Perching again on the bed, she spoke to Annie.

"I am so sorry, Annie. This is all my fault, Mr. Collingworth wanted me." Annie nodded and pointed to the key on the floor that she could see from her position. "You protected me. Oh Annie, at such a cost. I wish you had not. You know I am not a virgin. What was there to protect?" Annie pointed at her face where red bruises were beginning to show.

"Miss Wyndham!" Harriet turned at the voice of Mr. Parker. How long had he been there? How much had he heard? His expression told her he had heard everything.

"Well now you know, Mr. Parker," she said it bitterly.

At that moment, a leg came through the window, followed by the bulk of Mickleson. He looked at the startled faces and addressed Miss Wyndham, "He is dead, fell off the balcony and smashed his head open." She gave him a curt nod.

"Did he fall, or was he pushed?" Bertram looked up at the man.

"Do not ask me that question unless you want me to answer it." Mickleson turned to the bed.

Bertram had been considering the situation, having deduced what had occurred from overhearing Harriet talking to the maid. He looked up at Harriet who had moved out of Charlie's way, "I do not think anyone else is awake, so I suggest the following. We keep quiet and say nothing of this attack on Miss Brown. Mr. Parker and I will go and arrange things with Drum. He and Miss Cadman will be the only others we inform of the truth here. He will inform us all at breakfast that he has discovered Collingworth's body beneath the balcony and suspects that he fell trying to climb it."

"There is some scraping where I climbed up, so it could be assumed that was his doing," Mickleson added.

"Excellent!" Bertram looked at the big man impressed at the physical feat he had managed, he knew of acrobats who would not have attempted that climb.

"I suggest you go back to bed, Miss Wyndham." Mr. Parker suddenly spoke, "Horncastle and I will see to everything." There was a command in his voice that she did not appreciate, but she had just hurt him, she knew that, so she acquiesced and thanked him.

"I will have Drum send a maid to you in the morning, informing her only that Miss Brown is ill," Bertram confirmed.

Charlie had been murmuring to Annie and wrapped her up in the top blanket on the bed, cradling her easily in his arms, "I am taking her to our cottage. Could you ask Drum to wake Benjamin as early as possible and tell him to check on the sickly mare, then report to me."

"Of course we will, do not worry about the stable and Annie must not be concerned about leaving the cottage for a few days at least. I will come to her in the morning to see how she is faring."

"What comfort should that be?" The big man was bitter.

"I am not without experience in such matters," she said it quietly, looking at Charlie, but she knew Luke heard her. Then they all left her there and she collapsed onto the small bed to cry.

Bertram had hunted up Drum in his office and once he was suitably dressed, they walked out into the courtyard to where Parker was standing over the body of Collingworth. Bertram had explained the situation to Drum quietly as they had walked outside. The three men looked up at the balcony and then down again at the prone form of the man.

"He did not fall," Drum spoke for all of them.

"No," confirmed Bertram.

"Charlie killed him."

"Yes, he did the same as any of us would have done in his position." Parker spoke the words they were all thinking, and each thought of the person for whom they cared the most.

"We would have," Bertram confirmed again. "Let us lift him into the bathing room off the kitchens. There is a table big enough for him in there. Once everyone is awake we will inform them that his body was discovered in the early hours. As soon as it is daybreak, I suggest we send to his house for them to collect the body."

"You do not wish us to take care of that ourselves, sir?" Drum asked.

"No, I want as little as possible to do with the man and his family. Lord Freyley may wish to discuss it with you tomorrow, Drum. Keep to the story, you can say he must have got these scrapes and bruises climbing up. We all saw him drinking far too much. If he has further questions, refer him to me. Ah, you had better button him up, Drum!"

After taking the body to the bathing rooms and Mckinnon locking it securely, they all retired for the rest of the night.

In the morning, the guests were astonished by the news that Mr. Collingworth was dead. He had apparently been trying to get onto the balcony in front of Miss Wyndham's rooms and had fallen, cracking his head open on the stones below. What his aim had been in trying to get to her rooms was unclear, as she had slept through it all and had no idea. She confirmed that she had locked all the doors to her rooms that night.

After completing their breakfast, the three men, Mr. Chapple, Mr. Holder and Mr. Leake, with Mr. Chapple's sister, all made a hasty departure. Lord Freyley insisted he be shown where the body was discovered and where they had placed him. Bertram and Luke accompanied him, leaving Lady Freyley in the breakfast room, her only companion was Harriet.

"Miss Wyndham, I am glad to see you are much recovered from your cold."

"Thank you, My Lady."

"Are you certain that Mr. Collingworth did not make it to your room?"

"Quite certain."

"I do hope, Miss Wyndham, that if you found yourself in any kind of difficulty, you would consider me a friend you could confide in."

"Thank you."

"It would seem that Mr. Collingworth held a rather unhealthy interest in you, attempting to get to your rooms in this way."

"I believe his interest was more in Wyndham House than in me."

"Probably. You did not return his interest? I thought early on I detected something, but then Mr. Parker arrived."

"Yes, then Mr. Parker arrived. Though I fear he might be leaving soon."

"Not without visiting the Marshams first I am sure."

"I beg your pardon?"

"When Mr. Parker was in Bath five years ago, he became acquainted with the Marshams. They live further south of Bath, so do not often come to any of my dinner parties."

"They live near a pond that people skate on in the winter."

"Yes, that is correct, Greypond. How do you know of it?"

"Their daughter fell through the ice once and was rescued by a young man."

"Oh my word! I had clear forgotten that happened, that must be over twenty years ago!"

"Five and twenty I believe."

"How could you possibly know that my dear?"

"That was my mother, Eliza Marsham."

"Oh my word! Well, I recall she ran off and married in a hurry, but I had not realised to whom, as the family had nothing to do with her after that. So she married Mr. Eldridge, I do recall seeing him around here, he was rather sickly and of course I knew he was your father."

"He was sickly, he died on the day my sister and I were born."

"Oh, that is a sad story. Then she also married the lieutenant."

"Yes, he was the young man who saved her from the icy pond."

"I had no idea. Do you think he was in love with her all that time?"

"Yes, he was." The older woman gave a sigh at that information. "Now, I wonder what Luke Parker thinks he is up to with the Marshams? They did not come to my mother's funeral you know, and Mr. Harker told me he wrote to them many times about my sister and I. They never responded. I do not appreciate Mr. Parker keeping me in the dark over this."

"Does he know what relation they are to you?"

"How could he not?" Lady Freyley did not think it wise to point out to the angry, young woman that she had not and let the matter drop.

Annie Brown had not slept much. Charlie had carried her into the cottage behind the stable and placed her on his big bed still wrapped in the blanket. He had pulled another blanket over her and then laid on his back beside her on top of the covers. She had stopped crying at last and looked out of the blankets at him as he rested his head on his arm, its muscles straining against his shirtsleeve.

"I am sorry, Charlie." He turned then and looked at her.

"For what?"

"I fought him. I did fight him."

"I know you did."

"I would understand if you did not want to marry me now."

"Would you? I would not if I were in your position. I love you, Annie. That bastard can never change that and he will never hurt you again."

"Did you throw him off the balcony?"

"Yes."

"Thank you." He leaned in, brushed her cheek with his fingers and kissed her swollen lip with the merest of brushes of skin upon skin. It was so tender and so gentle that she did not flinch from it. She would never flinch away from him, because she loved him and knew he would never hurt her. Then she grasped his hand and looked at his fingers where the flesh was ripped and bloody.

"It is nothing." He pulled his hand away.

"It is not nothing, Charlie. You did this climbing that wall, I have no idea how you managed to get up there."

"I had to get to you. You needed me."

"I did, and you were there, I love you so much." She kissed each finger gently.

Before heading to breakfast, Harriet had called in to the kitchens for a word with Miss Cadman. She and Mckinnon were the only ones told of the attack on Annie. Harriet suggested a bath be taken to the cottage, if she could give a good reason to do so. Annie should want to wash the man off her body, she knew that only too well. She should visit her later in the morning after the Freyleys had left.

Fiona Cadman took care of the bath herself. She told the kitchen staff they had to manage without her. It should be good practise for the few days after her wedding at the weekend. Charlie carried the bathtub into the little kitchen in the cottage and she set about getting him and the boys to fetch and carry water, starting with the kettles and pots she had boiling on the kitchen fires in the house. Once the bathtub was filled, she shooed them out of the cottage and promised they could come in again when Annie was back in bed. The boys were asking questions of Charlie, but he would only say that their ma was not feeling well and needed some rest. He also cautioned them about talking to anyone else of it.

Fiona could not help but wince at the sight of Annie's face. She had a bruise down one side of it and a swollen lip. She walked her out of the bedroom and into the kitchen, holding her elbow all the way and noting the blood on her nightgown. Then she helped her step into the bathtub and handed her the soap.

"Thank you, Miss Cadman. This is very kind of you."

"Miss Wyndham suggested it. She thought you might like to wash that bastard off your skin." Fiona busied herself in the small kitchen.

"So everyone knows?" she hung her head as she said it.

"No, Drummond and myself only. They are not laying this at the door of the man who did it. Personally, I think he should be shamed into his grave."

"I think the fact that he is in his grave is sufficient punishment."

"I suppose so."

"It will not feel the same as this for you on Saturday."

"Oh, Drum could not wait until our wedding night. That deed is done. Though it was painful for a moment, he was loving and gentle and of course welcomed, so there is no comparison. What of Mr. Mickleson?"

"We are waiting until our wedding night."

"What if there is a child from last night?" When Fiona asked her this, Annie turned suddenly with a shocked look on her face. She had not considered it.

"Then it will be my child." A deep voice came from the doorway of the kitchen. Charlie had come to see if she was doing well. He had left her sleeping in the early hours and herded the boys away when they woke. He pointed outside, "those boys are not my blood, but I love them as if they were. Same goes for any child of Annie's."

"You should go, Mr. Mickleson. I will call you when Annie is back in bed."

"No, you should get back to your duties, I will help her." Fiona looked to Annie and she nodded, so she left them to it. Given what she had told Annie of Drum, she could hardly protest about impropriety.

Charlie picked up a cloth from a nearby cupboard and sat upon a stool beside the tub. Then he looked at Annie in the deep water which was cloudy with all the soap she had used to wash herself. He dipped a corner of the cloth into it and proceeded to wipe her face gently. She rose and he picked up a thin towel to dry her as she stood with her feet in the tub. He swallowed hard, because she was wet and naked and he wanted her, but he would keep his control.

Tenderly he rubbed the towel over her and wrapped it around her before picking her up and carrying her back to the bed. There Fiona Cadman had left a clean nightgown and had taken the other and the bloody blanket to clean. He put the fresh garment over her head, pulling the towel off her as it fell over her body, then he bent to dry her legs and feet. Once done, he flung the towel over his shoulder and lifted her legs on the bed to tuck her in.

"The boys are worried, are you well enough for them to come in and see you?" She put her hand to her face with a question in her eyes. "I think they should be told the truth. They survived on the streets over a year together, they are not that naïve." She nodded and he turned to get their boys who he knew were waiting impatiently outside.

They ran into the room, but Richie pulled up short as he saw Annie's face. While Arnie climbed up on the bed when she had patted the counterpane beside her, Richie rounded on his new father. "You hit her! You cannot hit her, I will not let you. You can hit me all you like, but never hit her." His fists flailed ineffectually on Charlie's hard stomach and chest. He did nothing to stop him, but looked up at Annie, helplessly.

"Richard Mickleson, you stop that this instant and apologise to your father!" Annie reprimanded him. "He would never hurt me, or you. Look at him taking all your punches. Now get over to this bed and sit on it with your brother." Richie hung his head and sat at the end of the bed, he chanced another look at her and saw her gentle smile. Then her head jerked to his father.

"I am sorry, Da." Charlie nodded.

"I was attacked by a man who was staying at the house last night. He was trying to get to Miss Wyndham."

"You stopped him," Charlie smiled at her as he said it.

"I had help," she gave a small smile back at him as anything further hurt her face. "Your father climbed up to the balcony and saved me." Richie and Arnie looked at the man they loved with even more admiration than they had before.

"Was it the man that they were talking about being dead?"

"Yes, he fell from the balcony."

"Did he get to you, Ma?" Arnie finally spoke up and pointed toward the lower part of her body, "Richie had men get to him, he said it hurt. He would never let them get to me, told me to hide until he got the money. Then we could eat." Richie's head hung even lower at that, then he stood and turned knowing they should want him to leave. Before he knew what was happening, he found himself in the strong embrace of the man he had hoped to call Father for a long time.

"Ah, Little Owl. Son! What a thing to have to do. You are so brave." Charlie held him close and felt his smaller body quake against his own as the tears fell. With his own legs feeling weak, he sat on the end of the bed and looked toward Annie. There were tears in her eyes. Arnie started to cry, too, he did not know he had said anything wrong and now everyone was crying.

"Sorry, Ma. Sorry, Richie!" he spoke through his tears.

"Do not be sorry, Arnie. It is important that we know this kind of information. We do not think less of either of you because of it. Richie did what he had to do to get food. No child should ever have to, but it is the way of things. Miss Wyndham is hoping to change that, at least around here. He also protected you, because that is what big brothers do." She took a deep breath, she had not planned to tell them all of what had happened, but now it felt important that she did. Richie's crying had stopped and he turned to look at her. "He did get to me, but your father stopped him. He was trying to get to Miss Wyndham because he wanted to be master of the big house, which should happen if she had to marry him. Never be afraid to tell us anything. We might get angry, but we will never hurt you and we will always be here for you. We are going to be a family officially when your father and I get married, but I think that we are already a family in our hearts."

"When you have a baby, will you still want us as your family?" Arnie had wondered about that.

"Yes, yes of course we will. When that happens, you will be a big brother, too, Arnold Mickleson."

Richie and Arnie clambered toward her and she held out her arms to them. "Be careful! Be careful!" Charlie admonished them.

"Mr. Mickleson, when are you going to learn that I am not such a frail thing that you have to save me from hugs from our sons?"

"If you are not frail, I want hugs, too!" He launched himself toward them with a roar, landing a hand either side of her embracing their boys. Then he leaned forward and brushed his lips gently across hers, before kneeling and grabbing each boy with tickling fingers. They all squealed with laughter that gladdened his heart so much, he paid no heed to the pain it caused his hands.

Harriet had been to see Annie later that morning. She had been surprised at how well the woman looked. Charlie had been right to bring her to the cottage. She was away from any speculation here and in the loving arms of him and her sons.

They talked over what had happened, what had been told to the guests and how she was feeling. Harriet made the suggestion that they consider marrying quickly. She would be prepared to pay for a special licence and they could be married right after Miss Cadman and Mckinnon on Saturday. Everyone should be going to the Lodge for the wedding breakfast she had planned for the Mckinnons and once they had left, she and Bertram would stand up with them for their own wedding. She thanked her and promised she should talk to Charlie of it. Harriet told her not to worry about coming back to the house for at least a week or two.

When Harriet returned to the house, she saw Mr. Parker in the hallway and he asked if he could be permitted a word with her. She nodded, and he followed her as she turned toward her study. She sat down behind her desk and motioned for him to sit opposite her. She could not hope to look at him eye to eye with them both standing. She already felt at a disadvantage now that he had learned of her indiscretion, she did not need another.

"I thought I might go and visit some friends over the next few days. I have dallied in doing so, though I have been here for a fortnight. I will return this coming Saturday for Drum's wedding, if that is acceptable."

"Yes, of course. Would this be the Marshams?"

"Yes, perhaps, one day, you might allow me to introduce you to them. They are very pleasant people."

"I am sure." He frowned at her, she seemed angry with him, but he was not sure why. Surely she did not wish to talk more of what had happened last night or about her revelation that he had overheard? "Do you talk to them of me very often?"

"Yes, I stayed with them five years ago, when I was here last. They were generous with their hospitality and asked me a lot about my family and the area where I am from. Of course, that included a lot of stories about Eastease, and you and your sister." She harrumphed and stood again, pacing behind the desk.

"Go if you must, sir, but please convey to the Marshams, that if they wish to hear stories about their grandchild, it might behove them to contact me directly. As they have never bothered to do so in the past one and twenty years, I do not see why they should be allowed access to information about my life from an indirect source. I do think, Mr. Parker, that you might have consulted me before ingratiating yourself with my mother's family. Until Saturday."

She marched out of the room and left him sitting there with a stunned expression. She hid herself in her rooms after that and when he had asked to speak with her again, she refused. He said goodbye to her from behind a thick wooden door, then he exited the house and mounted his horse. She watched from an upstairs room at the front of the house as he departed. As she watched his tall, familiar figure leaving her, she found herself humming a tune. It was the 'Loneliness' composition and when she caught herself doing it, she marched to her dressing room, changed into her riding habit and took Hudson out on a ride over to the lake.

Chapter Twenty-One

Luke Parker rode his mare out of Wyndham House grounds and toward the south, and the Marshams. The last time he visited them was five years ago. He met their grandson at a club in the town of Bath where he had a room. The young man insisted he come to their house, meet his family and stay for a while.

Now that he thought of it, Edward's grandmother asked him a lot about Eastease and the two girls that lived there. He refrained from discussing the events following the twins' sixteenth Birthday ball, that led directly to him travelling and ending up in Bath over a year later.

He had been happy to talk of his home, however, happy to relive the fun times he had as a child with the twins. They had raced around the graveyard playing games when they were allowed out of the boring church sermons. Maria daringly walked along the wall of the church, swung from trees and run as fast as him. Harriet tried to be daring, but was always more cautious. If ever she was caught doing anything naughty, Maria would call her by her own name, putting the blame on herself. Although often she did not have to do so, as the adults would assume it was Maria.

As he had talked, he was aware that he allowed his mouth to run away with him. Mr. Marsham, Edward's grandfather, would leave the room after barely five minutes and he had begged Mrs. Marsham to stop asking him, for fear he was insulting the man in some way that was beyond his understanding. He understood it now. Mr. Marsham was the one who had insisted there was no contact between the rest of his family and his granddaughters. Luke had been her grandmother's only source of information.

He thought of the night before, when Collingworth had died. He had wanted to kill the man for simply purchasing a dance of Harriet's from Leake, but Harriet dressed and acting very convincingly as her brother, had been so angry at hearing of it, that he had done all he could to soothe her anger instead.

When he had gone to bed that night, just down the hall from Harriet, his room almost opposite Collingworth's, he had told her to lock her doors. He was grateful now that she had listened to him. He had lain in his bed with his arms behind his head, knowing sleep was going to elude him. He was unsure how long had passed before he heard a scream.

Thinking directly of Harriet, he had grabbed his clothes, pulling on trousers and a shirt quickly. By the time he reached Harriet's door, still buttoning himself up, he knocked and called her name but heard nothing. Bertram was approaching from the other side of the house and suggested they try the dressing room door where the maid was sleeping. That man called out Harriet's name and she suggested the furthest room of this suite, which should belong to her husband if she married. They made their way through that room to the connecting door of the dressing room and as he stood there, he heard the words directly from Harriet's mouth that ripped into his heart. She was not a virgin. She had given herself to someone else, he knew who it was as he had only seen her distinguish one man in that way.

He had suspected that this was why there was one part of her reserved from him and that was the reason he had not declared himself to her. *"Be honest to yourself at least, Luke! You did not want her to refuse you and you could never see her again."* That was the truth. It had been painful enough not seeing her after that ball, and that had only been for a year and a half. He could not act upon his feelings now, she needed him. She was, as always, stubborn enough to see through her plan to perform her musical pieces in public. While he had no authority to stop her, he could at least ensure her safety. Where it should all lead, he was unsure, but apart from allowing her the freedom to pursue her passion that she otherwise should never have, he felt no good could come from it.

Edward Marsham had replied to Luke's letter that stated he was staying at Wyndham House. His friend had extended an invitation to him to stay with them at Greypond House. Greypond had been the family name before Edward's grandfather married the last of them. With the large pond, of the same name, nearby that many people came to skate upon in the winter, they had not changed the name of the house.

The Marsham's were finally out of mourning for the senior Mr. Marsham and Edward's father was now at the helm. Luke would be one of the first visitors to Greypond and he intended to talk to Edward of his estranged aunt and cousins, before he talked to Mrs. Marsham.

By the time he had finished his deliberations, he could see the outline of Greypond on the horizon, as it sat at the top of a hill. Excited to see his friend again, Luke squeezed his horse on.

Bertram sat in his own study considering the events of the previous evening. Though everyone else involved was thinking about the attack on Annie Brown, or the death of Collingworth, his thoughts were on a problem of his own making. His relationship with James Dawley.

James was spending almost every night in Bertram's bed, in his embrace, even if there was nothing physical between them. That fact was not the problem. He welcomed him, missed him if he was not there and turned to him often in passion. His feelings for James were not the problem, he enjoyed his company and his body, and that was the end of it. James' feelings for him were the problem. As he had the first night they spent together when he had declared *'I love you for saying so'* after Bertram had said he would have killed Davenport, he had proclaimed his love in similar ways over the past few weeks.

Last night, when their intimacy had culminated in a most tender and satisfying simultaneous peak, James had looked at him and said outright, *'I love you, Bertram'*, but he had not responded. The words stuck in his throat, as he felt it a betrayal to the memory of Phillip. Guilt already weighed upon him over the fact that he had accepted James in his bed and appeased the desires of his body despite his promises to Phillip. He wondered if his anger over the discovery of the letter to Davenport had only been an excuse. Each morning he determined that he should not allow those brown eyes and soft lips to sway him the next night, but he would stand on the window seat to allow James to untie his cravat and the soapy smell of the man would waft over him making him want to taste, nip and suck.

'I love you, Bertram' it was said with an expectant look in his eyes, but was met with silence. Then they heard the scream.

When he had returned to his rooms after seeing to the body of Collingworth, his bed had been empty. He had lain in it and could only smell James. He longed for his embrace and to be able to talk to him of what had happened. He slept fitfully and woke to the sound of movement in the dressing room. When he entered, James would not look at him and spoke to him only as *'sir'*. When he dressed him, he sat on a stool in front of him and fixed his eyes only on his tasks of buttons and cravat.

Before he had a chance to stand and walk away, Bertram grasped his face firmly in one hand and turned it to him. James eyes were still downcast, and he shook his head slightly, but he would not look at him.

"James," he said softly, "look at me... please." The beautiful brown eyes were rimmed in red and puffy. He had made him cry and the feeling of knowing that was a physical blow to his stomach. He released him.

"If that will be all, sir?" James stood and headed toward the door, before he could open it Bertram spoke.

"I need more time, James."

"That is an excuse, I know how you feel about me, even if you will not admit it to yourself."

"You have never loved another, James. It takes time to let go."

"That is unfair. You had not met me when you made that promise, you could not have known that there was someone who would love you and no one else. Phillip Wyndham certainly did not. You will not let yourself love me." He left the room then and Bertram did not stop him. Was there some truth to what James had said, or was there something else that he was not quite realising yet? He hoped James would forgive him. He did not relish the thought of an empty bed.

Luke enjoyed his first afternoon and evening at Greypond. The family that lived at the house were Dowager Marsham; her son, Mr. Marsham who inherited the estate from his father; his wife, Mrs. Marsham; their son, Edward and their daughters, Miss Catherine and Miss Louisa. Miss Catherine was due to be married shortly. The nuptials had been postponed after the death of her grandfather.

Luke had been relieved to hear of it and quickly imparted his congratulations. When he visited before at the age of seventeen, he felt the family hoped he might show some interest in their eldest daughter who was two years his junior. Miss Louisa had only been ten years old at that time. She was still much too young for his consideration.

As during his previous stay, at every opportunity Dowager Marsham asked him questions about his home, his father, said she was sorry to hear of the death of his grandmother a few years ago and then the questions about Eastease, the Harkers and of course the Wyndham twins came. The latter he avoided as much as he could. He was not sure she even knew of the death of Maria Wyndham or that Harriet was only a few miles away. This first dinner was not the time to broach it. Thankfully, Mr. George Egerton, who was marrying Miss Marsham, preferred the subject matter to be himself and Luke was happy to encourage him in it.

The following day, he took a ride with Edward. It was cold, but they soon warmed themselves and their horses with a race across the fields. As they reached the last field of Greypond's property, where the graveyard of an old church began, they brought their mares to a trot and then a walk, turning them back to the direction of the house. As they caught their breath and the horses snorted out white billows of warm air, Luke considered how to broach the matter of Edward's cousin to him. There was no gentle way.

"Do you remember I mentioned in my letter that I was staying with friends at Wyndham House?"

"Yes, you stayed there last time you were here, did you not?"

"Yes, we were invited to a gentleman's evening there, but you were unwell and did not attend."

"I remember that, I was as sick as a dog. The owner, Wyndham, died early this year and his nieces inherited."

"Yes, the Wyndham twins that your grandmother asks me so much about."

"She does seem very interested in Eastease. I did offer to take her there once, I was sure if we were in the vicinity we could trouble you to introduce us."

"Of course I would have, and I am sure she should have been welcomed. What do you know of your aunt?"

"My mother's sister?"

"No, on your father's side."

"My father does not have any siblings."

"Not anymore, she died in childbirth fifteen years ago."

"No, you are mistaken. I should know if my father had a sister."

"She left home over twenty years ago and married hastily. Her name was Eliza."

"No. Your information is incorrect. I do not know who is telling you these lies, but I *would* know if what you are saying is true. If this woman married hastily, I assume you are implying she was with child. Then she died in childbirth later. I should have cousins on my father's side, but I do not."

"You do," Luke huffed out a breath, "you have one cousin. Miss Harriet Wyndham is your cousin."

"No, that cannot be right. With her so close at Wyndham House, Father would have told me of her. But, I can refute you now, she is a twin, so if this were true, I would have two cousins."

"Her sister, Maria, died earlier this year."

"And the child from when this Eliza died?"

"Died at the same time as Eliza."

"I cannot believe it, Parker. I should know. My father would not keep such a secret from me, from the whole family. I could believe it of my grandfather, he was very straight-laced in his opinions. I am not conceding that I believe you, but if it were true, why not tell me of it before?"

"I only learned of the connexion myself yesterday when I left." Luke keenly felt the pain of Harriet's rejection and refusal to speak to him. "I have to tell you that Miss Wyndham was not pleased to learn that I had spoken of her so often when I was here last, but I had no idea."

Edward considered him for a moment, his friend had a sense of humour, but it would not be in his nature to trick him about a family situation of this kind. Still, what he was saying was so unbelievable. "I do not believe you, Luke. I will ask my father, he will clear all of this up. Miss Wyndham must be mistaken."

"She is not mistaken. She knows her own mother's maiden name and it is Marsham." Luke was getting frustrated with his friend not believing him, but he could imagine if it were Edward telling him of a secret his own father had kept from him, he would be as stubborn. He tried to think of some fact he could tell Edward, "Eliza Marsham fell through the ice on Greypond many years ago and Lieutenant Wyndham rescued her by jumping straight in after her." It was a story the twins had told each other often when they spoke of their parents.

"No, people always mistake that girl as a Marsham, but she was one of the servants. Every year when the pond freezes over there is talk of her." Edward's grandfather had done a good job, Luke thought.

"What was the servant's name?"

"Eliz..." the name caught in Edward's throat, "you must have heard me tell that story."

"When? The pond was not frozen by the time I left here. It was before Christmas. I was home for Christmas."

"Then where did you hear that story?"

"From the twins. They told it often about their mother and stepfather."

"I have to talk to Father." Edward squeezed his mount into a trot away from Luke. He followed and his younger horse caught up easily.

"Given the secrecy that has kept this from you, I think it might be better to talk to your grandmother first. If you have confirmation from her, then your father cannot deny it. However, I am concerned about breaking the news of Maria's death to her. I do not think she knows."

"You and I should talk to her after luncheon and then there will be no need to talk to my father. You will see you are wrong." But Edward felt a gnawing in his stomach that quelled his appetite.

"I will follow your lead on both." Luke was grateful his friend was no longer angry with him, even if he did not fully believe him yet.

Harriet's mood did not improve in the morning following Luke's departure. The offending person of Mr. Collingworth had been collected by his family. Bertram and Drummond had talked to the solicitor they had sent with the carriage and directed him to talk to Baron Freyley for confirmation of the particulars as that man had been staying at the house when the body had been discovered.

Charlie Mickleson and Annie Brown had agreed to her plan to be married quickly and quietly right after the marriage of Drummond Mckinnon and Fiona Cadman. All the arrangements for the wedding breakfast at Wyndham Lodge were in place and Bertram had organised the special licence for the Micklesons.

Harriet wandered the corridors of the lower level of the house. Her music room did not beckon to her and nothing in her study needed attention. She did not seek out Bertram, as his mood was not at its best for the past few days and she wondered if his back was giving him trouble.

The person weighing on her peace of mind, was Mr. Luke Parker. She had sent him away without settling her anger. Was it his fault that he had been kept in the dark as to the identity of her mother? She hated the thought that the people who had rejected her sister and herself for so long had learned so much about them through an unsuspecting Luke. It was not that she wished her family had taken her and her sister in when her mother died, but that they had not cared enough.

Certainly, she had no complaints with her upbringing or the care and love she had received from her guardians, but to have family that did not care that she had lost her mother, a brother, two fathers and now her sister know everything there was to know about her, made it feel as if they held all the cards and she none.

The only thing that pulled her out of her mood, was a visit in the afternoon by Mr. Chapple and Mr. Holder. They had met with her in the parlour and excitedly asked if it were possible to speak with her brother. Thankfully the weather was dry and she used the excuse that he had gone for a ride, and would pass on any messages.

"We have been given the opportunity to perform at a recital in Bath a week on Saturday. Do you think he would be willing? We should have enough time to play two of his three pieces and if well received the third piece as well."

"Yes! Yes of course he would be willing. That is wonderful news gentlemen, wonderful news."

"We should need to practise and we wondered if that would be possible here. Every day would be preferable."

"Yes, that would be most acceptable."

"You will inform him then?"

"Yes, come back tomorrow afternoon and practise."

Edward Marsham and Luke Parker requested an audience with Dowager Marsham. She had her own sitting room next to her rooms and they sat within after their luncheon. Edward had explained all the particulars that Mr. Parker was sure were about her daughter and had confirmed he had told him that she did not have a daughter. His father was her only child.

"Edward, dear boy, I assure you that Mr. Parker is quite correct. I did have a daughter named Eliza. She had twin daughters, Harriet and Maria Wyndham, and she did die in childbirth when they were six years old. Your grandfather disowned her and forbad me any contact, but I will not deny it when asked directly."

Edward sat back in his chair and blew out a breath. "Why does Father still keep it a secret? Does he know? He must know, he cannot have forgotten a sister. Luke, I am sorry for disbelieving you."

"I, too, apologise, Mr. Parker, for all the questions, when you did not know I was asking about my granddaughters. Could you provide me with more information now? I have heard nothing since last you were here and told me so many stories about your childhood with them. Can you tell me of their lives over the past five years?"

"Madam, I am sorry, but I cannot tell you much. Miss Harriet Wyndham was not happy to learn of my interaction with you and that you gleaned so much information about her life from me. I am sorry to have to inform you, however, that Miss Maria Wyndham, or should I say Mrs. Maria Brooks as she became, died last spring." The lady put a hand to her mouth at that, she wanted to ask him more questions, but knew that was not fair to do. Tears formed quickly in her eyes and trickled down her face.

"I am so sorry, Grandmother." Edward moved in front of her chair and knelt on one knee so he could cover her other hand with his own.

"She had two children. A boy and a girl. You are a great-grandmother." Happiness and sadness showed in her face at once as the tears continued.

"Luke! I have more than one cousin then?"

"Yes, I suppose so, once removed is it not?" Edward nodded and smiled.

"The only other piece of news I feel I can impart to you, madam, is that Miss Harriet Wyndham and her sister inherited Wyndham House, a few miles north of here. She is living there and has been for the past two months."

"She is here? Oh, so near and yet so far. Michael will never allow me to see her."

"Leave Father to me, Grandmother. Remember I am a trained barrister. I can make a good argument when the cause is just."

"If a reconciliation can be made, Mrs. Marsham, then it is possible that Miss Wyndham would be willing to make living arrangements for you. In that case, you need not adhere to your son's rule."

"My husband never even let me write to my daughter, or my granddaughters after she died, he monitored every letter I sent or received. My son has continued in the same vein. However, if I were to write a letter to Miss Wyndham, do you think you would be willing to give it to her?"

"I will, but please refrain from asking me any further questions."

Edward's father had been a much different situation to tackle. He had railed against Luke for informing the dowager of anything to do with his sister and nieces. He knew Maria Wyndham had died and that his mother had great-grandchildren; he also knew that Harriet Wyndham was running the Wyndham estate, which he thought disgraceful. Luke had become angry at that and informed the man in no uncertain terms that Miss Wyndham was completely capable of running that estate.

Edward, who had remained calm as his training had taught him, shrewdly asked his father where he had come by all of his information. At this question, his father had turned a rather peculiar colour and had been forced to admit that he had been receiving letters from Alexander Harker all this time, as had his father ever since the twins had arrived at Eastease. The letters had only arrived once or twice a year at most and contained the very basic information of their well-being, but they had all ended with the same offer that contact with the Marsham family should always be welcomed at Eastease.

Edward demanded the letters, but his father refused. Then he surprised both his father and Luke by declaring that he would be requesting an introduction to his cousin by his friend and hoped that he could manage a reconciliation between the family. If his father was not willing, then he need not be involved.

"I will cut you off, you will receive nothing and Greypond will be inherited by Mr. Egerton."

"You forget, Father. I am well placed to take care of myself. I do not place property and things over family. If Miss Wyndham is willing to reconcile, I am sure I would not want for a place to stay if ever I found myself in difficulties."

"If you leave now, you will never be welcome back here."

"Like father like son? Is disowning their children all the Marshams know how to do? I refuse to follow in your footsteps. Luke and I are leaving, we will find accommodation in Bath until he can arrange a meeting at Wyndham House. If Grandmother should like to come with me, she would be welcome."

"I will not let you have use of the carriage."

"Then we will rent one. Good day, Father."

"Mr. Marsham," Luke gave a quick bow to the man and exited with his friend.

Luke Parker returned to Wyndham House two days earlier than expected. He arrived in the afternoon and requested a meeting with Miss Wyndham. Drummond showed him into the parlour and Bertram soon arrived to share refreshments with him. He could hear music from the music room and assumed Harriet was playing with the other men.

Bertram quickly informed him of the recital they were planning to play at a week on Saturday and he shook his head, the small knot in his stomach growing a little larger. She was currently dressed as Henry Wyndham and practising with the other men. Bertram had left Mckinnon watching over them. They were planning to practise every day next week, too. Luke groaned, this was going to add to an already complicated situation.

He briefly told Bertram of his interaction with Harriet's family. Bertram confirmed that she had confided in him about the Marshams and that she was very angry that they had been informed of her. Luke explained how her grandmother had not been permitted interaction. She had not even been allowed to write to her daughter and granddaughters. Harriet's cousin, his own friend, had not even known he had an aunt on that side of the family.

Edward Marsham and Dowager Marsham were comfortably ensconced in rooms at a hotel in Bath and were hoping to be invited to Wyndham House to meet with Miss Wyndham. Meanwhile, Harriet was busy pretending to be her brother and preparing for her first public appearance. It all seemed rather impossible.

"You are forgetting we have two weddings three days hence and a wedding breakfast at Wyndham Lodge, too! We will be without Mckinnon and our cook for a week, and Miss Brown's bruises have not yet faded. We must take some time to plan our best course of action."

"There had better be no planning that does not include, Miss Wyndham."

"Indeed. You are learning well, Luke my boy! Let us go and see the lady concerned. They have been playing for two hours now. We should see the other men on their way and talk to her."

They stood and walked out of the parlour toward the music room. Luke wondered at their need to practise more as it sounded beautiful to him. Bertram opened the door for them and Luke saw once again the unusual vision of Harriet dressed as Henry. It was an odd sensation to desire someone that to the outside world was a man.

Harriet turned to smile at Bertram as he re-entered the room, then she saw the tall figure of Mr. Parker behind him and her fingers, for once, gave her away as they played completely the wrong notes.

"Mr. Parker! You have returned to us earlier than Harriet expected."
She did at least remember to use Henry Wyndham's voice.

Chapter Twenty-Two

The musicians left and Luke asked Harriet if she would mind changing back into herself before they talked. He had news of her family to impart. The three of them sat in the parlour with refreshments. The view was marred somewhat by the misty rain that had started to fall, but it gave a cosy feeling to the atmosphere as they sat in chairs close to the fire.

Luke had explained how he had talked to Edward Marsham, Harriet's cousin, about her and that the man knew nothing of her or even of his aunt. He talked of his friend fondly in the hope that Harriet should see fit to allow an introduction. Then he mentioned Harriet's grandmother and her demeanour became a little colder.

"She is a very pleasant lady, Miss Wyndham. All of these years without news of her daughter and grandchildren. Her husband received letters from Mr. Harker, but never allowed her to see them. Of course, she would not go against his wishes, for fear that she would be rejected by your mother and by you. Then she would have had no place to go unless her husband forgave her."

"Alexander would never have sent her away."

"But she did not know that because she never knew of his letters. Edward stole the letters from his father's study before we left and said she was distraught at reading them all. It is little wonder that she questioned me so hard about you when I was here last and since then, five years ago, she has heard nothing. I told her that Maria had passed. It was most difficult."

"I cannot even think about this now. The weddings are this weekend and I have to practise for the recital."

"Mr. Parker and I have discussed this, Harriet," Bertram interjected, "and with your agreement, of course, this is what we propose. You could meet with Dowager Marsham and your cousin at the hotel where they are staying. You and Parker could go after the weddings, so you should have time to toast the happy couple and then leave everyone to enjoy it without their mistress overseeing them. I will of course keep my eye on proceedings. If you should like to, you could meet them there a second time and invite them to the recital, where, oh dear, you were feeling unwell and unable to attend. They would be able to see and hear you play without knowing it is you."

"I would accompany them there and, again if you are willing, introduce them to Henry Wyndham. The following week, you can invite them here. What are your thoughts?" Luke completed the plan.

"I think you and Bertram are manipulating me admirably, but what if she does not like or approve of me?"

"She is probably thinking the same thing. Perhaps these letters will help you. Bertram and I will leave you to read them in private."

"No, stay, please."

Harriet opened the letter from Edward Marsham, who expressed his surprise in learning of this newly discovered relation and his hope that she could forgive his family. He was at her disposal if she would be willing to meet with him. Luke would attest to his being different from his father and grandfather. The second letter she turned over in her hands, the writing was delicate and feminine. A grandmother, her beloved mother's mother. Her chest ached, the resentment that had built in her mind around this woman who had rejected her own child, her own grandchildren, dissolved in the realisation that she had not been permitted contact. Swallowing back the tears so she could focus on the words, she cracked the seal.

My Dear Grandchild,

What words can I write within this letter to express how deeply sorry I am that we have been kept apart for so long? Your grandfather was most disappointed in your mother rushing into marriage with Mr. Eldridge. I think his greatest anger lay in her being unable to fulfil his own wish for her to marry Lord Fairforth, a man much older than dear Eliza.

Her disgrace was hardly noticed at the time and never spoken of now. Most people have forgotten we even had a daughter, a fact I believe your grandfather forgot himself quite often. I never forgot and have been miserable for the past twenty-two years having no contact with first Eliza and then you and your sister.

I could have been there when Eliza passed, I could have cared for the two of you, though it would seem in that department your father made a suitable choice. I know Mr. Eldridge was not your father in the truest sense of the word.

My heart is broken over the loss of your sister. I had no idea until Mr. Parker informed me today. I understand however, that she had two children and I am a great-grandmother. Edward and I are planning to take a trip to Lincolnshire to visit them, we hope it will be with your blessing and perhaps you will join us?

Mr. Parker refuses to tell me more of you and your activities, as he informs me you are displeased with his revelations to me in the past. Please allow me to assure you that I was deceptive in my motives for finding out more about you and these indiscretions are not this young man's fault.

He did advise me that you are running Wyndham House. That large estate with you alone at the helm. That the servants look up to and respect you and would do anything for you. Such loyalty is seldom seen in such households. I am so very proud of you, Harriet.

I can never forgive my husband and son for depriving me of my family for so long. Yet how can I then expect you to forgive me my weakness in not insisting I visit you, or simply to put myself on a carriage heading north? Had I known of the generosity of your guardian, Mr. Harker, and known that I should have been welcome at Eastease, I might have been braver, but I never saw that man's letters until today.

Your courage must have been inherited from Lieutenant Wyndham, for surely he must have had so much of it to serve in the Navy and fight at Trafalgar.

I request that you give this old woman a new lease on life. To accept my apology and allow me to try, at least, to make up for so much lost time. Yours

Susanna Marsham

Harriet looked up at the two men waiting expectantly. "Thank you for bringing my family back to me, Mr. Parker. I believe I should like to meet with them on Saturday, after a toast to the happy couple at the wedding breakfast. Would you please arrange that and accompany me?"

"It would be my honour and my pleasure, Miss Wyndham."

The wedding of Drummond Mckinnon and Fiona Cadman was attended by all of the bride's family. Additionally, everyone possible from Wyndham House was present, including the lady of that house, Miss Harriet Wyndham, and her friends Mr. Luke Parker and Mr. Bertram Horncastle. Mr. Horncastle stood up with Drummond Mckinnon, though most people had to strain their necks to catch a glimpse of the smaller man and the unusual sight of the Scot wearing his kilt. Miss Cadman was attended by her sisters.

They crammed into the small church that resided on the Wyndham estate and listened solemnly to the service given by Mr. Green, the clergyman. Once they were declared man and wife, Mr. and Mrs. Mckinnon made their way out of the church to loud calls and climbed aboard an open carriage that should take them the mile or so to Wyndham Lodge and their wedding breakfast. The rest of their guests walked behind the carriage, looking forward to the feast they were certain Wyndham House had provided for its butler and cook.

Remaining in the church were Miss Wyndham, Mr. Parker and Bertram Horncastle. Standing in front of the clergyman now were Charlie Mickleson and Annie Brown, they clasped each other's hands firmly. At either side of them stood a small boy. Mr. Green looked at the odd family in front of him and then glanced behind them at Miss Wyndham. She nodded for him to proceed.

When the ceremony was complete the two boys cheered and

jumped up and down. Mr. and Mrs. Mickleson turned to receive the congratulations of Miss Wyndham. "I have a gift waiting for you outside." They traipsed out to the front of the church and found a large, bay Shire. His coat was gleaming from being groomed and he stood at least eighteen hands by Charlie's estimation. For all that height, he was lean and muscular. His black mane contrasting with the bright bay coat. The white, long-haired socks were topped with black points.

He was harnessed to a good-sized cart with two rows of seats and plenty of storage room behind. A beaming Benjamin Bramley stood at the head of the horse.

"He is for me to use?" Charlie felt as unsure as he had often seen his boys when he presented them with something of their own.

"No, Charlie, he is yours, as is the cart. Of course, his care will be provided by Wyndham House as part of your stable manager's pay. Now I suggest you take your wonderful wife home and we will take your sons with us to the Lodge. As planned, they will be in the care of the Robertsons for the rest of the day and tonight."

"It is too much, Miss Wyndham," Annie spoke with obvious feeling in her voice.

"Annie, for the services and loyalty you and your good husband have given to me personally and the care of this estate, it can never be enough. Promise me, that if you are ever in need of anything, you will come to me." Embarrassed, Annie nodded. Charlie took a few moments to acquaint himself with the enormous horse, then handed his wife up to the cart. He looked down at his sons.

"Be good. I want nothing but good reports from Mrs. Robertson tomorrow." They both nodded obediently. "Have fun, too!" They smiled their wide smiles.

"See you tomorrow, Ma! See you tomorrow, Da!" And they waved them off to the cottage.

Benjamin Bramley drove the rest of them to the Lodge. He was allowed in for the toast of the happy couple and then he left with Mr. Parker and Miss Wyndham, driving them to Bath town centre to meet Miss Wyndham's family.

"I have no idea what to say to them," Harriet declared as the carriage made its way.

"Do not put so much importance on it. The fact that you agreed to meet with them is enough."

"Not important! It is only the first time I have ever met anyone from this side of my family. We never met Uncle Phillip on the Wyndham side either, but at least he wrote to Alexander and remembered us in his will." Luke smiled at her chiding him.

"You never came to Wyndham House as children?" he could not remember her ever speaking of it.

"No. I do not think young girls were his forte."

"You could thank her for her letter," he suggested.

They met in a private room of the hotel at which Mr. Edward Marsham and Dowager Marsham were staying. At first the meeting was awkward, Harriet knew that these people were her family, but they were strangers. Knowing she was nervous, Luke began talking of the wedding they had just attended and then of the gift Harriet had bestowed upon her butler and cook. They should be leaving their wedding breakfast to be driven to Weston-super-mare on the west coast, about a day's drive away. The man driving them had family in the area whom he would visit while they stayed three nights at Reeves, the new hotel at that location. The new Mrs. Mckinnon had never visited the sea, whereas Drummond Mckinnon had grown up in northwest Scotland.

"Thank you for your letter, Mrs. Marsham," Harriet spoke for the first time after the introductions. She had tried to think of a suitable opening to discuss the fact that she had been excluded from this family for her whole life, but Luke's suggestion was all that came to mind. She slanted a look at him, daring him to laugh, but his lips only twitched.

"My dear, a letter cannot possibly convey the apology due to you for the harm and the hurt my family has bestowed upon an innocent in this business, for surely that is what you are. I hoped you might consider it a start."

"I blamed you and Mr. Marsham for rejecting my mother. She was a wonderful mother and did not deserve to die the way she did, but I know now that you did not know any of that. You were not permitted to know. My anger and resentment cannot be directed at either of you. The only one I should direct it at is no longer alive."

"Well, we could have been reunited a year ago, if my son had not continued in the same vein as his father. I could have met Maria. If I had been as brave as you are, I could have defied my husband."

"How could you have known that you would have been welcomed? How could I have known you were being prevented from making contact? No, we cannot apportion blame to anyone in this room and we cannot look back and regret. We can only move forward, if we do not the future will be tainted. We deserve a good future."

"I knew I was going to like you, Miss Wyndham!" Edward had been listening to the exchange. His grandmother had asked him to allow her to make her apology to the young lady first. "I could not have put it better myself."

"I understand from Mr. Parker that you are a barrister, so that is high praise indeed, Mr. Marsham."

"How do you feel about us all making a trip to Lincolnshire? I should love to become acquainted with my other cousins, small though they may be and see where you grew up. I understand Maria's widower lives close by?"

"Mr. Brooks, yes he does. However, at the moment, I am afraid I am committed to remaining in Bath for a little longer. My half-brother is living at Wyndham House with me for the time being. He will be playing at a recital here next weekend and is using my music room to practise with the gentlemen with whom he performs his pieces."

"I was not aware you had a brother." Edward looked pointedly at Luke.

"On my father's side, before the lieutenant married my mother. Obviously, he did not marry the woman but allowed the boy to take the Wyndham name. Uncle Phillip provided for him until he was old enough to travel, he has been out of the country for the most part. We are very close in age."

"You mentioned 'his pieces'. He is a composer?" Dowager Marsham asked.

"Yes, he sent me pieces to play, music is a passion of mine. He has invited you to attend the recital if you are interested."

"That should be wonderful, would it not, Edward?"

"Yes, most acceptable."

While Harriet was meeting with her family, Charlie and Annie Mickleson were inside their little cottage behind the Wyndham stable. The mantle over the front doorway had been decorated with a pretty garland of late Autumn foliage and inside their kitchen was a large basket of food and drink. Annie poked through it and pulled out a bottle of wine with an exclamation.

"I think I would like a glass of wine right now. Would you, Husband?" He turned at her words and smiled. He liked to hear it, just to remind himself that he had gotten so lucky as to marry her.

"We could save it for before we go to bed." He was not sure whether she should want to receive him yet, but if she did, they could probably both do with a little wine to allay their nerves. She looked at him then, he was a big man, she had seen him with so much anger in his face, he had killed for her, but she was not afraid of him. She was not sure she was ready for the feeling of a man within her again, but she knew that she wanted it to be this man. It was not going to get any easier in her mind until she allowed him to take her to bed.

"We could drink some now and then go to bed." She suggested with a small smile.

His eyes met hers quickly at that. He had thought over this night, how he should have to take things slowly, be gentle with her, hold his own control. He knew how to give a woman passion, if he could bring that out in her, she should be sure to welcome him and this whole horrid affair with Collingworth could be one step further away. Some wine should help them both and he nodded.

They sat by the fire in their sitting room, they had arm chairs facing one another and they sipped their wine and looked at each other, saying nothing. This was not going to get them close she thought, so she stood and walked over to one side of his outstretched legs, he looked up at her and she ran her hand through his thick mop of black hair. Quickly, he reached out and pulled her into his lap.

"I want to kiss you, Mrs. Mickleson."

"Then I suggest you do so!"

He started the kiss light and tender, her lip had healed and he did not cause her any pain. He had kissed her this way a few times as she had stayed at the cottage since that dreadful night, but now he put more demand in the kiss, he found his hands moving into her hair and pulling out the pins that held it in check. Her long locks fell down her back and over her chest as they were loosened.

With her hair down, he could run his hands through it as he continued to kiss her. He moved those kisses to her face and down her throat as he allowed the back of his hand that ran through her hair covering her chest, to stroke the rise of her breast. She gasped. Joining their mouths once more, he moved fluidly out of the chair and rose with her in his arms, walking out of the door and up to their bedroom. The fire there had been banked down and the room was chilly, so he set her down to take off her boots and her gown before encouraging her to get under the blankets.

She watched as he stripped off his own clothes, leaving only his breeches on. She could not help licking her lips at the sight of his muscled chest and stomach, then she laughed at the thought that he certainly was a magnificent beast. He glanced at her, not sure what he had done that was humorous but pleased that she was happy. She pulled the blankets back for him to get into bed, but he walked out of the room and returned quickly with the two cups of wine they had not finished. She sat up and took hers, and drank the remaining wine with a quick couple of gulps. He smiled at her and did the same.

They snuggled together to generate some warmth and he pulled her to him so she could rest on his chest. "Annie, if you want me to stop at any moment you must say so and I will."

"I will not want you to stop."

"I will never hurt you."

"I know." She looked up at him then and kissed him, moving her body along his chest as she reached for him and made the kiss more passionate. His hands slid over her, pulling her completely on top of him as he pulled her chemise up and over her head, her dainty breasts rubbed against his firm muscles and she sighed. He stifled a groan as he felt himself grow against her. Kissing down her neck, he pulled her easily up above him and took one of those nipples hardened by the cold air, into his mouth, sucking gently.

She could not believe the sensation that flooded her. She had never thought a man should suckle on a woman's breast. If she had, she would have thought it a ridiculous thing to do, to behave as a baby in that way, but, by the way that part of him within his breeches pushed into her thigh, that he enjoyed it.

Before she thought about it, her legs opened and she straddled his hips. She still wore her drawers and they parted allowing her most delicate skin to rub against his breeches, but she did not feel delicate. The rough fabric enhanced the feelings he was giving her. Putting a hand either side of his head, she moved her other breast into his mouth. With her now supporting herself, his hands released her sides and cupped them. His thumb rubbed over the nipple he had been suckling.

"Yes." The word came out of her mouth involuntarily and she bit her lips together. His eyes flew to hers and though his mouth was still clamped over her nipple she could see a smile. When he did release her, and placed her back to his side, she felt a little saddened. The tingling feeling had been increasing in intensity and she wondered where it was all leading.

Charlie turned to look at her. "I think I should take off my breeches and show you my body. It should not be some mystery."

She nodded, curiosity building within her after feeling it against her. He unbuttoned his breeches and pushed them under him as he lifted his hips, then he reached within them at the front to hold himself and avoid any pulling as he pushed the breeches off and kicked them off his feet. He had taken off the blankets and lay there with his hand still covering himself, oddly shy for a moment. Her hand reached out to cover his and then cover him, as he slipped his hand away and back over hers. He encouraged her to make a fist around him, then moved his hand away. He tucked his arm behind his head, his other arm held her to his side.

As her hand moved he groaned, she moved her head to his chest and kissed him running her tongue over his nipple as he had done to her, not sure if it gave him as much pleasure. Then she stopped suddenly as she came to a decision. She laid on her back and untied her stockings and drawers, pushing them off her legs so they were both naked. She straddled him again and offered him her breasts. With a huge grin at the sight before him, he took a nipple into his mouth again.

This time there was no rough fabric between them and she felt the surprisingly soft skin of his arousal against that part of her that was

310

pulsing. She moved her hips to feel him against her and felt heat bursting within her core. They groaned at the same time and he lifted her hips up to stop the motion she was about to repeat. He would not be able to keep his control if she continued. Instead he moved his hand down her stomach and between her legs, into that soft hair and those soft lips. His fingers took over rubbing that point of heat that had her panting, and moaning for more.

He slipped a finger inside her and her eyes flashed to him a moment, before he circled again with his thumb. "If you should like to stay in control, Wife, I have no objection." He removed his finger and positioned his hardness at the point the finger had exited. Tentatively she pushed her hips down onto him and felt him enter her a little, then she pushed a little more and he slid in further.

My God, he was trying to hold on, but each little push took him to the edge of his control, moving his thumb back to that point that she had enjoyed him touching moments ago, he circled and at the same time pushed within her. With him fully inside her, a feeling of power and desire overtook her. She rose and fell over him again and again, his thumb continuing its circling. Finally, a wave of pulsing and feeling cascaded over her as she peaked, pulling him into her and allowing his ultimate release. She collapsed upon him with laughter and gasps. His breath ragged, he pulled her to him and covered them with the blankets.

"This is going to be a very interesting marriage, Mrs. Mickleson."

Harriet returned from the first meeting with her family members quite relieved and felt a weight lifted off her. She liked Edward very much and was surprised how easily she had found it within her heart to forgive the older woman. She visited with them in Bath twice more, declaring it a relief to get out of Wyndham House and the infernal repetition of the same three pieces of music. Luke raised his eyebrows at that, Harriet, it would seem, was quite an accomplished liar!

It was a busy week for both Harriet and Henry Wyndham. Finally, the evening of the recital arrived and many of the families who had left London at the end of the season and moved to their homes in the country, enjoyed an opportunity to gather in Bath. In amongst the audience was Dowager Marsham and Edward Marsham. Luke Parker joined them, sitting next to the older woman with her grandson the other side of her, and he introduced Bertram Horncastle who sat to his other side. He explained that unfortunately Miss Wyndham was unwell and remained at Wyndham House. Her grandmother was disappointed and showed much concern for her granddaughter's wellbeing.

When the players appeared on the small stage and bowed, Luke heard the dowager gasp. The familiar music began and he felt a tap on his arm. Looking at the lady to his right, he leaned over to hear her better. "That is Harriet, is it not?"

"I do not know what you mean, madam." Luke tried to make light of her comment.

"The pianist is Miss Harriet Wyndham. I should recognise her anywhere. How daring! So, there is no brother and the composed pieces are her own?" The lady seemed positively delighted with her granddaughter, so Luke smiled and then put a finger to his lips. She nodded and did the same. What talent and courage her granddaughter had, she was so proud of her.

The players received such a loud ovation at the end of their two pieces that they were allowed to perform a third. Mr. Chapple spoke out in his loud voice that their final piece would be one that was also composed by Henry Wyndham and that they had not performed it anywhere before this evening. It was entitled 'Family'.

Dowager Marsham put her hand to her mouth in surprise at the title and then applauded with everyone else as the players took their positions once again. Silence enveloped them before the piece began. The pianist played a light carefree melody to begin the piece that the flute joined in. A feeling of childhood came back to Luke, as he pictured himself running and playing with the Wyndham twins, then it fell into a deeper darker place that he imagined was her grief over the loss of her parents and her sister, then it moved to an optimistic sounding ending that resounded of hope and possibilities. When he turned to look at Harriet's grandmother, the woman had tears streaming down her cheeks. Edward even poked a finger at his eyes a little, while Luke's own were very damp.

The piece finally came to a close and the room erupted. Harriet sat at the pianoforte in shock, as usual she had lost herself in the piece and her playing. Without thinking, she slapped both hands up in front of her face, covering her nose and mouth. She looked over at Mr. Leake who was looking at her rather oddly. Standing she bowed with the other gentlemen and smiled broadly, she had never been so happy or felt so accepted. She looked over at Luke and felt a soaring in her heart at the sight of him. He was smiling broadly and applauding loudly with everyone else.

The journey home had been very pleasant. She rode in her carriage with Bertram and Luke and they talked nonstop about the performance. After the applause had died down, she had gone over to Luke for him to introduce her as Henry Wyndham to Edward and her grandmother. Though she saw a sparkle in the dowager's eye, she did not know that the lady knew it was her. Once they were safely in the carriage and out of earshot of anyone else, Luke imparted the news.

Mr. Chapple, Mr. Holder and Mr. Leake were all riding in their own carriage to Wyndham House to enjoy a celebratory supper and drinks. However, when the other men arrived, Mr. Leake unceremoniously walked in and pointed to Harriet. "Imposter!"

"What on earth do you mean, man?" Harriet tried to sound angry. That was not difficult, given that her triumphant evening was in tatters at that one word.

"I mean that you are Miss Wyndham, not Henry Wyndham."

"I most certainly am not! What an insult, I demand you take it back."

"I do not know how I have not seen it all this time! I have never seen the two of you together, and tonight when you covered your face and made me focus solely on your eyes I saw it."

"Of course we have similar eyes, we are brother and sister, you imbecile."

"Have you seen the two of them together?" he pointed in turn at his comrades and they shook their heads, though they were not as convinced as Mr. Leake.

"Well I have seen them together." Bertram said amiably, looking amused by it all. He did not want Leake to think him worried.

"As have I," Luke confirmed, too.

"I am not convinced. You are probably colluding with her." He turned to Harriet, his tone demanding, "put your hands over your face again, we will all see it then."

"I will not!"

"Then bring Miss Wyndham here so we can see you both together."

"She is staying with her family tonight and tomorrow. They were at the recital." Luke improvised quickly.

"Then drop your breeches, we are all men here."

"That is ridiculous, Leake," Holder joined into the argument.

"There must be some other way I can prove it. Name a task a woman cannot do. If I can best one of you at it the argument should be settled."

"I do not think that should be necessary," Luke cut in, sensing danger. "I must say I would expect the word of myself and Horncastle here to be sufficient."

Caught up in the idea of a competition, Bertram contradicted Luke. "I like the idea of a competition. Let us each think of a task, they will be performed tomorrow. Leake can be your champion and Wyndham, here, will be ours. If he can best you more often than not, Leake, you must concede your position." It was agreed, and drinks were served, each group of three taking to an end of the parlour as they discussed their tasks and tactics.

When Harriet went to bed that night, using the room adjacent to her own, she wondered what on earth Bertram had gotten her into, but she was determined to see it through in the slim hope that she could play another recital.

Chapter Twenty-Three

The following morning, Bertram and Mr. Chapple took a look at the list of challenges that were proposed. They agreed that the first should be riding. During a review of the horses, they decided the riders should use Hudson and Henry. They were so alike it was hard to tell them apart. As Henry Wyndham knew the horses a little, it was determined fairest that Leake should choose between them.

Leake was surprised. "Are they twins? I cannot tell them apart."

"Harriet knows." Wyndham stood to the side and Leake gave him a long look, then harrumphed.

"This is Hudson." Mickleson stood holding the reins of one horse, his son, Richie held the other. "Twins are rare in horses and would not be so big and strong as these boys." They were liver chestnuts, with white socks on all legs and a white blaze on their faces. Their manes and tails were flaxen, giving them a high-class look.

Wyndham kept his face neutral while Leake reviewed Hudson. Of course, he would rather Leake chose Henry, so when the man glanced his way, he looked down but let a small smile play on his face. Leake immediately thought the man happy he was going to choose that horse, and chose Henry instead. They all mounted their horses and Wyndham surprised Luke by springing up from the ground without assistance, pushing up with his arms and lifting a leg easily over Hudson's back.

Mickleson suggested they all ride out to the lake and detailed their route when they gathered at its edge. "It is about two miles around. First, make your way through the wood," he pointed to the left side. "The paths are accommodating, providing you duck a few branches. From there the bank of the lake begins to rise up from the water and at the top of a grassy slope, you have a choice which will test your capability."

He winked unseen at Henry Wyndham and explained, "You can continue around the lake getting up a good amount of speed and these boys are capable of plenty of that, or as they are sure footed, and if you are more daring, you could head your mount down a steep, rocky slope to the edge of the lake. The ground at the water's edge is firm from recent cold weather. It is a less steep climb back up to the higher bank and cuts out at least a third of the distance. From that point, it is an easier run back here, skirting the copse of trees to this side." He pointed to the right bank. "They are too densely populated to ride through."

They set off through the trees, taking different paths. Leake's took him nearer to the lake's edge and found himself ahead. Looking back, he could see Wyndham getting closer and ducked a low branch when he turned back. Wyndham found his way onto the same path as Leake. The man called out to him, which he realised belatedly was to distract him from a low branch. Just in time, he managed to lay flat on the horse's back. Scowling at Leake's back as he straightened.

They exited the wood and raced to the grassy slope, up to the higher bank, but when they approached it, Wyndham moved ahead quickly. He stood up in the stirrups, leaning his body forward behind Hudson's neck and keeping his heels down. Leake remained in the saddle, giving Henry no assistance at all. The lead allowed Wyndham to stop at the top of the rocky bank that led down to the water's edge and he gave Hudson a good look at it.

The horse nodded his head as if agreeing that it was manageable, and they started down. Wyndham had seen the best course over the rocks. They were big enough and mostly flat enough for horse hooves and he guided Hudson down as quickly yet safely as he could. He leaned back in the saddle to put the least amount of pressure on the front of the horse and avoid falling off over his neck.

He had felt, rather than seen, Leake thunder past them on Henry. Wyndham had guessed he would go for the longer, faster route. He was confident that Hudson was sure footed and allowed him a longer rein, so he could navigate over the rough terrain. If Mickleson was right and this route cut out a third of the distance, he was sure he could get back up and out with a good lead over Leake.

They reached the water's edge safely and rode at a steady canter. He held Hudson back from a gallop over the hardened mud to pace him for the climb back up to the higher ridge. Thankfully, this was easier than getting down had been as half of it was grass. Wyndham realised he was not as far ahead of Leake and Henry as he had hoped.

Leake had seen Wyndham take his horse down the slope, and knowing it was a shorter route rode his mount hard around the upper bank. When Wyndham, Horncastle and Parker had decided on riding as one of their choices, he had been surprised. If Wyndham was a woman, he should not be used to riding astride a horse nor could he ride as fast not being as strong. Now he was wondering if he had really seen what he had thought he saw when the recital finished last night. No, he was right, he was determined, this was Miss Wyndham.

The man and horse rose from the lower bank barely two lengths ahead of him and he continued to urge Henry on. What he had not considered, however, was that his horse had been running fast the whole way around, whereas its almost twin, had seemingly enjoyed a pleasant canter by the water. As he tried to pull closer, Wyndham legged the less winded beast into a full-on gallop that even with a fresh horse Leake doubted he could match. By the time he rounded the last grouping of trees, he could see Wyndham slowing his horse as he reached their friends, receiving loud congratulations from them all.

Dismounting, Wyndham walked Hudson around cooling him off and as Leake approached, the stable manager, still sitting astride his enormous Shire, requested he do the same with Henry. Parker put out an arm to hoist Wyndham onto the back of his own horse, the man leapt up easily as if he did so every day. Leake had a little more difficulty joining Chapple on his horse and they led the tired stallions back to Wyndham House and the stable.

Luke talked to Harriet, enjoying the feeling of her arms around his waist. "I never doubted your horsemanship and I never will."

Leake's first choice was fencing. Wyndham and Leake stood opposite each other on the same grassy spot, by the small wall, that Nathaniel and Bertram had months before. "Best of five hits, gentlemen." Bertram gave the signal. Wyndham bowed, but Leake performed his quickly and was attacking the moment Wyndham straightened.

"A hit," Wyndham spat the words at him, disgusted. They fought again, and this time Leake found a way through with a hit to the chest. He pressed it there hard enough to cause a bruise, not knowing he was hitting Harriet's bindings. Leake's next hit would win him the challenge! It had been a long time since the colonel had taught Harriet to fight, she had to focus and look for the other man's weaknesses. Wyndham had seen an opening, in the second, but was hit before he could take advantage of it. This time he spotted it, avoided a hit to himself and took the hit on Leake instead.

Foolishly, Leake did not defend that weakness the second time, so Wyndham took advantage once more. With the score even, and them both breathing hard, they took their stances for the last. Wyndham thought he, had seen the man's weakness show again, but he had feigned it and delivered his own hit.

"Nothing to be ashamed of." Bertram tried to console him.

Chapple agreed. "He is the best swordsman of any of us."

Wyndham snorted and walked away saying, "Then the shame really depends on how good the two of you are, does it not?"

Mr. Parker sidled up to her as she stalked away. "There is no need to be rude to Chapple, he is being a good sport about all of this, I do not think he believes Leake."

"Thank you, but that is not why I am upset."

"Why then?"

"Never tell the colonel I lost, will you?" Luke smiled at that.

They were tied, one task a piece. The final outdoor task was shooting. Harriet had wanted to be sure to choose at least two physical challenges so she did not seem weak, and had assured Bertram she was a good shot. They had left Mckinnon in charge of the preparations, while they partook of some luncheon. Leake enjoyed his meals at Wyndham House. He particularly liked the sweet cakes and pastries they served at luncheons. Wyndham stayed away from them and ate a lighter meal.

By the time they headed outside to the opposite side of the house to that of the stable, Leake was yawning. Mckinnon had set up a table, fifteen paces away from a grouping of trees.

"Gentlemen, as you see, I have pinned a piece of paper to each of three trees at the front and one piece on a tree at a further distance. The pistols on the table here are loaded. You can choose, three shots at the three nearest, or two and a riskier shot at the tree five paces further back."

He held out his fist with several pieces of grass in it. "Shortest piece shoots first." Wyndham's was longer, so Leake stepped up and picked up each pistol and shot at the trees. Then they walked with Mckinnon to check his success. He had hit all three closest papers to differing degrees of accuracy. Mckinnon circled each hole.

Wyndham stepped up after the pistols had been reloaded. Carefully, he shot all three and, when finished, they all approached the trees. As the papers came into view, Leake began to laugh. "You missed every one. Every one!"

"Did I?"

Mckinnon reached the papers first. Pulling one down he inspected it more closely and gave a startled looked up at Wyndham. He handed it to Leake. "Look at the circle I drew." Leake stared, the edge of the circle was broken, what had appeared to be one shot hole, was actually two. Leake strode to the next tree and yanked at the paper, the circle was broken there, too. Pulling down the final one, he laughed.

"It does not matter, you missed this one."

"I did not aim at that one." At that, Bertram smiled at Wyndham and moved to the furthest tree, pulling down the paper target. Almost centre to the paper, was the hole of a ball shot.

"Wyndham wins!" He held it up.

As they walked back into the house, Luke could not help but whisper in an aside to Harriet, "Where *did* you learn to shoot?"

"Helena."

The fourth challenge, Leake's second choice, was declared cards. Unfortunately, this was not one of the colonel's strengths that he had taught his ward. Hence, Wyndham lost to Leake very quickly.

Now they were tied again and the fifth task, Harriet's final choice, was chess. Leake, shook his head. "I do not know how to play."

"Then you must forfeit!" Bertram declared, "making Wyndham the winner by three tasks to two."

"Can I not have my second play in my place?"

Bertram looked to Wyndham. "It is up to you, sir." He looked at Leake and then to Bertram. It would not feel as if he truly won, were the man forced to forfeit, and he did not want to risk suggesting another task. The last one the other man had chosen was drinking and he was well aware of his disadvantage there, whereas he felt chess was his particular strength.

"Who is your second?" Mr. Chapple cracked his knuckles with a look of glee. Chess was a favourite of his. "Then let us play, man."

Chapple was white and moved first. His strong opening gambit was a familiar one to Harriet, Harker used it often when teaching her to play. Eventually, she had found a way around it and beaten him, but it had been long and required tempting the opposition to take two key sacrifices.

As the game with Chapple dragged on, he became less confident observing Wyndham's less predictable movements. He did succumb to the temptation of Wyndham's first sacrifice and was satisfied it was a mistake when he saw him scowl. When Wyndham moved his second sacrifice piece, he lifted his hand from it and then, as if realising his mistake, made to move it back.

"Too late, man. You released it." Chapple took the piece with glee. His satisfaction lasted only a few moments, before his opponent made his next move and his mistake became clear. There was no escape from the checkmate and seeing how cleverly he had been manoeuvred, he knocked over his king. "Excellent game, sir. Well done."

"Thank you."

"Wyndham wins. No need for the final task. The most it would garner would be a tie." Bertram declared, and Luke looked relieved. Leake moved forward to bow to Wyndham.

"My apologies, sir. A woman could never have bested me, or Chapple here. Obviously, what I observed was simply familial resemblance."

"Apology accepted, of course. You still plan to stay for dinner I hope? You can depart in the morning."

"Excellent!" Holder, who had not been happy about all the anger between his friends, looked forward to a more relaxing dinner.

The meal was enjoyed by all, music began the discussion, but conversation soon moved to the day's events. Leake felt he was coming out of the retelling rather worse than Wyndham, especially when Bertram pointed out Wyndham had not asked for a second in playing cards. Bertram was sure to have won. Then Chapple said that he had played chess for him. "Well there is one way we can settle this as *men*," he suggested and tapped his wine glass for a refill from Mckinnon.

Wyndham, who was feeling emboldened from all the praise in shooting and riding, as well as Chapple talking of his unusual chess tactics with considerable respect, finished off his wine and indicated Mckinnon should refill his glass, too.

Bertram was laughing and enjoying himself in a way he had not since Phillip hosted his all male dinner parties. It was only Luke who seemed to see the danger and perhaps Mckinnon, too, as he looked to Mr. Parker often.

The meal was finished quickly and drinking copious amounts took over, with Wyndham matching Leake glass for glass in wine and then in port. Much hilarity ensued as each glass was consumed, with the other men joining in sometimes, all except for Luke.

When Harriet looked over to him, her eyes unfocused and put her hand on his cheek tenderly, saying, "Dearest Luke, loyal Luke." He smiled at her with a shake of his head. Her cheeks suddenly turned pale, and her eyes rolled back in her head.

Luke grabbed the hand she had put to his cheek, lifting her up from the chair slightly, he ducked his head under her arm and let her limp body fall over his shoulder. Turning, he could see Mckinnon opening the door for him and he stepped out with Harriet, Mckinnon closed the door on the laughing men.

"Mrs. Mickleson is with her family, I will call her in to help." Mckinnon made to move.

"No, Drum. Let her stay with them. This will be an all-night situation and not my first of this kind, either helping or needing the help."

"But..." Drum was unsure.

"I would never... You know that, Drum. She could not consent in this state and I would never..."

"Yes, sir. I will send up some supplies, have them left in the dressing room. Make sure to use Mr. Wyndham's bedroom."

"Thank you, Drum."

Luke laid a passed-out Harriet on the nearest couch in the bedroom that adjoined her own via the dressing room. Then he shrugged out of his coat and waistcoat and searched under the bed for the chamber pot. Moving to the dressing room, he found another and some cloths. There was water in a basin on the washstand and in the pitcher beside it. Filling a cup, he dipped a cloth in the basin and returned to the room.

"Come on, Harriet, sit up." He pulled her up to a sitting position and holding her face in his hands he tapped her cheek gently. She murmured and opened her eyes, looking vaguely at him. He grabbed the nearest pot as he saw her eyes widen and her pallor grey. Just in time he got the pot to her face as she cast up her accounts. When she seemed to be finished for the time being, he set the pot down and picked up the wet cloth, applying it to her head and dabbing gently at her mouth.

She groaned, "Help me get this off." She gestured to her coat and waistcoat and he helped her with them. The movement made her head spin. As she retched again, he grabbed the other pot. "Oh God, I feel so bad."

"It was idiotic and unnecessary, Harriet."

She looked at him with as much sarcasm as she could muster. "Really? Thank you for pointing that out, sir, or I might never have realised." She vomited and again he wiped her mouth and offered her the cup of water to swill with and then drink a little.

"I was stating what was obvious, I suppose. Though you did not find it obvious before you started drinking."

"Help me get this off, I cannot breathe." He untied her cravat and undid the top button of the shirt.

"Did that help?"

"No, this," she began to pull frantically at the binding beneath her shirt.

"Harriet, I cannot."

"I cannot breathe, Luke. Please." He stood her and looked in her eyes as she swayed slightly. He pulled her shirt up over her head and looked for the end of the binding that had been tucked in under her armpit. Releasing it, he wound the binding into a ball, as he fed it around her.

Reaching both his arms behind her, she swayed toward him as he passed the ball of cloth from hand to hand, then brought it to the front again to repeat the process. As the binding released, he could see the mounds of her breasts swell as they were freed. Turn by turn brought his first sight of them closer and yet, in this moment, he knew he was not permitted to touch or kiss as he desired.

The last ring fell from her as he put his arms around her the last time. Her nipples, hardened in the cold air, brushed against his ribcage through the thin material of his shirt. He held his breath. She slumped back down on the couch, her hands circling over those mounds to relieve them. He glimpsed a bruise from the fencing and swore.

"Thank God! That must be the worst thing about pretending to be a man." Harriet sighed in relief.

Luke stood there opened mouthed entranced by her moving hands, but when he heard her retch again, he moved quickly to assist her. Noticing a coverlet over the back of the couch, he draped it over her back and again applied the wet cloth to her face and wiped her mouth.

"Wait here, I will find your nightgown." Leaving her with one chamber pot, after emptying all the contents into one, he picked up the used cloths and returned to the dressing room. Two more chamber pots had appeared there as well as a pile of clean cloths. "Thank you, Drum," he said aloud to the empty room, leaving the used pot after covering it with a cloth.

Finding a nightgown laid out and ready for its owner, he picked that up, too, and returned to the room. Harriet had taken off her boots, laid down on the couch and closed her eyes, wrapping the coverlet around herself. She opened one eye when he came in and held up the nightgown. Without a second thought, she pushed the coverlet off her shoulders, stood and pulled down her trousers. She worn nothing underneath and stood completely naked in front of him.

He should look away, but could not. Desire flooded his loins as he gazed at her lean, lithe body. He stood transfixed as he held out the nightgown he had bunched up to put over her head. She walked toward him, avoiding the nightgown and moved into the circle his arms made with it. She pressed herself up against him, her hands busying themselves untying his cravat.

"Harriet, no," he spoke on a whisper and then with all his self-control and much regret, he put the nightgown over her head and allowed it to fall down her body, covering her.

"Of course not," she said resignedly. "Now you know about Davenport, you do not want me."

"It is not that."

"Then it is my sister. You still love her. I understand. Everyone loved her."

"No, Harriet. I have always loved you."

"Exactly."

He picked her up in his strong arms and walked through to the other bedroom with her. Depositing her gently onto the bed and pulling the covers over her. He set a chair beside the bed with a chamber pot on it and some cloths over the back of it, then he refilled the cup with water from the pitcher and brought it over to her.

Tears spilled down her cheeks, and he sat on the edge of the bed to reach over and wipe them away with his knuckles. "You do not want me."

"I want you more than anything else in the world."

"Then kiss me and hold me."

"Firstly, your breath smells, so I am not going to kiss you. Secondly, you are drunk and do not know your own mind. Ask me again when you are sober, and I will gladly oblige you." She looked at him, so sensible and strong. She knew she would not ask him when sober. It would not be fair to him. He loved Harriet and she was not Harriet. Thinking of her sister, she became maudlin again.

"I loved her, too, you know, so how can I blame everyone else for loving her? You loved her more, your grandmother, too, of course. Mr. Brooks did not look at me in any particular way, but the day after she came back he could not keep his eyes from her. Davenport, I cannot blame her for him after the way he treated her. He beat her you know."

"So I understand."

"It should have been me, he only decided to take her because she would be less trouble than me. That is what he told me."

"Trouble is more interesting." Luke spread his hands out at their situation, which made her laugh a little, then he stroked her short hair. "Tell me what happened between you and Davenport."

She told him how she thought that finally someone held an interest in her, rather than her sister. It was intoxicating to think that he cared for her and he made her feel special. She did not even see that he was doing the same with her sister. She fancied herself in love with him. Nathaniel trusted him and so she felt she could, too. The morning after the ball, she met him at the shelter. Thinking they were to be married, she welcomed his attentions and then the situation had changed. When she was at her most defenceless, he turned on her. She had asked him to stop, but he laughed and told her to blame Alexander and Nathaniel.

Knowing the kind of man he was, she had let her sister ride away with him. Lied to give them time to get away even, but when she returned to Eastease, her sister did not blame her.

"I doubt your sister would have been able to come here and be as successful as you at running this house. Nor could she have won the challenge that you did today."

"You think you could have beaten me?"

"I do not think I should have fared any better than Leake."

She smiled at that and her eyes fluttered close. He watched her as she fell asleep and put a hand to his heart. He had not thought he could love her more, yet hearing her story made him realise how strong she had been to hold her head high again. That she had kept that secret and still had the courage to come here to do so much, had increased the love he held for her. He had to ask her to marry him, he could not go on living without holding that beautiful body against his own.

Feeling that she was out of the woods and should sleep until morning, he left her and moved back to the other room to tidy up. Rather than leave and go to his own bed, he decided to sleep nearer to her. He wanted to be close if she needed him. Stripping off all his clothes he slid gratefully under the blankets of what was supposedly Henry Wyndham's bed and fell asleep.

Chapter Twenty-Four

Leake woke before dawn from a restless night's sleep, with a pounding headache. He lay in the luscious bed within a large room and took a moment or two to work out where he was. Wyndham House of course. He ached from the horse ride the day prior and the headache was from the port. They had drunk so much of it he felt they must have drunk the place dry.

Now he recalled, the big fellow had carried a passed-out Wyndham over his shoulder and out of the dining room. Grimly, Leake felt that meant he had won the challenge if you discounted the chess. What had Wyndham said just before that happened? He remembered thinking it was odd. He had put his hand to that man's face. *'Loyal Luke,'* that was it. He had to get out of bed and find some hair of the dog.

Parker's room was opposite his he recalled, as he stepped out into the corridor. He went to knock on it, but there was no reply. He opened it a crack. The curtains were open and the dim light the windows provided showed an undisturbed bed. The man must have stayed with Wyndham all night. Again, his addled brain registered this as odd. He headed toward the stairs and then remembered that the rooms with the wider corridor, set back from the top of the stairs, were Wyndham's.

Walking to the door, thinking if the man was awake he should tell him that he lost, he knocked and entered. What he noticed first was Parker's golden hair on the pillow and then seeing a bare leg and arm hanging off the bed, out of the bedclothes. The man was sprawled on the bed on his stomach. There was no sign of Wyndham, who must have stepped out. They had shared a bed and not only that, but it looked as if Parker was naked.

Walking directly to the bed, he unceremoniously pulled back the covers to reveal that Luke was indeed without clothes. "You dirty bastards! They string men up for this kind of disgrace. You will go to hell, God will see to that."

Luke, who had protested loudly at the cold air reaching his body so quickly, pulled the blankets back to cover himself and looked up at Leake. "What on earth are you doing in here, man?"

"I should ask the same question of you, but I would say it was obvious what happened here. Did you take advantage of a drunken man? Are you that depraved?" Luke, who was not hungover from the drinking the night before realised how damning his presence in this room seemed, but how could he explain it without revealing Harriet's secret? He could not, so he said nothing of it.

"It is not what it seems."

"Is it not? Let us allow the magistrate decide that! Get dressed, I am going to wake Chapple and Holder." Luke did not resist, the magistrate around here was Lord Freyley, it was probably best if he spoke to that man directly.

Annie woke Harriet with urgency in her voice. "Miss, Miss, you must wake. It is Mr. Parker, you must wake."

"What? What is it, Annie? What about Luke, Mr. Parker?"

"They have taken him to Lord Freyley. He has asked Mr. Marsham to meet him there. Charlie sent Benjamin to fetch him, took a spare horse with him to save time. Mr. Parker's instructions were not to wake you, but I took it upon myself. I knew you would want to know."

"Of course, Annie. Thank you. Why? Why have they taken him?"

Annie blushed. "He slept in *'Mr. Wyndham's'* bed. Mr. Mckinnon told me he helped you last night, I should have been called."

"It was fine, Annie. Luke took good care of me." She was sure he had, but some of the memories of the night before eluded her.

"Well, that Leake fellow found him naked in the bed and assumed that he had slept there with Mr. Wyndham. He called him some rather unsavoury names and woke his friends so they could take him to the magistrate."

"Lord Freyley." Harriet had sat up in the bed quickly, but her head ached so much she rested it in her hand. Annie thrust some water into her other hand and she swallowed some, but it was an effort, given her stomach's reaction. "Why did he not just tell them it was me?"

"Having spent most of the day yesterday convincing him you were a man, I am not sure he would have believed Mr. Parker. I imagine, Mr. Parker did not want to betray your secret either."

"So he is willing to hang to keep it? That is ridiculous. There is nothing for it but for me to reveal myself. Have Charlie saddle a horse for me and then come back and dress me. I will wear my gown with breeches beneath. Forget the wig, I will simply wear a bonnet." Annie held up the rolled-up bindings, which forced Harriet to recall exactly how they had been removed the night before and how she had stood naked in front of Luke, she slapped her hand over her mouth as she recalled propositioning him. What must he think of her now? "No need, Annie," she said simply.

Luke stood in front of Lord Freyley with his clothes in rather more disarray than he would have liked. The baron, being an early riser, was fully and rather more correctly dressed, and sat behind his big desk while Mr. Leake told the tale of how he had discovered Luke in another man's bed. Halfway through his diatribe, Edward Marsham was shown into the room and introduced. Presenting the baron with his card that bore his credentials, he requested a word in private with his client, Mr. Parker. The baron acquiesced, and Edward led Luke to a private room indicated to him by the butler.

"What on earth is going on, Luke? The man you sent could not tell me much other than you were being brought here."

"That man speaking in there, Leake, found me naked in Henry Wyndham's bed this morning."

"What? Luke, I never realised. I thought you were rather sweet on my cousin."

"No, man! For God's sake. Henry Wyndham is your cousin."

"That is a tenuous link, but I suppose, as he was Wyndham's son before he married my aunt, it could be argued."

"No," Luke was shaking his head again. "Harriet is Henry Wyndham."

"No! Not the man we met at the recital? The pianist?"

"One and the same."

"Now I must be angry with you. What were you doing in Harriet's bed?"

"No, Harriet's bed is in the adjoining room. She was sick after getting drunk with those men, dressed as Henry. She passed out and I took her into Henry's room, but then moved her via the dressing room, to her own. I was tired, but wanted to be on hand if she needed me."

"So you slept in the other bed and he came in and found you."

"Exactly."

"Why did you not tell him all of this?"

"Firstly, Harriet had just spent the day challenging and besting this man. Secondly, if her secret is revealed, she will not be allowed to play publicly again. She is so good Edward and she loved it so much. If I can get out of this without revealing it, I think it should be best."

"It might put a taint on you, a suspicion of impropriety."

"I am hoping that Harriet will agree to marry me and that might settle all of that."

"You are finally going to ask her?" Luke gave him a weak smile. "Then let us enter the fray my friend."

When they returned to Lord Freyley's study, Leake had finished telling his story. The baron thanked them for joining them at last, with a hint of sarcasm and requested Luke tell his side of the story. Edward spoke for him.

"My Lord, I believe Mr. Parker was alone in the bed when Mr. Leake walked into the room."

"But it was Mr. Wyndham's room, I have been informed."

"Yes, but Mr. Wyndham was not present at any time when my client was in that bed."

"Then, where was he?"

"He was in the dressing room. He was sick and chose to sleep in there."

"Why did he not simply sleep in his bed and Mr. Parker here sleep in his own room?"

"Mr. Parker wished to be close by in case he was needed. Wyndham had drunk a considerable amount and had passed out earlier, prompting my client to carry him to his rooms."

"I am afraid, I should need testimony from Mr. Wyndham himself before ruling on this." The door opened and Harriet stood there.

"Miss Wyndham insisted, My Lord. She said it is pertinent to the case you are hearing." The Freyley butler allowed Harriet to enter at his master's nod.

"Harriet... Miss Wyndham, there is no need, your cousin has this in hand."

"Mr. Parker, if the truth does not come out now, then your good name could be tainted forever, I will not allow that just so my secret can be kept. My Lord, I am Henry Wyndham." She removed her bonnet and revealed her short hair.

"This is not Miss Wyndham," Leake shouted it, "it is Henry Wyndham in a gown."

"I assure you, My Lord, I am Harriet Wyndham."

"Not possible. Henry Wyndham bested me at riding and shooting yesterday. I was not bested by a woman! Check under the gown, then we will know for certain."

"No!" Luke and Edward chorused, both rising quickly to protest.

"A little decorum, gentlemen!" Lord Freyley quieted them all and looked at Holder who was standing closest to the door. "Call my butler back in."

"My Lord." The tall butler bowed again as he entered the room.

"Please ask my wife to attend me here as soon as possible." The man left and they all sat in silence for a moment until Lord Freyley could not contain his curiosity any further. "How did you best this man riding and shooting?" Harriet told the tale of the challenges the day before, finally leading up to the drinking and Mr. Parker aiding her whilst sick, explaining that was how he ended up in what was seemingly the room of Mr. Wyndham.

"Young man, if you were in Miss Wyndham's room at night alone, you should really consider making a proposal."

"Nothing would give me greater pleasure, My Lord."

"I do not think that will be necessary, My Lord."

They replied simultaneously and Luke looked sharply at Harriet, but she looked straight ahead. Edward turned to give his friend a shrug. Fortunately, at that moment, Lady Freyley entered the room.

"Ah, there you are, my dear. I need your aid in this most perplexing case. This gentleman claims to have found Mr. Parker naked in the bed of Mr. Henry Wyndham. Mr. Wyndham was not present at the time. Mr. Parker claims Mr. Wyndham was sick and sleeping in his dressing room, and he slept in the bed to be of aid in the night. Now here is where it gets really interesting. Miss Wyndham claims that she *is* Mr. Henry Wyndham and has shown me her shorn hair as proof. She slept in her own room also connected to the same dressing room. Mr. Leake believes that this is Mr. Henry Wyndham pretending to be Miss Wyndham and demands we check under her skirts. What do you say?"

"Well I can look, sir, if that is your wish, but I can assure you that this is Miss Wyndham and she has indeed been impersonating her own brother all along."

"Nothing escapes you, my dear. Once again you impress with your keen observations. Let me ask you this. What would you say if Mr. Leake here says he was bested at riding and shooting by Mr. Wyndham just yesterday and a woman could not possibly do that?"

"I would say that Miss Wyndham is a most talented and determined woman. I should not be surprised at all to learn of it. Now if you no longer need Miss Wyndham to aid you, I request I be allowed to have a moment with her."

"Certainly, my dear." Lady Freyley left with Harriet in tow.

"She is not even going to look?" Leake was incredulous and spoke without thinking.

"Do you doubt the integrity of my wife, man?"

"No, My Lord. I apologise."

"My ruling is that you were misled about the personage of Mr. Wyndham and Mr. Parker here is free to leave. If I hear a single murmur against his name or any hint that the true identity of Mr. Wyndham is revealed, I will be making sure it is known by everyone exactly how she got the better of the three of you gentlemen."

"Yes, My Lord." All voices concurred.

"Mr. Marsham, admirable work. Please advise your cousin that I recommend Mr. Wyndham recommence his travels directly and indefinitely. However, I hope to hear more of his compositions in time."

Harriet followed Lady Freyley to a pretty sitting room. It was bright and made her wince as her head still hurt.

"Are you well, Miss Wyndham?"

"A bad headache. The challenges with the men yesterday included drinking a lot of port."

"Here my dear, have a glass now. *'I pray thee let me and my fellow have, A hair of the dog that bit us last night, And bitten were we both to the brain aright.'*"

"Really? I am not sure my stomach can take it." Lady Freyley insisted and handed Harriet a glass. She politely took a sip and her stomach protested. She placed it on a nearby table.

"I am sorry your ability to play in public is to be curtailed. I thoroughly enjoyed your playing the other night. I knew it was you."

"Lord Freyley is right, nothing escapes you! However, I am not prepared to keep playing at the expense of Mr. Parker's reputation."

"What of your own? You did not think of that or that he wished to save your reputation?"

"There are two differences. I actually committed the acts that my reputation must suffer, Mr. Parker did not. Also, mine may only result in some social news and snubbing, where as Mr. Parker would risk the gallows. There is no comparison."

"You are right, but knowing my husband, who has his faults it is true, those men should be advised not to mention any of these events to a soul."

"I am planning a trip to my family in Lincolnshire. I will be taking Mr. Marsham and the dowager with me if they are willing. I plan to ask

Mr. Parker to stay at Wyndham House and aid Mr. Horncastle in anything."

"I think that might be the best solution and hopefully it will all have blown over by the time you return."

"Could I trouble you to assist with anything needed in getting things started at the Lodge? I should like Rebecca Robertson to have a woman to turn to for any issues."

"It would be my pleasure and I actually wanted to talk to you about that. Mr. Collingworth's estate was in rather more difficulties than suspected. It has to be sold to settle the debts. His sister has been left with nothing. She is a well-educated lady and I wondered about her taking the role of governess."

"I only met her briefly at a handful of events. Is she at all the same as her brother?"

"Not at all. In fact, I think she will benefit from not being downtrodden by him any longer."

"Then I leave it in your capable hands to make the arrangements as soon as she is willing to move. Could I ask you to trouble the baron to look in on the stable occasionally? Mickleson is travelling with me and bringing his whole family. Mr. Parker is capable, but an additional eye, especially one of his experience, should be welcomed. If he feels there are good men from Collingworth's stable, then perhaps he could discuss them working there with Mckinnon and Bramley?"

"Certainly, when do you leave?"

"Today, as soon as I can return to Wyndham House and ready myself." She stood, knocked back the last of the contents of the glass with a shudder and bid the lady farewell. As she exited, she ran into Mr. Marsham and outlined her plan to him. She asked Mr. Parker to return with his friend and aid him in preparing to depart.

"I can accompany you to Eastease, Miss Wyndham."

"I would prefer it if you would remain here and oversee things at Wyndham House with Bertram. I plan to be back in a month, certainly before Christmas."

Lord Freyley stood tall in the doorway of his wife's sitting room after all the young men and Miss Wyndham had left. She was busy writing something at her feminine desk and he reviewed her while he watched. She was a little larger than she was when he married her, but that was to be expected when she had borne him six children. All but one of them had reached adulthood and the loss of their last child had been a heavy blow to them both. She still took care of her appearance and to him looked a lot younger than he, with his grey hair and lined face. She caught him looking at her and raised her eyebrows.

"Oh to be young and foolish do you not think, my dear?" she teased.

"Their manner astonishes me. Were we ever so foolish?"

"I think there were times, a long time ago." She sounded wistful.

"Miss Wyndham did not fool you."

"I rather think that I put the idea into her head. She is a very talented composer and as a man would be revered. It must frustrate her."

"Are you frustrated, my dear?"

"I live vicariously through hearing of their stories and romantic entanglements."

"You do not wish for a romantic entanglement of your own?" He had often feared her disinterest in their marital bed was only with him and not the whole process entirely.

"Only if it were with you, but as that side of our relationship has waned for you, I do not think about it and remain happy with the other side of our lives." He stared at her, his mouth opening and closing a few times as he took in her words. Realising that this meant she would receive his advances, he licked his lips and looked down at her ample bosom as his blood stirred his body.

He walked to her and pulled her to her feet. "For such an intuitive woman, you have severely misunderstood my feelings on this subject." He crushed his mouth against hers and pulled her soft curves against his leaner form.

Gasping when he released her, she managed only to say, "I have missed you." Then he was pulling her from the room and up the stairs. She wanted to protest that it was still morning, but she wondered why and followed him willingly instead.

Bertram had woken late as the drinking had continued for quite some time after Luke had hauled Harriet up to her rooms. He was surprised to learn, as he sat down to a hearty breakfast, that no one would be joining him.

They had all dragged Parker up to Lord Freyley's house. He was apparently accused of spending the night in Henry Wyndham's bed and taking advantage of that man in his drunken state. He should have laughed except it hit a little too close to home. He was grateful, for once at least, that James had not spent the night in his bed.

Many of the staff were rushing about as Harriet had decided she needed to create some distance between herself and the inevitable uproar at the revelation she was about to make in order to clear Parker's good name. She should be leaving that day for Eastease for a month and taking all the Micklesons with her, as well as her grandmother and cousin.

Bertram fully expected Parker to go with her and therefore looked forward to some peace around the place for a while and perhaps a chance to reconcile with James. The man was being stubborn. It had been a fortnight since he had touched him, other than his valeting duties and enough was enough.

Surprisingly, Harriet had requested Parker remain with Bertram at the house and they waved to the full carriage as it left. Bertram turned to talk to Drum and they walked into the house leaving Luke to watch the carriage disappear. Hence, he did not see it stop further down the driveway and another figure climb on board and sit next to Mickleson.

As Bertram readied himself for a pleasant dinner with Parker, there was a knock at his door. He had wondered where James was, as he had not appeared in the dressing room. It was getting ridiculous if he was going to knock and wait for Bertram to grant him access before coming in.

"Come!" he shouted in his annoyance and stared at the man who stood there.

"Sir, I wondered, as James has left with Miss Wyndham, if you would like me to tie your cravat this evening?" Mckinnon offered.

Bertram staggered backward at this news, it was as if James had aimed a pistol to his chest and fired. More painful than anything he had experienced, even in the hardest years of his life. Drum quickly reached out to steady him. "I am sorry, sir, I assumed James had told you himself.

Miss Wyndham agreed he could act as valet to Mr. Marsham on the journey. It must have been quite a disagreement if he did not tell you."

"Did he say... Is he planning to return?" he choked the words out, grateful it was only Mckinnon there to witness his pain.

"I do not know, sir."

Later, Bertram cried as he lay in the bed he had shared with the man he finally admitted, at least to himself, that he loved. The grief he felt at James' leaving was worse than any he had felt after Phillip's death and he wondered now if he had ever loved Phillip at all.

The next evening after dining, Luke sat in the new parlour at Wyndham House with Bertram. Both were miserable. They had exhausted the subjects of the challenge, Leake's accusations and Harriet leaving the day before and neither wanted to discuss anything else.

Mckinnon cleared his throat and approached Luke. "Miss Wyndham requested I wait until after dinner tonight before giving this to you, sir."

"Thank you, Mckinnon." He took the letter and cracked the seal.

Luke,

I am sorry for leaving you this letter, rather than discussing this in person. However, I am a coward. I could not bear to see the heartbreak on your face when I tell you what I need to tell you. I also apologise for asking Mckinnon to delay in giving this to you. I did not want you to stop me from leaving or catch up to us. I need to see my family alone and by that, I mean Alexander and Nathaniel. I am drained and I need filling up with their embraces and love.

I find I am thoroughly ashamed of my behaviour the other night, drinking so much. I have never done so before and I have to say the sickness last night and this headache today has schooled me to never do so again. That my behaviour could have resulted in your imprisonment, or worse, frankly scares me. I must apologise for trying to tempt you into being less than the splendid gentleman you are. I know you suggested I make you the same offer when sober, but I cannot. There is a reason for this and I have procrastinated in telling it to you, because I have enjoyed your company since you returned to Eastease for that Christmas ball. If I am honest I have to say I have enjoyed your company since we met when we were six years old. All I ever wanted to do was impress you with my daring and adventurousness.

I am procrastinating in this letter, too, it would seem. I love you, Luke. I have always loved you, but you preferred my sister, as everyone did. I teased you because I wanted to make you feel some of the pain I was feeling at seeing you distinguish her. I thought I had no hope, so when Mr. Davenport arrived, I felt there was someone who finally loved me and not her. Of course, I was very mistaken in his character.

Here is my confession. I am not Harriet Wyndham, I am Maria Wyndham. It was Harriet who left with Mr. Davenport and married him. I was so ashamed of what I had allowed to occur between he and I, that I pretended to be Harriet and everyone assumed it was Maria who had eloped. When Alexander left to pursue Davenport to Scotland, Nathaniel told me he knew I was Maria, but he wanted me to continue pretending to be Harriet. Ultimately, when the real Harriet returned to us, his plan worked and Davenport released her.

This pretence has all been worth it for those few short years Maria Brooks had with her new family. The price that has been hardest to pay was that it put me so close to you and yet all the time I knew I was deceiving you. I could never accept you with that between us, but now I believe you must detest me.

My heart is broken knowing that you will never look at me again the way that you have recently, particularly the way I recall you looking at me the other night just before you covered me with my nightgown.

I hope you will find another to love and if she loves you even close to the amount I love you, you will be a very happy man. Maybe then you will find it in your heart to forgive me. I do not think I can ever forgive myself.
Yours'

Harriet

Luke handed the letter to Bertram. He would have to leave for Lincolnshire in the morning and hoped the man should understand. Bertram's eyes raised at the mention of the nightgown, but nothing else was new to him. Harriet had told him everything else, except that she loved Luke. That he had worked out for himself, because he had eyes.

"What will you do now?"

"Follow her to Lincolnshire and ask her to marry me. I love her, Bertram. Not the woman who married Davenport and Brooks, but the woman who came here and turned this house on its head. The woman who pretended to be a man and was better at it than any man of my acquaintance. The woman who can melt my heart and bring me to tears with her compositions and playing. All that is about," he pointed to the letter, "is a name. I am not in love with a name. I am in love with the most incredible woman."

"Will you allow me to accompany you?"

"I would welcome the company, it is a long journey, but I hope to catch them somewhat and arrive perhaps only the day after, so I will be on horseback. I have wasted too much time. I knew she held a part of her back from me and I thought it was her interaction with Davenport. I did not propose before because I sensed something. I feared her rejection and never being able to see her again. Will Mckinnon be able to manage without you, Harriet and Mickleson?"

"Well, Drum?" Bertram turned to Mckinnon who was standing in his usual spot and grinning from ear to ear.

"Of course, sir. Perhaps we could impose upon Baron Freyley to check in on the horses a little more often, but Bramley has been learning a lot from Mickleson."

"Then we leave first thing in the morning."

"At first light."

Bertram Horncastle stood in front of the mirror in his rooms later that night a little more optimistic. His sadly tied cravat hung limply around his neck. He was in a sorry state since James had left with Harriet. After their words a fortnight prior, James had continued as Bertram's valet and said nothing further to him about their relationship. Nor did he spend any more time in Bertram's bed and he had missed him. Now he had left to return to work at Eastease.

In the morning, he and Luke would travel to Lincolnshire and Eastease to find the two people they loved. Bertram was confident Luke would be successful in his proposal to Harriet, he feared that his task may well be a more difficult one, but one worth earning, that much was certain.

Chapter Twenty-Five

It had been three months since Harriet Wyndham had last been seen at Eastease. Despite the cold, she leaned her head out of the window to see the familiar rooftops and chimneys appear in her view. How odd she thought, that though she loved it still, she now considered Wyndham House her home and missed it.

She was very grateful, when she entered the house and saw Alexander and Genevieve in the entrance hall waiting to greet her. She quickly found herself embraced by both of them and tears welled in her eyes.

"I am so happy to see you both, I have missed you so much."

"We have missed you, too, Harriet. Why do you not introduce us to your travel companions?"

"Yes, of course. As I detailed in my letter, this is Dowager Marsham, my grandmother, and Mr. Edward Marsham, my cousin. Grandmother, Cousin, this is Mr. and Mrs. Harker."

"A pleasure to meet you both, we have your rooms ready, would you like to refresh yourselves, before we partake of some tea?" Alexander suggested.

Trish Butler

"That would be most welcome." The dowager was pleased to be given time to compose herself somewhat and followed the housekeeper up the stairs on the arm of her grandson.

"Could I speak with you both?" Harriet asked. Alexander nodded and led her to his study while his wife followed.

Gennie and Harriet sat together holding hands on the loveseat, while Alexander pulled an armchair closer to them and looked at his ward. She looked tired, was that from the journey or was there something else?

Gennie prompted her gently. "What is it, Harriet? What has brought you back to us? Not that we are unhappy to see you."

"I have made a mess of everything." She told them of pretending to be Henry Wyndham and how wonderful it had been to play her pieces in public. Then of how Leake had accused her of being Harriet Wyndham and Bertram's idea of the challenge. How she had bested Leake for the most part and details of the chess match, that interested Alexander.

"Well, that is all very peculiar, but how have you made a mess? If they believe you are Henry Wyndham, your only problem is that you can never be both Harriet and Henry at the same time." Gennie was thinking of the practicalities of it.

"The game will be up sooner or later, however, and those men will not be happy that you misled them." Alexander could not say that he approved of Harriet's behaviour, but he knew how talented she was, he could certainly imagine her in a recital and could not wait to hear her compositions himself.

"The game *is* up. I drank too much and was sick. Luke, Mr. Parker I mean, carried me up to Henry's room, which adjoins my own. He helped me, and to be on hand in case I was sick further, he slept in Henry's bed. One of the men found him there in the morning and assumed he had spent the night with Henry Wyndham! They took him to the magistrate, to Lord Freyley."

Alexander looked angry. "Setting aside, for the moment, the fact that Mr. Luke Parker was in your rooms, what happened with the magistrate?"

She looked sheepish at that and detailed what had happened. She ended by telling them how Lord Freyley had insisted that Henry Wyndham continue his travelling abroad, indefinitely.

"Lord Freyley seems to be a very sensible and fair man. It would seem that you have escaped it all with little damage to your reputation. A trip home was a sensible choice. Let those men forget it all."

"Home." Harriet looked wistful.

"What is it, my dear?" Genevieve asked her.

"This will always be my first home, but I really feel that Wyndham House is my home now."

"That is a good thing." Gennie squeezed her hand.

"I am glad I have Bertram, Mr. Horncastle that is, and Mr. Parker taking care of it for me while I visit here."

"Ah, well, I had a letter from Luke Parker the other day. He expects to be back at his home in Eastcambe tonight and requested he be permitted to visit here tomorrow morning." Alexander informed her.

"He is coming here tomorrow?" she looked panicked. "I had hoped for more time."

"More time for what? It is only Mr. Parker, he is so amiable, surely you have not argued."

"No, but I think we might tomorrow. I told him that I am Maria."

"Have you not told him that before?"

"Why should I? It is supposed to be a secret. He is in love with Harriet and he wants to marry her. He has not asked me outright, but he will not, now I have told him I am not her."

Gennie looked at her with a soft smile, "what did he say when you told him?"

"I did not, I left a letter. I could not face him, he will be so hurt."

"My dear, you have been Harriet for five years, do you not think that it is you he is in love with and not your sister?"

"But he loved her first and he will never forgive me for lying for five years."

"Must one only ever be in love with the first person they loved? That should be a poor state of affairs for Mr. Brooks. I am sure at some point he will marry again."

"Well, Mr. Parker and Mr. Horncastle are both visiting in the morning. We will be sure to give you some privacy to work things out, but not in your rooms! You may own your own property now, but here you are still my responsibility." Alexander brought a smile out in her with his protectiveness.

"Let us go and talk to our other guests. Helena and Nathaniel are coming for dinner tonight."

"Wait, Bertram travelled with Mr. Parker?" she groaned. "Can no one follow my instructions?"

"Now you know how it feels!" Alexander laughed as he followed his wife and Harriet out to the parlour to talk to the Marshams.

Harriet sat in front of her mirror as Annie fixed her wig in place for dinner. She had sat here year after year and before that in Maria's room that her grandmother was using for this stay. It seemed small. How was it possible that in four months Eastease had become too small for her? She thought that was the way of things, children grew up and flew the nest.

Her nest was waiting for her in Somerset, near Bath. She thought about what Gennie had said and hoped that Luke would forgive her for lying about her name. If he felt he loved her as Harriet now, regardless of his feelings for her sister in years past, then she would accept him, because she could not imagine sharing that enormous nest of hers with anyone other than Mr. Luke Parker.

"You look determined, my dear!" Dowager Marsham stood at the door looking at Harriet in the reflection of her mirror.

"I am thinking of birds flying out of the nest." She smiled warmly at the older woman whom she found she had come to love in a short time. She reminded her of her mother, what memories were left of her at least, and had encouraged the woman to tell tales of her mother when she was younger as they had travelled north. "You look beautiful, Grandmother."

"As do you, Harriet. Talking of birds, a little one told me that Mr. Parker will be visiting here tomorrow. I like that young man very much. Sensible and amiable, but strong. Good looking, too."

"Yes, he is all of those things. I like him very much."

"I am glad to hear it."

"There you are, Miss. You look perfect."

"Thank you, Annie. No need to aid me tonight, I can manage, and I imagine that Mr. Mickleson will be eager for help with the boys as he does not have the distraction of the stable to manage here."

"Oh, he has already been assisting Adam. He cannot help himself where horses are concerned. They are keeping the boys busy."

Harriet and her grandmother entered the drawing room together. Almost as soon as she crossed the threshold of the room she was embraced by Helena and then they were both taken into strong arms that almost lifted them off the ground.

"My two favourite girls!" Nathaniel almost shouted it in his exuberance.

"I am sure Isabella will not like to hear that!" Helena laughed releasing Harriet and allowing him to take the younger woman into his arms by himself.

"My three favourite girls!" He was unabashed, then whispered in her ear, "I missed you, Harriet." She squeezed him in return and released him so she could introduce her grandmother.

Throughout the dinner there was talk of Harriet's music, how she made contact with the Marshams again and the challenge she won against the men. Nathaniel of course picked up on the fact that she lost the fencing and berated her for it.

"She won the shooting, however, my dear," Helena interjected, "I think that must be due to the excellent tutor she had."

"And who was that, Mrs. Ackley?" Mr. Marsham asked her.

"Me of course!" She laughed easily at her scowling husband.

"I taught her to ride!" Nathaniel was not going to be outdone.

"But she rode astride because of my influence!" his wife countered.

"I taught her chess. She found a way through that strategy because I never let her win." Alexander joined in with a laugh.

"None of you taught her to play I believe," the final word was to be the dowager's, "that talent is hereditary as I would be happy to demonstrate after dinner!"

The playing went late into the evening. The dowager did indeed perform marvellously and Harriet played her compositions, receiving much praise from everyone present. In between, the colonel played for Helena, who sang as beautifully as always.

When they finally retired for the evening, Harriet walked down the west wing corridor with her grandmother holding on to her arm.

"You and your sister found yourselves a wonderful family in the end."

"Yes, we were very lucky."

"And the men picked well with their wives."

"Yes, though both ladies put them through their paces at first. Genevieve and Helena have been my older sisters or even mothers. They have helped me tremendously."

"I regret, I truly do. To think that I could have had this connexion with you all this time."

"There is no point in regret, Grandmother. We have each other now. Will you come and live with me at Wyndham House? There is plenty of room."

"What will Mr. Parker say about that?"

"It is not his decision."

"Yet."

"We will see tomorrow, when he visits."

"After that, see if the offer is still to be made. If so, I should be very happy to accept."

"Goodnight, Grandmother."

Luke Parker and Bertram Horncastle arrived at Eastease promptly the following morning. They had stayed the night before at the Parker household which was halfway between the town of Grantham, about ten miles west of Eastease, and the village of Eastcambe. Bertram was greeted warmly, he had stayed at Eastease when he came to Lincolnshire to deliver his nephew back to his home. He was shown into the parlour where Mrs. Harker, Mrs. Ackley, Mr. Marsham and the dowager were waiting for him.

Mr. Parker was shown into Mr. Harker's study where the master of the house looked at him sternly, while Colonel Ackley stood looking formidable. Feeling at a distinct disadvantage in power and strength, Luke stood as tall as he could, his only advantage his height. He was not offered a seat.

Noting that the colonel was going to remain standing, Harker walked around to the front of his desk and leaned back upon it, looking at Luke. "I am given to understand from my ward, that you were alone in her rooms with her a week ago, while she was incapacitated by a considerable amount of alcohol."

"Yes, sir." Luke could think of no defence that would not sound weak, so he simply agreed with the man to take the sting out of the accusation.

"I would like you to explain yourself."

"I do not know how much Miss Wyndham has told you?" He framed it as a question in the hope that they should reveal what they knew and he did not offer up more information than Harriet had told them and get her into trouble.

"Oh no, Parker," the colonel joined the fray, "you are sorely mistaken if you think we should give over our advantage so easily. You must assume we know everything and tell us the truth. That is your only option here if you wish to leave with your family jewels intact." Luke did his best to refrain from covering the front of his breeches at this comment, but could not help flinching.

"We know of the challenge, and that after 'Henry Wyndham' won, there was a lot of drinking. You can start there," Harker began for him.

"I did not drink much, I was concerned she might reveal herself when inebriated and I would have to defend her." He could see this earned him a little respect, particularly from the colonel, but he knew he would need every ounce of it when they knew the truth. "Finally, she turned to me and I could see she blanched suddenly. Her eyes rolled back and before she could fall face down on the table, I grabbed her and picked her up over my shoulder. Drummond Mckinnon, he is the butler as you know, Colonel, opened the door to the hallway and I took her straight upstairs, using Henry Wyndham's room in case any of the men were watching.

"Mckinnon had said he should get her maid, but Annie had recently married, and I knew this could be an all-night endeavour. I was not even sure Annie would be able to manage it, so I told him not to bother her. I have been in that situation myself and seen a couple of friends through it. Best to get what drink you can up and out, rather than let it go through your body.

"In the room, I put her on a couch, got the chamber pots ready and woke her up. She was sick, a lot. I helped her clean up, we talked, she was sick again. Feeling the worst was over, I carried her to her own bed. She cried a little, talked about her sister and fell asleep. I slept in Henry Wyndham's bed in case she needed me."

"Then the man came in who thought you had slept the night with Henry Wyndham and he took you to the magistrate," Alexander provided.

"Yes, Miss Wyndham had just spent the day convincing him she was a man, it would have been difficult to persuade him otherwise at that moment, especially as he was still suffering from the heavy drinking the night before."

"So, you informed the magistrate of it all?"

"Well, no. I hoped as 'Henry Wyndham' had not been there when I was found that Edward could get me out of it without revealing Harriet's secret."

"Good Lord, man! Why would you risk that?" The colonel exclaimed.

"You did not see her perform at that recital. She was astonishing. Her own compositions, with all the separate pieces for different instruments that she had worked on with those men. They respected the hell out of her as a man and she deserved it! Her performance was wonderful, she is a natural. Of course, performing as a woman would be frowned upon. Her work would have been mocked. They tell 'Henry Wyndham' how superior his playing is to that of his sister, can you believe that? Harriet really deserves better."

"We did hear her pieces last night, they are astonishing." Alexander smiled at him, but the colonel was not going to let him off so easily, even if he did stand up for Harriet and try to keep her secret.

"Yes, all very lovely, but you are forgetting one thing here. You were alone in her rooms with her and she was drunk! You could have taken advantage of her and she might not even have remembered it. Did you undress her before you got her into bed?"

"What? No! I did not *'get'* her into bed, I carried her to her bed and put her in it. The damn woman undressed herself, it was all I could do to cover her up with her nightgown. I would never do that to Harriet. Never!" He was getting angry and it was not often that happened.

"Why have you not offered to marry her, instead of putting her reputation at risk?" The colonel was not done, feeling he had his prey cornered.

"Why do you think I am here now? I thank you for this welcome, but I do wonder why you are on your high horses with me, when I have done nothing to hurt her. All I have done is take care of her. I would have proposed sooner if I had been certain of her regard. I feared she might reject me and I could not be there to protect her if she was discovered as Henry. Where was all your anger and righteousness with Davenport, after what he did to her? He told her he compromised her to get his revenge on the two of you." He wondered if he had gone too far when the colonel stepped forward, but he was damned if he was going to be raked over hot coals for loving and caring for Harriet. He stood his ground.

"What would you have us do? We could not make him marry both of them. If there had been issue, I would have married her."

"Your answer would have been to force her into a marriage with a man she considers a father? How self-sacrificial of you. Well you would not have had to, as I would have married her. Gladly." Colonel Ackley sat down suddenly, the anger knocked out of him. "Now, gentlemen, if you would excuse me, I would like to talk to Miss Wyndham and see if I can convince her that it is she I am in love with and not her sister. I hope if I am successful, you will both give your blessing to our marriage."

The two men nodded, although it was not a question. "She is in the music room," Alexander told him as he rounded his desk again and plopped into his chair, with an approving glance at his friend.

Outside the music room door, Luke took a calming breath and straightened his coat. That breath was knocked right out of him at the sight of her at the pianoforte. She looked up as he entered and gave him a small, uncertain smile before she stood to curtsey in response to his formal bow. Neither of them said anything.

He walked over to her and took her hands, then they sat on the wide stool together, as they had so many times when she played. "Forgive me for coming straightaway, I had to, after reading your letter."

"You are not angry with me for lying to you for five years?"

"No. I should apologise. I am the one who has been lying, and for much longer than five years."

"What can you mean?" She frowned at him.

"I mean that I never loved your sister. I have always loved you, Maria." She gasped at his use of her real name, but shook her head.

"No, you paid all your attention to her."

"It may have seemed that way, but I did that to appease my grandmother. She thought you were trouble. She was right, but I loved that trouble. You were so happy, the slightest thing thrilled you, and you talked of all the places around the world where you were going to travel."

"I never managed that though, did I?"

"It did not matter, your stories of places and people were wonderful, exotic. My young heart did not stand a chance." She laughed at that and it made him glad. She nodded when he asked if she would hear him out.

"After your ball, I heard that Davenport had eloped with you, with my Maria. I was dismayed. I was heartbroken. I did not blame you, but how I hated him. So, I left, I travelled to some of those places you talked of and then, when I returned to England, I went to Bath. I had never been there and thought it better than here, where you were not. Eastease without you would have been dismal.

"How fateful it was that I should meet with your cousin of all people, when I did not even know of the connexion. We were invited to an evening at Wyndham House and who should I run into there but Davenport himself. Your sister was not present.

"He taunted me, saying he had married the twin that I had favoured, for had I not wanted Harriet Wyndham for myself? I hardly dared to believe that it was true. All this time, you had not run away with him, but I had run away from you, Maria. I was so foolish. His words did not have the effect he had hoped for, but then he did deliver the blow. He said that he had taken your virginity before he left. He laughed at that. I should have killed him, but all I could think of was getting back to Eastcambe to see if it was truly you who remained. I chose not to believe what he said of you, but you confirmed it that night Collingworth fell to his death.

"I saw you again at the Christmas ball four years ago. It was you, I could tell, but you were different, reserved, and pretending to be Harriet. I mentioned it to the colonel and he asked me to go along with it. Pay attention to you at least for a little while, then I could stop visiting if that was my wish.

"Of course, it was not my wish, so I played along, but I was afraid of asking you to marry me. Part of you seemed out of my reach and I feared you rejecting me and never being allowed to see you after that. I thought perhaps it was because of Davenport, if he had broken your heart, or hurt you in some way. I had no idea you thought I was only distinguishing you because you were Harriet! What a tangled web we were caught in!

"When you asked me to allow you time in Bath to find yourself, I desperately wanted to follow you straightaway, but I also hoped it might allow you time to find that exuberant, adventurous side of yourself. When the colonel and Bertram arrived back here a few weeks ago, they teased me about Collingworth showing an interest in you and I jumped at the chance to accompany Bertram back to Bath. I was not going to let you slip away again.

"I was delighted to find my adventurous Maria had appeared once more."

"But how did you know it was me, Luke? When you saw me again at the Christmas ball my manner was as Harriet's. Even Alexander did not know."

"Do you remember how we used to play in the graveyard of the church when we managed to escape from the boredom of a sermon? There was a tree that grew close to the wall and you would walk along the wall and then swing from a nearby branch." She nodded and smiled at the recollection. He had swung right behind her, but her sister had not dared. "One Sunday, you caught your hand on part of the branch as you let go and cut the back of it, right here."

He picked up her hand that was gloveless while she had played, and ran his thumb over the soft part between her thumb and forefinger. There was a thin silver scar there that was barely visible, she gasped both at him stroking her hand and at the truth in his story. "I pulled out my handkerchief and pressed it on that cut to stop it bleeding."

"I remember. I remember the feel of your hand in mine, just as it is now. I looked at your hair flopping forward as you looked intently down at my hand. I wanted to reach out and touch your hair. How old were we then? Twelve?"

"You were, I had turned thirteen. I must have dreamt of kissing your hand for months afterward... years." He brought her hand up to his lips and rubbed the lightest of kisses upon that scar, as he looked into her eyes.

"You never faltered in calling me Harriet. How is that, when you knew who I was?"

"That was easy. After visiting with you and your sister, my grandmother would ask me about Harriet. I would always talk about you, but call you Harriet. I know that I must continue to call you Harriet, but just for one question would you allow me to use your real name?"

"Yes, Mr. Parker, you may."

"Miss *Maria* Wyndham, I have loved you since the moment I first laid my eyes on you when we were six years old, and I know now that you have felt the same way about me for all of that time. Would you do me the honour of marrying me?"

"Yes, Luke! Oh yes. I do love you. Yes, I will marry you."

At that, he put a hand gently up to her face and brought his lips to hers in a tender caress. She leaned in toward him and poured all the love she had for him into that kiss, deepening it and sliding her lips over his. His tongue dipped into her mouth and she moaned with the sensation of it. Remembering where he was and the verbal threats he had received from the colonel, he reluctantly pulled away.

"Can we get married tomorrow? Do you not think we have waited long enough?" Harriet asked with lips that had reddened through his attentions.

"Yes, we have waited long enough. I would marry you this very moment if it were possible, but we may have to allow a week at least for preparations."

"I will be Harriet Parker. Oh, there will not be a Wyndham at Wyndham House. There will be no more Wyndhams."

"I had thought about that in the moments on my journey here that I dared to hope you should accept me. How would you feel about us both changing our names and becoming Mr. and Mrs. Wyndham-Parker?"

Chapter Twenty-Six

Harriet and Luke walked to the parlour hand in hand. Upon hearing the loud voice of the colonel as they approached, Luke dropped her hand quickly. She looked up at him and laughed. "Did he have words with you over being in my rooms the other night?"

"It was not so much the words, but the threat of the injury he was thinking of inflicting." He clasped his hands in front of himself at this and she laughed again.

"You survived and he always values people who can stand up to him." She pushed open the door and entered with Luke right behind her. Everyone turned to look at them.

"Well?" Colonel Ackley was not one to mince his words.

"She has accepted me."

"Of course she has!" Genevieve stood and walked over to Harriet, grasping both her hands she pulled her further into the room. "Congratulations, Harriet. You, too, Mr. Parker, and welcome to the family!"

More congratulations were given and received and then the

question of when they were to be married was addressed. Harriet insisted they should return to Wyndham House before Christmas and therefore should be married as soon as possible. She favoured the next day, but Mr. Harker insisted that Mrs. Hopkins should not have time to make all the preparations needed.

"We do not need a big wedding as you and Gennie had. I would prefer a smaller gathering." They finally agreed on ten days hence. Luke and Harriet should ride that afternoon to the church and speak to Mr. Brooks about a licence, then they should go to Bernier House where Luke's father was visiting and advise him of their plans. Luke could stay at Redway often over the next few days, saving him the longer journey to his home and allow him to be on hand to manage any wedding preparations set to him.

Mr. Horncastle was offered a room at Eastease until his return to Wyndham House. How fortuitous it was that he, Mr. Marsham and the dowager should be there for the nuptials. Everyone returned to Eastease for dinner that night, the additions included Luke's father, Mr. Parker, and Mr. Brooks. All of the decisions they could make that night were made and all of the tasks that needed to be done before the wedding took place, and after to get them on the road back to Bath were allocated. They were all exhausted by the time they retired to their rooms that night.

Bertram Horncastle was back in the room he had occupied at Eastease when he had stayed there last. He and James had been very discreet on that visit. It should not do to be discovered here and James had not spent the night with him. Now he was alone. He did not know where to find James. Was he somewhere in this house? Was he staying with his mother? He dared not ask.

He sat on the small couch and put his face in his hands. He would not cry again. He had cried enough over this man. He was here and he should find him at some point during his stay. He had to. There was a knock at the door and he quickly swiped away the few tears that had escaped before he got control of them.

"Come!" The door opened and James stood there.

"May I serve you, sir?"

"James! You are here. I was unsure where you were and hoped to find you soon."

"Mr. Watkins asked me to serve you, as I have done so before. So here I am."

"Thank you, James. Thank you for agreeing to serve me, so I could talk to you. I need to talk to you. Why did you leave?" James turned and for one panicked moment, Bertram thought he was going to leave. Instead he closed the door.

"We both know why I left, sir."

"Please, can you stop calling me *'sir'*? Call me Bertram or nothing at all."

James said nothing. Bertram slipped off his shoes and stood up on the couch.

"Can you get this cravat off me? The damn knots have been digging into my throat all day."

"Yes, s..." James stopped himself in time and could not help a small smile. He was thrilled to see Bertram there, though he knew it was only to be at the wedding of Mr. Parker and Miss Wyndham. On the long journey back, he had regretted his hasty decision to accompany Miss Wyndham on her trip. She had not questioned him after he said he was concerned for his mother after her last letter.

He did love Bertram and he had missed him since he had put their relationship back on a master and servant footing a few weeks ago. What did it matter if Bertram never admitted it? He knew he loved him. He stepped over to the couch and tackled the knots, looking at Bertram's face. He hesitated a moment, the man's cheeks were damp. His eyes looked a little red and he sniffed a couple of times. Had he been crying when he walked in?

"Who tied this monstrosity? This might take a while."

"Thank you." Bertram chanced a look at the younger man. It was now or never. "As I said, I did want to talk to you. I have been in contemplation and searching my heart for some time now. I am afraid that what I discovered was not particularly pleasant." James fingers slowed on the knots as he listened intently.

"I do not think I ever loved Phillip Wyndham, James. I was in a bad situation when he brought me to Wyndham House. He gave me shelter and cared for me. He gave me what I had never had with anyone else, intimately at least. I think what I felt was a deep gratitude toward him and I still do to some extent. But I did not love him. Back then, I thought that what I felt was love, but the truth is that I convinced myself of it because I could not leave him. I was afraid to return to the life he had taken me from. I came here to tell you this, because it may change your opinion of me. It turns out I am not a nice person, I allowed Phillip to treat me in any way he liked, because I wanted to stay at Wyndham House and enjoy its comforts. I was no different from a whore."

"I cannot blame you for that. I am fortunate that I worked for a good master here and a good mistress at Wyndham House. Not all are so. Some men and women have to make very difficult choices for their own or their family's welfare. I am glad you were able to travel here for Miss Wyndham's wedding and tell me all of this."

"For Harriet's wedding? No, not at all. That is a happy coincidence. I came here for you, James. To take you home. I realised that I was not in love with Phillip, because your leaving hit me harder than his death. I was rejected by the people who should have loved me at such an early age, that I had cocooned my heart away from sight for a long time. You broke that cocoon open and I was scared to come out."

James' hands were shaking as he loosened the final knot in the cravat. He could hardly believe what Bertram was saying. Then Bertram grasped his hands that were still at his neck, James' eyes met his and they gazed at one another. "I...I love you, James. Oh my God, how I love you."

He barely finished the words before James' lips were upon his. The kiss was hard, hungry and pulled the passion out of him in such an animal way, but in this moment, it was not what he wanted. "Wait, wait," he pushed the words out between their lips and James pulled away from him, a confused look on his face. "What you do to me when you kiss me in that way, is primeval, but we cannot. Not here. What I want to do right now is kiss you lovingly." He took James' beautiful face in his hands and brushed his lips gently, keeping them soft as he slid them over his. The love he held for this man washing over him as he slid his hands into James' hair and then down his back.

James was overcome with the tenderness and the love he could feel from Bertram. His own heart seemed to swell with it and his knees felt weak. Feeling the man shake in his arms, Bertram pulled him down to sit on the couch with him while he still kissed him, all the while keeping it tender and loving. His hands stroked James' back as the kiss continued. Finally, they broke apart and Bertram turned to lean back and rest his head onto James chest. James leaned back into the corner of the couch.

"I am happy to sit here with you and talk. Tell me of your time since leaving Bath. How is your mother? Just stay with me a while and talk to me." James draped his arm over Bertram's shoulder and let his fingers stroke his muscular chest. They stayed in that embrace and talked of what had happened since they had last seen each other, then they talked of the upcoming wedding.

"I wish I could marry you, Bertram. I do love you so much. I worried that you might think I did not anymore, when I left."

"I did not think that. I knew you loved me. You are the first person who truly does. I would marry you, too. Are you attending the wedding?"

"Yes, some servants, who are not involved in the preparations here are allowed to attend at the church. There will not be many people on either side as it is."

"Then when Luke says his vows to Harriet, know that I am sitting there and saying the same to you in my mind."

"And when Miss Wyndham says hers, I will be saying my vows to you."

"You do not need to obey me, James. I would prefer that you did not have to serve me in any capacity, but if you did not, we could not be together with such ease, and of course no one can tie my cravats as well as you. Within our rooms, however, we can behave as equals in the way I consider you in my heart. Only obey me in one thing." Bertram turned his head to look in James' eyes.

"What would that be, my love?"

"Never leave me again."

"Till death us do part."

"Yes, till death us do part, but I hope that will not be for a very long time."

Ten days later, Harriet Wyndham joined Luke Parker in front of Mr.

Brooks in the little Eastcambe church. As the clergyman read out the reasons for marriage, he looked at the face that was so familiar to him, and yet so different in every way to the face of her sister, his wife. He was happy to be marrying her to this fine, upstanding, young man.

He turned to Mr. Parker. "Luke Parker, wilt thou have this woman to thy wedded wife, to live together after God's ordinance in the holy estate of Matrimony? Wilt thou love her, comfort her, honour, and keep her in sickness and in health; and, forsaking all other, keep thee only unto her, so long as ye both shall live?"

"I will." As Luke answered, Bertram mouthed the words sitting a few pews back on Luke's side of the church.

Mr. Brooks turned to Harriet and smiled, "Harriet Wyndham, wilt thou have this man to thy wedded husband, to live together after God's ordinance in the holy estate of Matrimony? Wilt thou obey him, and serve him, love, honour, and keep him in sickness and in health; and, forsaking all other, keep thee only unto him, so long as ye both shall live?"

"I will." She turned to Luke as she said the words, and Bertram turned slightly to see James sitting on the other side of the aisle and smiled when he noticed his lips moving.

"Who giveth this woman to be married to this man?" Colonel Ackley and Mr. Harker stepped up and confirmed they did. Mr. Harker, standing closest to Harriet, took her right hand in his and handed it to Mr. Brooks. He in turn took Luke's right hand and placed Harriet's in it. Then he prompted Luke to repeat his vows to Harriet line by line. Unknown to all but James Dawley, Bertram mouthed his vows, too.

"I, Luke Parker, take thee, Harriet Wyndham, to my wedded wife, to have and to hold from this day forward, for better for worse, for richer for poorer, in sickness and in health, to love and to cherish, till death us do part, according to God's holy ordinance; and thereto I plight thee my troth."

Mr. Brooks instructed the couple to loosen their hands, but neither wanted to let go, so he simply turned them so that Luke's hand lay on top of Harriet's and prompted her in the same way he had with Luke. The eyes of the congregation were on the couple making their vows at the front of the church. No one noticed two pairs of eyes that were not, those of James Dawley and Bertram Horncastle. James mouthed his vows as Harriet repeated hers, and gazed at the only man he had ever loved or ever would love and that man gazed upon him.

"I, Harriet Wyndham, take thee, Luke Parker, to my wedded husband, to have and to hold from this day forward, for better for worse, for richer for poorer, in sickness and in health, to love, cherish, and to obey, till death us do part, according to God's holy ordinance; and thereto I give thee my troth."

Luke then put a ring on Harriet's fourth finger and repeated the customary words, "With this ring I thee wed, with my body I thee worship, and with all my worldly goods I thee endow: In the Name of the Father, and of the Son, and of the Holy Ghost. Amen."

After reading out the solemn prayer, as they all knelt, Mr. Brooks moved to join their hands together, but once more found there was no need. Holding them on his own palm he announced, "Those whom God hath joined together let no man put asunder." Bertram risked a quick look at James and gave a solemn nod.

Mr. Brooks continued, "Forasmuch as Luke and Harriet have consented together in holy wedlock, and have witnessed the same before God and this company, and thereto have given and pledged their troth either to each other, and have declared the same by giving and receiving of a ring, and by joining of hands; I pronounce that they be Man and Wife together, In the Name of the Father, and of the Son, and of the Holy Ghost. Amen."

As the newly joined couple exited the church, Harriet turned toward the graveyard. She walked to her sister's grave and placed the posy of autumn foliage she had held in her hands at the base of the headstone. "Luke has promised we will return by April first for our birthday, dear sister. I hope you approve, I love him so much."

The wedding breakfast, which was held at Eastease, went very smoothly, as all events at that estate tended to do, despite only a little over a week's notice to prepare. Mr. Harker and Colonel Ackley stood together and watched Harriet Wyndham-Parker move gracefully around the room with her new husband in tow. No longer could they consider her their ward, her wealth far exceeded either of theirs and they had raised her to be a loving, caring and considerate person.

As they looked at each other and smiled rather self-satisfied smiles, their wives joined them. "We fail to see what the two of you are looking so smug about," chastised Helena in a way that she knew her husband loved to be teased, "I think she has turned out well despite the two of you!"

"I credit your wives, actually," Gennie joined in the teasing.

"I was thinking of our own 'wedding night', my dear." Colonel Ackley turned that smug smile toward her.

"What wedding night?" Alexander teased his friend, "You have yet to make that legal."

"If this oaf thinks I will vow to 'obey' him, he can think again!" She gave her 'husband' a winning smile. "However, we made our own vows, which are as binding in our hearts as anything legal."

"You can hardly be the one to talk of wedding *nights*, Alexander!" Genevieve admonished him. "You were unable to wait until nightfall, as I recall."

"I wonder if they will wait? Mr. Parker has been invited to stay for the evening and night at Bernier House, so they will be at the Parker residence alone," Helena speculated.

"I do not want to think of it! He has only had to wait ten days, I would think he could control himself enough." The colonel grimaced as he spoke.

"Fifteen years and ten days," Helena corrected him. "Hush, here they come."

The happy couple arrived in front of the four of them with huge smiles upon their faces. "We have said our thank yous and goodbyes to everyone. We will be on our way and return in the morning ready to set off for Wyndham House."

"We hope to visit next year, after Gennie's confinement," Alexander confirmed.

"That would be wonderful!" exclaimed Harriet with a look to Luke who nodded.

"However," he added, "your visit might have to wait a year. With my wife's agreement, I plan to take her abroad. There are a few places I believe she should like to visit and I am sure her brother, Henry, will manage to meet us here and there. I am hoping I will be able to hear him play a few times more, before we return."

"When might that be?" Nathaniel smiled broadly at the younger man, knowing now that he was leaving Harriet in good hands, as he knew how she had longed to travel when she was younger.

"Assuming we are blessed, I hope it will be when we have children of our own."

"That is the most wonderful gift you could have given me, Husband!" Harriet glowed with her love for him.

"Congratulations, Harriet. Congratulations Luke. We are all so happy for you." Genevieve grasped a hand of each of them and Helena did the same forming a circle.

"Yes, congratulations!" then she whispered something in Harriet's ear and stepped back to her own husband, with a quick wink.

As they rode in the Wyndham carriage to the Parker household, Luke asked her what Mrs. Ackley had whispered to her. "It is not relevant to us, but something about Wyndham House. When the time is right, I will tell you."

He nodded and pulled her over to him so he could kiss her in the same way he had after his proposal had been accepted. This time he did not have to pull away.

They did wait until after dinner before retiring to bed, however, Luke had been sure to ask the butler to make it an early and short meal, informing the man they had eaten plenty earlier in the day. Harriet had not brought Annie with her and had assured the butler that she did not need a maid. She did not want someone who should question her need for a wig.

Uncertain of Luke's preference, she had entered his bedroom with it on. He deferred to her and she confirmed it would be more comfortable and practical to take it off. She hung it on a chair, hoping it should keep much of its shape and style ready for the morning.

Luke was already lying in the bed with his nightshirt on. Harriet had tied a dressing gown over her own rather revealing nightgown as it was sleeveless and the room was cool. She slipped the dressing gown off her shoulders and placed it on the same chair, before climbing into the bed with him. She was shaking in anticipation of what was to come. She remembered often how her body had felt before Robert had turned on her and that she hoped to feel the proper culmination of that act when her husband should tell her how much he loved her.

She laid on her back next to him and waited. He moved over her and smiled. "You are so very beautiful, Harriet." His hand ran over her side and to the mound of her breast as he leaned over to kiss her. He massaged her breast through the silk fabric and moved more on top of her to allow his other hand to pull aside the fabric covering the other breast. Kissing down her neck, he took the nipple into his mouth and ran his tongue over it.

Harriet was enjoying this sensation, she felt a tingling thrill through her body from his attentions. She could feel his arousal against her body and pushed against it.

"No, wait, I will not be able to hold back if you do that."

"Sorry."

"No, no need, just let me set the pace." He continued to massage and lick her breasts, which caused her to open her legs. She desperately wanted to writhe and push against him, but he had told her not to. She groaned in desire and frustration and he lifted his head. "Am I hurting you?"

"Not at all, I'm enjoying it. I'm sorry, I couldn't help it." Was she to refrain from all demonstration of passion she wondered?

He seemed pleased that she was enjoying it and moved between her legs, holding himself above her. As he pushed her nightgown to her upper thighs she offered, "I can take it off, if you wish." She longed to feel his skin against hers, but he shook his head. He reached his hand under his own nightshirt and pulled himself from under that fabric to under hers. She saw nothing of him at all, though she had tried to look.

He pushed himself within her, gently at first and then with more urgency. She could recall the feel of a man within her, though she never liked to put it in context, but this felt different, she felt stretched and pushed to limits that made her body pulse, her earlier frustration forgotten as she raised her legs more and welcomed him into her.

She looked up at him and smiled, her lips parted as another groan escaped her. "Oh Luke, yes!" she could feel a mounting pleasure, but before she could reach it, he groaned, too, and collapsed on top of her. The pressure within her lessened and the pulsing stopped. Surely, he should continue his attentions?

Luke rolled off her, "Harriet, that was magnificent. I have waited so long to take you in that way, thank you for giving yourself to me." He pushed her nightgown down and tenderly covered her breast. "I hope I was not too ungentlemanly. You were very accommodating." He pulled her to him and kissed her forehead. Holding her to him.

Ungentlemanly? She did not want him to be a gentleman in bed, she wanted him to be a man, she knew he would not hurt her. Accommodating? She was not there only to please him, she wanted pleasure for herself, too.

Before Maria had married Mr. Brooks, Helena had come to her room next to Harriet's. Maria had been crying and upon hearing it, Harriet had gone across the sitting room they shared to the door of her sister's bedroom. The door was ajar and Harriet had listened as Helena had spoken to her of the pleasure a woman could have if her husband was willing to learn. She had also assured Maria that during her first time with Mr. Brooks, he may not be able to control himself much as he was a virgin. He should learn how to and the colonel was planning to speak to him of it all. She thought that Luke had taken other women when he travelled and thought her lost to him, so it was simply a matter of him learning to control himself, was it not? She was sure a few moments more or more attention to her body should have resulted in her own peak.

What should she do? She lay comfortably in his arms and wondered how best to approach him about it. He loved her, he had said that his grandmother had warned him she was trouble, but he had loved that trouble. He had enjoyed the adventure of her being Henry Wyndham and the tasks that she had taken part in, at least until the drinking. Then she recalled the look he had given her when she had stood naked before him. She wanted him to look at her that way again and this time be able to take her in his arms and do whatever he pleased to her. Surely, he did not only wish to have this kind of fumbling connexion while they still wore their night clothes?

Finally, she recalled Nathaniel's advice when she had asked him about Collingworth disagreeing with her. She rolled her eyes at the thought that she had ever considered him someone she might possibly marry. Nathaniel had said that if you loved someone then you worked out your differences, tried to accommodate their point of view, change. He had advised her that it could be a painful process.

She was not going to wait, because if she needed Helena's help or Nathaniel to speak to Luke in the same way he had with Mr. Brooks, that should have to take place tomorrow before they left for Wyndham House.

"You are very quiet, Harriet. Have I upset you? Did I hurt you?"

"You did not hurt me, Luke. I do not think you ever could. I am a little upset, however." He sat up in the bed, leaning back against the pillows as she moved to sit with her legs curled under her so she could look directly at him. He did not look at her, but he did not seem angry. "Look at me, please Luke."

"I cannot, you look wonderful in that nightgown and it is gaping, so I can see your breast. I should not look at you that way, I am sorry. I do not want to demean you that way."

"Demean me? You think by looking at my breast you demean me?"

"Not just looking, but it makes me think about the many things I would like to do to your body. Things that I have thought about in the past. I do not want you to feel obligated to do anything with me because I am your husband. You are an intelligent, talented and most beautiful lady. I cannot believe my good fortune that you married me, and I want to make you happy. You were so obliging allowing me to kiss your breasts."

"Luke, when you kissed and suckled me, it shot thrills through me from my breast to here," she pointed between her legs. "Before Maria married Mr. Brooks, Helena talked to her of a woman coming to a peak in the same way a man does."

"I do not think that is true, Harriet. Is it?"

"I think it is. I have not experienced it, but just now I came very close to... something. If you truly want to make me happy, you could touch me, look at me, allow me to push against you and groan in pleasure. In fact, anything else that you have thought of doing with me in the past and things we have not thought of yet. I want it all and I want it with you."

"Are you sure, Harriet?" Now he did look at her, but he looked in her eyes. "I want all of that but I find when I think of it, of doing more, I cannot hold myself back."

"Helena said that a man can learn to control himself. I believe the colonel controls himself very well."

"How can you possibly know that?"

"I have stayed at Redway. While Eastease is a large house and I have never heard anything of Alexander and Genevieve, you can hear a lot more of the goings on at Redway. Their loving lasts quite some time!"

"I have disappointed you."

"Not at all! I am confident that as we both seem to be willing to try things, we will enjoy ourselves learning. In the same way as learning to play the pianoforte. I could not have hoped to sit down and know how to play a concerto the first time. It takes practise and trying hard. I believe we have a lifetime of practise if we should wish it."

"And you promise you will tell me if I hurt you or do anything you do not like?"

"Yes, and you will promise to do to me everything and anything you desire?"

"Yes, if you will do the same to me." They smiled at each other as she nodded.

"Then I will tell you that I would love to feel your skin upon mine. I want to see you look at me the way you did when I stood naked in front of you when I was drunk. This time, you need not resist me."

"Harriet, I do not know how I found the strength within me to do that."

"You will find it again, I am sure of it. Then draw on that strength, so you can prolong your enjoyment and therefore mine." She moved in toward him and kissed him, her nightgown gaped open and when she pulled away he looked down at her breasts, considering.

"Wait there." Getting out of bed, he pulled on his breeches and buttoned them just enough to contain himself, then he stripped off his nightshirt and moved to the fire. It had been banked down for the night, but he soon had it blazing. He pulled blankets and pillows off the bed, and laid them on the floor in front of the hearth.

She watched his actions wondering what he was planning. She had been thrilled, when he pulled off his nightshirt, to see the strong muscles in his back and across his chest. Those along his arms curved and bunched as he set to his tasks. He returned to her side of the bed and held out his hand to her. Eagerly she grasped it and followed him to the blankets, she was surprise when he stood her to one side of the fire, rather than have them lie down upon them. He kissed her long and slow, a deep kiss that had her pressing her breasts into his ribs. He ran his hands down her back and to her rump, giving it a friendly tap. Then he released her and moved to sit in the highbacked armchair opposite her.

The fire blazed as she stood there in only her silk nightgown. The light from it played upon her pale skin and the shine of the fabric where it clung to her curves. He was not sure he could control himself, but he was damn well going to try. The pleasure in looking at her and knowing what he was going to do with her sparked its way through him. He had held it in check before, she was right, he could do it again.

Harriet stood there a little uncertain after her initial bravery and pleasure. He had not said what he wanted her to do, but sat there looking at her with that expression on his face she had seen before. It was a mixture of desire and trying to control himself. A perverse pleasure overcame her, knowing she was affecting him this way and could cause him more pleasure just by exposing herself to him.

The thought caused her to quiver and the silk shimmered, then she reached a hand up to the strap of the nightgown and pushed it off her shoulder. He jolted in the chair at her action, but stayed sitting there, so she clasped the nightgown at her chest as she pushed the other strap off the other shoulder. She waited and looked at him, his gaze giving her confidence and at his nod she released the garment, dropping her hands to her sides.

It shimmered down her body a liquid that touched every curve as it fell, pooling at her feet. He followed its progress and then looked up from it over her body. He drank in the sight. "Come to me, Wife." He sat up straight and she stood between his legs. Her breasts at the perfect height for him to take a nipple into his mouth.

Earlier, he had been tentative and gentle, now he did what he wanted. He rolled a nipple roughly with his tongue, then sucked it out to a peak. The other he circled with his thumb as his fingers kneaded flesh. Her knees buckled as she groaned out her passion, so he released a breast and wrapped an arm around her in support, a large hand cupping a buttock as he pulled that mound of soft hair onto his chest. He felt himself move to the edge of his control as he struggled to rein it in, but he was not finished with her yet. He longed to draw it out, but knew he could not last that long. He vowed he would learn to control himself more, she was right, this pleasure was theirs for the taking.

He turned her and sat her on his lap, hooking her legs over his knees to open her and leaning back in the chair so she could lay back upon him. One arm wrapped around her and the hand cupped a breast toying with its nipple, while the other hand reached down between her open legs. "Guide my hand to where it gives you the most pleasure, my love. You are so lovely and I am longing to take you again, but I want to see you reach this peak first."

His words allowed her to abandon all her inhibitions. She put her hand over his as he explored her delicate folds. When his fingertip found a particularly sensitive spot, she gasped, he circled it and she groaned, "Yes, Luke, there, more, please!" He continued his efforts with both hands as she writhed on top of him. Her bottom rubbed against him, but he silently named all the places he had visited on his travels to distract himself.

Harriet could not believe the feelings he was bringing out in her, the way he allowed and wanted her to surrender her body to him. As his long fingers worked their magic, she felt a change within her. The pulses grew more and more urgent in their demand and she began to think she could not bear more when they finally cascaded over her. Stopping his hand, she clasped it between her legs as she jerked against his palm.

She had hardly caught her breath when he lifted her up and placed her on her back on the blankets. He ripped at his breeches, pulling them off his legs. This was when she saw him for the first time. The bulge in the front of his breeches that she had inspected when they had talked of her needing something for 'Henry's' trousers, was nothing compared to what she was seeing now. No wonder she had felt such a feeling of being filled by him. She opened her legs to accept him eagerly and as he entered her he groaned her name. "Maria, my Maria."

He had felt such a need to enter her, he had thought he would not last a moment, but he found a scrap of control and held himself above her. He looked at her flushed with the peak he had brought out in her, feeling her pulsing around him. Enjoying prolonging it as much as he could, he finally collapsed upon her.

They laughed together and he pulled the two pillows over to their heads as he once again laid her by his side close to the fire. This time their legs entwined and his hand stroked down her slender, naked back. He was not planning for them to have much sleep that night.

"I knew that I loved trouble."

"You called me Maria."

"I thought I might save it for these moments. Is that acceptable?"

"Yes, just never call me Henry in your desire!"

"On that, my love, I believe we can agree."

Epilogue

A week later, the Wyndham-Parkers arrived at Wyndham House. There was much in the way of congratulations and then a surprise. They had written ahead confirming their marriage and Lady Freyley had insisted that there should be an event at Wyndham House the Saturday evening following their return. She had taken it upon herself to make all the arrangements.

The evening was a grand affair, with dancing and food, and of course plenty of wine flowing. Harriet performed two of her pieces with Mr. Chapple and Mr. Holder. Those two men had decided that it should better suit them to continue to work with Mrs. Wyndham-Parker, although she obviously could not perform at public events. Mr. Chapple had said that he should love to hear any further pieces 'Henry Wyndham' might compose. When they had found a third and fourth to join them, they would play publicly again.

A little over a month later, they celebrated Christmas. Bertram woke in the morning with James in his arms. He shifted slightly to reach over to the table by the bed where he had placed a small gift. James woke and smiled at him.

"Merry Christmas, James."

"What is it?" he took the gift that Bertram offered him.

"Open it and find out." It was a gold wedding band on a chain.

Bertram took it from him and as he placed the chain over James' head he recited the words, "with this ring I thee wed, with my body I thee worship, and with all my worldly goods I thee endow."

"Bertram." James looked at him tenderly.

"There is more. I have drawn up a will so that everything I own will become yours if I die before you, which is most likely as I am older. You will be provided for. Mr. and Mrs. Wyndham-Parker have told me they plan to build me a house. It will be a bit further along from the Lodge. Not big, but enough for us should we wish to live away from the house, as it should be most natural for me to take my valet with me. It will belong to me and therefore, when I die, it will become yours."

"That is most considerate, but I do not plan to live without you, so you had better not die. Merry Christmas, my love."

When Harriet and Luke had been getting married in Lincolnshire, Lady Freyley had established Miss Collingworth at Wyndham Lodge. Lord Freyley, who had been pressed upon to visit Wyndham House's stable more often with the absence of Bertram and Luke, as well as Harriet and Mickleson, had been very impressed with young Benjamin Bramley. His own stable manager was getting on in years and as involved as he was in his own stable, he felt he would favour a younger man at the helm, who could learn his preferred way of doing things.

Lord Freyley had left Benjamin a list of tasks to complete before his next visit to Wyndham House, but the poor lad had to confess that he could not read. He suggested to the young man that he should learn as much as he could from Mickleson upon his return, and learn to read and write. If he could do that, then Lord Freyley should consider him for the position at his own stable when it became available.

When the Wyndham-Parkers had returned, Benjamin had asked about learning to read and write and they agreed, if Miss Collingworth was willing, that he could join the children at the Lodge learning their letters.

In the spring of 1818, Luke and Harriet Wyndham-Parker began their travelling. Firstly, as promised, they travelled back to Eastease to celebrate her first solitary birthday with family and to visit Maria again. After leaving Lincolnshire, their travels took them to many places, including Paris, Rome and New York. Henry Wyndham did indeed play his compositions at several places they visited, and composed more pieces, including a wonderfully soothing piece he had named 'Love'. When opportunity arose, he sent them to Mr. Chapple to look at and work on the other instruments' pieces.

Annie, who was expecting her own child when the Wyndham-Parkers left, did not travel with them. Instead, Harriet took one of the young girls who had been first amongst the homeless children who had made their way to Wyndham Lodge. She had learned well and made an excellent lady's maid.

Upon discovering she was with child when they were in America, Harriet and Luke returned to Europe and she gave birth to their identical twin boys when in Portugal. As soon as they were sure all was well, they headed back to England, and Bath.

Several things had changed since they had left over a year before. Dowager Marsham, who had indeed been invited to live at Wyndham House, worked with Lady Freyley often at Wyndham Lodge, raising money from wealthy families to support the young ladies that lived there and learned to become accomplished.

These ladies became governesses or they found a suitable marriage. Sometimes they did both. Monies supporting the homeless children that came to work and learn there came from Wyndham House and another surprising source, Lord Lorlake.

Annie Mickleson had given birth to a baby girl and soon after, it was easily established from the baby's dark hair and intense eyes that she was certainly her father's daughter. When Harriet returned, Annie was again with child, and she agreed they should have to add rooms to their cottage behind the stable.

The charming Benjamin Bramley had soon persuaded Miss Collingworth to spend time teaching him separately from the children, although they were under the eagle eye of Mrs. Robertson. When he convinced the governess that he would go to the ends of the earth for her, and Lord Freyley, impressed with the man's efforts to better himself, rewarded him with the position of stable manager at his own stable, he proposed marriage. Miss Collingworth became Mrs. Bramley. She continued as governess at Wyndham Lodge and was expecting their first child.

At a celebration for the return of the Wyndham-Parkers, Mr. Chapple and Mr. Holder introduced their two new group members to Mrs. Wyndham-Parker. The four men were seen often at Wyndham House practicing the new pieces from Henry Wyndham that Mrs. Wyndham-Parker had brought back with her. She directed them with regard to each piece and was always present at their recitals.

Mr. Henry Wyndham never returned to Bath. However, his music compositions did make their way there over the years, from whatever country in which he was currently residing.

Consequently, it was not until late in the summer of 1819 that Harriet and Luke rode out over their land to the wood that lined the large lake on their property. The weather had been warm and the ground around the lake was dry. Following the instructions that Helena had given her on her wedding day, Harriet tied their horses to trees at the edge of the wood and led her husband through them to a well-hidden inlet of the lake, that had a nice mossy patch of grass close to its edge. The water was clear and deep. She pulled Luke to her and kissed him passionately.

"Would you like a swim?" she asked him, unpinning her hair, that had grown longer since her last performance as Henry Wyndham, and kicking off her riding boots.

"I do not really want to ride back to the house in wet breeches."

"Then do not swim in your breeches." She had been unbuttoning the front of her riding habit as she spoke and allowed it to fall off her shoulders to the ground. She was wearing nothing underneath. With a laugh, she clambered up to the large rock. Looking back, she could see her husband stripping off his clothes as eagerly as he had that first night they had spent together, then she dove into the shimmering, warm water.

~The End~

Acknowledgements

I dedicate this book to Barbara Baker and Luis Fernando Jiménez. Both of these wonderful people think that my daughter is amazing, which I cannot disagree with, and know that music is part of your soul and can fill you up with any emotion you choose. Thank you for your help with getting my musical terms correct and helping me make Harriet sound as accomplished as we know her to be!

As always, I would like to take a moment to acknowledge the love and support of the most important person in my life, my courageous daughter, Emily.

This is a story about a woman who finds the path to the occupation she wishes to pursue, blocked by sexism, and ignorance to the capability and creativity of the female brain. Recapturing her long-lost courage, she embraces her gift of music and finds a way to share it with the world.

Thank you to my draft readers Cheryl Duffy, Pat Marsden, Melissa Kremmel and my sisters Janine Westgate and Rachael Nash. Your insights into my characters and enjoyment of my stories helps and supports me immensely, in keeping focus and making sure I do not stray away from my characters' true selves (it really does happen!) This process would not be half so much fun without all of you!

Once again, I have the pleasure of thanking Adriana Tonello for her marvelous cover design, as well as the map and all the other images within the book. We moved inside for the cover, and her background painting has not diminished in its vibrancy or beauty for that. '*Though I am often in the depths of misery, there is still calmness, pure harmony and music inside me.*' ~ *Vincent van Gogh*

Thank you to my wonderful and compassionate sister-in-law, Billie Henry, who helps me with all my horse terms. Her insights often provide me with a different situation than I had planned. You really give some truth to my stories about the horses and their characters.

A special thank you must go to Gordon Brooks, who reviewed some of my battle and fight scenes. His practical experience so valuable, when mine is only from books, TV and movies.

Special thanks to Chris for spending his valuable time and sharing his opinions on two of my favorite characters, Bertram and James. My aim was to show this relationship as tender and true as any relationship in my books and I hope that I have achieved that.

Also, special thanks to the Theatre Royal Bath, and especially Christine Bayliss, Hon. Archivist. While this book is a work of fiction, it is wonderful to have some semblance of truth. Thanks to Christine my characters attend an event that actually happened! She even found out that it got delayed a day because of rain, which provided me with a situation that made at least one of my characters rather frustrated!

Thank you to my 'sister author' Amy McCoy for her advice, and her time and patience listening to me talk of books and plots. You keep me motivated and I hope I do the same for you.

Thank you to my own mother, Gal Junie, and my mother-in-law, Margaret Butler for your continued support and belief. Both of you listen patiently to me babbling on forever about my books and take time to read, and hopefully enjoy, them.

Thank you to my colleagues at Connecticut Family Support Network, I appreciate all that you do to help families of children with special needs. Thank you for helping me, not only with my own daughter, but also encouraging and supporting me in my writing.

To all women, we are lucky not to have to face the challenges of our female forebears. They paved the way for more equality, but remember that we are not there yet. We need to continue, in whatever small or large way we can.

Thank you all!

Trish Butler

Without courage, we cannot practice any other virtue with consistency. We can't be kind, true, merciful, generous, or honest.

~ *Maya Angelou*

*In secret we met
In silence I grieve,
That thy heart could forget,
Thy spirit deceive.*

~ *George Gordon Byron*

About the Author

Trish Butler is the author of the Redway Acres series of books.

She was born in Norwich, in the county of Norfolk in England and moved to Connecticut in the US, in 1999.

Currently, she works as Communications Director for the Connecticut Family Support Network (CTFSN) a non-profit organization that helps families with children with special needs.

Redway Acres is mostly set in Lincolnshire, Cambridgeshire and Norfolk in the UK, which is an area that Trish knows well.

She has always wanted to write a book and at age fifty, finally realized that dream.

Read her blogs about her process, Redway Acres and its inhabitants at her website www.redwayacres.com

#RedwayAcres

Previous books in the Redway Acres series

Redway Acres – Book 1 Helena

Set in early 1800s, England...

Mrs. Helena Andrews is the widow of Captain Andrews who died in battle. Leaving all she knows behind her in Norfolk, she travels to Lincolnshire to live with her grandfather, Redway Acres stable owner, George Stockton. There she will raise her daughter.

After the death of her grandfather, she is left to run Redway by herself. She makes friends with an old widower in a ramshackle cottage, the family from a local, grand estate and their friend, a colonel and second son of the Earl of Aysthill, Nathaniel Ackley.

She is an opinionated woman in a man's world, who loves horses and her daughter, and will stand up for those who are in need.

Her story is one of horses, strength of will, music, friendship, love and loyalty.

Redway Acres – Book 2 Maria

Set in early 1800s, England...

Maria Wyndham is the younger and more vivacious, twin stepdaughter of the late Lieutenant Mark Wyndham.

After their mother's death, she and her sister, Harriet, move to Eastease in Lincolnshire, and become wards of the lieutenant's friend, Alexander Harker, and his cousin, Nathaniel Ackley.

Just in time for a ball for the twins' sixteenth Birthday, a friend of their stepfather and guardians, Robert Davenport, arrives to lavish them with gifts and to dance.

Family and friendship bonds are pushed to the limit, as Maria's story plays out. She finds her strength of will to survive and pursue her own happiness.

Maria's silliness and love of life, often hide her intelligence and loyalty, in this story of sisters, and a girl, too soon pushed into the world of a woman.

Redway Acres – Book 3 Martha

Set in early 1800s, England...

Martha Hopwood, who lives with her sisters and parents in Cambridgeshire, meets a gentleman named Mr. Samuel Woodhead, a friend of Alexander Harker of Eastease in Lincolnshire.

Mr. Woodhead takes up residence at the nearby estate of Copperbeeches and pursues Martha both in Cambridgeshire and at Eastease, when her family is invited to visit there.

His sudden departure from Eastease, when all were still asleep, prompts Martha to consider an alternative future. Martha pursues her independence, until the return of the gentleman who stole her heart, and upon whom her family's financial future may depend.

In a time when a woman could not be married and independent, Martha Hopwood has to consider where her true future lies.

Made in the USA
Monee, IL
22 September 2020